I really was d

I grabbed the counter, shaking so har[...] [...] What was *wrong* with me?

"Sav? Sav! What is it?"

I could hear my friends' voices, distant, muffled. I shook my head, my focus turning inward. What was going on with my body? Was this a sign that the bloodlust was about to take over completely or something? No, it couldn't be. I'd felt the bloodlust before. It hadn't felt anything like this.

"What's wrong with her?" Michelle asked in a high voice.

"I don't know. Get a teacher," Carrie ordered.

Anne moved toward the door, but I grabbed her arm to stop her. "No, wait. It's not…" I closed my eyes and mentally searched for the source of the pain. "It's not me. I mean, I'm okay."

"Then what's the matter?" Anne said, crouching down in front of me.

I shook my head again. "I don't…"

And then I knew. "Oh, God. It's Tristan," I whispered.

* * *

Praise for *CRAVE,* Book 1 of The Clann.

"An enticing mix of forbidden love, magic, betrayal, and heartache, this romance will leave you craving more."
—*Mundie Moms*

"Melissa Darnell has written a beautiful love story centered around the supernatural world. There is nothing sweeter than forbidden love."
—*Realm of Fiction*

"A spellbinding, compelling, and completely enjoyable debut, *Crave* had me flipping pages until there were none left to flip."
—*Electrifying Reviews*

Books by Melissa Darnell
from Harlequin TEEN

The Clann series in reading order

Crave
Covet

and coming in 2013

Consume

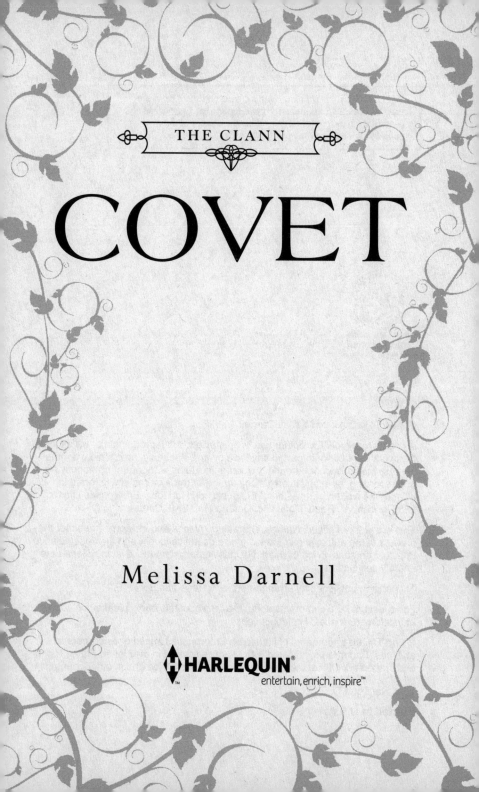

THE CLANN

COVET

Melissa Darnell

HARLEQUIN®
entertain, enrich, inspire™

Recycling programs
for this product may
not exist in your area.

ISBN-13: 978-0-373-21056-5

COVET

www.HarlequinTEEN.com

Printed in U.S.A.

To the moms (in order of appearance in my life):
Joyce, Janet and Judy, for showing me so many different ways
to be a strong woman, mother and wife.

To my dad, Joy and my father-in-law, Mack,
for showing me the many sides of being a father and a husband
with such honesty, wisdom and humor.

To Dawn: thank you for being the older sister I've always wanted!

And to the real-life grandmas who inspired the character of Nanna:
Mamaw and (in memory of) Nanna.

I love all of you guys!

CHAPTER 1

SAVANNAH

The vampire council's private jet, a giant cocoon of white leather and exotic wood trim, hummed a false lullaby around us, trying to lure me into sleep. But even though I was warm and safe within the arms of the only boy I'd ever loved, I couldn't give in to the exhaustion dragging at my body. Not yet. There was so little time left to enjoy this doomed illusion of peace and perfect happiness. I needed to fight the urge to sleep as long as I could.

Beside me, Tristan Coleman had already lost that battle. He sat slumped in a corner of the sofa we shared near the rear of the cabin. Though his chin with its dusting of three-day-old whiskers rested awkwardly on his chest, a slight smile deepened the corners of his lips, and his arms, so solidly wrapped around me, never budged. Trying to protect me even while he dreamed.

I should have been protecting him instead.

Despite the soft leather beneath us, Tristan had to be uncomfortable. After all, unlike me, he was human and his body could only take so much abuse. When his eyelids had first begun to droop hours ago, I'd tried to convince him to move to one of the reclining chairs or to at least take the entire sofa for himself so he could stretch his long body out properly. But Tristan had refused, insisting on sleeping upright so we could continue to sit close together.

Knowing what was coming for us, I'd given in. Selfish though it was, I didn't want to let go of him yet, either.

One stray golden-blond curl, rebellious like its owner, flopped over his forehead. Carefully I reached up and smoothed it back, forcing my eyes to look past the sharp contrast between my pale skin and his rugged tan.

In a few hours, even the right to that small touch would be lost forever.

I tried to memorize every detail of his face, normally so hard with determination or blinding everyone nearby with one of his infamous grins, now softened at the edges by sleep and his mistaken belief that everything was okay. He had no idea what sacrifices I'd made to get the vamp council to release him after they had used him and his powerful, magic-laced Clann blood to test my self-control. Handcuffed to a chair in a cement-lined interrogation room next door, he hadn't heard the torturous promise I'd made to that circle of cold beings. A race I was slowly but surely turning into.

I could have told Tristan the truth after the council released us from their Paris headquarters. But I hadn't, partly because I was dreading his reaction, but mostly because I wanted to be with him, as happy as possible, every last second that we had left together.

The muscles in my chest tightened, refusing to let my lungs expand fully, and another tear slipped down the side of my nose. Stupid tears. My eyes hadn't stopped leaking for more than a few minutes at a time since Tristan and I had safely exited the council's underground labyrinth of tunnels.

Knowing what I had to do for Tristan's own safety once we returned to our hometown in Jacksonville, Texas, I feared the tears would never stop.

There were so many perfectly logical and good reasons why I was all wrong for Tristan, why I *had* to do as promised and stop seeing him. My mind understood. Why couldn't I make my heart agree?

Dropping his head back against the sofa, Tristan sighed and snuggled me closer. And though I knew I should move away, keep him safe by putting physical distance between us, I gave in one last time to my heart. Closing my eyes, I nestled my forehead where his neck and shoulder met, a curved space of heat and strength that seemed to have been sculpted especially for me. Drawing in a deep breath, I could just make out the lingering crispness of his aftershave left over from Friday morning, the last time he'd had access to a razor. And beneath that, the barest hint of the precious and oh-so-forbidden Clann blood he had been forced to shed for my test. A test I almost hadn't passed. A test that had nearly cost him his life.

Swallowing hard, I pushed that dangerous memory away.

Soon. I would keep my promise to the council soon. Just… not yet. A few more hours while we were escaping the laws of gravity and the Clann and the vamp council in this plane together, a few more precious memories to make before we were grounded once more so I could be sure I would remember how it felt to be held and loved by him. How it felt to wrap my arms around his waist, feel the press of his hard chest against my cheek, hear his heartbeat pounding beneath my ear. To feel the illusion of safety while cradled within his arms, his strong hands on my hip and back cupping me as if I were a precious treasure instead of the monster that I truly was…

"Savannah," a familiar voice whispered like an annoying mosquito near my ear.

"Mmm," I mumbled, wanting that voice to go away. Only one male's voice was welcome right now, and that one wasn't it.

"Savannah, wake up," Dad insisted, his whisper slightly louder but still far too soft for Tristan's human ears to hear.

Scowling, I cracked one eyelid open.

"We are an hour away from the Cherokee County Airport, and the pilot warned that we will be landing in bad weather. You should call your grandmother and mother and let them know." Dad held out a black cell phone stamped For In Air Use Only in gold letters.

I took the smartphone, and Dad returned to his recliner at the front of the cabin.

Worried my talking would wake Tristan, I tried to ease out of his arms, intending to move closer to Dad's end of the plane. But as soon as I moved, he woke up.

"Sorry," I whispered. "I need to make some calls. Go back to sleep."

"I'm all right." He tugged me back onto his lap, brushing his nose against mine in a too-familiar, silent request for a kiss. At the last second, I turned my head so his lips touched my cheek instead. He leaned his head back to search my face, his heavy-lidded gaze hurt and confused.

"We shouldn't…not until we land and you can draw some energy." Thanks to the demon Lilith, the creator of my father's race of hybrid vamps, I could drain energy with a bite or a kiss, a fact I had only recently been reminded of. As long as we were away from the ground, my kiss could kill Tristan, despite his being the son of the most powerful family of witches in the Clann. His ability to pull energy from the earth through direct contact with the ground was the only thing that had saved him a few days ago after too long a kiss with me and a fight with his fellow Clann member Dylan Williams. If I hadn't been able to drag Tristan over to some nearby grass where he could draw replacement energy, Tristan might have died that night.

He frowned but nodded, letting me slide over to sit at the other end of the short couch. As soon as I was settled again with my legs curled up between us, he rested a hand on my ankles below the cuffs of my slacks. His unusual need to maintain constant physical contact with me over the last few hours made me wonder. Did he somehow know what the council had made me agree to? Or had the council's test simply left him on edge and worried about me?

I covered his hand with one of mine and tapped numbers on the plane's phone with the thumb of my free hand.

My home phone rang four times, then the answering machine clicked on. I glanced at my watch, which was still set on Central Standard Time. It was 10:00 a.m. on a Sunday. Nanna, whom my mother and I had lived with most of my life, should be home and getting ready for church. As our church's pianist, she never missed the Sunday service. Why wasn't she answering?

I tried again, thinking maybe Nanna was in her room getting dressed. Again, I got the answering machine. Unease crept in as I left a message.

I called my mother's cell phone next. At least her whereabouts weren't a mystery. She was probably still on her latest sales trip.

Mom answered on the first ring, making me jump. Unlike Nanna, Mom seldom had a signal while she was delivering safety products and chemicals to forestry clients out in the fields and woods.

"Oh, hey, Mom. Just wanted to let you know I'm okay and—"

"Savannah! Oh thank God. I, we, your grandma…" She was on the verge of shrieking, her normally low voice pitched high enough to hurt my ears and make me wince. "I'm on my way home now. But I'm still hours away from Jacksonville and—"

My hands convulsed around both the phone and Tristan's hand. "Whoa, Mom, slow down. What's going on?"

Eyebrows pinched with concern, Tristan flipped his hand under mine and laced our fingers together. Grateful for something strong and solid to hold on to, I squeezed his hand.

"Sav, they took Nanna! They called me, and—"

"Wait a minute. Who took her?" What little warmth my body had drawn from Tristan's drained away. Had the vamp council gone after my grandmother now?

"The Clann. They called me, asking about that Coleman boy as if I would know where he is. For some reason, they think you two are involved. I tried to tell them it was a mistake, that you'd never break the rules like that. But they didn't believe me."

Oh God. The Clann knew. Dylan must have told them he'd caught Tristan and me kissing after dance team practice Friday night.

I eased my hand away from Tristan's and back into my own lap. Frowning, Tristan sat forward on the edge of the couch, resting his elbows on his knees as he watched me.

"They insisted he was with you," Mom continued. "I told them he couldn't be, that you were on a trip with your father, and they went crazy! They said they have your Nanna, and they won't release her until we bring the Coleman boy back. I tried calling her, but she's not answering."

Holy crap. "Mom, hang on. Let me get Dad."

Dad must have been listening at the front end of the cabin, because he immediately joined us and took the phone. While Mom filled him in, I returned Tristan's stare and tried to absorb my mother's words.

"The Clann...they've kidnapped my grandmother," I whispered, hardly able to believe the words coming out of my mouth even as I said them.

"They wouldn't do that," Tristan insisted. "There's been a mistake."

I told him word for word what my mother had said. By the time I finished, his face had turned pale and his left knee was bouncing out a rhythm only a hummingbird could appreciate.

"I'll fix this," he promised. "Let me use the phone and I'll call my parents."

"Joan, we are half an hour from the Rusk landing strip now," Dad told my mother. "I will straighten this out and call you back when I have news." He ended the call then handed the phone to Tristan.

Tristan tried reaching his father first, then his mother and even his sister, Emily. Scowling, he tried a few other descendants' home and cell phones. No one was answering.

"I don't understand. Wouldn't they be waiting for your call?" I said.

"Yeah, they should be. Unless..." Tristan looked away for a moment, then his gaze snapped back to mine, his jaw clenching. "Unless they're already meeting at the Circle and using power. If they've raised enough power together, sometimes it blocks incoming radio and cell phone signals."

"Why would they be raising a lot of power?" I asked, hopeful the Clann did this at all their meetings for ceremonial purposes or something.

Tristan stared at me in silent answer, and my stomach twisted.

This wasn't the norm for the Clann. Which meant they were doing something to Nanna…

Bile burned the back of my throat, and I couldn't look at him anymore. If anything happened to Nanna, if Tristan's fellow descendants did something to her to try and find Tristan, the fault would be ours. We'd broken the rules to be together. I'd thought the vampire council was our only real worry, that the Clann couldn't do anything more to my family since we'd already been cast out due to my Clann mother marrying my vamp father before my birth.

I was wrong. And now Nanna was paying for it.

"Take your seats and put on your seat belts," Dad muttered, breaking the long silence. "We are landing."

I avoided making eye contact with both him and Tristan as we moved to the recliners and belted in, then gripped the armrests as my heartbeat hammered in my chest.

Please don't let it be too late, I prayed.

As soon as the jet touched ground and finished a short taxi, I unbuckled my seat belt and jumped up. Dad was faster, though, reaching the door before I could even blink. He got it open and the stairs unfolded so we could run down them to the rental car he'd called ahead and had delivered. The sky, which should have been a bright spring blue, was an ominous shade of dark gray, the storm clouds blackening out the sunlight so much it appeared to be almost dusk. Wind whipped my curly hair into an untamable red cloud, using the strands to slap first one side of my face then the other.

I got into the rental car's backseat, Tristan right behind me. Automatically I reached for his hand then froze. We were six miles outside of Jacksonville now. I'd promised the council I would break up with Tristan once we were home.

Not yet. Not till we sorted out this situation with Nanna and the Clann.

At my hesitation, Tristan glanced at me and frowned. "We're going to fix this, Sav." He squeezed my hand.

Forcing a nod, I swallowed hard against the knot tightening in my throat and looked out the window as Dad took off north on Highway 69 for Jacksonville, going fast enough to make the pine-tree-covered hills feel like a roller-coaster ride through the woods.

I spent the trip into town silently wrestling with the guilt crawling over my skin and clawing at my insides.

What had I done?

I never should have let Tristan talk me into breaking the rules with him. If I hadn't, Nanna would be safe right now.

And yet I couldn't even begin to imagine going through life without having felt Tristan's love. What we'd shared was a part of me now. It had changed everything...how I looked at the world and the future, how I felt about myself and others. When I was with Tristan, I felt solid and real and grounded and...good. Like being half vamp and half Clann was just circumstance, not who I really was. Like I could become anything I chose, not what others chose for me.

Except that wasn't true, because I couldn't change or choose what I was. Believing otherwise was every bit as much a lie as the ones I'd told my family for the last six months in order to be with Tristan. Which meant, no matter how much Tristan and I loved each other, this relationship was wrong. It was a selfish love that had nearly killed Tristan and might be hurting Nanna even now.

How had I gotten here?

I used to think of myself as a good person. But the truth

was I was a monster inside and out, and not just because my vamp side was starting to take over. How many people had I hurt? Maybe I could excuse accidentally gaze dazing those boys from my algebra class last year, and even gaze dazing my first boyfriend, Greg Stanwick. I hadn't understood what I was then. But I had always known dating Tristan was wrong, and still I had made that choice over and over for months. There was no excuse for it, no matter how wonderful it had felt.

I just prayed I had the strength and enough time left to fix what I had done.

Once we reached the center of Jacksonville, Tristan directed Dad to turn right on Canada Street and stay on it all the way out of town past our high school and still farther to the Coleman house, where apparently the Circle was located. Today was the first time I'd even heard of the Clann's secret meeting place.

I knew when we reached the edge of the Coleman property, because all the houses on the right side of the road ended. Five minutes later, Dad slowed the car and turned onto a gravel driveway barred by a huge wrought-iron gate. Tristan rolled down his window, leaned out and punched in a code on a pad housed on a gunmetal-gray pole near the driver's side window. The gate slowly rolled open.

I wanted to jump out and shove it open faster.

The driveway was long and curving, lined with some type of hardwood trees I couldn't recognize in the gloom, their branches lashing in the wind. A few raindrops pattered on the windshield and roof. Dad didn't bother to turn on the wipers. The trees ended suddenly as the drive circled in front of a three-story brownstone mansion, its every light blazing. I tried not to compare it to Nanna's single-story, single-bathroom, three-bedroom brick home where I'd grown up.

At least thirty or more vehicles lined the drive in front of the house. We added one more to the collection as Dad parked. We got out of the car, and Tristan led us around the outside of his house. More threatening raindrops fell, surprisingly cool on my skin despite the humidity. Once in the dark backyard, we all broke into a jog. I had time to recognize the yard as the same one in the dreams Tristan and I had shared many times over the last few months. Then we plunged into the even darker forest that ringed the yard. As soon as we did, I could feel it…a too-familiar prickling sensation of pins and needles down my neck and arms. Youch. A sure sign that descendants were using power nearby.

The woods seemed familiar, intensely so, as if I knew the location and size of every pine needle above me and just how the springy green moss below my feet would feel if I weren't wearing shoes. The moss grew everywhere, carpeting the forest floor and growing up the sides of the pines. When I caught glimpses of the clearing up ahead, I realized where I was.

This couldn't be the Circle.

We were in Tristan's and my dream woods, the ones where we met when our minds connected while we were asleep. Even the clearing was almost exactly the same. There was the stream, which ran across the mossy circular clearing where we'd danced and talked for hours. But where was the short waterfall that always spilled past the boulders and fed the stream? Maybe that had been an imaginary addition from Tristan?

Both sides of the stream were filled with descendants, too many of them to count. They gathered like giant crows circled round the harvest, their faces hidden in shadow beneath their blue and black umbrellas. Had my mother come here as a young girl with Nanna for the Clann meetings, maybe carrying her own dark umbrella in case it rained? It would explain why Mom liked to work in the forestry industry…

she'd grown up trampling through woods rain or shine for social gatherings.

On the far bank of the stream, where in our dreams Tristan and I usually sat or lay on a picnic blanket talking, sat a stone chair occupied by Tristan's dad, the Clann's leader, Sam Coleman. Behind him hovered Tristan's mother, Nancy, and Tristan's sister, Emily.

Yep, this was definitely the Circle. And we were so in trouble.

Then I looked up and gasped. Floating several feet above the stream, as if hung by invisible wires, was Nanna.

CHAPTER 2

TRISTAN

Savannah's grandmother, Mrs. Evans, appeared to be awake but immobilized in the air. The Clann must have caught her before she could get dressed; her long cotton nightgown floated around her legs and bare feet in slow motion as if she were a ghost. Savannah took a step toward her, and the descendants began to mutter. Hearing them, Savannah froze, her eyes narrowing and turning moss-green. A sure sign she was beyond ticked off.

"Mom, Dad, what are you doing?" I shouted to be heard over the wind and across the Circle's clearing. I had to put a stop to this before somebody got hurt.

"Tristan!" Mom screamed, darting out from behind Dad's throne. She took two steps toward me then stopped, her joyous smile flashing into shock, then fear, and finally settling into horror as she stared at Savannah. "No, it can't be true. Tristan, how could you? I told them you would never—"

"Son, do you know what she is? What her father is?" Dad's voice boomed throughout the clearing. "They're—"

"I know," I said. "But obviously I'm fine. There's no need to do this. Let her grandmother go."

Savannah looked up at her trapped grandmother again. Mrs. Evans's papery face twisted horribly, as if she were silently screaming in pain. Eyes shining with unshed tears, Savannah reached for her grandmother's feet, but even her toes were out of Savannah's reach.

This was insane. What did the Clann think it was doing, dragging an old lady out of her own home and off to the woods in her nightgown? Mrs. Evans would have every right to hex us all the minute they freed her.

"Let her down," I yelled, losing control over my temper.

The wind died, but the smell of ozone sharpened the air with the promise of more rain.

In the resulting silence, Dad said, "It's not that simple."

What?

Rocking back on my heels, I searched his face for some clue as to what he could possibly be thinking. I could tell from his overly formal tone that he was still in Clann leader mode, probably too aware of the audience of descendants surrounding us. But he wasn't thinking right. This wasn't about Clann and vamp politics. No matter what, no matter how powerful the Clann was, we didn't do *this*.

"It is simple," I said. "This woman had nothing to do with my disappearance."

"We know where you were," Dad said. "We know the vampires—that…girl's father—kidnapped you. Now tell us the truth, son. Are you okay? Did they hurt you? What questions did they ask you? Are they trying to figure out our weaknesses?"

Savannah took a step forward. "They're not trying to start

another war, Mr. Coleman. They just brought him in to test me, to see if I'm a danger to anyone. And my dad wasn't the one who took him. No one in my family had anything to do with Tristan's involvement."

"They didn't kidnap me. I went voluntarily to help Savannah," I said, desperate enough to lie at this point.

"Tristan, don't," Savannah hissed.

I didn't look at her, my gaze locked on the only person here who had the power to decide. My father.

Dad's face darkened. "So Dylan was right. You are dating her."

I didn't hesitate to answer him. "Yes. I love her."

The descendants gasped. Savannah froze. I fought the urge to smile as a weight I hadn't been aware of fell away from my shoulders. This was it, the moment I'd been waiting for, when the Clann would finally be forced to give us our freedom.

Beside our father, Emily slowly shook her head, one corner of her mouth deepening in that look that always said, *Oh, little brother, you've gone and done it now.*

Widening my stance, I crossed my arms and met her stare head-on. Emily might be older than me and think she knew it all, but she had no clue what it felt like to be in love, to need someone like I needed Savannah. In her own way, my sister was even more of a player than I used to be, ready to drop a boy from her dating schedule for the slightest reason. She'd never dated anyone longer than a couple of months, never broken any rules, Clann or otherwise, just to be with someone. And she'd certainly never be willing to leave the Clann if that was what it took to be with the person she loved.

But I was. And it was time the Clann knew it.

"It's time to let go of the past," I said, raising my voice so everyone could hear and not just my parents. "We've been at peace with the vamps for decades now. How long does that peace have to last before we can get over our old prejudices and fears? I love Savannah, and she loves me. And I'll do whatever it takes to make you see we're meant to be together. Including leaving the Clann if necessary."

"Tristan!" Mom gasped as Dad jerked forward in his seat, his bear-paw-size hands gripping the carved armrests.

Lightning flashed in the distance. A few seconds later, thunder rumbled out a warning of the storm's approach.

"He believes he loves me," Savannah said. "But the truth is…this is all *my* fault."

What the…?

I turned to her, sure I'd heard her wrong.

"Continue," Dad commanded.

She swallowed hard, refusing to look at me. "I'm half vampire. All this time, your son believed he was in love with me because my vampire side basically…well, put a spell on him. I gaze dazed him with my eyes. He couldn't help himself."

She'd lost her mind. The stress of facing down first the vamp council and now the Clann must have made her go nuts. She knew the gaze daze didn't work on me!

"I knew it," one of the Brat Twins crowed. I couldn't tell if it was Vanessa or Hope. "I knew she had freaky eyes." Their mother shushed her into silence.

"Savannah, stop it," I growled, clenching my hands at my sides so I wouldn't give in to the urge to shake some sense back into her. "You know the gaze daze doesn't affect me."

"Apparently it does." She kept her voice loud so everyone could hear what should have been a private argument between us. "Why else would you suddenly decide to break the Clann's rule this year and date me, if not for being gaze dazed?"

Half vamp or not, she had the worst poker face I had ever seen. She knew she was outright lying to everyone. But why? It didn't make sense to throw herself off a cliff now, when the truth was finally out. We were almost home free. All we had to do was stick together and refuse to back down, and the Clann would be forced to see reason.

"You know why," I murmured, taking a step closer to her. But she quickly stepped back, maintaining the distance between us. "Sav, don't do this. Just tell them the truth."

She shook her head, her eyes melting back to a dark slate-gray in sadness. "You're gaze dazed. You'd say anything right now in order to be with me."

"See?" Mom hissed to no one in particular as she glared at Savannah. "I told you Tristan would never willingly break the rules. She was making him do it."

Savannah nodded. "Yes, I was. And I'm very sorry. I didn't understand what my vamp side could do. But now that I know what I am and what I'm capable of, I can promise you..." Her throat worked as she gulped.

"Sav, don't," I said through gritted teeth.

She straightened her back and lifted her chin. "I promise you I will no longer be involved with your son in any way. As long as you agree not to punish Nanna or Tristan. Nanna didn't even know about us, and Tristan—"

"No," I shouted, her words clawing at my insides. "I knew what I was doing. Don't listen to her. She's lying to try and—"

"How do we know you'll keep this promise?" Dad asked, ignoring me.

"Because..." Savannah's voice wobbled. She cleared her throat and tried again. "Because I already made the vampire council the same promise. And they'll be checking on me to make sure I keep it. Just like I'm sure you will be."

She was lying. She had to be.

I searched her face. But this time, she was telling the truth. It was all right there for me to see in the trembling of her chin, the tears gathering in her eyes, the sudden slouch of her shoulders.

She'd promised a bunch of strangers that she would break up with me. Hours ago. Long before we ever got on that plane together in Paris. Before she sat curled up against me, letting me hold her, watching me smile and even fall asleep, letting me believe everything was finally working out for us.

All that time, she had been planning *this*—to break up with me. To *dump* me. And I hadn't guessed a thing.

The wind returned, whipping Savannah's long red curls into a frenzy that hid her face from me. The gusts tried to rock me off balance, but I couldn't feel them.

"We agree to your request," Dad said.

With a nod of his head, Sav's grandmother began to lower to the ground.

Savannah turned to watch her ease ever closer. I should be reaching out to help her catch Mrs. Evans, but I couldn't move. I was frozen, a statue ready to be pushed over and smashed into pieces.

This wasn't happening. Sav and I were meant to be together forever. She knew that. She loved me. I knew she loved me. She was just taking the easy way out, caving under the pressure because she couldn't see how close we were to freedom.

I had to stop this somehow, find the words to undo what she'd done.

I forced one foot forward, then the other, finally closing the distance between us. "Savannah, don't do this. You know we're meant for each other." I reached out and touched her upper arm, silently begging her to face me. "Don't give up on us."

She still wouldn't look at me.

"Savannah," Mrs. Evans gasped as the last of the elders'

magical hold on her fell away. She collapsed forward, and both Savannah and I managed to catch her dead weight.

Then two pairs of hands grabbed my arms, dragging me backward and forcing Savannah to take her grandmother's entire weight on her own. They went down to the ground together.

As soon as my captors set me back on my feet, I turned to snarl at them.

Dylan Williams and another descendant two years younger than us. I should have known.

"I warned you, man," Dylan murmured, sneering from underneath his too-long blond hair.

Cursing, I tried to break free, but the elders must have been lending their power because I couldn't shake my new jailers' grip. Their hands were like metal cuffs.

The wind tore through the clearing again, carrying with it a chorus of shrieks from the descendants. Savannah's father had darted out from the surrounding pine trees to kneel on the soggy ground with his daughter and former mother-in-law.

Hands rose all around us in silent threat. I tried to think of a spell to block them, but Savannah was faster.

She threw out her arms. "No! Wait, he's my dad, he's just here to help."

She and her father crouched together on either side of Mrs. Evans, their matching silver eyes warily scanning the tense line of descendants.

"Let him be," Dad said, and everyone slowly lowered their hands.

Savannah looked down at her grandmother. "Nanna, are you okay?"

Mrs. Evans reached up with a gnarled, shaky hand, which Savannah took. And that's when the clouds finally let it rip, dumping sheets of rain on the Circle and everyone within it.

SAVANNAH

Nanna's pulse skipped all over the place beneath the crepe-like skin at her wrist. She'd always been the strongest member of my family despite her age. When had Nanna become so fragile?

I leaned over her, trying to use my upper body to shield her as the clouds rained down their own stinging punishment on our heads. Despite my best efforts, within seconds we were both soaked.

Dad laid his cheek against her chest for a few seconds, then straightened up and leaned toward me.

"Her heart is damaged," he murmured near my ear. The wind did its best to tear his words away before I could catch them.

"I fought too hard," Nanna whispered, and even with my vampire hearing, I had to lean close to her mouth to hear her. "I was a foolish old woman. I shouldn't have tried to fight them."

"It's going to be okay now. Dad and I will take you home." I wiped the water from her cheeks.

But Nanna shook her head. "Too...tired." Her grip loosened on my hand.

"Someone help her," I shouted at the shocked faces around us. Were they so cold and uncaring that they would let an innocent old woman die right in front of them? She used to be one of their own!

But as the wind grew stronger and tried to steal their umbrellas, the descendants stumbled back beneath the shelter of the trees.

They weren't going to help.

Then a single man stepped forward into the sheets of rain. As he strode over to us, I recognized him as Dr. Faulkner, the Brat Twins' father and a surgeon at the local hospital.

"I'm a doctor. I can help." Dad moved out of his way, and Dr. Faulkner knelt at Nanna's shoulder, ignoring the wet moss that quickly soaked and stained his slacks. He pressed two fingers at the side of her neck while checking his watch.

The pulse in her wrist stopped beneath my fingertips.

"Nanna?" I shouted over rumbling thunder as I repeatedly patted the back of her hand. "Nanna!"

Time slowed and the roaring wind blocked out all other sound, making the moment surreal, like a movie I was watching instead of living. I saw Dr. Faulkner use his hands like electric paddles to zap Nanna's chest, making her lifeless body jerk. Tristan's dad ran over to us as if in slow motion, abandoning his throne to kneel on the soaked sponge that the moss had become, joining Dr. Faulkner's attempts. Their combined energy made Nanna's upper body lift several inches off the ground with each electrical jolt, then land with a small splash in the growing puddles beneath us. I tried to think of something I could do to help, but Clann rules had forbidden my family to teach me anything about magic. I wasn't yet a full vampire, either, so I couldn't turn Nanna into an immortal. Despite all the fears of both the vamp council and the Clann regarding what I might be able to do someday, the reality was I was powerless to save even my own grandma. All I could do was cause destruction and the threat of another war between the species.

And make dumb decisions that resulted in my grandma fighting for her life in the woods during a storm.

Mr. Coleman and Dr. Faulkner fell into a rhythm as a two-man team, taking turns zapping her chest, checking her pulse and blowing air into her mouth. I lost all sense of time as they worked for minutes that could have been hours, the rain soaking through their clothes and hair and eventually pouring in tiny streams down their arms.

Nanna never woke up.

Eventually, the men's hands withdrew from Nanna's too-still body. Dr. Faulkner was saying something to me. But I couldn't hear him.

"What?" The dreamlike feeling of shock drained away, leaving me soaked and chilled to the bone. Only then did I realize the wind had died down again and it was only my blood rushing in my head that was causing the roaring sound in my ears. "Is she all right?"

I reached past Mr. Coleman to pat Nanna's cool cheek, willing her to wake up. "Nanna? Can you hear me? Come on, Nanna, you've got to wake up. I've got to get you home now and into some dry clothes. Wake up, Nanna. Come on, wake up!"

Her eyes remained closed.

I circled around Mr. Coleman, kneeling so I could lift her head and shoulders and cradle them in my lap. She was still asleep, but she would wake up soon. I just needed to elevate her head, help her breathe easier. All she needed was a little time to come around.

I looked up at the sky, ignoring the flock of crows beneath their umbrellas still lingering at the edges of the clearing. At least the storm seemed to be passing. The thunder and lightning had eased, and the rain was coming down in actual raindrops again instead of a waterfall. That was good. Dad could carry Nanna back to the car now. We'd get her home and into a hot shower to warm her up, then into some dry clothes. She'd tell me how to fix her a cup of hot tea the way she liked it using some of her homegrown mint leaves....

A heavy paw of a hand rested on my shoulder.

I looked up at Mr. Coleman, but he was too blurry to see clearly no matter how much I blinked. All I could make out was his bushy white beard.

"I'm so sorry, Savannah. We tried everything. But...she's gone."

"No." She wasn't. She was just asleep. Raindrops splattered over Nanna's cheeks again, gathering in the deep laugh lines at either side of her mouth, and I wiped them dry.

"Savannah, it is too late," Dad said, standing at my other side. "There is nothing else we can do."

"No." I shook my head, staring at Mr. Coleman, willing him to help me. "Use your powers—"

"We did," Mr. Coleman said.

"Then try something different!" I turned to Dr. Faulkner. Why was I the only one here still fighting for Nanna's life? He fixed people for a living *and* he was a descendant. He had to be able to heal her. "You're a surgeon. Can't you go in and magically repair her heart?"

He shook his head. "I tried that. But I wasn't fast enough. There was years' worth of damage to the tissue. She must have had heart troubles for a long time now. Didn't she say anything to you?"

I stared down at Nanna's face, at her chest that refused to rise or fall. She had kept so many secrets. She hadn't even told me about my family's past until I was fifteen.

But why keep this secret? If she'd only told us, we could have done something to help her get better, made her lay off the fatty fried foods or helped her work out or something. Didn't they have surgeries and transplants for this kind of thing?

I tried again, asking both Mr. Coleman and Dr. Faulkner at the same time. "But you can still fix it. You can do a spell or—"

Mr. Faulkner shook his head again. "We can only do so much. We can't bring the dead back to life. At least, not with a soul—"

"Then bring her back without one!" I said, my hands aching to slap him. He was just refusing to help because we were outcasts, because I was a half-breed. "She's my grandma! You *killed* her. Do whatever you have to do, but bring her back!"

"No." Mr. Coleman's tone was final. "We don't do that. It's against Clann law to create zombies. And that's all she would be, a zombie, no personality, no true life within her. Just an animated corpse. Is that what you want, what your grandmother would want?"

I almost said yes, but the words choked in my throat. Nanna would be horrified and furious if she could hear us now. She couldn't stand to watch zombie movies and refused to read books about them. Even if I could convince the Clann to bring her body back to life, it was useless if it wouldn't really be her again.

"Please, there has to be something…." I whispered, staring down at the tiny wrinkles in Nanna's thin eyelids. I stroked her soft cheeks, then stopped as I realized she was already turning cold and losing her color.

No. This couldn't be happening. She couldn't be gone.

"I'm sorry. But there's nothing more we can do," Mr. Coleman murmured. "I swear, if we could bring her back for you, or undo what's been done here today, I would make that happen. But even descendants have limits."

So that was it then. Like me, even with all their supposed power, the Clann could only take Nanna's life, not bring it back. Nanna was really gone. I'd gotten here too late to save her after all.

And now I had to say goodbye.

"Nanna," I whispered, the ocean of ache in my chest spreading over my body to make my limbs so heavy I could hardly move. The ache bubbled upward, rising to fill my throat and burn my eyes and the inside of my nose, until I felt sure it would push right through my skull. If I had been standing, it would have knocked me over like a tidal wave. But I was already on my knees, and all it could do was bend me in half over my grandmother's body and leave me gasping for air.

I wrapped my arms around Nanna, lifting her to me in a one-sided hug, remembering all the times she used to hold me in her lap and rock the both of us in her rocking chair when I was little. And how she used to kneel just like this on her knees day after day, despite her joints getting creaky and popping with age, so she could talk to the herbs and fruit plants she so carefully tended in our backyard. It was the last time I would ever hold my grandma, the woman who had helped raise me, who at times had been there for me even more than my own mother.

She was gone. Because of *me*.

"I'm so sorry, Nanna." I couldn't say it enough. A lifetime of apologies wouldn't make up for what I'd done.

"Savannah," Mr. Coleman said. "Please accept my deepest apologies for your loss, and also pass on my condolences to Jo—to your mother. None of us intended for this to happen. I just wanted my son back safely, and we thought your grandma knew where… I never dreamed…"

Words apparently failed the big bear of a man. I looked up and discovered tears in his eyes, which were lined copies of Tristan's, giving me a glimpse of the man Tristan would someday become. A future I would no longer be a part of.

Hands covered my own, easing my fingers loose. Confused, I looked down to see Dr. Faulkner trying to release my hold on Nanna.

On Nanna's body. Because she wasn't here anymore.

I let him take her weight and lower her body to the ground. I couldn't move, couldn't feel my legs or arms anymore, couldn't even feel the clothes that were plastered to me along with strings of my hair along my face and neck.

What should I do now? What did normal people do when their loved ones died in their arms in the woods? There must be a procedure, certain steps of some kind that should be taken by someone. But my mind didn't seem to want to work to figure it out. Wiggling my hands, I discovered my fingers had somehow become buried in the earth. When I lifted them, clods of moss and mud clung to me. The same mud that would be all over Nanna's back now.

Nanna wouldn't want this. She wouldn't want me to sit in the mud sobbing over her body, especially not in front of the descendants who had cast her out and turned their backs on her. She would have demanded that I get up, put on a strong front, hide my pain. Show them just how strong the Evans women could be. Focus on what needed to be done, and break down later in private.

For her sake, I took a deep breath and tried to wipe my hands clean on my pants, only to discover my shirt and slacks were covered in streaks of mud. I would have to wait until I was home to clean my hands of the mess.

Home. Where Mom would be waiting soon for an explanation. Oh God. She didn't know yet....

"We'll help you with the arrangements," Mr. Coleman murmured, and Dr. Faulkner dipped his head in agreement.

What would Nanna have expected of me now?

"I think...she would have wanted to die at home in her sleep," I said to Dr. Faulkner. "She wouldn't want everyone to know..." Unable to say the rest of it, I gestured at the mess of it all, the slop of the mud and rain and grass stains all over Nanna's once-pristine nightgown, which she'd always been so careful to bleach a blinding white.

"I'll make that the official report," Dr. Faulkner replied as he, Dad and Mr. Coleman stood up, too.

I looked around the clearing, for the first time seeing again the horrified audience watching my every move. They stared at me, many of them whispering amongst themselves, as if this were a play they were watching but weren't really a part of. Didn't they feel *any* guilt for Nanna's death? Or was I the only true murderer here today?

Mr. Coleman turned in a slow circle, drawing everyone's attention and silence. "Today's events will never be spoken of. Is that clear?"

Slowly the descendants nodded, though my vamp abilities allowed me to pick up the general reluctance rolling off many of them as the crowd broke up and walked away in small groups through the woods.

"Savannah…" Sounding as if he were choking on my name, Tristan tried to cross the distance between us, but Dylan and another boy held him back. Cursing, Tristan fought against their hold.

Needles stabbed at my skin, a sign of his growing power level. Tristan was getting ready to use magic against them.

"Tristan, stop," I called out. I looked at his father. "Can I…?"

Mr. Coleman's gaze flicked down at Nanna's body, then he nodded.

More pain bloomed inside my chest, trying its best to rob me of air. Part of me screamed that I'd already lost enough, that I needed to hold on to what happiness I could. That I wouldn't survive losing anything else in my life right now.

But I had to. I'd made two promises now. And it was for his own safety.

I forced my numb feet to carry me over to Tristan. Moss squished beneath my shoes with every step I took, the sound loud enough to be heard now that the storm was nearly gone. It took far too few steps to bring me to the end of the only true love I'd known.

I tried again to memorize Tristan's face…to see every line across his forehead, the full curves of his lips, now flattened and thinned by anger and guilt and panic, the raindrops dripping from those curls, darkened like antique gold, around his face and clinging to the back of his neck. At the edges of my vision, all around us were reminders of the moments we'd experienced in our shared dreams of this place…so many kisses while lying together on a picnic blanket as we'd talked for hours. The pine trees with their heavy boughs swaying in the storm's retreat, the way they had swayed around us as Tristan and I had danced together barefoot on the mossy ground. Those same trees had been lit with thousands of tiny Christmas lights for my birthday last November as I'd kissed imaginary red velvet cake from Tristan's lips.

And now here we were. We'd finally come to the real clearing in the real woods to create another memory. A memory I would never be able to erase, no matter how much I would want to.

He stood as if frozen as I closed the final inches between us. "Sav, I'm so sorry. I never meant for this—"

"I know," I murmured. "I'm sorry, too. But the council and the Clann are right to want us to stay away from each other. It's better that way. Safer."

"No, Sav—"

I pressed cold fingertips to his warm lips, the water sliding down his face and around my fingers like tiny streams flowing around rocks. I closed my eyes. I didn't want to see his face when I said the next words. If I did, I might not be able to say what had to be said.

Standing on tiptoe, I kissed his cheek, tasting the raindrops on his skin, lingering so I could inhale his faint cologne mixed with the ozone scent of the rain and feel his warmth against my skin one last time. Then I stepped back, my eyes still closed, holding on to it all as tightly as I could even as I made myself let him go.

"We have to end this. Please don't try to see me anymore. This is the right thing to do. Someday you'll understand."

Before he could say anything to change my mind, I turned and walked out of our woods for the last time. Somehow I kept myself from looking back.

But I already knew I would be spending the rest of my life looking back on today, on the last few months, on every choice I had made, and wondering. What if I had been stronger? If I had only managed to resist the way I felt about him... If I had only followed the rules...

Nanna would still be alive.

CHAPTER 3

The next few minutes while I waited in Dad's rental car were a blur as the pain finally had its chance to claw through me. At some point an ambulance arrived. It turned around in the driveway then backed up in the yard behind the Coleman home. Two emergency workers got out and unloaded a metal gurney, carrying it into the woods between them. Eventually they came back, slower this time, the gurney between them supporting a bulky black bag.

I looked away then, burying my face against my forearm on the dashboard.

Eventually Dad came back to the car and got in. He sat there for a few seconds in silence. Then he awkwardly patted my back. The attempted comfort from him was so unfamiliar that it was like a little mental shake, reminding me I couldn't fall apart, not yet. We had to tell Mom first.

Dad started the car and followed the circle drive back to the road. Then we headed for my home.

Nanna's home.

"Have you called Mom?" I asked, my croaky voice forcing me to clear my throat.

"No."

"Then don't, not yet. I don't want her to hear while she's driving."

He checked his watch. "She should be home in half an hour or so."

Neither of us spoke again until we reached the house.

Every window of my home was dark when we pulled up onto the short, pine needle-blanketed driveway. The descendants had closed the front door but not locked it behind them after taking Nanna against her will. As we entered the house, I cringed, sure the place would be wrecked by a magical fight. But they must have snuck up on her and knocked her out before she had a chance to react. Everything was just as I'd last seen it.

I turned on the living room lamp, grabbed a handful of towels from the linen closet in the hallway and gave Dad a couple so we could dry off. I would change later, after Mom came home. I was afraid to go to my bedroom before we talked; I might give in to the urge to fall apart again.

I sank down onto the piano bench, the only furniture in the room that wasn't upholstered and wouldn't get wet from my clothes. Then I toed off my soggy sneakers and peeled off my soaked socks, trying to find any mental distraction that I could.

The house was so silent. It was hardly ever this quiet around here. Usually Nanna would have the TV on in the dining area so she could listen to it while cooking in the kitchen or crocheting in her rocking chair. Or she would be in the living room on the piano, filling the house with hymns as she practiced for church.

I turned to face the upright piano, laying my hands over the keys, feeling their cold, smooth surfaces, so like my skin right now. I'd never noticed before, but the keys in the center around middle C had rougher spots on them from being played more often than the ones at the far ends. I touched the surfaces where Nanna's fingertips had worn off the finish. Nanna had tried to teach me to play, but I'd never managed to read music well.

There was a cracked, leather-bound hymnal still open on the sheet music ledge. The last thing Nanna had played was "Amazing Grace." One line seemed to jump off the page at me....

I was blind, but now I see.

I had to get up, get away.

A truck engine rumbled up to the house and died, quickly followed by the slam of a door. Dad and I shared a look.

Mom was home.

I wasn't ready for this.

My fingers knotted and unknotted, twisting around each other countless times in the few seconds it took her to reach the front door and open it.

Mom blew in like a tiny tornado. "Savannah! Good grief, you're soaking wet. Did you shower with your clothes on?" Stepping over the threshold, Mom closed her hot-pink-and-brown polka-dotted umbrella, gave it a quick shake over the cement stoop, then rested it against the fake-wood-paneled wall.

She turned to face me, arms open wide for her usual welcome-home hug. But I couldn't move. My legs seemed locked into place. Her gaze darted to the right, and her smile faded. A tanned hand drifted up to fluff her frizzy bottle-blond hair. "Oh. Hello, Michael. I thought you would just drop Savannah off."

He nodded his greeting.

Frowning, Mom shut the heavy oak door behind her. "So where's Nanna? You didn't call, so I assumed—"

"Mom, you should come sit down," I interrupted, dreading her reaction and yet needing to get this over with.

She blinked a few times and then eased into the upholstered rocking chair, making its sagging springs creak in protest. Kneeling at her feet on the worn-out green-gold carpeting we'd tried a million times to convince Nanna to let us replace, I held Mom's hands and tried to figure out how to tell my mom I'd caused her mother's death.

"Mom, Nanna's…"

"Oh no," Mom whispered, her hazel eyes rounding. "They killed her, didn't they? Didn't they?" Her voice rose to a shriek. "I knew it! I knew they would murder her someday. Those hateful, spiteful… Oh sweet God. I should have been here, helped protect her. I shouldn't have been on the road so much. I was gone all the time, I made it so easy for them…."

"No, Mom. It's my fault," I blurted out.

"Wh-what?" she whispered.

I couldn't look at her. I stared at the carpet, and I confessed it all…dating Tristan and hiding it from everyone, the fight Friday night between Dylan and Tristan after dance team practice, the vamp council's watchers at my school. And then the council's test in Paris, and getting Tristan home again only to discover we were too late. I couldn't make my voice any louder than a whisper as I told her how Nanna had died in my arms despite everything Mr. Coleman and Dr. Faulkner had tried, and how the doctor thought Nanna must have had a heart condition for years. And finally, how I had promised both the council and the Clann never to see Tristan again, and then I'd kept that promise and broken up with him.

There was silence in the room as Mom processed it all. Then she jumped to her feet and went to stand by the dark stained bookcase with her back to Dad and me. For long minutes, the only sound was the ticking of the ornately engraved silver-and-red clock on top of the piano and Mom's harsh, fast breathing.

"Mom?" I felt like a little kid again, so small and scared. I'd never seen her so furious she couldn't even look at me. I'd always followed the rules, done everything I could to be a good girl. Until this year. Until Tristan. And now I had broken our family apart.

I got to my feet, my cold clothes sticking to my skin. I took two steps in her direction, not daring to move any closer. "Mom, I am so sorry. I can't even tell you how sorry I am. I didn't know...I didn't believe the Clann would ever do something like this. When they found out about you and Dad, all they did was cast you and Nanna out. And the council...taking Tristan like that..." How could I begin to explain how everything had seemed like no big deal, until it had spiraled completely out of control?

"You are your mother's daughter, aren't you?" she murmured, her shoulders sagging, and the disappointment, the utter defeat, in her posture was worse than a slap in the face could ever be.

Then she turned toward me, and I could see the tears pouring down her cheeks. I couldn't hold back my own tears and sobs any longer.

"Come here," she said, holding out her arms, and I was a first-grader all over again, running into my mother's embrace for comfort. Only this was no skinned knee or bruise from falling off my bicycle in the street. This was so much more, and I would never be able to make all my mistakes from this year right again.

I told her I was sorry, over and over, even as I knew no amount of apologies would bring Nanna back to us.

"Shh," she whispered, running a hand over my hair just as

she used to do when I was little, but it only made it so much worse because I didn't deserve to be comforted or forgiven.

She shook her head, filling my nose with her favorite Wind Song perfume, and sighed. "You didn't know what the Clann was truly capable of because I didn't want you to know. I tried to shelter you from all that ugliness, just like your grandma tried to shelter us both from her health problems, apparently." She leaned back, cupped my face between her calloused hands and gave me a sad smile. "I had really hoped you wouldn't ever have to experience the same troubles your father and I went through. And yet history just keeps on finding a way to repeat itself, doesn't it?"

She looked over my shoulder at my father and her eyes grew even sadder, which I hadn't thought possible.

The air whooshed out of her in the heaviest sigh I'd ever heard from her. "Where's Nanna's...?"

"It is all being taken care of, Joan," Dad said with a softness I hadn't thought him capable of. "Though of course there are other things to discuss when you are ready."

She nodded. "Savannah, why don't you go get some dry clothes on. Rest if you feel like it, and tomorrow we'll talk some more, okay?"

I nodded, so empty and tired now, it was all I could do to drag myself into my room and change into a giant T-shirt to sleep in. I slid under the blankets, my feet bumping against a stack of freshly folded laundry Nanna must have left at the end of my bed for me to put away.

I fell asleep with my fingertips rubbing the soft twisted nubs of the lavender-colored afghan Nanna had crocheted for my sixth birthday.

TRISTAN

I paced the length of my room from the bathroom door to my desk then back again, my fists curling and uncurling. What an unbelievable mess this morning had turned into, and just when I thought I'd finally figured it all out for Savannah and me.

I tried the knob on my bedroom door. An electric jolt zapped my hand, forcing me to let go with a yelp and a curse.

My parents had put one heck of a spell on my door to keep me here. No doubt the window was covered, too.

Would they let me out for dinner? For school tomorrow?

Growling out a sigh, I sat on the edge of my bed and dropped my head into my hands.

I needed to get out of here, get to Savannah. Be there for her while she dealt with all of this. She talked about Mrs. Evans all the time. Her grandma had been like a second mother to her, especially since her mother was on the road all the time. Losing her would be devastating for Savannah. She would need all the support that she could get right now.

I should be there with her. Instead, I was a prisoner in my own bedroom. And because of the other spells my mother had placed on this room years ago, I couldn't even dream connect with Savannah as long as I was locked up. The only time we'd been able to connect our minds in our sleep was when I camped out in the backyard.

If I smashed my desk chair through my window, would that break the spell on it, too?

A sharp double rap on my door made me jump to my feet. "Yeah?" I said.

The door swung open. Emily poked her head in. "Hey. Thought I'd see how you're doing."

I frowned at her. "How are you able to open the door without getting zapped?"

"Selective spell. Mom set it to work only on you. Don't try walking through the doorway just because I opened the door, though. The minute your toe hits the threshold, you'll get thrown back on your butt. And trust me, you'd remember the experience afterward." At my raised eyebrows, she added, "What, you think you're the only one around here who's ever been grounded?"

Grumbling under my breath, I dropped onto the edge of my bed again with my back to her. Man, this sucked. Why couldn't I have been born into a normal family?

"What in the world are you listening to? Is that...Phil Collins?"

It was. Not that it was any of her business. Rolling my eyes, I leaned over and turned down the volume on my docking station. Then I flopped back on my bed.

"Raiding Dad's music collection again?" Grinning, she stepped the rest of the way into my room.

I sighed and stared at the ceiling. "Come to gloat that you're the angel of the family again?"

"Well, it's not like you make it a hard achievement for me." She sat down on the corner of the bed nearest the door. "Seriously, little brother. What in the world were you thinking, pulling that stunt out there? Did you really expect the Clann to just roll over and give you whatever you wanted because you threw out an ultimatum?"

"No." Well, maybe I'd hoped.

"Then what exactly *did* you think would happen?"

I shrugged. "Either they'd accept Sav and me, or I'd leave the Clann. Just because I was born into this family doesn't mean I don't have a choice about anything."

She snorted. "Yeah, right. Like Mom would just let you quit and throw away all her plans."

Honestly, I didn't care what Mom wanted anymore. This was my life, not hers. "Any idea when they'll let me out of here?"

"I heard Mom on the phone. Sounded like she was leaving a message with the school office. You're out with the flu for at least a week."

A whole *week?*

As I stared at her in disbelief, she added, "They want you to have some time to calm down and see reason. Well, that and for the gossip to die down."

Unbelievable. They still didn't get it.

I slammed the heel of my fist against the mattress. "I need out of here *now.* Savannah just lost her grandma. And no telling what hell she'll be catching from her parents, too. She needs me to be there for her."

"Well, I guess she'll just have to face Hades on her own for a while, because you're not getting out of here anytime soon."

I cursed loudly. Emily didn't even flinch.

"You know, you could get out sooner."

That got my attention. "How?"

"Just tell Mom what she wants to hear. Tell her you're sorry, and you were wrong, and you still want to become the next Clann leader."

"And that I'll never see Savannah again?" I didn't bother to keep the sneer out of my tone.

One blond eyebrow arched in her trademark *well, duh* look.

I returned to staring at the ceiling. "Not gonna happen. I meant what I said out there. They can't make me stay in the Clann. And if I'm no longer a member, their rules don't apply to me anymore."

"Maybe the Clann rules wouldn't. But our parents' rules would."

I clenched my teeth and focused on not breaking anything.

Emily huffed out a long and noisy sigh. "Lord, you're hardheaded. I know you like Savannah and all, but honestly, she can't possibly be worth all of this."

"She is. And I don't just like her. I love her. I've never felt like this for anyone. Ever. I'm not giving her up just because our parents are a bunch of bigots."

"So you're going to stay grounded for the rest of your life?"

"They can't keep me in here forever. Eventually they've got to let me out for school."

"Not if they sign you up for homeschooling."

I raised up on one elbow. "They wouldn't do that."

She shrugged. "They might if you push them far enough." When I kept staring at her, she glared at me. "Do you really not know our parents *at all*? They're going to do whatever it takes to get it through that thick skull of yours that she's off-limits! Just let her go, Tristan."

"Never. Not as long as we love each other. Besides, our parents can only control me till I turn eighteen. Then I'm out of here and they won't be able to do anything about it."

"Oh, I see. Planning on falling back on that trust fund."

"Yep."

"Except who do you think holds the strings to that, too?"

Mentally I cursed. I hadn't thought of that, but I should have. This was why Emily was the brains behind most of the trouble we used to get into as kids. "Fine. Then I'll get a job."

"Doing what, genius? Folding burritos at a fast-food place? You think you're going to be able to support the both of you on that? Because I can guarantee you her parents aren't going to become your biggest fans anytime soon. Her dad looked ready to kill you in the Circle. And now that you two basically went and caused the death of her grandma, I can't see her mother liking you much, either. The only way she'll be with you is if she runs away from home."

"The Clann caused Mrs. Evans's heart to fail, not Sav and me."

A long silence. "Savannah didn't seem to see it that way."

I'm so sorry, Nanna, Savannah had whispered over and over while holding her grandmother's body.

As if Savannah blamed herself for Mrs. Evans's death. "I'll make her understand it was the Clann's fault."

"Good luck with that when you're grounded to your room till you turn eighteen."

Mom had taken my cell phone, house phone and computer, too. My left foot started to jiggle. "Let me borrow your phone."

"No way! Then Mom would take it away, too. And before you ask, you can't borrow my laptop, either. I'm not losing my social life just because you've gone nuts over one of the few girls on the entire planet that you can't have." She hopped to her feet. "Face it, little brother. You've had your fun, but your fling with Savannah is over. The sooner you move on and find someone else, the better it'll be. For the both of you."

She walked out the door then hesitated. "Oh yeah. And Mom sent you this." She used a foot to push a wicker and wood tray with a can of soda and a sandwich on a plate across the threshold into my room. "PB and strawberry jelly. Your favorite."

Like I would eat that. Mom had probably laced it with more spells to make me forget about Savannah or something. "I'm not eating till they let me out of here."

A slow grin spread across her face. "Stupid, but admirable. I'll sneak you in something to eat."

Could I trust whatever she brought?

Her grin turned into a laugh. "It'll be safe. Pinky swear."

"Thanks, sis."

Now if she could just find me a spell strong enough to bust out of this joint.

SAVANNAH

As I stumbled out of bed the next morning, I felt like one of my glass ballerinas, cold and brittle and way too breakable.

My eyes were scratchy and so puffy I could barely open them at first.

I desperately needed some caffeine.

Dragging myself down the hall, I headed for the dining table, already looking forward to that daily cup of Nanna's homegrown, old-fashioned steeped tea. Two things stopped me in my tracks.

My father sat at the dining table with my mother. I couldn't remember them ever sitting at a table together. They'd divorced when I was two and barely managed to speak nicely to each other over the phone since, much less actually sit down to a meal together.

The other thing that made my muscles lock up was the realization that I'd never have Nanna's homegrown tea again. At least not carefully measured out and steeped by her own hands.

"Hey, hon, how are you feeling?" Mom hopped up from her usual seat at the dining table and went into the kitchen to fix a plate of something I knew I wouldn't be able to eat.

How did I feel? Like a traitorous, rule-breaking, lying murderer. "Fine," I muttered, sinking into the chair next to Mom's. Which left me facing Dad.

I caught myself staring at him. Seeing him at Nanna's dining table was too weird.

Mom set a plate of nuked waffles in front of me. My stomach rolled over and threatened outright revolt as I stalled for time by cutting up the dripping, sticky plate of guilt into the tiniest pieces possible.

Mom sat down, clasped her hands on the table, then exchanged a look with Dad.

My instincts went on alert.

"Savannah, we need to speak with you," she began.

My gaze shot to her face, then Dad's. "Okay."

"Your father and I have been talking," Mom continued.

"And we both feel that you should live with him for a while. At least until you graduate from high school."

I stared at her, my brain scrambling to understand words I never thought I'd hear her say.

"Over the next year as your vampire side continues to develop, you are going to need me nearby to teach you how to recognize and control each new ability," Dad said.

"Why can't I just call you for advice?"

"This is not just your mother's and my wishes. The council has also...requested that I stay near you during this crucial time." Which wasn't a surprise, considering they'd threatened before to require me to live with my father in order to balance out the "effects" of living with former Clann descendants all my life. "If the bloodlust increases in strength, a phone chat is not going to do much to help control you."

"Control me? You really think I could become that big a threat to others?"

"It is possible, unless we are proactive in recognizing the signs leading up to such a situation and act quickly."

I tried to imagine living with him, but it was hard. Until this weekend, I'd seen him only twice a year for an hour-long dinner, during which we'd both pretended to eat and care about each others' lives. So I didn't have much personal experience to support my imagination.

"And this is what you want, too?" I asked Mom, desperate for her to say no, that she wanted me to keep living with her. All my life, my family had consisted of Mom and Nanna and myself. Now Nanna was gone and they were talking about taking me away from Mom, too.

"Hon, this is the best choice possible. For everyone," she said.

"I will of course be purchasing a home for us here in your hometown," Dad added. "So you need not be concerned about relocating to a new school or leaving your friends and dance team."

"Why would you do that?" I blurted out in confusion. If he was trying to reassure me, he'd just failed big-time. While descendants were spread out worldwide, Jacksonville was the Clann's home base and therefore had the highest concentration in any one area. The temptation of being surrounded by hundreds of descendants and their powerful, magic-laced blood would make his existence here unbearable. The only upside to moving in with my father should have been getting away from the Jacksonville Clann.

And avoiding the temptation of getting back together with Tristan.

"The council wishes it," was all he said.

Maybe the council wanted to continue to test me by making me stay here another two years?

"Well, at least I can still come visit you here on weekends, right?" I asked Mom.

"Hon, please try to understand, Nanna's social security checks barely helped us make ends meet. Now that she's gone, there's no way I can continue to make the payments on this place."

Dad scowled, and she rolled her eyes. "Yes, Michael, I know you've offered to help with that. But it wouldn't be right now that we're no longer married. I'm not your responsibility anymore, remember?"

She turned to face me again. "Besides, this place is too big for me to live in alone. I'd have to get fifty million cats just to keep me company."

A reluctant smile bunched my cheeks and pushed the tears out of my eyes. I sniffed and wiped my cheeks with the back of my hands. "That'd be attractive."

She smiled. "Exactly." She took a deep breath, then dropped

the biggest bombshell of all. "But the main reason is, now that your grandma is gone, her magic has begun to fade. Within days it will be gone completely, depending on how strong each spell was and how recently she strengthened it. That includes the dampening wards here." She didn't quite meet my eyes as she said that last part.

Oh. She was talking about the bloodlust-dampening spells only Nanna had known how to make, because she was the only descendant with magic abilities who had ever wanted to dampen a vampire's bloodlust—mine, in this case—without actually repelling the vampire completely.

As a teenager Mom had chosen to let her abilities atrophy like an unused muscle. But that decision couldn't erase her lineage. She was still a descendant with the Clann's powerful blood running through her veins, the kind of blood that was almost irresistible to vampires.

Without the dampening wards on my home, I might begin to feel the bloodlust for my own mother. And now those wards were beginning to fade.

I shuddered. As much as I hated it, there was only one thing to do. "I guess we'd better start packing."

CHAPTER 4

I should have tried to enjoy my last week in my childhood home. I also probably should have called my friends and mentioned that I would be moving in with my dad soon. But Mom had already called their parents to let them know about Nanna's funeral, and the rest they would find out about once I was back at school next week.

Right now, I had zero desire to talk to anyone. Talking to my friends would mean lying about how Nanna really died and why I was moving in with my dad, and I was already crawling around under enough guilt as it was. While my best friend, Anne Albright, knew a little bit about the Clann's abilities from helping Tristan ward off the algebra classmates I'd accidentally gaze dazed last year, she had no idea I was a dhampir, or even that vampires existed in the first place. My friends wouldn't see it that way, but I knew without a doubt that the less they knew about the vampires and the Clann, the safer they would be.

As a result, the week passed quietly and much too quickly.

Mom and I stayed busy packing up the house and putting it on the market. Mom had decided to sell the house and use the money for my college fund and to buy herself an RV so she could expand her sales territory. We'd thought, due to the lingering effects of the recession, that the house would take at least a few months to sell. But it found a new owner within days, to the surprise of Mom, me and the real estate agent. Apparently two companies had seen it on the internet the day the agent posted it and entered into a bidding war, driving the price up way higher than we'd set it. The winning bidder had also paid cash in full and skipped the usual house inspection so they could close within days instead of a month. Their only stipulation was that we vacate the premises as quickly as possible, apparently because they intended to put it on the rental market immediately.

All too soon, a stranger became the owner of our childhood home.

Later that week, we went to Tyler in Mom's truck to do some serious RV shopping. Dad had tried to talk me out of going with Mom. But she'd insisted if I could be trusted to go to school with the Clann, then I could be trusted to go shopping with my own mother for the day. Dad had argued that going to school with descendants only put me in large classrooms with them, not tiny truck cabs. But Mom said that was ridiculous and she wasn't discussing it any further with him.

Still, to be on the safe side, Mom took one of Nanna's most recent dampening charms with her in her pocket, and for added measure I kept my window rolled down. Just in case.

Halfway to Tyler, I finally gave in to the curiosity that had been bugging me for days.

"Mom, did you ever go to the Circle when you were in the Clann?"

She made a face as if she'd just smelled a skunk. "Unfortunately, I spent half my childhood there. Not only is it the place where all the major Clann gatherings are held, but it's also a safe place where elders can take descendants to train, especially the kids who are having a tough time learning to control their abilities. They've got a bunch of safeguards around it to keep out v—" She glanced at me. "I mean, outsiders, and to prevent descendants from accidentally setting the trees on fire or blowing up anything beyond its border. And believe me, I probably tested those wards more than all the other descendants combined."

"Then how did Dad and I get past the wards?"

"Your Clann blood will always allow you to enter the Circle. And if you were there and even thought that your dad should be allowed in, then the wards there wouldn't stop him, either. That's how the wards were set up, so we could pick and choose which allies to allow in during times of danger."

"So all I had to do was think 'let Dad in' and it did? There's no magic words that have to be said first?"

"Nope, not usually. Clann magic is mostly based on will-power and focused intention, not fancy words or magical candles and herbs." She blew out a noisy breath between her lips, making a sound like a horse so I would smile. "When I was your age, I would have given anything if only our abilities required eye of newt and hair of dog to work. Then I wouldn't have had so much trouble controlling them."

"Why not just do a spell on yourself to get rid of your abilities?" It seemed obvious to me. There must be some catch.

She burst out laughing. "Oh hon, don't you think I thought of that already? I tried a million times as a teen! But there are some things that are fundamental to our nature and can't be stopped with just willpower. Remember how Nanna gave you those special daily teas to hold off your puberty so we could try to prevent your vamp side from developing as long as possible? Remember how well that worked in the end?"

Did I ever. My body had ended up going to war with itself last year and I'd nearly died until Nanna's spell-laced teas flushed out of my system.

"But what about Nanna's bloodlust-dampening spell? Doesn't it affect the fundamental nature of vamps?"

"In a way, yes. See, the vamp wards work on your brainwaves by putting out a kind of targeted energy field that interferes with certain frequencies of thought. But that's almost like creating a sonar signal set to a frequency our ears can't pick up. That's not affecting anything on a cellular level.

"The bloodlust, however, isn't about your mind or emotions—it's in a vamp's genetic coding to crave blood. So the bloodlust-dampening spell has to work on that same DNA level. And that is some deep magic. It's like nothing the Clann normally teaches descendants nowadays. Which is why Nanna had to turn to the old ways from our Irish ancestors to find a way to make the dampening spell. She said there's a reason the Clann doesn't use the old ways anymore, because they're too dangerous. She even hinted that she had to make some sort of personal sacrifice every time for it to work. That's why she refused to write down the process or teach it to anyone. She was afraid other descendants would be desperate enough to try the spell regardless of the consequences."

I stared out at the highway ahead, both my mind and my heart racing. Dr. Faulkner had said Nanna died of heart complications, that her heart had years worth of scar tissue on it. But she'd never told us she was having health problems.

Could her heart disease have been connected to the bloodlust-dampening spells she'd done for my parents for years, and later on our own home so I could continue to live with her and Mom safely?

No. No, I was already at fault enough for the Clann imprisoning Nanna in the Circle. My vamp side couldn't be even more of a cause for her heart failure. She'd died because she'd fought against the Clann too hard that day, and because of the high cholesterol foods she ate, because she never exercised, because her genes had predisposed her to heart disease.

And yet…it fit, didn't it? If she were giving up part of her life or her health in some way in order to overcome the vamp's basic craving for powerful Clann blood, she wouldn't tell her daughter what Mom's love for Dad had cost. And she definitely wouldn't discuss it with her half vamp granddaughter.

Oh God. Nanna, what did you do to yourself?

I stared out my open window, biting my knuckles to keep from crying out loud as tears slid down my cheeks. The guilt, ever present in my gut, rose up to claw at my lungs, making it hard to breathe. I couldn't break down, not here, not now, when Mom was so excited about picking out the RV she'd always wanted. I'd already taken so much from her. I couldn't ruin this day, too.

"You okay, hon?" Mom said. "You got awful quiet there all of a sudden."

I cleared my throat, grateful the wind had dried the tears on my cheeks almost as soon as they fell, and forced a smile into my voice. "Sure! Just looking forward to seeing which RV you pick out."

"So what's with all the Clann questions today?"

I shrugged one shoulder. "You know, just…thinking about things."

"Missing your Nanna?" Her murmur was low and heavy with sympathy, nearly causing more tears to spill from my eyes.

I nodded. Closing my eyes, I tried to make my mind go blank. And yet flashes of that day in the Circle still managed to slip through…all those descendants watching Nanna die, watching me fall apart, listening to us as Mr. Coleman of-fered his condolences.

There had been something odd in Mr. Coleman's tone, a strange little catch as he'd almost said Mom's first name.

Desperate to change the subject, I blurted out the question, "Did you know Sam Coleman very well?"

"He was the future leader when I was growing up. Of course I knew who he was."

That didn't really answer my question. Safely dry-eyed now, I risked a glance her way. Her hands were gripping the steer-ing wheel so hard her tanned knuckles had turned white.

"He mentioned you," I said. "You know, when Dad and I were at the Circle."

She didn't look at me.

The seconds ticked by.

"Mom?"

She sighed. "I dated Sam Coleman when we were in high school."

Whoa, totally not the answer I'd expected. "Was it... serious?"

"Serious enough that he asked me to marry him at the be-ginning of our senior year."

"But you didn't because...you met my dad?"

She shook her head. "I told Sam I couldn't marry him months before I ever met your father. I didn't even want to be in the Clann, much less married to its future leader, no mat-ter how much I cared for Sam. So we broke up."

"And then you met Dad and ran off with him."

She nodded.

"Did you really love Dad? Or was it just because he was a vampire?"

She looked at me then. "Oh Savannah. Not everything's so cut and dried. I think, looking back now, that it was probably a little of everything. Michael was so handsome, and dangerous, and yet so polite and protective of me. It was easy to fall for him. The fact that loving him finally gave me the perfect way out of the Clann just added to my feelings for him."

"I thought anyone who wanted out of the Clann could leave anytime." She made it sound like some kind of gang or something.

"They can…if they don't have a mother like mine. Mom was determined to keep me in the Clann as long as she could. She always thought I'd change my feelings about our abilities, that I'd come around eventually and take up my training again."

"But then the Clann found out about you and Dad and kicked you out."

"Yes. Unfortunately my plan backfired a little. I never thought they'd blame Mom for my choices and kick her out, too."

I was starting to get why she'd run away from Jacksonville with Dad for years and come back only because of me. And why she'd chosen a sales rep job that kept her on the road so much of the year.

She wasn't just running away from Jacksonville or the Clann here, or avoiding causing me to feel the bloodlust around her. She was trying to run away from Sam Coleman and her past, too.

I couldn't blame her for that. If I thought leaving Jacksonville would really help me forget all my mistakes, I would run away from home so far and so fast and to heck with what the vamp council wanted.

Unfortunately I wasn't as good at living in denial as Mom was. No matter how far away from this town I ever managed to get, I would never escape the reflection in my mirror or the memories of the choices I had made.

But if running away made Mom happy, then that was what she should do. At the very least, she'd be safer away from the Clann headquarters. And from me and Dad.

It was a relief to arrive at the RV dealership. Normally Mom was a real pain to shop with because she tended to fall in love with everything in sight and become unable to choose. But this time Mom had done her research ahead of time and was surprisingly decisive about what she wanted in her new home on wheels. She test drove only two before she settled on a sleek travel trailer that could be pulled behind her truck so she could leave the trailer at campgrounds while she went into the fields and woods delivering chemicals and safety equipment to forestry clients.

She wore a triumphant smile as she signed the paperwork then towed it home. As she showed off the long-awaited trailer's updated interior features to Dad, her voice glowing with pride and excitement, I realized I was just the tiniest bit jealous of her.

At least one of us had her freedom.

The funeral on Saturday was even harder to endure than I'd expected. I couldn't look at Nanna's body, lying in the open casket at the church where she'd played the piano every Sunday, couldn't let myself think about her death or its possible causes, couldn't look at my mother who, despite all her excitement over her new home, was sobbing and clearly brokenhearted at having to say a final goodbye to her mother. When the new pianist played Nanna's favorite, "In the Garden," it was all I could do not to join my mother in sobbing.

The preacher's words were a blur both at the church and at the burial site in the Larissa Cemetery outside town, where all our family were buried. Even though it was only April, it was already hot enough to make everyone sweat under the glaring sun. The heat baked the mounds of carnations covering the casket, pushing their sweet perfume out into the air. I tried not to breathe deeply, but the stench of those flowers of death seeped inside me, clinging to the lining of my throat and lungs.

I knew I would hate the smell of those flowers for the rest of my life, however long that turned out to be.

After the preacher's final words were delivered, Mom spoke to all of Nanna's many friends while I gave Anne, Carrie and Michelle each a quick hug of thanks for coming. As soon as I saw my friends, I realized how much I'd both missed them and dreaded seeing them again. But for that day at least, none of them seemed to expect me to explain anything, which was a relief. Then my parents and I returned to Nanna's home to change and finish the last of the packing.

Dad had already found a house in town. It was a decrepit, crumbling two-story that might have once been a Victorian. The house looked like something the Addams family might live in. Worse than its appearance was its location, though… it was right across the railroad tracks from the Tomato Bowl, where the local high school and junior high football and soccer games were held. The only upside was that I wouldn't have a long walk after the home football games next year.

Dad said he'd chosen the house because it was the perfect renovation project to showcase his historical restoration company's abilities. I hoped they worked fast. Really fast. At least money would be no object. According to him, one of the advantages of being an ancient vampire with the ability to read human minds and actually live through several centuries of history was that he'd gotten really good at picking stocks.

On Sunday, Mom and I said a long, silent and teary goodbye to our home and each other. Then Dad and I moved in to our new home in progress, and Mom moved into her travel trailer and hit the road. True to his word, Dad had the movers set up my old bed in the new house. At least I wouldn't feel weird sleeping in an unfamiliar bed tonight, just a strange and dusty room surrounded by boxes of my things. I'd washed all my clothing before boxing it up, though, so I would have clean clothes until the washer and dryer were delivered and hooked up sometime next week.

Now if I could only get used to all the creaks and groans of my new home.

Nighttime, when I had nothing to distract me while I waited to fall asleep, was the worst. Even as little kids, Tristan and I had used our built-in abilities as descendants to psychically reach out and connect our minds in our dreams. We'd dream connected so often, especially during our recent months of dating, that it felt weird *not* to dream about him now. Another habit I was struggling to get used to breaking.

It would be so easy to close my eyes and reach out to him with my mind. To meet him like the hundreds of times I had before, always in the moonlight, usually in an imaginary version of the backyard behind his house or the Circle in the Coleman family woods. To see him smile, feel his fingers lace through mine, his lips against mine...

I lay there in my old bed in my new bedroom in the dark, watching the pine trees in the backyard sway in a breeze as if they were dancing. Dancing like Tristan and I used to do with our arms wrapped around each other as if we were two trees that had grown intertwined, never to be pulled apart. I had been so stupid, so naive to think he and I could make it last in spite of all the people and beliefs and fears against us.

Stifling a groan, I curled into a ball and pressed my pillow over my head, wishing I could press the memories out of my mind.

★ ★ ★

The alarm went off way too soon the next morning. Between fighting nightmares of Nanna and memories of Tristan, I hadn't gotten much sleep. Groaning, I slapped the clock's off button. Ugh, time to get ready for Charmers practice before school.

The thought made me freeze. Would Tristan be there?

I'd called Mrs. Daniels yesterday to let her know I'd be returning to practice today. I should have asked if Tristan would be there, too. Surely he wouldn't. His parents would keep him as far away from me as possible. Maybe I'd get extra lucky and they had even pulled him out of the history class we shared every other day, too.

I tried to relax as I got ready for school. I'd considered microwaving a bowl of oatmeal in the kitchen in a feeble attempt to recreate Nanna's cooking, but one look at the grubby mousetrap of a room and I changed my mind. Vampires couldn't eat regular food, so Dad probably wouldn't think to renovate in there for a while. There was no way I could choke down anything from that nasty, cobweb-draped dungeon until I cleaned it up. Besides, knowing my luck lately, if I tried to use the microwave I'd probably end up starting a house fire from the old wiring.

I should tell Dad I was leaving. But where was he? I followed the sound of hammering to the living room—then my feet skidded to a stop. My father had his head stuck inside the fireplace, his entire upper body swallowed within its cavernous darkness. Clouds of soot poofed out with each blow of his tools.

He was wearing…jeans? I'd never once seen him in anything but a suit.

"Uh, Dad?"

He ducked out of the fireplace. "Good morning, Savannah. Sleep well?"

Oh yeah, like a baby. "Um, you're working on the fireplace yourself?"

"Yes. It just needs a little cleaning to remove the nests inside. Then it should work fine."

I had a sudden vision of him trying to start a fire and blowing up the house. I cringed. "Shouldn't you hire a professional?"

"I am more than qualified to serve as a chimney sweep, Savannah."

Maybe he had a point. He was old enough that he'd probably been around when chimneys were invented. "I've got to go. Charmers practice." I checked my watch. "Which I'm going to be late for if I don't get moving."

He nodded. "What time will you be home this evening?"

"I don't know. We've got more practice after school."

His dark eyebrows shot up, hiding themselves under the wavy black hair that had flopped out of its usual precisely combed style onto his forehead. "You do not know what time the after-school practice will end?" His tone sounded either suspicious or accusing, I couldn't figure out which.

I stared at him. The man had had almost no involvement in my life for years. Now he'd decided to be a control freak just because I'd been forced to move in with him?

"Savannah, I am not your lackadaisical mother or grandmother. I will need to know your daily schedule with precise times at which to expect you home each day."

Lackadaisical? Did anybody even use that word anymore? And besides, my mother and grandmother had raised me just fine. Just because I made one mistake that caused a huge mess...

Fine. I saw his point. "Usually I do know what time practice will end. But right now the Charmers are getting ready for our annual Spring Show in a week. So we'll be practicing every morning before school starting at 6:45 a.m., and again after school until at least seven or eight o'clock. I never know when the evening practices will end exactly, because it depends on when each group of girls decides to quit for the day, and I have to stay until the last person leaves so I can lock up the building. So that's really the best guess I can give you. Would you like me to call when practice ends each day?"

"Yes, please do. I programmed my number into your phone." He reached into his pocket, pulled out my phone and tossed me the digital dog leash.

I dropped it into my blue leather Charmers duffel bag and turned toward the freedom of the front door.

"And Savannah?"

I stopped and looked back over my shoulder, trying very hard not to huff out a sigh of impatience. If he kept this up, I'd never get to practice on time.

"If you begin to feel strange in any way, do not wait to call me." His tone was a stern warning.

Or else I might go on a killing spree before he could get to me and stop me? Yeesh. "Yes, Dad," I muttered then made a hasty escape.

Annoyance continued to knot my stomach during the short drive across town to the school's front parking lot.

As I walked across the dark campus, I remembered how scared I had been with the watchers there. Now that I was turning into a full vampire, I was the scariest thing imaginable here.

Shaking my head, I headed up the sports and arts building's cement ramp toward its blue painted rows of doors and then had to stop as a sharp pain spiked through me.

For the first time in months, Tristan wasn't waiting for me.

My steps became jerky as I forced my legs to move. I swallowed hard and searched for the right key to unlock the doors.

This is all wrong, a voice at the back of my mind moaned. He should be here, leaning against the doors, as perfect-looking as a catalog model. He should be reaching out to hold my thermos of tea, made fresh by Nanna, while I struggled to think straight.

But I didn't have my usual cup of tea from Nanna. And I was alone.

Inside, I stopped, too aware that I was the only person in the dark, empty building. I scowled. I had been just fine before Tristan came along. I'd been in this building alone countless times and had never felt lonely.

I had to get used to being on my own again.

I trudged across the foyer, flicked all four light switches up in one swipe, then continued up the stairs, my footsteps echoing in the half-lit stairwell, every step seeming to whisper, "Alone. Alone. Alone."

Gritting my teeth, I pulled open the upstairs hallway door and entered the pitch-black third-floor hall. The door slammed shut behind me, making my shoulders hunch up.

I pushed onward, my eyes adjusting quickly to the dark. I unlocked the dance room doors and turned on the lights. And froze as I was confronted by another crime scene. Right there by the stereo, Tristan and I had sat on the floor, sharing pizza in the semi-darkness for our first date. And then we'd danced together, a silly waltz to make me laugh, then a slow dance until I'd melted into our first kiss since the fourth grade.

Right there in that dance room was where I'd also first unknowingly drained him of energy.

Enough. I shook myself, breaking free of the paralyzing memories and guilt. I had a job to do.

A familiar ache welled up in my chest and stomach, and

this time it wasn't from the memories. Oh no. Only one person caused *this* sensation.

I was no longer alone.

I whirled around and sucked in a breath. "Tristan!"

He lounged in the hallway's entrance, leaning one broad shoulder against the wall, arms crossed. He stared at me, his green eyes the color of a deep pine forest today. "Good morning, Savannah."

I gulped. So wrong for my heart to leap at the sound of my name spoken in that deep, rumbling voice. So wrong of my feet to want to take off running toward him.

"We need to talk," he said, his tone like a brush of his fingertips across my cheek.

I struggled to make my body move toward the Charmers director's office door. Routine. Focus on the morning routine.

I fought to keep my voice even. "What are you doing here? Didn't your parents—"

"In spite of the local rumors, my parents don't actually rule the world."

Frowning, I got the office door unlocked. I walked inside, turned on the overhead lights, then headed for the closet door on shaky legs. "The Clann would disagree with that."

Closet door unlocked, I reached inside for the jambox and Megavox case. And sucked in another sharp breath as Tristan cupped my upper arms, his big hands warm and gentle on my bare skin below the sleeves of my T-shirt. I nearly moaned at the contact.

"Sav, please stop for a minute and listen to me."

Oh sweet lord. How was I supposed to withstand that soft, deep voice pleading with me? I closed my eyes and prayed for strength as everything inside me begged me to turn around and hug him.

"I'm sorry about your grandmother."

His words were velvet-covered blows to my stomach. I couldn't breathe.

"You have to know I never imagined anything like that would happen."

"But it did," I croaked, still facing the closet. "Because of us." *Because of me.*

He pressed his forehead to the top of my head, his sigh warm in my hair. "We didn't do that. The Clann did. I know how much you loved her. We tried to save her. You, me, your dad and mine, even Dr. Faulkner. She knew you loved her and were trying to help her."

Bitter acid rose up as a sour taste at the back of my mouth. "She shouldn't have even *been* there. And she wouldn't have been if we hadn't broken the rules. We never should have gotten involved with each other."

"No, the Clann and the vamp council never should have barred us from seeing each other."

Strength slowly seeped back into my body. "Keeping us away from each other was one of the few things they did right."

"Savannah, I love you," he whispered, his voice harsh, as if the words were torn from his lungs. "And I know you love me."

I wouldn't lie to him. I nodded.

"Then why can't you see how this isn't about whether to follow the rules or not? The rules are wrong. If ever two people were meant for each other, we're it. We don't have to let them control our lives. You and I determine our future, not them."

I turned to face him then, needing to see if he was truly this delusional. Didn't he get it? This wasn't about what I wanted, or even what he wanted anymore.

"I'll leave the Clann," he said, speaking fast now. "You

know I never cared about being in it anyways. Then they can't stop us. Their rules won't apply to us anymore."

"And break your parents' hearts?" Oh lord, how badly I wanted it to be just him and me, free from the rules, free to be together. But then we'd be just like my parents, always on the run, always hiding. There was nowhere we could go to be together beyond the reach of the Clann or the vamp council. Even if he wasn't in the Clann anymore, he'd still be a descendant. And I would still be a vampire.

His lips thinned. "They'll get over it, trust me."

"And the vampire council?"

"We'll talk to them, convince them that our being together isn't a danger to their peace treaty."

"Tristan, you don't get it. We're not Romeo and Juliet. There's a reason the Clann and the council hate and fear each other. We're a *danger* to each other, whether you're in the Clann or not. You could set me on fire with one snap of your fingers. And I could kill you just as easily. As long as vamps and descendants are each others' biggest threats, they're always going to be enemies. You and I will never get permission to be together."

"Just because they have the power to kill each other doesn't mean they have to. We can show them that, make them see that they can choose to coexist in peace. Don't you see? You and me together...*we're* the proof they need to make them believe it can be done."

"Not everything's a simple choice like that."

"Sure it is. You could have bitten me a thousand times by now, but you never did. Right?"

"What about all the times I kissed you?"

He hesitated. "So you took a little energy. It was worth it."

"It put you in danger. *I* put you in danger. I took a little bit of your *life* every time we kissed. That's not a choice I can make, either. It's automatic. There's no way to turn that off."

He scowled. "So we'll keep working around it. You're not a danger to me."

He was an idiot. Or suicidal. How could he not see the truth, how impossible this whole situation was? No matter how much we loved each other, no amount of love or wishing would change the fact that I was a threat to his life every second we were alone together. Even now, right this second, he was in danger. And he refused to see it.

I would save him from himself and *make* him see.

I stepped closer to him and rose up on tiptoe, finally giving in to the need to press against him. He groaned, wrapped his arms around me, and ducked his head.

I kissed him, parting his lips, purposefully deepening the kiss past sweetness straight into mind-wrecking loss of control. His energy poured into me, a heady rush of power that sang through my veins like liquid lightning.

He moaned into my mouth, and even his breath was food. I didn't even have to work for it. All I had to do to drain him was kiss him. There was no internal on and off switch, no controlling the flow of energy from him to me. I was an endless, bottomless cup that would take every drop of his life until he was gone. And there was nothing I could do to change that ability.

He staggered backward to the wall, pulling me with him. And still we kissed, his fingers spread wide over my back, mine threaded into the soft, unruly curls at the nape of his neck. His heart pounded against my chest, its rhythm slowly growing fainter.

I was killing him. And part of me didn't want to stop.

His knees shook against my thighs then gave out. He slid down the wall to the floor.

Only then did I break off the kiss with a gasp and step away from him. He sat on the gray industrial carpeting, struggling for breath, and that struggle brought tears to my eyes.

"How do you feel?" I whispered.

"Wow," he whispered, his eyes dazed.

My hands ached to reach out to him again, to pull him to his feet. To pull him closer for another kiss. "Can you stand up?"

He laughed, unaware that I was crumbling to pieces inside. "You'll have to give me a couple of minutes to recover here."

He'd just proven my point. And my biggest fear.

"How can you refuse to see how dangerous I am to you? How dangerous every vamp is to every descendant? You can't even stand up after one kiss from me. If another vampire were here right now, would you have enough energy to protect yourself?"

He frowned, his eyes blinking fast as if to clear his vision. He was so stubborn. But I would save him, no matter what it took. I had to. I couldn't live in a world without him in it, even if I couldn't be with him.

I leaned closer to him until my lips hovered over the vein pulsing sluggishly at the side of his neck. I could hear his heartbeat, faint and slow like a low chord softly played on an unseen piano over and over. He could never know how precious that music would always be to me.

The memory of how sweet and good his blood had tasted filled me with such an incredible ache that I was momentarily frozen.

I pushed the memory away. Just more proof that I was a danger to him every second we were together.

I pressed a shaky kiss to the side of his cheek instead, breathing in his crisp scent, feeling the rasp of stubble from a few whiskers he'd missed shaving this morning in front of his ear.

"No matter how much I love you, no matter how much I wish I could change what I am, I can't. And neither can you. Sometimes love doesn't conquer all. Sometimes we just have to let go. The Clann and the council, they just want to keep us safe from each other. Listen to them. Help me keep my promise to them. Let this go."

Let me go.

Help me find a way to let you go.

Help me rip out my own heart here, I might as well have said.

CHAPTER 5

TRISTAN

Red strands of her hair tickled my cheeks, their lavender scent filling my nose and adding to the buzz in my head. Did she have any idea how much she wrecked my mind, my control? How much I'd missed even the scent of her perfume all last week? How, even now, without any power to stop her or protect myself, I was still happier than I'd ever been?

When I was around her, my world made sense. I knew who I was. I'd never known what I'd wanted out of life before her, other than to play pro football. I'd drifted through each day, doing exactly what my parents expected of me. I'd dated other girls. A lot of them. Blondes, brunettes, redheads, they'd all made me feel the same…nothing more than casual friendship. They were great to hang out with, but none had ever made me wonder what they were thinking or doing when we were apart. I never wondered how they were getting along with their parents. I never worried that no one else recognized how amazing they truly were. I didn't miss them when I couldn't talk to them, and I hadn't been torn to pieces when I stopped dating them.

I'd never *needed* any girl like I needed Savannah.

Sluggish as my thoughts had become, I heard the goodbye in her voice, in her words, saw it in her tear-filled eyes. She was letting me go.

I had to stop her.

She turned away, dragging a sleeve across her cheeks as she left the office and headed down the hallway toward the back stairs that led to the stage.

I struggled to my feet. My legs didn't want to work, but I forced them to move. I caught up with her halfway down the hall. "Turn me."

She stopped so suddenly I had to grab the wall to keep from running over her. She looked at me over her shoulder, her eyes pale silver now and round with shock. Then she was on the move again. "I can't."

"Think about it, Sav. If I was a vamp, we wouldn't have any problems, would we? You couldn't drain me, and the vamps and Clann wouldn't have to worry about protecting their peace treaty." And my parents wouldn't have an excuse to keep us apart anymore, either.

"There's a reason I'm the first known dhampir of our kinds, Tristan. Descendants' bodies reject vamp blood. Every descendant who has ever attempted to turn died."

"So they claim. But when's the last time anyone actually tried it? I'm willing to risk it. There's got to be a spell to help the process or—"

"No way. I'm not risking your life." Backstage now in the pitch black of the wings, I heard her set down the portable sound system with a thud. Metal clanged as she opened the fuse box on the wall, probably using her vamp eyesight to see in the dark. The stage lights came on.

"I could find another vampire to help me."

"No, you can't. Everyone knows who you are. No vamp would go against the council like that." She slammed the fuse box door shut, the sound echoing in the empty wings. Then she took the portable sound system out to the front corner of the stage, crouching down in the shadows beyond the reach of the overhead stage lights in order to set up the music in the jambox.

I squatted in the shadows beside her as I always did during sound system setup, our knees touching, her arm brushing mine as she worked. In the beginning last fall, I'd done it to try to get her to recognize her feelings for me. That had been before she'd known even kissing me could be a problem. Back when all I'd needed to do was get her to admit she was falling for me.

Now we knew what we felt for each other, and it still wasn't enough. Not as long as my parents, the Clann and the vamp council were determined to keep us apart.

"What if I got everyone to change their minds about us?" I had no idea how I could pull that off. But there had to be a way.

She looked at me, her still watery eyes filled with a flash of hope that squeezed my insides like a vise. "How?"

I didn't have an answer yet. But I would, no matter what it took. "I'll find a way."

"Mr. Coleman, what are you doing here?" Mrs. Daniels called out as she entered the theater through the audience area doors. "I don't believe you're supposed to be helping us anymore."

Great, just what I needed. "That's a misunderstanding—"

"I don't think so. I spoke with your parents last week. Their intentions were very clear." Mrs. Daniels took her usual seat in the back row.

Savannah quickly wiped her face dry then went back to working on the sound system. Obviously she would be no help here.

I jumped off the stage and strode up the aisle to Mrs. Daniels's row. The woman's gaze was every bit as frosty as Savannah's when she was trying to shut someone out.

"Ma'am, I still want to help out with the team," I insisted, trying my most charming smile on her. It always worked on the teachers and the ladies in the front office.

One blond eyebrow arched. "No one stays on the team in any capacity without their parents' consent, not even volunteers on the stage crew. School rules. You'll have to take it up with your parents if you want to help us out again. Until then, I'll have to ask you to go to the front office, where you've been reassigned as an office aide for your first periods from now on." She flipped a page on her clipboard, silently dismissing me.

Great. Now how was I supposed to talk to Savannah, be with her at all, without the Clann seeing? The only class we had together was history every other day with Mr. Smythe, Dylan Williams and the Brat Twins...four descendants who would be extra vigilant in spying on us now.

I glanced back at Savannah. Her shoulders hunched in response, but she refused to look up.

Fine. Savannah had made herself clear. Until I found a way to change the rules, she wouldn't see me, and there would be no point in arguing with Mrs. Daniels.

But Savannah was wrong if she thought I'd given up on us. I *would* find a way to change the rules. Somehow.

SAVANNAH

My friends fell silent as I joined them at our usual table in the cafeteria on my first day back at school. I wasn't hungry, but I'd skipped breakfast, so I'd grabbed a bag of chips and a Coke. And tried to ignore the ache that being within a hundred yards of Tristan always caused. Usually he sat outside at a tree during lunch. Today he was sitting by his sister at the Clann table and staring at me.

In the silence, my chip bag cracked like a gunshot as I tore it open. But I'd pulled too hard. The bag ripped in half, exploding harvest-cheddar-flavored chips all over my lap and the table in front of me.

I sighed. "Good thing I wasn't hungry."

"Sav…" Anne began, and I cringed at the hesitant sympathy in her voice. I knew what was coming. Most of the Charmers and Mrs. Daniels had all used that same tone of voice to offer their condolences about my grandmother earlier this morning.

I looked up, found all three of my friends staring at me with drawn, sympathetic faces. I held up a hand. "I know y'all are probably worried about me. And I appreciate it, really I do. But I'm okay. Honest."

They nodded too quickly and too hard.

Desperate to change the subject, I pasted on a smile and looked at Michelle. "So what's the latest gossip? Did I miss anything good last week?"

Michelle opened her mouth, then bit her lower lip. "Um, actually, all the hottest gossip has been about Tristan and… you."

Oh no, we were not going there. "Okay, then I've got some news. I moved in with my dad last week."

"What the heck?" Anne gasped. "But how…I mean, I thought he lived in another state. Will you have to transfer?"

"Nope," I told her. "He bought that old Victorian place across the railroad tracks. You know, the one you can see from the Tomato Bowl? He's fixing it up as a local showcase house for his renovation company."

All three pairs of eyes widened.

"Oh, Sav, that's terrible," Michelle whispered, as if I'd just stated that I had some incurable disease. "Everyone knows that house is haunted."

"And extremely unsafe," Carrie added. "No one's lived in it for decades. It must be in terrible condition. Probably filled with lead plumbing and asbestos, too."

"Well, it does need a lot of work," I replied, making a mental note to get some bottled water to keep at the house. "But that's my dad's specialty. His business's whole focus is on renovating historical homes and restoring them to their former glory. So he'll probably have it all fixed up in no time." I hoped.

"Have you seen any ghosts yet?" Anne asked before taking a long chug of her soda.

"No." I laughed. "It is a little spooky though. Dad says it gets so noisy at night because all the wood and plumbing expands or contracts or something with the change in temperature from day to night. My room has a great view, though, and it's about four times the size of my old one. So everyone will finally have plenty of room for our sleepovers."

I smiled and looked around, expecting them to at least get excited about that. Instead, everyone was suddenly very busy eating or gathering up their trash.

They were freaked out by my new home, and they hadn't even seen the inside yet.

I thought about the houses they all lived in...Carrie's brick lakeside home, Anne's pristine modern brick home in town by Buckner Park. Even Michelle's house, while not always the tidiest because of all her little brothers and sisters, was fairly new.

And now they thought they'd get lead poisoning if they came over to my house.

I snagged a chip from my lap and chomped on it in silence.

Then I felt it...the hairs at the back of my neck stood on end, like someone was staring at me.

Slowly I looked over my shoulder.

Tristan.

My lungs tightened, refusing to expand. Would he come over, insist on arguing with me again about things I had no power to change, make another scene in front of the Clann kids?

But he only sat there staring, his jaw set, his eyes that shade of dark emerald they always turned when he was angry or upset.

Maybe he'd finally started to see the reality of our situation.

My head said I should be relieved.

But all I felt was the aching need to cry.

TRISTAN

I tried to find that old confidence inside me that I was right and somehow I'd find a way to change the minds of the vamp council and my parents. But my parents refused to talk to me about it, my mother even going so far as to threaten to take away my truck keys and ground me if I said Savannah's name one more time in her presence. And I had no way to directly contact the vamp council.

By Friday night, as I sat in the high school theater while the Charmers performed their Spring Show onstage, I knew there was only one solution to all of this.

I had to become a vampire.

I had no way to convince the Clann or the council to change their rules. But if I became a vamp, then there wouldn't be any danger in being with Savannah. They'd have to leave us alone.

Savannah would never turn me herself, even if I tried to make her lose control of the bloodlust. She believed the myth that vampire blood killed descendants. I'd have to convince another vamp to do the deed. But who? I knew only one vampire. Her dad. And I had no idea how to convince Mr. Colbert to turn me, or even where they lived.

I knew someone who might know their new address, though. And she was in the phone book. I slipped out of the theater to make the call. Thankfully she answered.

"Hey, Michelle, it's Tristan Coleman. From first period office aide—"

A loud squeak made me hold the phone away from my ear. What the heck?

"Michelle? Are you still there?" I asked, wondering if her phone had died.

"Yep! I'm here," she breathed.

Okay. "I know it's weird for me to call you like this, but I was hoping you could do me a huge favor. Do you know Savannah's new address? I need to talk to her father."

"Say no more," she said, her voice rising with each word. "I always thought you two would make the perfect couple."

That made two of us.

"They bought that old haunted house across the tracks from the Tomato Bowl. You know, the green-and-white Victorian?"

"Yeah, I know the one you're talking about." I was already headed down the ramp to my truck in the back parking lot. "Thanks, Michelle."

"You know, Savannah's been really sad this week. Everyone says it's because you two were secretly dating and then broke up, but she won't talk about it at all. Did you dump her?"

"No. It was the other way around actually."

Silence. Finally she said, "Well, I hope you get back together."

"I'm sure trying."

"Good luck!"

I thanked her, then ended the call, got in my truck and headed across town, trying to plan what in the world I could possibly say to convince her dad to turn me when I couldn't even convince his daughter.

At the house, I parked by the curb, turned off the engine, then sat for a few minutes listening to the ticking of my truck's engine as it cooled down.

Was I doing the right thing? Or should I do what everyone else wanted and let her go?

I closed my eyes, and as always Savannah's face was right there in my mind waiting for me. I had a thousand memories of her...as a sweet little girl with flowers in her hair giving me the softest of kisses on the playground in the fourth grade... dressed as a breathtaking angel dancing barefoot with me in the leaves outside this year's masq ball.... She feared she would lose control and kill me, but all I knew was the innocent, loving side of her. Everyone wanted me to see her as some kind of monster. But I didn't know how to do that.

I couldn't give up on her. Not yet. Not if there was one last shot at making everything right again.

I got out of my truck and walked across the front yard, still clueless as to what the heck I would say to her dad. The front porch creaked as I stepped onto it. I paused, my pulse pounding. Was I nervous about the creepy house, or talking to her dad?

Both, I decided, but kept going anyway. The loud whine of a saw started somewhere deep inside the house, and I froze at the front door. A chain saw? Oh man, this was like every horror movie I'd ever seen come straight to life. Still, I went ahead and knocked. A vampire would hear me even over the saw.

The noise stopped, and too soon, the door opened.

The only time I'd seen Savannah's father was on the return

trip from the vamp council's headquarters in Paris. Mr. Colbert had appeared every inch the vampire then in a polished suit, his emotionless face set like carved marble.

Tonight, he wore a button-up shirt, sleeves rolled to the elbows, and jeans, both covered in dirt and sawdust. He seemed nothing more than an average guy hard at work on his house.

And I'd come to ask him to turn me into a vampire.

Mr. Colbert didn't seem surprised that I was there. But he didn't invite me inside, either. "Hello again, Tristan. How may I help you this evening? Savannah is not home."

"I know that, sir. That's why I'm here now. I need your help."

He stared at me, unmoving. I'd hoped we could have this talk inside. Not that it would have been any easier there. I cleared my throat.

"I love Savannah. And this isn't some teenage hormone thing, either. I've loved her since we were kids. I've never felt anything even close to this with anyone else. And I know she loves me, too."

My heart pounded harder. It didn't help that he could probably hear it. My hands turned hot and damp. I shoved them inside my front jeans pockets.

"You know the promises she has made." He wasn't asking me.

I nodded anyway. "The council and the Clann are afraid she'll kill me and break the treaty. Savannah's afraid of that, too. But I think there's another option."

A single thick black eyebrow rose in silent question. The way he was able to stand so still was more than a little unnerving.

If I was successful tonight, would I be able to freeze like that, too?

"You could make me a vampire."

Seconds ticked by. A breeze kicked up, making the trees rustle behind me. The wind wasn't strong enough to dry the sweat running down my back, though.

Finally, Mr. Colbert stepped away from the door. "Come inside."

Was that his way of agreeing to turn me?

Heart racing, I entered the house, my every step making the hardwood floors creak and groan. He shut the door behind me then led the way to a dark maroon leather couch in the room to the right. Sawdust made the floor slippery and the air smell like pine, and tools lay all over the place.

He gestured toward the couch, and we sat at opposite ends, angled to face each other.

As soon as I was seated, he asked, "You are really willing to give up your humanity for my daughter?"

I didn't hesitate. At least this much I was sure about. "Yes, sir."

He studied my face. "You seem confident. But perhaps that is because you do not know what being a vampire is truly like. Shall I tell you?"

Less sure I wanted to hear this, I forced a nod. Might as well find out the gory details of what I was getting into. Though part of me would rather find out later once I was turned and couldn't be tempted to chicken out.

"We vampires are an evolved species," he began. "Things that were once dire problems, such as daylight, are no longer threats to us. It may seem that we are the perfect beings, able to walk among humans, appearing relatively normal, with only fire, staking or decapitation to worry about. We are immortals. No sickness will ever harm us, and we will never age past the point in life at which each of us is turned. We are able to read the minds of fellow vampires and humans, but not descendants. We gain great speed, strength and agility."

He paused, letting silence fill the room so long I was forced to reply. "Doesn't sound like being a vampire is all that tough so far."

His silver gaze, a more intense version of Savannah's, locked onto me. "Yes, it would seem so. But within hours of first awakening as a vampire, you feel a thirst that is like nothing you could ever imagine. It is the bloodlust clawing at your very insides, the craving for human blood, and any human's blood will do. In the first few weeks, many vampires accidentally kill even their loved ones because of this blinding thirst."

Okay, not so great to be a vamp in the beginning. "But it goes away, right?"

"The bloodlust lessens after a while. But it never completely goes away. And being around someone like yourself with such powerful, magic-laced blood in your veins presents special challenges. That power calls to even the oldest of vampires as strongly as if we have just been turned. Even at my age of over three hundred years, I find it difficult to be around a descendant for long."

I shifted uneasily, making the couch creak. "But you can do it. I mean, you married Sav's mom. And you were around a bunch of descendants in the woods a couple weeks ago and you were okay."

His lips stretched into a cold smile. "With Savannah's mother, I had the assistance of a charm her mother created for me—a spell that only Savannah's grandmother knew, which dampened the bloodlust and made it bearable. And in the forest with the Clann, it is true that I managed not to attack anyone, but it was a great struggle not to. If I had been younger, I might not have had the control to stop myself."

I turned my head to stare at the empty black opening of the fireplace. "So I wouldn't be able to be around my family for a while."

"If it even worked. Unfortunately, it is impossible to successfully turn a descendant."

I stared at him again. "I've heard the stories. I don't believe them. They're just lies to keep descendants from trying to become vamps."

He was gone and back so fast I felt a breeze, returning to stand by the coffee table with a knife and two saucers. "I will prove it is the truth. Cut yourself, just a little, please, and catch the blood in a saucer. Then add my blood to yours and see what happens." He sliced his finger, and a dark red puddle rapidly formed in one saucer. Then he handed me the knife, his finger already healed as if it had never been cut in the first place. "When you are done, we will continue this discussion outside."

Then he was gone, leaving the front door open. Apparently he didn't want to test his control around a bleeding descendant. Was it really *that* big a problem?

I cut my finger like he had, letting the blood drop onto the clean saucer. When the pool was roughly the size of a dime, I used the knife to scrape up a few drops of his blood from the other saucer and drip it into mine.

I'd thought he and everyone else had been lying. But when I saw the two combined types of blood turn into one thick, gooey black circle that smelled like rotting roadkill left in the sun, then sizzle and give off tendrils of smoke, I knew it wasn't a myth. And that was from a few drops of vamp blood. What would more vamp blood do inside a descendant's body?

There was no way to turn me into a vampire.

I noticed a piece of paper stuck to the back of the saucer. A Band-Aid. I tore its thin wrapper open with my teeth and covered the cut on my finger, then headed out to the porch on shaking legs.

"If you knew, why bother telling me what being a vamp

is like?" He'd been toying with me since I got here, making me think I had a shot at becoming a vampire and being with Savannah forever. If he hadn't been her father, I would have been tempted to punch him.

"So you would know just how impossible it is for you two to be together."

I stared at the street lamp, its light throwing long shadows across the yard.

Sheer desperation made me say, "There has to be a way we can be together. If you love her, tell me what to do, what to say to make them change the rules. You know it can be done. You did it yourself. You married her mother. Give us the chance to have that, too."

"But it did not work. Even after Savannah's mother was kicked out of the Clann, our union was a danger to the peace treaty because of what it produced."

"You mean Savannah."

He nodded. "You two could produce another dhampir like her if she does not fully turn vampire first. And the council, as well as the Clann, will never allow that to happen again."

An image flashed before me of a little girl with curly red hair like her momma. And maybe green eyes like her daddy. I'd never thought about being a dad someday, but something clenched in my chest all the same, making it hard to breathe.

Mr. Colbert didn't seem to notice. "That child would be a danger to vampires and descendants alike, even more than Savannah is. Like Savannah, it could grow into a fully immortal vampire with its father's legendary Coleman magical abilities, or into the next Coleman witch with the speed, strength and agility of a vampire. Either way, it would present enormous risks. Risks that the council—and I am sure the Clann—will never consider acceptable."

I couldn't be turned into a vampire. And as long as I was

still human and Savannah could still have kids, the Clann and the council wouldn't let us be together. "What happens if she fully turns?"

"There will still always be the risk that she could end your life. Your parents will not care whether you are a member of the Clann. You will always be their child, and they will do whatever is necessary to protect you." He turned to me now, placing a hand on my shoulder. "If there was a way for you and my daughter to be happy together, I would do everything in my power to assist you. But there is no way the rules will be changed for you. And I can promise you from experience that even the strongest of love cannot long survive being on the run, or some of the tactics either side might employ in an attempt to draw you out of hiding." His hand fell away. "The constant hiding alone drove Savannah's mother away from me."

I wanted to believe he was wrong, that things would be different for Savannah and me. That what we had together could survive anything, including being on the run from the council and the Clann.

But what if he was right? The Clann had already taken Sav's grandmother from her. Would my parents be desperate enough to go after Sav's mother next? Or her father? Would the vamps go after Emily to get to me?

Savannah and I could never live with ourselves if any of that happened. Savannah was struggling to deal with her grandmother's death as it was.

And that's when it hit me. There was nothing left to try. The Clann and the council were going to get their way, no matter how much Savannah and I wished otherwise.

No amount of football game losses could have prepared me for the crushing defeat that slammed me now. I'd never been in this situation before. I'd always been able to find a way to get what I wanted in life. Not because I was spoiled, as Emily teased me, but because Dad had always said if you wanted something enough and kept working at it, you'd find a way.

He was wrong. The one thing I wanted more than anything else in life was to be with Savannah. But I couldn't. Not now, and if her father was to be believed, not ever. Not as long as the Clann and the council hated and feared each other.

I made my feet carry me down the porch steps to my truck, and then I headed for the prison that my home had become.

CHAPTER 6

SAVANNAH

Tristan had given up.

Until that moment, I hadn't realized just how much faith I secretly had in him. Tristan was a fighter at heart, and he almost always got what he wanted. He wanted us to be together again, so if there was a real solution, he would find it.

Except this time he obviously hadn't.

He didn't have to tell me it was truly over. I could feel the frustration and despair rolling off of him every time we passed each other in the main hall between classes. I could see it in the bleakness in his eyes, in the defeated slump of his shoulders. And most of all in how he couldn't seem to look me in the eye anymore.

It was over.

I tried to tell myself that it wasn't the end of the world, that maybe someday my heart would heal and I'd find someone new.

When the lies didn't work, I tried to throw myself into school and Charmers stuff with the hope that, if I could just stay busy enough, then eventually I would find a way to breathe deeply again without that aching need to cry.

There wasn't a real sense of time passing over the next few weeks while I waited for our sophomore year to end. At home, I filled every spare second by helping Dad remove old wallpaper and flooring in the house. Unfortunately, this still left me with far too much free time now that the Charmers Spring Show and team auditions had passed. Team auditions day had been the one day when I actually hadn't had a single free moment for four blessed hours, as I'd had to shoulder all the manager workload while both of my fellow sophomore managers successfully re-auditioned for the team. I tried to be happy for them, and happy that it left me as the only choice for head manager for next year. Most of all, I tried not to regret the fact that the vamp council had banned me from ever dancing in public again so I wouldn't accidentally reveal my vamp side to humans. I doubted I could even remember how to dance now anyways.

In March, the team also held officer auditions. Mrs. Daniels had me stay late after school that day to run the music while she and two judges scored the candidates on their officer solo and group routines. Bethany Brookes became one of the junior lieutenant officers, which didn't surprise anyone. She was a good leader for the team, always willing to help others, always so happy and sweet and outgoing. It was like she had this perpetual ray of light beaming on her everywhere she went. Probably why her nickname on the dance team was Lil Miss Sunshine.

I wished I could be like her. But everything about my life was the polar opposite of hers. While Bethany was spinning in the spotlight, I was huddled in the dark backstage, and I couldn't find a way out. I wanted to be the girl I was a year ago, before I got sick and learned all my family's secrets, before I took a chance and let myself fall for a boy I could never have. Before Nanna died, and Mom was gone all the time on the road.

But I couldn't go back, and I couldn't change what I'd done or stop what I was now becoming. All I could do was fake a smile for my friends at lunch every day and pretend everything was all right.

And make sure I never looked back over my shoulder at the Clann table or the boy I could never be with again.

"Savannah?" Anne asked, her voice louder than usual in the cafeteria.

I jumped, knocking over my drink in the process. We all dived for napkins to sop up the spill while I muttered apologies. Well, there went my liquid lunch. All other food smelled too gross to eat lately.

"Are you in?" Anne repeated once Lake Savannah was managed on the table.

"In?" I stared at her in confusion. I really needed to stop spacing out so much around others.

"To go shopping this weekend," Michelle answered, staring at me. When I didn't answer, she added, "For dresses for the semiformal spring dance? We're going to the mall in Tyler this Saturday." Her tiny frame practically bounced in her seat.

A semiformal dance? Why would I want to go to that?

Carrie stared at me as if I were a new species of germ under a microscope.

Anne just rolled her eyes. "Earth to Miss Space Cadet. The dance is in two weeks. We're all going. Including you."

Cringing, I opened my mouth to argue.

Anne shook her head, her chestnut-colored ponytail swinging wildly. "No way, don't even think about bailing on me.

These two have dates. I don't. Therefore you will be coming with me. I am not standing on the sidelines alone the whole night."

"Then why go—" I began.

"For the dresses, of course!" Anne grinned. "Hey, don't look at me like that. Even tomboys like me enjoy playing princess every once in a while."

Carrie snickered.

Anne ignored her. "Come on, Sav. You never do anything with us anymore. Just because we're not cool like your precious Charmers…"

It was my turn to groan and roll my eyes. "Don't start with that again."

Anne bared her teeth in the semblance of a smile. "Then don't make me! Come shopping with us. Come to the dance. Pretend to be human again for a change."

I froze. Did they know…?

No. No way could they guess my secrets. I was just being paranoid.

But maybe, just to be safe, I should try harder to fit in and be normal. "Fine." I sighed, already regretting giving in. "Let's go shopping this weekend."

Michelle squealed and started raving about some prom magazines she'd bought to help prep us for the occasion. I nodded and tried to look interested.

Suddenly, the full meaning of Anne's words registered with me.

"Wait a second." I turned toward her. "Why aren't you going with Ron?" She and Ron Abernathy had been dating for months, just like Tristan and me. In fact, their first date had been at the Charmers' masq ball last October.

Where Tristan and I had danced together outside in the

leaves, the full moon's light making his fake knight's armor shine as if it had been plated in real silver...

"...so we're not seeing each other anymore," Anne finished in a mumble.

I'd spaced out again and missed hearing her answer. Geez, I was a crappy friend lately. "I'm sorry, it was too loud in here. What did you say?"

Anne stared at me then shrugged. "I said he and I got into an argument and I broke up with him. We're not together anymore."

"What was the fight about?"

Anne gathered up her things. "It was...family stuff. I really don't want to talk about it. And the bell's about to ring anyway. Come on, let's go."

I opened my mouth to argue but the bell rang, cutting me off. Then I got a good look at the set of Anne's chin. Stubborn as she was, I wouldn't get anything more about it from her today.

Obviously something major had happened that I'd missed either because I hadn't been paying attention or she hadn't wanted to tell me. When had she broken up with Ron? Had she been upset and I hadn't even noticed? Had she tried to call to talk about it?

I caught up to her at the trash cans. "Anne, wait. At least tell me when you broke up with him."

She took her time pouring her soda into the trash. "It was the week after your grandma..."

Oh. So that's why I hadn't heard about it. "I'm sorry I wasn't there for you. That week was—"

She gave a quick shake of her head. "Don't worry about it. I would have been out of it, too. Ready for third period?"

Part of me wanted to push her harder, find out what had

happened. She had seemed completely blissed out every time Ron was around. What had changed?

Then again, who was I to try and pry the details of a painful story out of her? It wasn't like I'd told her anything about my own breakup with Tristan. Or how Nanna had really died, or my family's many secrets....

Yeah, I was definitely in no position to be nosy.

But it was one more thing between us pushing our friendship apart, and I didn't know how to fix it.

And yet, I had to try.

I did my best to stay in the present and pay attention that Saturday when we all went dress shopping in Tyler, first at the mall then at several boutiques Michelle had looked up. I wanted to care about dresses and hairstyles and the merits of gold jewelry versus silver and rhinestones versus pearls. Maybe if I pretended hard enough, I could forget about the reality of my crazy, messed-up life and be normal again, at least for a little while. And maybe then the growing distance between me and my friends would disappear.

I tried to act excited as I gave Michelle total freedom to put together my look for the dance. But she didn't make it easy when she picked out a long black satin dress with a plunging neckline and sequined straps. Black. On a vampire. It was so cliché it was ridiculous. Except she didn't know what I was turning into, and she insisted it made my pale skin and red hair glow. More like glow in the dark. Still, what did I care how I looked? I wouldn't be there with Tristan, and I would never be interested in anyone else. So as long as it made Michelle happy, it was fine with me.

"Hey, Sav, are you okay?" Michelle asked, surprising me from my thoughts as I sat in Anne's desk chair the following Saturday night. I hadn't even noticed her walk over.

Anne continued to tease Carrie mercilessly about being too wimpy to let Michelle apply her mascara. Carrie calmly ignored her as she sat on the daybed and put on mascara with the help of a small compact mirror.

"I'm fine," I lied to Michelle, having to swallow back a lump so I could talk.

Carrie suddenly swiped Anne on the tip of the nose with the mascara wand, leaving a big spot of black. Anne screeched and stole the mirror, then licked her finger to wash off the spot. She called Carrie a rude name then stuck her wet finger in Carrie's ear, making the blonde shriek out a few choice words about Anne's germs.

"Watch your mouth, missy!" Carrie's mother yelled from the living room where all three sets of their parents waited, no doubt armed with cameras and video recorders.

My mother was on the road somewhere in Arkansas tonight, unaware I was even going to the dance. I hadn't mentioned it to her, and apparently neither had Dad. And of course the idea of being here to record the night in a scrapbook had probably never even occurred to my dad.

Did vampires scrapbook?

Probably not. They wouldn't want a visual record of just how long they had lived.

"But Mom—" Carrie began.

"Carrie Lynn, you watch that mouth or you'll go to that dance with a mouthful of soap."

That made me crack my first sincere smile of the evening.

Michelle giggled, then dropped to her knees beside me on the thick carpet. "It's good to see you smiling again."

I blinked at her, unsure how to respond. "Sorry. Guess I've been a bit of a downer lately."

She shrugged. "I would be too if I lost a guy that hot and then he turned around and started dating Bethany Brookes like it was no big deal." Scowling, she sat back on her bare feet. "I thought you two were going to get back together! Especially after he called me the night of the Charmers Spring Show."

Wait, what? It felt like my eyes were about to pop out of my head as I struggled to choose which question to ask first. And how did she even know I'd been dating him? I hadn't told anyone but Anne. Someone else must have blabbed. Maybe someone in the Clann, like one of the Brat Twins? Or maybe a Charmer...one of the dancers or managers might have put two and two together after noticing Tristan and I were both gone from school and Spring Show practice at the same time and then he quit volunteering to help the team.

That answered how Michelle might have heard about us, but not the rest of it.

I took a breath and started with one question at a time. "He's dating Bethany?"

She nodded, her hazel eyes big and solemn. "Rumor has it they're going to the dance together."

Wow, he sure waited a long time to get over me and move on.

Once again, I found myself trapped in a battle between my head and my heart. Logically I knew I should be happy for him. Bethany would make him laugh, go to parties with him, eat lunch in the cafeteria with him and the descendants. His parents would probably adore her, too. If I really loved him, I should want nothing but the best for him, right?

My heart said it infinitely preferred for him to be as miserable as I was for the rest of his life.

I sighed and moved on to the next question. "Why did he call you the night of the Spring Show?"

"He wanted to know where you had moved to. He needed to talk to your dad, I think. He made it sound like he wanted to get your dad's permission to date you publicly or some-thing."

My breath caught in my lungs and refused to budge. There was only one possible reason that he would want to talk to my dad. And it wasn't to get permission to date me publicly. Dad didn't have that kind of clout with the vamp council. But he could turn a human into a vampire.

Why was I surprised that Tristan would have asked my dad to turn him? Of course Tristan would have tried everything he could think of to get us back together.

Michelle glanced over her shoulder then shot to her feet. "Anne, you stop that right now! You're going to ruin my cre-ation."

Still in shock, I barely had time to move my feet out of her path before she took off across the room to grab Anne's wrist and wrench a brush away.

"But you left all this down," Anne complained from where she was leaning down in front of her vanity trying to pin up the hair at the nape of her neck.

"Those curls are supposed to be down," Michelle argued, batting Anne's hands away. "It adds to the cascade effect."

"More like the sloppy effect," Anne muttered back. "It looks like I didn't use enough hairspray or something."

I clutched the sides of the chair by my legs, staring down at the black satin shimmering over my knees. Tristan had gone to ask my dad to turn him.

And yet now he was dating someone else.

What had Dad said to convince Tristan so completely to give up on us?

The doorbell rang, announcing the arrival of Carrie's and Michelle's dates. I went through the motions of posing for group shots in the living room while their parents buzzed around us, their camera flashes blinding me as my mind circled in confusion. Tristan's actions didn't make sense. First he made me think I would never get him to see the reality of our situation. Then he apparently went on a suicide mission to my dad to ask to be turned even though he knew the turning process could only result in his death and the start of a brand-new war between the vamps and the witches. And now just a few weeks later…he was dating Bethany Brookes.

The camera flashes stopped, but my thoughts didn't. Nor did the lump in my throat go away.

Michelle and Carrie rode with their dates in Carrie's car, and Anne and I followed in Anne's truck to the JHS campus where the dance was being held in the cafeteria. I was momentarily distracted by the process of trying to exit the truck without revealing my underwear to everyone in the parking lot. Slits in dresses were both a blessing and a curse, allowing us to walk but making the climb out of a truck a real problem. Then we were all together again and stumbling on our heels across the parking lot and into the cafeteria.

The inside of the circular room had been transformed for the night. The dance committee, headed by the senior cheerleaders, had chosen Night at the Movies for the theme. We navigated our group around twelve-foot-high cardboard reels of movie film and equally giant buckets filled with yellow and white balloons tied in bunches to look like enormous popcorn, as a white fog from an unseen fog machine swirled around our ankles. Most of the tables and chairs had been removed to allow room for dancing, so we cut straight across the room toward the back.

Anne led us all up a set of carpeted stairs I'd never paid attention to before. They ended at a loft space above the kitchens and serving area. Tonight the second floor was decorated with a shimmering silver curtain backdrop and several movie reels as props for professional photos, which Anne insisted we had to have taken of our group right away in order to beat the line she was sure would develop soon.

Wait a second. Photographs. Now that I was definitely turning into a full vamp, were photos a problem? I'd had plenty taken before, of course. And earlier at Anne's house, I'd been too in shock about Tristan to think about all the pictures the parents were taking of us.

But now I had time to think. And freak out. Wasn't there some rule about how vampires couldn't show up in photos? What if that was true? I'd never asked Dad about it. We'd covered everything else…the bloodlust, draining with a kiss, stakes, decapitation, holy water, garlic, crosses and churches and Bibles and holy ground and fire, even how our hybrid race of vamps was supposedly the creation of the demoness Lilith, who according to Jewish myths was once the true first wife of Adam. But vamps and photos? Nope, we'd missed that one. Was my vamp side developed enough that this would apply to me too now? Would I simply not show up in the photos and freak everyone out later?

A quick call to Dad would clear the question right up. I fumbled in my handbag for my cell phone.

"Sav, it's our turn." Anne tugged at my wrist.

"Wait, I just need to make a quick—"

"Later," she said, pulling me ever closer to the silver tinsel-draped backdrop where the others were already being posed by the photographer.

I found Dad's number on speed dial. "Okay. Just let me call my dad first."

Anne snatched the phone away just as I hit the call button. "And to think you used to hate these things! Five seconds, pretty princess, then you can make your precious phone call."

"Would you give me that?" I lunged for the phone, but

she was faster, dropping it down the front of her dress into her cleavage.

"Anne!" I gasped.

"Not going after it there, are ya?" She snickered. "Now turn around and say cheese."

I turned toward the photographer's voice and formed some semblance of a shocked smile.

Then I heard Dad's voice coming from between my best friend's boobs.

Silence reigned for five long seconds as Dad called out my name in question.

Then everyone erupted in laughter. Even me. And oh, man, did it feel good to laugh like that, as if I was taking my first deep breath after drowning for months.

Anne's cheeks turned pink as she bent forward at the waist and reached down the front of her dress. Then her head popped up as she gasped. "Oh no."

"Savannah? Savannah! Are you okay?" Dad yelled from somewhere below Anne's chest. Judging by the rectangular bulge now at Anne's stomach, the phone had slid way past her bra.

The group laughter turned hysterical at that point, and my eyes teared up as Anne shimmied and wiggled, trying to get the phone out of her dress.

"Oh no, my makeup jobs!" Michelle wailed as apparently Carrie and Anne both teared up, too. "Come on."

Michelle hustled all of us, still laughing, down the stairs toward the bathrooms.

"Quit bumping me or it's gonna fall out and break on the stairs," Anne hissed, still clutching the phone at her stomach, as we passed another group headed up the stairs. They froze and stared at us in horror.

"Dad, hold on, I'm fine," I called out toward Anne's stomach. "Just…" I was laughing too hard to breathe properly. "Just hang up. I'll call back and explain later, I promise."

In the bathroom, we all grabbed handfuls of toilet paper and tried to repair our eye makeup as best we could. I'd never had much on to start with, thank goodness. But Carrie looked like a raccoon, which made me laugh even harder.

Anne went into one of the two stalls, her expression sour. "I should throw this darn thing down the toilet."

"I am still here and waiting for an explanation." Dad sounded more than a little tense.

I snickered behind a hand to muffle the laughter. Bet he'd never been in quite *this* position before.

"Oh, um, sorry sir," Anne said. "Just let me get you out from under my dress…"

"I can assure you I am presently nowhere near you or your dress," Dad snapped. "Are you girls high on something?"

Carrie, Michelle and I all howled with fresh laughter.

Red-faced, Anne finally emerged from the stall and held out my phone.

"Ew, you are going to wipe it off, right?" Carrie's nose wrinkled with disgust.

"It wasn't… I had a shower this… Oh fine." Giving up, Anne wiped the phone with a paper towel, hanging up on my father in the process.

Oooh, that was going to tick him off for sure. "Better let me call him back quick," I said, still smiling as Anne gave me the phone. I found his number, hit the call button, lifted it to my ear, then pretended to sniff my phone. "Hey, Anne, you wearing a new perfume tonight?"

That set Carrie and Michelle off into fresh giggles.

Dad answered on the first ring. "What is going—"

"Sorry, Dad," I interrupted the potential tirade. "I was going to call you and ask you if it was okay for me to get photos taken here at the dance. But Anne stole my phone and hid it in the only, um, pocket she had in her dress. And then she had a…wardrobe malfunction and had trouble getting the phone back out." A snicker escaped me. "I'm sorry if we worried you."

A long pause filled the connection before he cleared his throat. "Well, at least you sound as if you are having a good time for a change. Call me before you leave."

His words surprised me. He was right. I was actually having a good time. A great time, in fact.

Now if I could just avoid seeing Tristan dancing with Bethany all night…

CHAPTER 7

TRISTAN

It was a dumb thing to do, going out to Drip Rock Road. I was already running fifteen minutes late in picking up Bethany, and my favorite hilltop was in the opposite direction of her house.

Still I found myself driving out there, needing...something. Fresh air. Quiet. A few minutes of freedom.

My parents had kept me on total lockdown every minute I wasn't at school. They'd let me loose tonight because I'd taken Mom's repeated, not-so-subtle suggestion and asked Bethany to go with me to the dance. Not because I had any interest in Mom's choice of replacement girlfriends. I just needed to see Savannah outside of class one last time before the school year ended.

So I'd called Bethany as instructed last week. And then I'd thrown on the tux Mom had rented and left the house tonight with the corsage Mom had picked up for Bethany. But when it came time to exit my driveway and cross the road to the country club subdivision where Bethany's house was, I'd turned in the opposite direction and come out here instead.

Even though the sun was setting, the air was still warm with no breeze to cool it off. The darkening sky over the pines below shimmered from the heat. And it was only the start. In the coming weeks as summer came on full force, being outside past eleven in the morning would become pure torture. Already it felt like I'd stumbled into a swamp. Even the air was trying to choke the life out of me.

I glanced at the corsage, waiting like a silent demand from my mother on the dashboard of my truck. Mom would be ticked off if she knew I was letting the corsage wilt instead of rushing straight over to Bethany's with it like the good little boy Mom expected me to be.

I looked at the hills around me, and then to the sky. In the east, the first stars were just starting to wink into view. And I wondered for the thousandth time where Savannah was right now. Was she at Anne's house with her friends, getting ready, smiling into a mirror while those long fingers of hers fixed her hair and makeup?

Was she thinking about me at all?

I knew she was going to arrive at the dance looking more beautiful than ever. Earlier this week in the office, I'd picked up an image from Michelle's thoughts of Savannah in a long black satin dress. Michelle had been really proud about finding that dress for Savannah. If Michelle's memory was anything to judge by, she had a right to be proud. Savannah was going to look even more stunning than usual.

Tonight, watching Savannah but unable to hold her in my arms or dance with her was sure to be an exercise in torture. Especially with another girl on my arm all night.

A smarter guy would have stayed home.

Except I couldn't. Just like I couldn't convince myself to give up on us. I'd tried. Over and over, I'd told myself that there was nothing we could do. There were too many powerful people standing in our way. But every time I told myself to let her go, everything inside me rebelled. I couldn't imagine my future without Savannah in it.

How could two people seem so perfect together, be so happy together, and yet be so wrong in so many others' eyes?

There had to be an option I was missing. Maybe I was too close to the problem. Or maybe I didn't know enough about the council. My parents I understood…they were just trying to protect me. They couldn't understand that Savannah wasn't dangerous to me. But if the council could be convinced to change their minds about Savannah and me, and if I could create a bloodlust-dampening spell that would make it safe for Sav to be around me, surely my parents would change their minds, too. There was no way their fear of vamps could be stronger than their love for me. I knew that, deep down, they wanted me to be happy. I just needed a way to get rid of their fear.

I'd thought Savannah and I were it, that our love would be the proof everyone needed to break down the fear and hate on both sides. Now it looked like we would have to get rid of the prejudice before we could be together. But how?

Savannah knew more about the council than I did. If I could get her to talk to me, we could figure something out together that might appease the council. But she wouldn't talk to me, because she was listening to everyone else, letting their fear beat her down and convince her to stop fighting for us. And yet I knew she loved me. There wasn't a single doubt in my mind about that. Yes, we'd both kept the secret about her vampire side from each other. But what we'd felt together hadn't been a lie. The way we'd talked, kissed, held each other, the way she'd looked into my eyes so many times…I'd never felt anything more real, no magic on earth stronger, than that.

I would never feel anything like it again.

But I couldn't fight this battle alone. I needed Savannah's help. How could I convince her that we could make this work when she wouldn't even talk to me?

Magic. I could do a spell that would allow her to feel how I felt. I could literally give her my confidence, my faith and belief in what we had together. Then she'd have the confidence to want to fight again.

The cafeteria would be dark during the dance. Surely there would be the perfect opportunity to pull Savannah out of sight at some point. If the spell worked, she would agree to dream connect with me later tonight. And then we'd figure out a new game plan together.

What spell should I use? Dad had never taught me how to give someone confidence.

Then again, why worry about using a specific spell anyways? Using magic wasn't about the words I said. It was about focusing on what I wanted to make happen, injecting those intentions with my willpower, and then releasing the spell so it could take effect.

As I got back into my truck, feeling for the first time in weeks like I could breathe again, I created the spell in my mind.

"I want you to feel what I feel, Savannah," I murmured as I started my truck's engine. "I need you to have faith in us like I do. I need you to want to keep trying, to fight back with me, to help me find a way to change their minds." I envisioned those thoughts filling with energy. And then I released them into the air toward where I figured Sav would be by now…at the dance.

I carefully turned toward town and headed down the hill. I

could pick up Bethany and be at the dance in fifteen minutes. The spell would probably take effect immediately. I hoped it lasted long enough. Once I got to the cafeteria, I would need a few minutes to find Sav, another minute or two to talk to her and get her to agree to dream connect with me tonight.

The truck rushed down the steep road, which was straight for a long stretch. But I could see the sharp curve ahead. I tapped on the brakes to slow down for it.

Nothing happened.

I pressed the pedal all the way to the floorboard. The brakes didn't respond, the truck still picking up speed as the curve drew closer and closer.

Muttering a curse, I tried downshifting to force the transmission to slow the truck. But it was too late.

Jaw clenched, I gripped the wheel as hard as I could and tried to turn the truck with the curve, but I was going too fast. The truck rocked onto its left wheels and kept right on going. The world flipped over and over as glass shattered and rained through the air. My seat belt jerked tight, slamming the air out of my chest.

Maybe I shouldn't have tried to use magic and drive at the same time, was the last thought I had.

SAVANNAH

I hung up the phone, and that's when I heard him. It was like Tristan was right behind me, whispering in my ear.

"I want you to feel what I feel, Savannah," he murmured. "I need you to have faith in us like I do. I need you to want to keep trying, to fight back with me, to help me find a way to change their minds."

His voice was so clear inside my head that I actually whirled around, thinking he must have snuck into the bathroom after us.

But he wasn't there.

I popped my head outside the door. No Tristan in sight, not in the short hallway leading to the bathrooms or in the cafeteria-turned-dance-floor beyond.

"Savannah?" Carrie said, pausing in the process of reapplying her mascara. "What's wrong?"

"Nothing." I forced a smile. "Just thought I heard someone yelling for us outside."

I shut the door again, pretended to check my makeup in the mirror.

And then it hit me…wave upon wave of pain over my entire body. Pain on a level I'd never experienced before, not even during that week when I was sick my freshman year as the start of puberty awakened my two genetic sides and caused an internal battle between them that nearly killed me.

Oh sweet God in heaven. I really was dying this time.

I grabbed the counter, bracing my hands on the cold laminate, my legs shaking so hard I was afraid I would fall down without the sink's support. What was *wrong* with me?

"Sav? Sav! What is it?"

I could hear my friends' voices, distant, muffled. I shook my head, my focus turning inward. What was going on with my body? Was this a sign that the bloodlust was about to take over completely or something? No, it couldn't be. I'd felt the bloodlust before. It was nothing like this.

"What's wrong with her?" Michelle asked in a high voice.

"I don't know. Get a teacher," Carrie ordered.

Anne moved toward the door, but I grabbed her arm to stop her. "No, wait. It's not…" I closed my eyes and mentally searched for the source of the pain. "It's not me. I mean, I'm okay."

"Then what's the matter?" Anne said, crouching down in front of me.

I shook my head again. "I don't..."

And then I knew. And in that moment, I actually wished it had been the bloodlust or any other new vampire development in my body. Anything other than what my heart, my instincts, my very soul said it was.

"Oh God. It's Tristan," I whispered. I didn't know how I knew. But I knew. Something was wrong. He was hurt badly. And I had to tell someone.

"Huh?" Anne said.

My eyes flew open as I pushed her to the side and fumbled with the bathroom door. But it was locked.

"Is Emily Coleman here?" I asked, trying to get the lock turned on the knob.

"Who?" Michelle asked.

"Tristan's sister!" My shaking fingers couldn't manage to work the lock properly. Stark fear combined with desperation, turning me into something close to an animal. I wrapped both hands around the knob, heard a satisfying breaking of wood and groaning metal, and the doorknob came off in my hands. I tossed it to the floor with a loud clang.

"Savannah!" Carrie gasped.

But I was already headed out the door and down the short hall toward the strobing lights and shallow pool of balloons in the middle of the cafeteria, searching for a certain blonde who ought to be here. The senior cheerleaders always ran the semiformal dance; it was their way of helping to raise funds to support the cheer squads. Emily had to be here somewhere.

Bingo. The punch table.

"Stay here," I shouted to my friends, and something in my expression or my tone made them listen to me for once.

I tried not to run, settling for pushing my legs into the longest strides I could manage in these stupid heels on the slippery floor.

Emily's head popped up when I was still halfway across the dance floor. She must have read something on my face because she stared at me as I approached.

"Tristan," I gasped when I finally reached the table and leaned across it. "Something's wrong. You need to call him."

Her eyebrows drew together in worry or confusion. But at least she grabbed her phone and tried to call him.

"He's not answering," she shouted over the music.

"He's hurt somewhere. We have to find him," I told her as she circled around the table.

"How do—"

"I don't know how. Maybe he was doing a connection spell or something. I thought I heard him talking to me, and then I felt his pain." Even as I led the way across the cafeteria, I could still feel an incredible amount of pain throbbing throughout my body.

I pushed the doors open too hard. They slammed into the brick wall of the building. Emily's eyes widened.

But it didn't matter. Nothing mattered except getting to Tristan in time.

"Where's your car?" I asked her.

She turned right, and I spotted the infamous pink convertible in the row closest to the sidewalk.

"What are you doing?" she asked as I grabbed the passenger door's handle.

"I'm going with you," I said.

"You can't. You two are not supposed to —"

"I can still feel his pain." In fact, it was stronger now that we'd left the cafeteria. "I think we can use it to find him."

"You can't be serious."

I opened the door and slid in.

Huffing out a loud sigh, Emily got in, started the car and

headed out of the parking lot. At the stop sign, she said, "Which way?"

I twisted toward the left, and the pain was a little less. "Go right."

Our progress was too slow as we repeated the process at every intersection. But my feelings were all we had to go on. Emily had tried calling her parents, but they had no idea where Tristan was. Apparently he was supposed to have picked up Bethany half an hour ago but never showed up. Emily ended the call without explaining why she was worried about him or that I was with her.

Ten minutes later, we found ourselves heading out of town toward Drip Rock Road.

"Why would he be out here?" Emily muttered.

I had to wonder the same thing. It was in the opposite direction of Bethany's house.

But I couldn't worry about that right now. I could barely breathe, the pain was so strong. "He's close. Go slow," I said.

Thankfully she slowed down. Otherwise we might have ended up with flat tires from the glass in the curve of the road, which she narrowly avoided running over.

Tristan's truck had taken out a huge section of wood and barbed wire fence as it either rolled or plowed through the ditch and field, coming to a stop right side up several yards off the road. I didn't remember getting out of the car or even pulling to a stop. I just found myself running through the field toward that crushed-in hunk of metal and praying that he would be okay.

As I ran around to the driver's side, I felt all his pain stop like a switch had been flipped off.

"Tristan!" I screamed, grabbing the handle of his door. But the twisted door wouldn't budge. "Emily, I can't feel him anymore. Call for help!"

I reached in through the broken-out window, carefully found the side of that strong column where his pulse should be throbbing out a steady beat to me. It was there, but just barely.

"Tristan, please," I whispered. "Please don't go."

CHAPTER 8

Emily finished talking to someone on her phone. Then she reached past me and touched her brother's shoulder.

"Oh God," she gasped. "Tristan, don't you dare die on me!" She yanked repeatedly at the door handle, her once smoothly styled French twist flying loose in all directions.

"Together on three," I told her, grabbing the windowsill of the door, ignoring bits of glass as they ground into my hands. "One, two, three."

We jerked as hard as we could, and the door burst open so quickly we landed on our butts in the grass. I scrambled to my feet, fighting the stupid heels as they sank into the soft dirt. Emily must have more practice with heels. She was already back at Tristan's side, her hand pressed to his shoulder again.

"We have to get him out," she muttered. "Then I can work on him better."

"Do you know what you're doing?" I asked. What if moving him made his injuries worse?

"We have to try. The ambulance won't be here for another five or ten minutes. And his pulse—"

"I know." I didn't want to hear her say what I already knew, that his heartbeat was way too weak. That we were losing him.

We couldn't lose him. I couldn't lose him. I didn't care if I couldn't be with him. I had to know he was alive in this world somewhere. Otherwise I'd go crazy.

"Okay, get his feet," I said as I grabbed his shoulders and tugged him toward me. Emily squeezed in between me and the door and freed his feet from the twisted frame and steering column.

Somehow we got Tristan out of the truck and onto the ground. I cradled his head in my lap, stroking the blood away from his forehead, while Emily knelt on her knees at his side.

"There's so much broken," she whispered.

"Please," I murmured, begging her, begging God, begging a universe that had been nothing but cruel to me, in the hope that maybe it would finally answer just one request.

Emily closed her eyes and pressed her hands to Tristan's chest as if she were about to do CPR. But she never pushed down. Instead, she sat perfectly still, her palms laid flat on the stained red and white shirt. The skin on my arms and the back of my neck erupted in prickles of pain far stronger than I'd ever felt before, even when Tristan was using magic while fighting Dylan. That had been a fire ant attack. This was like being in the middle of a swarm of really ticked off wasps. God, she was a strong witch. But was she strong enough?

If only I'd been allowed to learn how to use magic....

I bent over him, the pain in my chest my own now, the staggering force of it curling me over. Blood streamed from a gash in Tristan's forehead near his left temple, and the bloodlust was there in the distance, wanting my attention. But nothing could dull the sheer terror pounding through my veins now, not even the bloodlust.

"Please, Tristan, stay with me," I whispered against his forehead, my lips moving against the only clear area at his right temple, his hair brushing my nose and cheek.

And then I heard it. A strong, solid heartbeat, followed by more of the rapid, barely-there taps.

"Again, Emily," I whispered.

More pinpricks stabbing at my arms and neck as she ramped up the energy level.

Another strong heartbeat beneath my fingertips. And another. And another, each one evening out the rhythm into a steady pulse again.

Tears streamed down my face now. I looked up at her for confirmation, needing to know I wasn't imagining it.

"He's coming back!" she cried out, grinning.

"That's it, Tristan," I murmured, stroking bits of glass out of his hair. "Keep fighting. Come back to us." *Come back to me.*

Wailing in the distance. The ambulance was here. They pulled to a stop on the road, two figures jumping out from the cab to unload a gurney from the back end of the vehicle.

"He's going to be okay now, I think," Emily murmured. "A few stitches here and there and some broken bones that'll have to be reset, which I'm sure the Clann will help heal faster. But he'll be okay."

I held Tristan's right hand as the emergency workers wrapped a brace around his neck then got a stretcher under him so they could lift him up onto the gurney. When they carried him toward the van, I kept holding on, walking beside Tristan. He still hadn't woken up. I needed to see those green eyes looking back at me before I could be sure he'd be all right.

"Ma'am," one of the emergency workers said to me. "You have to let go so we can load him."

"I want to go with him."

Emily laid a hand on my forearm. "You can't. I called my parents. They're on the way to the hospital already. They'll be there waiting."

"I don't care. I have to go."

"You can't," Emily said, more firmly this time. "You know what will happen."

"Please," I begged her. "I have to know he'll be all right."

"He will be. But you have to let him go now." She leaned in close and whispered, "Please don't make me use magic on you to save you. I know you love him. I promise I'll call with updates."

At that moment, I almost hated her. But some more logical part of me made me let go of his hand and step away.

"What's your friend's number?" she asked as the emergency workers slid Tristan into the ambulance.

"What? Why?"

"Because I've got to follow them. You need someone to come pick you up."

I told her Anne's number, and she punched it in. She didn't have to say much before Anne agreed to come get me.

"She says she'll be here in ten minutes," Emily said after ending the call. "Now what's your number?"

I looked at her in confusion, my mind too focused on the closing ambulance doors to be able to process her question.

She touched my shoulder. "Savannah, I need your number so I can call you with updates."

"You'll really call me?" I asked.

A smile tugged at her lips. "I said I would, didn't I? Didn't Tristan ever tell you I always keep my promises?"

So I told her my number. Then I wondered where exactly I'd left my phone. Maybe Anne had it.

She punched the number into her phone. "Are you going to be okay till she gets here? Do you want me to stay with you?"

"No!" Panic made me nearly shout. The driver for the ambulance threw a quick glance over his shoulder as he climbed in behind the wheel. "No, please follow them." She would be my only contact at the hospital. My only way of knowing if Tristan got worse.

She hesitated then gave me a quick, fierce hug. "Hang in there. He's going to get better. Then he'll be right back to his usual spoiled-rotten self in no time. And, Savannah?"

The ambulance drove away, its taillights fading down the road toward town. "Mmm?"

"Thank you."

I looked at her then. "Thank me with updates."

"I will. I promise."

And then she was gone, her car's lights following the ambulance.

Suddenly I found myself in a field at night all alone with only Tristan's wrecked truck to keep me company. And yet I couldn't manage to dredge up a single ounce of fear. As long as Tristan was going to be okay, nothing else mattered much.

A bit of movement in the distance at the edge of the woods drew my attention. In the moonlight, it looked like a person entering the woods. The figure was too far away for me to make out details before the trees and the darkness swallowed it up. A neighbor come to watch the local drama? Probably.

My gaze dropped to the heap of metal between the tree line and where I was standing. I stumbled back to the totaled vehicle, stopping by the driver's side opening. Remembering the sight of Tristan slumped there unconscious and bleeding. As if they had a mind of their own, my fingers reached out to trail over the ripped leather headrest, and I shuddered.

I had nearly lost him tonight.

Anne found me there some time later. She touched my arm and gasped. "Sav, you're like ice! Are you okay? What's going on?"

"Tristan totaled his truck. Emily said he'll be okay."

"Come on, let's get you warmed up."

I followed her to the road where she'd left her truck running. We climbed inside, and she cranked up the heater as she headed back into town.

"Do you have my phone?" I asked, feeling numb from head to toe. I couldn't even feel the heat that my ears said was blasting out of the dashboard vents. "Emily promised to call with updates."

"Sure." She started to toss it to me, hesitated then just set it on the seat between us. I grabbed it between both hands and held it to my chest, vowing to sleep with the once hated device if necessary till I knew Tristan was okay again.

"I told the girls we'd meet them at the Sonic as planned," Anne said as she turned onto the main strip.

I glanced at the clock on the radio and was shocked to see that it was nearly time for the dance to be over. How long had Emily and I worked in that field to save Tristan?

I could feel Anne's curiosity like a steady hum as she drove. But she managed to hold her questions at bay until we found a parking space at the Sonic and she placed an order large enough to sink a ship.

"Want anything?" she asked.

"A Coke float would be good." It was all I figured I'd be able to keep down, as bad as my stomach was twisting. Mom always claimed the combination of acid and dairy products in a Coke float could balance out any upset stomach. I was about to put her theory to the test.

Anne kept the heater blasting until after the food arrived.

Then she turned it off. "Sorry, but I'm dying here. Are you still cold?"

I honestly couldn't tell. I was always cold lately. "I'm fine, thanks. And thanks for coming to get me and everything."

"No problem. But could you at least tell me what the heck is going on? You took off with Emily like a pair of bats out of Hades. Next thing I know, she's calling me and asking me to come pick you up from some field in the middle of nowhere by Tristan's wrecked truck. I didn't know you two were even friends."

"We're not. Not really. I just…" Oh lord. I was a crappy liar on the best of days. How in the world would I ever even begin to tell a lie well enough to cover up tonight's events?

I rested my head on the seat's headrest and closed my eyes, my earlier exhaustion returning with a vengeance. I was so done with all of this. The secret keeping, the loneliness, the guilt. I just couldn't handle it anymore. Maybe Carrie and Michelle didn't need to know. Carrie would never believe me anyways, and Michelle would end up accidentally blurting it out to someone someday. But Anne was like the Fort Knox of secrets. She'd never once betrayed someone's secret, no matter how mad she might be at them.

So I told her the truth. "I'm half vampire, half witch."

CHAPTER 9

In the process of tearing open a packet of salt, Anne ripped too hard and the salt went flying. I opened one eye in time to see tiny white crystals cover the steering wheel and the seat between us. Maybe it was safer to keep my eyes shut. Then she could have whatever facial reaction she needed to and my feelings wouldn't be hurt.

"You want to run that by me one more time?" Anne said.

I started at the beginning, explaining about the vamps and the Clann, my dad and mom's illegal relationship and how it resulted in Dad's removal from the council and Nanna and Mom's removal from the Clann. The truth behind Nanna's death and my growing abilities and my breakup with Tristan. I told her everything, risking opening my eyes toward the end, leaving nothing out. It was the first time I ever saw Anne ignore a cheeseburger. But she was handling it so much better than I'd ever expected her to. At least, so far.

When I was done, I felt…lighter. This was the first time I'd ever willingly shared the truth about myself to someone normal, someone who was outside of all the Clann and vamp weirdness.

I watched her face now. Would she freak out? Would she worry that I would bite her someday or use a spell on her or something?

She was silent for a long time. Finally, she took a long slurp of soda, blinked twice and said, "Wow. And I thought I had family problems."

A short laugh escaped me. "You have no idea."

"My mother would crap kittens if she knew all this."

Uh-oh. Maybe she wasn't such a Fort Knox for secrets after all? "You can't tell her, Anne. Or Carrie or Michelle or anyone else. Consider this the biggest secret you've ever had to keep."

She snorted. "Oh please, you know me. Have I ever once spilled a secret?"

"Not that I know of. Which is why you're the only normal human I've told this to."

She grinned at that. "You consider me normal? Oh man, you do have some weirdos in the family closet then."

"Ha, ha," I said. "But seriously, Anne, this is a big deal. And there's something else." I winced as I added, "Not only can you never tell anyone about this, but you also can't sit around thinking about it, either. Both the Clann and the vamps can read human minds."

That wiped the smile off her face.

"Exactly," I said. "Now you see why I waited so long to tell you?"

"Yeah. Though if you *had* told me sooner, at least I could have been a better friend for you. You know, been more supportive for you when you were going through all this stuff." Her tone was soft, almost apologetic. And Anne was never soft.

I almost didn't know how to react. "Sorry. I was just trying to protect you. And I didn't realize you'd handle the news this well." I stared at her. "Actually...why *are* you taking it so well?" Most people would either laugh at me, think I was nuts, or freak out completely.

In the process of grabbing a French fry, she froze. "Let's just say...this isn't the strangest thing I've heard lately."

"Really? What could possibly be any weirder than finding out Jacksonville is secretly run by a bunch of power-hungry magic users and your best friend is half Clann and half vampire?"

She took a deep breath. "I...can't tell you."

Now it was my turn to do the slow blink thing. "Why not?"

"Because it's someone else's secret and I swore I'd never reveal it."

"Whose secret is it?"

"Can't tell you that, either." She chewed a small handful of fries now, cramming them in like she thought it might buy her some time before my next question. Except I knew how often she talked with her mouth full.

"Anne, what's going on?"

"I can't tell you!" she mumbled around the food. She started to stuff in more fries, then hesitated. "Hey, you can't read my mind, can you?" The tiniest hint of anxiety shot out of her, rasping over my already frayed nerve endings like a quick brush against sandpaper.

"No." At least not yet.

The wrinkles in her forehead smoothed away as she took her time swallowing.

All of a sudden, my door flew open. If not for the seat belt I was still wearing, I would have fallen out of the truck.

"Hey, freak. Did you run off to try and save your lover boy?" Dylan Williams said.

I straightened up, the edges of the seat belt digging into my hands as I clutched it. "How did you know—"

"Everybody knows," he said. Darkness emanated from him like a bad cologne, making me want to shrink away. Somehow I managed not to flinch. "Rumor has it that Romeo tried to off himself inside his truck tonight."

"He wouldn't do that," I said, trying to sound confident.

Dylan shrugged. "Rumor also has it that his brakes might have failed."

Everything inside me went still. "Who told you that?"

"Oh, a little birdie." He smiled.

An awful thought came to me then. "Did you do something to his truck?" I leaned toward him now, ready to grab him by the throat if he said yes.

His eyebrows shot up, and he drawled, "Now why would I do that?"

"Oh, I don't know, maybe because you're evil," Anne said.

He stared at her over my shoulder. "Be careful or you might find out just how evil I can be, Albright."

Was he threatening my best friend?

I would kill him.

I reached for my seat belt, so mad I couldn't get the stupid buckle to work. "If you so much as—"

He laughed. "That's right, Colbert. Now you're getting a clue." He leaned in close and whispered, "So why don't you just leave town before anything else bad happens to someone you care about?"

"Oh please," Anne said. "Do you really think you're scaring anyone?"

His gaze flicked to her. He smiled slowly. "You know, I'm really looking forward to school next year. It's going to be fun teaching you to respect the Clann."

On pure instinct, I reached out, intending to grab him, slap him, something. I couldn't even see straight, I was so furious.

Laughing, he dodged my hand then turned and strolled

back across the raised cement area between the rows of vehicles to his own car.

I would *kill* him. I would find a way and I would rip his throat out. If he'd hurt Tristan tonight… And he'd just threatened to hurt Anne next…

Dimly I heard someone saying my name, felt someone grab my wrist.

"Savannah! You're going to break the seat belt!"

I blinked a few times, turned toward the voice, found Anne biting her lower lip as she tugged at my hands, which were still scrabbling at my seat belt buckle.

"Whew! When did you get such a temper? I thought I was the one who needed anger management courses around here." She grinned.

I stared at her. "Did he just say that he was responsible for Tristan's accident tonight, or was I hearing things?"

Her smile faded. "I think he was just messing with you about that. He's a piss-ant, nothing more. He's not smart enough to attempt murder without killing himself in the process. Can you see him even figuring out where the brake lines on a truck are? He'd probably wind up rolling the truck over himself if he even tried looking for them."

"But he did threaten to hurt you," I said. "You heard him say *that* at least, right?"

She rolled her eyes. "Oh please. He's all talk and no bite. Besides, if he did try to come after me, I'd just shoot him with my new bow and arrows."

Did I hear her right? "Uh, bow and arrows?"

"Yeah. My grandpa sent me the newest pro series Firestorm compound bow for turkey season. I've been dying to try it out."

"Since when did you take up bow hunting?"

"Since I was five. It's a family thing. My grandpa owns a

company that manufactures them. Don't you remember me talking about it? I must have mentioned it at least a thousand times by now."

I vaguely remembered her grossing us all out at lunch with stories about deer hunting every November with her uncle. I definitely remembered her mentioning that deer hunting included dousing herself in deer urine. But I sure didn't remember her ever mentioning what kind of weapons they used. "I knew you like to hunt, just not with bows and arrows. Isn't that kind of...old-fashioned? Why not just use a gun?"

She took a long, deep breath. "Oh dear lord. Promise me you'll never say that again. First off, no one goes hunting with a gun. Guns are for hunting *people*. Rifles are for hunting *animals*. And secondly, my grandpa would skin me alive if he ever heard I was using anything other than a compound bow made by his company. Besides, compound bows are more fun to use than a rifle and a heck of a lot harder to shoot yourself with." Her face wrinkled into a frown. "Though I guess if you were a complete idiot you might accidentally shoot yourself in the foot. Or if you had the worst luck on the planet, a crappy shaft could explode and stab you through the hand. And of course you have to use proper technique so you don't derail the string and kill your arm or take out an eyeball or something..."

Before she could get any further on a roll here, I jumped in while I still could. "Has your grandpa's company been making bows a long time?"

"Yep, going on forty years now. Want to see some pictures?" Before I could answer, she dove across the seat, opened the glove compartment and rooted around until she found a catalog. "Check out my new Firestorm." She jabbed a finger at a page. "Isn't it awesome? Mine's black, though. I'm gonna call it the Black Widow. I can't wait to take it on night hunts for wild hog."

She had to be joking. "Er...wild hogs?"

She nodded quickly several times, her eyes round. "The durn things are taking over everywhere! They're a total menace, which is why you can hunt them all year round without a license. Uncle Danny and I already went on a couple of hunts this year, mainly just to scout out the local population, and nearly got ourselves killed the first time out. Those hogs are crazy aggressive."

I studied the complicated-looking device in the catalog. Compound bows weren't anything like what I'd expected a bow to look like, consisting of a futuristic design with a lot of holes for the main part. At each end of the main section were even stranger looking pulleys and not one but three strings stretching between them. It looked like something out of an *Aliens* movie. How did one even go about *shooting* this thing?

I flipped through a few pages and had to stop as the color of one particular design leapt off the catalog page. "They make them in pink camo?"

She grinned. "Yep, that's one of the Rookie models. I had one kind of like that for my first bow."

I tried to visualize a preschool aged Anne running through a field with a giant hot pink compound bow and shooting arrows as Dylan ran away screaming like a little girl. A reluctant half smile loosened the muscles in my jaw. Now that would be fun to see. Unfortunately, in real life Dylan would never run away. He'd just stand there and hit her with a magically produced fireball or something.

I handed the catalog back to her, my attempt at a smile fading. "Listen, Anne, you really should be careful. I know you think you're tough enough to handle anything Dylan might throw at you. But the Clann…they're way more powerful than you realize. Even Dylan's got a few tricks up his sleeve that a compound bow probably wouldn't be much use against."

"*Pfft.* Bring it on. I'd like to see him try. He'd never even see or hear me before it was too late."

She pretended to hold a bow in her left hand and pull back an imaginary arrow with her right. She made a short whooshing sound, apparently to simulate releasing the arrow, followed by a soft whistle and a grin.

I shook my head and sighed. Anne already knew the Clann could do magic. She'd heard the rumors right along with everyone else in Jacksonville. And she'd even seen some of their spells' smaller effects when she helped Tristan hide charms in my duffel bag and locker to block my gaze daze victims' stalking attempts last year. But what she hadn't seen was just how quickly descendants could throw power at people to knock them off their feet and even almost kill them.

If she'd been there the night Tristan and Dylan had gotten into a magic fight, she wouldn't be so quick to wave off my warning now.

Michelle and Carrie pulled up beside us a few minutes later with their dates. The driver's side window was down, and I heard them saying my name then something about Tristan and Emily and a car wreck. Hot news spread fast in Jacksonville, and no topic was hotter than Tristan.

Carrie glanced up at me, grabbed Michelle's hand, and they both turned pink.

"Um, what do you guys want to eat?" Carrie said to everyone in the car.

While they placed their order, I checked my phone for missed calls or messages. Nothing yet. Just to be sure, I double-checked the signal. Maybe Emily hadn't had a chance to go somewhere private and call me?

When the food arrived for Carrie and Michelle's car, Anne got out to bug them through the passenger windows while they tried to eat. But I was rooted to the seat with worry.

Emily should have sent an update by now. What was happening at the hospital with Tristan? Was he going to be okay? Maybe no news meant he was still undergoing X-rays or something. Unless...

No, I refused to think like that. He was going to be all right. He had to. Emily had done enough to keep him alive until he could get to the hospital and the Clann could take over. And there was no way they would allow their future leader to die.

But that didn't mean a few descendants might not still want Tristan out of their way. And if anyone had a motive for wanting to hurt Tristan, it was Dylan. What had he said the night he'd caught Tristan and me kissing after Charmers practice? Something about how the pictures he was taking of us would ensure the Clann would remove Tristan's dad as Clann leader.

Sounded like a motive to me.

Part of me agreed with Anne. Dylan seemed way too stupid to manage something as complicated as messing with someone's brake lines. Then again, maybe he'd finally discovered how to use the internet or read a book. Miracles could happen, especially for someone as driven as Dylan. He was dedicated to getting Tristan's family ousted as the Clann leaders, enough to get into a spell fight with Tristan on school grounds and nearly kill him in the process. How much further would he have really had to go to tamper with Tristan's truck tonight?

And if he was capable of messing with Tristan's truck, then he was also more than capable of going after someone else. Someone outside of the Clann without any power. Someone like Anne, whose working parents had few if any political connections around here.

What if his idle threat had really been a promise to try to hurt her next year?

I had to find a way to protect both Tristan and Anne.

If I'd only grown up learning how to use magic like the rest of the descendants, I could make protection charms for them. I could also help heal Tristan, if only from a distance.

But I couldn't protect or help anyone, because my mother and grandmother had promised the Clann that they would never teach me to do magic.

Which seemed incredibly unfair. Why shouldn't I be allowed to use an ability I was supposedly born with? If I did have any of the Evans magic in my blood, then it was as much a part of me as having two hands and two feet!

Dylan and the Brat Twins only messed with me and my friends because they knew my family had promised never to teach me how to protect myself against them.

Then again, Mom and Nanna had made that promise. *I* never did.

If only I had access to some spell books...

"Finally!" Anne said as she helped Carrie and Michelle and their dates throw away their trash. Then she hopped back into her truck and started the engine. "Time to party!"

Half an hour later and minus Carrie's and Michelle's dates, we all crowded into Anne's room in our PJ's and settled in for a movie fest. Thankfully the girls chose a comedy instead of their usual romantic favorites, and they pretended not to notice my phone attached to my hand all night.

Emily texted at eleven to say Tristan was okay and sleeping peacefully. Finally I could breathe deeply again. It was going to be all right. I still didn't know how to protect him or Anne from Dylan. But Tristan was alive and recovering. For now, that was enough.

As my friends alternated between laughter and gasps over

the movie, I let their happiness soothe my raw nerves. It was the first time I'd found a good use for my usually annoying ability to sense others' emotions. Slowly but surely, the tension eased out of my neck and shoulders, and I found I could even smile sincerely again.

When I'd watched the ambulance take Tristan away, I had thought I would never survive the night. At the very least, I'd expected to pace for hours alone in my bedroom, sick with worry and fear. No way would I have imagined spending the rest of the night in my comfy cotton pajamas with my three best friends, huddled around the TV in Anne's bedroom, alternately groaning or grinning over a movie about a crazy bunch of bling-wearing, Segway-riding vamps. And yet, that's exactly how one of the hardest nights of my life ended.

Tonight, I had faced my two greatest fears. Almost losing Tristan had shown me that, as long as he was alive somewhere on this earth, I could survive pretty much anything else the world had to throw at me. It had given me the courage to face my second biggest fear and tell my best friend the truth, something that I'd been too scared to even attempt for over a year now. And I'd discovered that Anne was capable of being a far greater friend than I'd ever given her credit for.

The resulting relief meant, instead of being able to outlast everyone like I usually did, this time I was the first one to crash, my phone still clutched like a magical talisman in my hands under my pillow. I thought I felt Anne throw a comforter over me at some point, which made me smile. Who knew she had a mothering bone in her body? Then I was out cold.

A buzzing in my hand woke me the next morning at eight-thirty. Emily's text message read:

24 stitches on head, 26 staples on lft. arm, 2 brkn ribs, lft. leg brkn 2 places reset & cast, lft. wrist brkn reset & cast. T pretty as ever. Says brakes failed???

CHAPTER 10

I had to read it three times, twice to get over the numerous injuries listed, and a third time to make sure I'd read the last part right. The phone's plastic case creaked in warning as I gripped it too tightly.

Brake failure. Just like Dylan had oh-so-casually suggested. Could he really be behind it?

He could have heard about it from someone else in the Clann, or even from someone at the sheriff's department and used the rumor to mess with me, as Anne had suggested.

But if Dylan hadn't tampered with Tristan's brakes, then why had they failed?

An image flashed through my mind of a dark silhouette ducking into the woods after Tristan's wreck. Could it have been Dylan?

But how would he know where and when the brakes would give out?

Anne was right. Dylan probably wasn't that smart.

Unless he was smart enough to pretend he wasn't.

Okay, this was getting ridiculous and giving me a headache. I was just being paranoid. Brakes failed all the time, right?

In a relatively new, perfectly maintained truck? *Sure* they did.

I got dressed in the bathroom across the hall, then gathered up my things as quietly as I could. The girls must have stayed up pretty late last night after I conked out; Michelle and Anne always snored, but Carrie didn't usually unless she was pretty tired. All three were sawing the logs loudly this morning.

I carefully stepped over Michelle and Carrie on the floor and tapped Anne on the tip of her nose where she was ticklish.

"Mmph?" she asked, one eye cracking open as her hand flopped up to rub her nose.

"I've gotta go. Family stuff."

"Mmkay," she muttered.

I started to turn away, then remembered. "Oh, can I ask you a huge favor? Could you burn my dress for me please?"

Her eyes squinted open at that. "Huh?"

I checked to make sure Michelle and Carrie were still snoring, then whispered, "It's got you-know-who's blood all over it." It was black so you couldn't really see the bloodstains. But if I brought it home, Dad would definitely smell the blood and know I'd been around Tristan right after his wreck.

Her nose wrinkled. "Well, that sucks."

I started to reply, then caught her grin. Vampire jokes. "Oh ha ha. Think you're funny?" Grabbing the corner of her pillow, I gave it a quick jerk out from under her head, then dropped it on her face.

Her snicker, along with her promise to get rid of the evidence, came out muffled.

As I eased out the front door and down the sidewalk to my truck, I tried to hold on to last night's sense of relief and gratitude that Tristan was okay. But those question marks at the end of Emily's message kept bugging me.

Tristan had nearly died last night. If Emily and I hadn't gotten there in time, or if Emily hadn't known how to heal him, he would have.

Could someone actually have tried to kill him? And if they had, would they try again?

When I arrived home, Dad was waiting for me in the kitchen with a mug of hot chocolate. He must have nuked it as soon as he heard the sound of my truck in the driveway.

"Thanks," I said and took a sip, grateful for the warmth. Then I peeked at him over the cup. "Did you hear about the wreck?"

He nodded. "I have a connection at the hospital."

I didn't even want to know what for. I focused instead on keeping my tone calm and even. "Emily texted me this morning. She said he's okay other than a few stitches and some broken bones the Clann will help to heal faster. But he said his brakes failed and that's why his truck wouldn't slow down for the curve in the road. Also, there might have been somebody in the distance, watching."

It wasn't a lie. I just didn't clarify who actually saw the watcher in the distance. Everything Dad knew, the vamp council would too the next time he was called to Paris to report to them. They would read his mind and pick up everything whether he wanted them to know it or not.

If Dad suspected I wasn't telling him everything, he chose not to question it.

"This is disturbing news," he muttered. "Is there any reason to believe the brake failure was an accident?"

"Emily doesn't seem to think so. Tristan's truck was new, and he was serious about taking care of it." He'd even nagged me a few times about getting my truck's oil changed for winter. "If the brakes quit working, it's either some kind of man-ufacturing problem, or…"

"Or someone is attempting to start another war," Dad fin-ished, going still as only the older vamps could. "I will alert the council."

He disappeared into the living room. I stayed in the kitchen at the small table, letting the heat from my mug seep into my hands. I was so tired of being cold all the time.

He caught me shivering when he returned to the kitchen. "Cold?"

I nodded. "I was thinking of getting a little heater for my room."

"You are anemic. It is a symptom of the change. We must train you how to hunt and feed soon."

The small amount of hot chocolate in my stomach threat-ened to make a comeback. "Gross, Dad. Forget it. I'm never going to…feed." Even saying the word was utterly repulsive.

"Savannah, it is what you were born to do."

Yeah, thanks to him and Mom deciding to break the rules and hook up.

He sighed. It was one of the few human things he still did. "Resisting your nature is both foolish and unnecessarily dan-gerous to any human you come into contact with."

"Giving in to my vamp side is what's dangerous," I argued. "I don't need blood to survive. I'm still half human." So far.

"And yet you continue to lose weight," he said.

"So my jeans are a little loose lately. It's just stress. I'll gain it back soon."

"Not if you do not obtain the proper nourishment to meet your body's changing needs."

"They're not changing. I'm fine eating regular food still." I tried to put on my best poker face. Like I even had one.

"What do you eat, precisely? And do not attempt to lie to

me anymore. I have seen the food stores in our kitchen, as well as how little you spend on lunch each day. Why do you think I encouraged you to shop for your own groceries? You are free to buy anything you wish to eat, and yet you still eat nothing."

Stupid credit card receipts. I should have known he would use any and all means to watch me.

I drew in a breath through my nose, held it, then let it out slowly so I wouldn't give in to the urge to throw a tantrum like a kindergartner. "If you're going to spy on everything I do, you can have the credit card back."

"It is for your own safety. And others'. Or do you intend your first victims to be your friends?"

"Of course not!"

"They will be, unless you take better care of yourself. Your body will force you to find nourishment sooner or later. Either you choose what that nourishment is, or it will decide for you."

"Fine," I snapped. "I'll try to eat better, okay? But human food only."

"Why do you have to try? Is it not easy for you to eat?"

I stared down at my still mostly full mug. A few months ago, I would have chugged it down in a matter of seconds. "Everything smells gross lately."

"It is another symptom. Soon you will have the bloodlust for humans as well as descendants."

I really didn't want to hear it. "Do we have to talk about this right now?"

"You cannot run from what you are, Savannah."

"I can try," I grumbled.

"You will fail. And when you do, innocents will be harmed, and you will never be able to forgive yourself."

I glanced up at him. "You sound like you're talking from experience."

He didn't reply, which meant the answer was yes.

So my seemingly perfect dad had screwed up once or twice, too. That was both disturbing and comforting in a weird way. If he hadn't always been perfect, then he couldn't expect me to be perfect, either.

"You must face the facts. You are unique with unique needs."

"How can I forget it, what with you and Mom and the Clann's constant reminders." My hot chocolate had gone cold. I jumped to my feet to reheat it in the microwave.

"Reminders?"

"Savannah, how are you feeling?" I deepened my voice to mimic him. "Savannah, how was your day? Anything strange happen today, Savannah?" The microwave dinged. I grabbed my mug, set it on the counter, jerked the silverware drawer open to get a spoon, and the drawer handle came off in my hand.

Growling, I held out the flimsy hardware to him. He accepted it without a hint of surprise.

"Stupid knob. That's twice since yesterday!" I muttered as I grabbed a spoon then hip bumped the offending drawer shut again.

"Your strength is increasing. We will need to practice hiding it when you are in public."

"Forgive me if I don't jump at the chance to play vampire." Maybe extra marshmallows would make the hot chocolate taste better. I dug through the pantry for them.

Suddenly Dad was standing beside me, his white-silver eyes boring into mine. "You cannot *play* at what you are. Like it or not, your vampire side is growing stronger. You are my daughter and my responsibility. I *will* see to it that you learn how to survive in this world we are forced to deal with. You will learn how to feed properly and safely. And you *will* learn how to control your abilities enough to blend in with human society. I will not see you killed by the council or turned into some sort of lab experiment by humans because I loved you too much, gave in to your wishes and neglected to teach you how to evade detection."

Yeesh! I'd never seen Dad furious before. He was pretty darn impressive at it. I swallowed hard. "Fine. Whatever makes you happy, sir." I mimicked a little salute.

"What would make me *happy* is if you start your training right now."

"Now?" I squeaked. I'd been awake for barely an hour. And it was a Sunday. Couldn't I go to my room and chill out for a while first?

"Now." He pointed at the living room.

Grumbling about dictatorial control freak vampires, I stomped into the living room. I turned and faced him, my arms crossed over my chest.

"Teenagers," he muttered before doing that annoying vamp blur thing to reappear a couple of feet away from me.

"Are you going to teach me how to do that, too?" I asked, only half sarcastic now.

"Actually, I am going to teach you how not to do that. At least, not without deciding to. Moving faster than the human eye can see will come with time and feeding, along with steadily increased strength, whether you want these abilities or not. The point of our training will be to teach your body how to retain control and self-discipline so that you do not accidentally reveal how fast and strong you are around humans."

I groaned. Why did my parents always have to take the cool out of everything? I was half witch, but no one would let me learn to use magic. Now I was becoming a vamp, and no one wanted me to have fun with that, either!

"Fine. So then what, I just practice moving slow and acting weak all the time?" I made my voice as high as it would go and batted my eyelashes. "Oh no, this bag is just too heavy. Won't someone please help me carry it?" I reverted back to my normal voice with a grin. "Easy. Done. Training's over."

Dad glared at me. "Ignoring what will soon come naturally to your vampire body is not going to be so easy. You will have to be vigilant not to give away your true abilities. The best way to remember to do that is to make it a habit for your body to move slowly. It will feel awkward at first, so you must practice to allow your body to grow accustomed to the sensation. We will also work on teaching your muscles using kinetic memory."

I stared at him, completely lost now. "Connecticut what?"

"Kinetic memory. You have not heard of this?" His eyebrows shot up. "Dancers use it all the time. Your muscles have their own memory. If you repeat the same motions often enough, your muscles will begin to remember those movements for you. Then your mind will have to remember less for you, and moving humanly slow will once again feel natural to you."

I sighed. "If you say so. So what, I just pretend to be a mime and do everything in slow motion?"

One corner of his lips twitched. "I was thinking more along the lines of tai chi."

I stared at him. "Isn't that what old people do in the park?"

"People of all ages practice tai chi as a way to focus and quiet their minds while teaching their bodies to have control and self-discipline." He sounded a little huffy. Did vamps ever get self-conscious about their real age?

Then I thought about what he'd said. Control over my body. Now *that* I could get excited about. "All right. What do I do?"

★ ★ ★

We trained for two hours, slowly going through several tai chi moves that became almost like a dance routine. Well, a really flat-footed ballet routine, maybe. Still, there was something soothing about tai chi, even if it was a little strange at first.

It reminded me of when I first started taking dance in the ninth grade, before my vamp abilities began to develop and the vamp council banned me from dancing in front of others. Of course, I had a lot more grace now. But it was still new and awkward, learning the precise positioning of each move and trying to teach my body how to go through the new motions far slower than it wanted to. The challenge of it had the added benefit of taking my mind off other things.

And my mind could definitely use a break.

We stopped for lunch. I wanted to skip it, but Dad insisted we experiment with fruits and steamed vegetables I normally wouldn't consider eating much of. Since I refused to drink blood, he seemed bound and determined to find the healthiest human food I could stand to eat and then fill me up with a week's worth of it.

It wasn't all bad, though. I discovered that my new favorite foods were canned pears and steamed carrots. Their soft textures didn't hurt my extra-sensitive teeth, which seemed to ache all the time lately, and their flavors were subtle enough not to send my stomach into immediate revolt. I also found I could stand vegetable juice, though it had to be watered down so it wouldn't make my taste buds scream in pain.

Apparently vampires had extremely delicate palates.

We practiced more tai chi after lunch, focusing on breathing techniques this time, and the hours somehow slipped by unnoticed.

"Thanks, Dad," I murmured as the light streaming in

through the wooden blinds at the living room windows began to turn more orange and fade. "I really needed this."

He returned my smile with a gentle one of his own, looking for a brief moment like any other human father might. "You are more than welcome. Tai chi has always brought me great peace when I needed it most. I can only hope it provides you the same." He glanced at the darkening world beyond the windows. "Unfortunately we will have to conclude today's training now. It is growing late and I have not fed in a week, so I must leave for a while."

Peaceful feeling gone.

He talked about feeding on some poor person as casually as if he were mentioning that he needed to make a quick run to the grocery store. Even if that person was a so-called evil-doer, as he referred to them, it was still wrong to go shopping for a blood donor like it was no big deal.

I went to my room, put on my headphones, cranked up the music and tried not to think about my dad and his "grocery shopping." Or how I might end up just like that soon.

CHAPTER 11

TRISTAN

"Quit faking, I know you're awake," Emily grumbled from somewhere at my right side.

I cracked one eyelid open. The coast was clear, no parents or other descendants in sight. "Hey. How'd you know?"

She shrugged and crossed her arms.

"Where's Dad and Mom?"

"I told them to take a break and go get something to eat. You know, I've gotta say, I always knew you were a brat, but this totally takes your selfishness to a whole new level. I ought to hit you, but I'm pretty sure the nurses would throw me out."

"What? What the heck did I do? Shouldn't you be giving me some sympathy here instead of grief? I'm *wounded*."

She rolled her eyes. "Oh please. Like I'm really buying that whole line from last night about your brakes not working. Everyone knows you weren't supposed to be out there. They think you tried to kill yourself in your truck."

"Give me a break. I needed some fresh air, that's all. Mom and Dad have been treating me like an inmate lately. Can't a guy get two minutes to himself without everyone assuming I'm suicidal?"

Emily stared at the floor. She looked like she was ready to swing a bat at my head.

Then I noticed the tears gathering at the edges of her eyes. "Aw, sis, don't cry. I'm all right now."

"No, you're not, you moron. You crushed practically the whole left side of your body! It's going to take months to heal you."

I glanced down at myself. Was she serious?

"And you nearly died. Did you know your heart actually almost stopped beating? If not for Savannah—"

"Wait, what? What does Sav have to do with this?" I didn't believe her about my heart nearly stopping. She was being a drama queen. But her mentioning Savannah was pretty random for her and a huge coincidence for me.

Had my truck wrecked because I'd unleashed that spell for Savannah while driving? Maybe the energy blasted out my brake system or something.

"She was the first one who knew you were hurt. She came tearing across the cafeteria at the dance to tell me she could literally feel your pain. She didn't know where you were, but we were able to use that pain connection to tell if we were getting closer or farther away from you. Then we found you, and she helped me pull open the door and get you out. And then…" She took a shuddering breath. "Then I had to do a healing spell on you to keep your heart going."

"Huh." So the connection spell had worked. Though not exactly in the way I'd meant it to. Sav was supposed to have felt my emotions, not my physical pain.

Her eyes squinted in sudden suspicion. "What did you do? You were out there using power, weren't you?"

Time to switch gears. "Is she okay?"

"Is she— You nearly *died,* you idiot! Are you not hearing me? Your heart almost *stopped!* You even managed to make *Dad* cry."

I cringed. Maybe she wasn't kidding about the near miss after all. "Okay, okay, I hear you, stop shouting. But I don't know what to say about it. Thanks for bringing me back?"

She scowled at me. "You're welcome. And yes, she's fine. When your heart started to fail, so did whatever spell you'd put on her." She leaned in closer and hissed, "You do know our parents would go mental if they knew about that, by the way."

I tried a smile. "So don't tell them."

Emily sighed loudly. "What spell did you use, anyways?"

I tried to shrug, forgetting about my hurt arm and wrist, and had to freeze and hiss through the resulting pain. When I could think straight again, I answered, "I just wanted her to feel how I felt."

"A love spell?" She made a face as if I were too pathetic for words. Maybe I was.

"No, not exactly. She already loves me. I just wanted her to feel confident about us again."

She stared at me then slowly shook her head. "Oh wow. You are really and truly a lost cause, aren't you? How many times, in how many ways, by how many different people, do you need to hear that you two are over, and furthermore, were totally and impossibly doomed from the start? She's the *enemy,* Tristan, plain and simple. Let her go already."

Okay, now Emily was starting to tick me off. "I thought you were supposed to be the smarter one here. I mean, okay, maybe I shouldn't have tried to do a connection spell on her. I can see now that it wasn't such a smart move." At least not without better planning first. "But why is it so hard for *you* to see how we've been brainwashed? All of us have, on both sides! We shouldn't even be enemies in the first place. We should all be working together—"

The door to my room opened, and Dad and Mom came in. I had to endure several long, excruciating minutes of Mom's teary hugs before she finally gave me air to breathe again and backed off. In the meantime, Emily got up out of their way. I thought she was leaving, but she stopped and leaned against the doorjamb.

Dad stood at the foot of the bed watching me, his face scrunched up in an expression I'd never seen him make before. He patted my right foot under the sheets. "Glad to have you back with us, son. You sure worried us for a while there."

Emily threw me an I-told-you-so look.

"Um, sorry about that. I swear it was an accident." How many times would I have to repeat that before everyone got the message? "I tried slowing down in time for the curve, but the brakes never responded. By the time I tried to downshift it was too late and I was going too fast to be able to take the curve."

Mom grabbed a tissue from a box on the bedside table and dabbed at her eyes.

"I don't suppose my truck…" I began.

"Totaled," Emily answered without even a hint of sympathy. "It's scrap metal now."

Aw man! I'd loved that truck. It was the one space I had that was truly mine.

Not to mention, Sav had once ridden in it beside me on a date.

"Tell you what," Dad said. "Why don't you worry about recovering over the next few months, and let your mom and I worry about getting you some new wheels."

"Thanks, Dad," I said.

Spoiled brat! Emily slowly mouthed.

Mom glanced at her, and Emily put on a sweet smile.

"I'm going to go call everyone with an update," Mom murmured and headed out the door. Shaking her head, Emily followed her out, leaving me alone with our father.

He dropped heavily into the room's only chair.

"You look tired," I said, studying the lines radiating from the corners of Dad's eyes and the heavy bags beneath.

"You sure gave me a few extra gray hairs."

I grinned. "Impossible. It was all gray already."

Dad snorted, but at least he was smiling. After a few seconds, though, that smile faded again. He sat forward, his elbows braced on his knees.

"Look, son, you can tell me the truth, and I swear it'll stay just between us. Was it really—"

"Dad, I'm not lying. The brakes weren't working. Can't you get a cop or a mechanic or somebody to take a look at it?"

He stared at me. "You're that certain about it?"

"Yeah, I am."

"All right, I'll get somebody to look it over." His thick eyebrows drew together. "Is anything going on at school that I should know about? Anybody who might want to mess with your truck?"

"You mean other than the Williams family?"

We shared a look.

"Other than them, no," I said.

He searched my face as if he thought he'd find a different answer hidden there. Finally he sighed and leaned back in his chair. "Well, at least one good thing came out of it all. Your mother agreed to let you play football again next year. If you're physically recovered enough to."

My pulse sped up at that. "She did?"

He nodded. "We thought… Well, maybe we've been pretty tough on you this year. Football used to keep you mostly out of trouble. And your punishment for using magic on Dylan in public has lasted plenty long enough to satisfy any descendants who matter."

"Think Coach Parker will let me back on the team after all this time?"

Dad grinned. "You let me work on that. Just focus on healing up as fast as you can, and we'll get you all the field time you can handle next fall."

"Thanks, Dad."

My family went home to get some rest and returned later to bring me a few things to clean up with as best I could in bed. When Mom answered a call on her phone, Dad quietly leaned in to mutter that he'd had a mechanic look at my truck and the brake lines had been ripped loose, but they couldn't tell if it happened before or as a result of the wreck.

Dr. Faulkner also stopped by later that afternoon to show me my X-rays and talk about the recovery plan. When I saw the X-rays, I realized why everyone had been so freaked out. I hadn't just broken a bone or two. When my truck's driver's side door had crunched in on me, it had practically shattered my left wrist and my left leg below the knee. I'd also gotten several deep cuts from broken glass, one gash across my forehead, and two or three more on my left shoulder and forearm where apparently I'd tried to hold on to the steering wheel while being tossed around like a sock inside a dryer.

Even with my family and the local descendants helping with long-distance spell work, it was going to be at least a week before they could reknit my bones enough to allow me to leave the hospital, and a month in casts and on crutches.

That was the last time I *ever* used magic while driving. Just in case it was the reason my brake lines blew out.

By Monday afternoon, I was sure it was going to be the longest week of my life. I'd never realized how much I needed two hands until I temporarily lost the use of one of them. I couldn't play video games. Shaving, even with the help of a nurse to hold a mirror for me, was a joke and left me with nicks all over the left side of my face where I couldn't seem to angle the razor correctly. There was nothing worth watching on TV. And I'd already seen all the movies they had in the nurse station's library.

And my last plan to find a solution for Savannah and me had failed. Big-time.

So when a familiar girl poked her head in the doorway, I was pretty happy about it. Even if the girl was a blonde instead of a certain redhead, at least Bethany was someone to talk to who could distract me from the frustration brewing inside my skull like a spring twister.

She returned my smile as she came into the room. "Hey, champ. How are you feeling?"

"Better now that you're here. You wouldn't believe how boring this place is."

Sinking down into the chair, she opened her Charmers bag. "I brought you your homework for the week. I hope you don't mind? Your mom asked me if I could pick it up for her from the front office."

"She called you?" Mom sure was turning on the matchmaker skills lately. Either she really liked Bethany, or she was pretty worried about me.

"Um, no. I called her to see how you were doing and asked if it would be okay to stop by." She took out a stack of books, each one with several loose pages stuck inside. I tugged one paper free, glanced at the notes, and groaned.

"Oh man, this is going to suck."

"Having trouble in history class?" she teased after glancing at Mr. Smythe's notes.

I thought of Savannah, how her long legs looked tucked up under the desk beside mine in that class. "Always."

"If you need a little help this week, I could work with you on it."

I debated for about two seconds, just long enough to remember how ticked off Emily was at me right now. No doubt she was going to be too ticked off to offer much help with homework this week.

"Sure, that'd be great. Thanks."

She grinned, her cheeks turning pink. "It's no problem. The Charmers don't have practice this week or the next so we'll have more time to study for finals. So I can come right after school. And in the meantime…want to start with today's lineup?"

I sighed. "Yeah, why not? It's not like I've got anything else planned."

Laughing, she pulled a textbook from the stack and we got to work.

Bethany turned out to be a much better tutor than my sister. For one thing, she had way more patience when the deeper context of the English lit reading assignment was lost on me. She also didn't whack the back of my head if a certain redhead came to mind and I spaced out every so often.

When somebody came in with a tray of food at six o'clock, followed by my mother, I think we were all surprised, me most of all. Where had the time gone?

I pretended to eat the craptastic food until Mom left to find a spoon to eat her own takeout with.

As soon as she was gone, I hissed, "Quick, save me! Eat this before she gets back."

Bethany frowned at my tray of food. "Um, why?"

"Because it tastes like dog sh—er, crap—and I don't want to have to listen to everyone's nagging if I don't eat it."

She burst out laughing. "Oh, but it's okay to torture me with the bad food? I don't think so."

"Aw, come on, Bethany! Don't you have any sympathy?" Putting on my best puppy-dog face, I pointedly draped my free hand on my arm cast.

She ignored my plea while gathering up her things. "Sorry, champ, but I'd better head home before my mom gets worried. She knew I was stopping by here, but it's later than she probably expected."

Mom had left the door propped open. I could hear the determined, steady clacking of her heels returning down the hall.

"Bethany, please!" I held out the bowl of creamed corn. "At least toss it in the trash for me or something."

Biting the corner of her lip for a few seconds, she finally grabbed the bowl and dumped it in the trash under the sink. She was just putting the bowl back on the tray for me when Mom reentered the room.

"There you go, all salted and peppered as requested," she said with a bright smile.

"Oh, men can be such babies when they're sick or injured, can't they?" Mom agreed with a smile.

"Well, I'd better go now. See you tomorrow?" Bethany said to me.

I nodded, shoving the gelatinous gravy around on top of my turkey while Mom moved to prop up the pillows behind my back.

"Thank you for coming, dear," Mom murmured to Bethany before returning to her pointless attempts to make me more comfortable.

At the door, behind Mom's back Bethany mouthed, "Mc-Donald's?" while using a pointer finger to draw imaginary golden arches in the air. I nodded frantically.

Mom made me lean forward so she could stuff an extra pillow behind me. I craned my head around her and mouthed, "Big Mac!"

Bethany shot two thumbs up then ducked out.

By the time Bethany returned the next day, I couldn't tell if I was happier to see her or the McD's bag she pulled out of her duffel.

"Oh man, you're an angel," I mumbled around the biggest mouthful of Big Mac I could manage.

She laughed as lettuce dripped onto my hospital gown.

I scarfed down the food and promised to pay her back as soon as my jailors returned my wallet. She hid the empty trash inside her duffel bag, and then we tackled the day's homework.

When Mom showed up later for a visit, she frowned and sniffed the air. "Is that...takeout I smell?"

Smiling, Bethany put a demure hand up in front of her mouth. "Oh, I'm so sorry, Mrs. Coleman. That was me. I just burped."

I covered up a snort of laughter by pretending to sneeze.

"Oh here, dear." Mom reached for the box of tissues on the bedside table. "Don't hold in your sneezes like that. It'll inflame your sinuses."

Mom held a tissue in front of my face. When I stared at it, she gave the tissue a shake. "Blow."

"Mother," I muttered through clenched teeth, feeling my face heat up.

"I should go." Bethany gasped, her face turning red as she

no doubt choked on the urge to laugh. "See you tomorrow, Tristan."

I was still blowing my nose for my mommy as Bethany ducked out the room, leaving a trail of giggles echoing down the hall.

Over the next few days, the routine repeated, thankfully without any repeated nightmarish demonstrations of my mother's overprotective style of parenting. Bethany's visits quickly became the highlight of the day, mostly because of the food she smuggled in, but also because she was nice. I'd never really had a chance to talk with her before; at Charmers practice when she would come over, I had always kept the chats short so we wouldn't make Savannah jealous. And in school we were always in a hurry to get to our next class.

Other than the occasional teasing about my being a momma's boy, Bethany actually had a great sense of humor. She also wasn't afraid to boss me around when I tried to slack off during the tutoring sessions and watch TV instead.

On Friday Emily finally got over being ticked off and stopped by to bug me. Bethany was still there when my sister arrived. Other than a quick flash of raised eyebrows, Emily was nice enough not to make a big deal about Bethany's visit. At least at first.

"So, sis, you going to bring me here next week for my physical therapy sessions? The doctors said I'll have two or three a week, maybe an hour or so each. We could probably schedule them in the afternoons if you want." School would have half days all next week, with two final exams each day. I would be released from the hospital on Saturday so I could get rested up in time to attend them.

"No can do," Emily said while making a point to bite into a quarter-pounder with extra cheese. Her obvious attempt to torture me wasn't working, though; I'd already inhaled a custom triple-decker from Dairy Queen an hour earlier courtesy of Bethany.

"Why can't you give me a ride?" It wasn't like she would be sleeping in all week. She had to take final exams, too, and pass them, in order to graduate. And since it would be weeks before I could drive myself again, I would already be hitching a ride with Emily to school every morning.

"Because after the exams, I have to stay for cheerleading practice with the varsity Maidens. And then after that, I'll have to drive to Tyler to the University of Texas campus to practice with the college squad."

"Now I know you're lying," I grumbled. "It's the end of the school year. What can you possibly need to practice for now?"

"Lots of stuff," she snapped back. "The UT cheer squad competes at cheer camp every summer, so we have to start getting ready for it as soon as possible. And since it's a coed team and I have zero experience doing coed stunting, trust me when I say I need all the practice I can get with them. And I'm still working with the Maidens squad this month because I have to train my replacement for next year's team captain. The Maidens voted in Sally Parker."

I snorted. "Well, there goes our varsity cheer squad for next year."

Even Bethany giggled at that, though she tried to cover it with her hand.

Emily sighed. "Yeah, I know what you mean. The Maidens went for sweet and stupid instead of diabolical genius. I can't really blame them, though. It was either her or Vanessa Faulkner. Nobody else wanted it."

I shuddered. "Good choice." Vanessa was so mean she would run everyone off the team in no time if they'd chosen her for captain.

Clearing her throat to hide another giggle, Bethany rose and picked up her things. "I'd better be going. Good luck next week."

"Thanks," Emily and I both replied.

"Hey, thanks for all the tutoring and the…well, you know," I finished lamely, not wanting to mention the takeout and give Emily any more additional blackmail to use against me with our parents.

Emily's eyebrows rose again at that.

"Sure!" Bethany said. She started out the door then stopped and turned back. "Hey, I could give you a ride to your physical therapy sessions next week. If you can get them set up after lunch, we could grab a bite to eat then head straight from school to here."

"Okay, but this time the grub's on me," I said. "Otherwise the deal's off."

"You drive a hard bargain. See you Monday after school." With a wave, Bethany turned and headed down the hall toward the elevators.

Emily cleared her throat loudly.

"What?"

"She seems really nice."

"Yeah, she's not too bad."

Emily threw a balled-up napkin at me. Bored, I used a little power to make it stop midair then reverse direction and zoom back at her. Laughing, she mimicked me, holding up a hand to halt the napkin.

"I think she likes you." She flicked her wrist and the napkin headed my way again.

I caught it without touching it, bouncing it in the air a few times with my energy. Shrugging in response to her comment, I made a thumping motion at the napkin and it flew through the air to circle around Emily's head.

Ducking, she froze the napkin ball between her hands. "So unless you actually like her back, you might want to be careful."

We pretended the napkin was a basketball for a while, dribbling it off the ceiling, the walls, the TV screen, trying to outdo each other's crazy bank shots.

"Why can't she just be a friend?" I suggested.

"A girl who's just your friend? I didn't think you knew how to do that."

"Maybe I should learn. Lots of guys have female buddies, right?"

"Mmm." She caught the napkin as it veered off the bathroom door, deftly sending it sliding across the top of the window blinds. "Well, I guess you could always try it and see how it turns out."

"Wow, knock me over with your faith there, sis." I frowned and grabbed the napkin. Pretending it was the tip of an invisible sparkler now, I tried drawing shapes in the air with it.

Emily stole it back. "I just think you're going to have a tough time keeping it at just a friend thing with her." She made the napkin draw the shape of a giant heart.

"What if I'm upfront with her? Tell her right from the start that I'm not looking for a girlfriend." Not unless it was Savannah. "Then she won't expect anything beyond friendship."

She sighed. "Good luck with that."

The door opened and Mom came barging in like the head of a small SWAT team on the offense. "What are you two *doing?* I could feel the power use from the parking lot!"

Emily dropped her hand and the napkin hit the floor and rolled out of sight under the rocking chair. "Nothing. Just talking."

"Yep. Just talking." I put on a big smile.

Mom glared at both of us then sighed. "I'm going to see

about some DVDs or something to keep you two out of trouble. While I'm gone, be good!" Muttering about packing her wild heathen children off to stay with their cousins in Ireland for the summer, she swept out again.

"She doesn't really mean that, does she?" I asked with a frown. "She remembers she agreed to let me play football again, and that I've got physical therapy and then football training starts up right after that, right?"

Emily snickered. "You better hope she does."

The napkin hit my temple out of nowhere, and the game was back on.

I meant to have the "only friends" talk with Bethany the following week. I even opened my mouth, the words right there ready to be said, when we stopped by Taco Bell for lunch Monday after the day's final exams.

But then she hopped up to get us sauce, mild for her, medium for me, and when she returned she brought a stack of napkins.

"In case you decide to drool again," she joked, plopping the napkins on the table between us.

And in the middle of teasing her back, I forgot about having the talk with her.

Savannah looked ready to cry on Friday when I awkwardly hopped and lurched up the steps into Mr. Smythe's portable building for the history exam. I'd finally started to get the hang of this whole crutch walking business, though my good arm's armpit was killing me. The leg cast was heavy, so it took some effort to get it positioned under my desk after I sat down beside her. By the time I was all tucked in and ready to talk, Mr. Smythe was passing out the exams and telling everyone not to say a word or we would get automatic Fs for cheating.

Afterward, Savannah took advantage of how slow my injuries made me and shot out of class like a bolt.

So much for one last talk before the summer break.

CHAPTER 12

SAVANNAH

The summer break couldn't come fast enough.

All I wanted to do was hole up in my room and escape the constant bombardment of everyone else's emotions slamming me every time I left home. I'd thought the ability had calmed down. But lately my own emotions had been a nonstop roller-coaster ride, making it harder to control sensing others'. Thankfully, I was about to get several blissful weeks of solitude. As usual, my friends' parents had filled up their summer with family babysitting for Michelle, candy-striping and volunteering at a nursing home for Carrie, and church camp and helping bale hay out on her uncle's farm for Anne. Even the Charmers wouldn't need me for a couple of months. The team would be going off to dance team camp for a week, then the officers would be at leadership camp, then we'd have all of July off and wouldn't meet back up until the team's annual boot camp week and slumber party in August just before school started again.

All I had to get through was the junior summer party that first Saturday after school let out for summer break.

But what should have been a simple lake party turned out to be way tougher than I'd expected. I'd braced myself for the onslaught of emotions that hit me when I entered Bethany's family lake house and dropped off two bottles of Sprite, my contribution to the food table. But then I headed downstairs and out onto the private pier just in time to hear Bethany telling everyone that she was dating Tristan now.

Tristan was already dating again? He'd just gotten out of the hospital! How could you go on dates wearing two casts and covered in staples and stitches?

For a few seconds, I couldn't even move from the doorway, the slapping of the waves of water against the pier doing nothing to soothe me or cover up Bethany's voice as she chattered on about how she was driving him to his physical therapy sessions three times a week and home from school every day in between, and where they'd eaten lunch together, and how bravely he was fighting through the physical therapy to recover as fast as he could for football training season.

If I'd eaten any lunch, I would have lost it all over the pier right then and there.

Tristan was dating Bethany. Not just taking her to a single dance. Actively, continuously dating her.

A few heads turned my way, and someone nudged Bethany's shoulder. She looked up, saw me standing there, blushed, and stopped talking.

Feeling too many eyes on me, I pasted on a smile, waved hello to everyone then went to sit at the edge of the pier with the two girls who had been managers with me this year until they'd re-auditioned and made the team for next year. I pretended to listen to them, though I actually had no clue what they were talking about.

Bethany resumed recounting all her recent dates with Tristan, this time in a whisper. But of course my stupid vamp hearing had no trouble picking up every word.

I'd thought I knew Tristan, but lately I couldn't figure him out. Even before the wreck, Tristan's decision to take Bethany to the dance had confused me. First he'd promised to find a way for us to be together and even asked my dad to turn him. A week later he was taking someone else to the dance. At the dance, I'd thought I heard him telling me to have faith in us, that we'd find a solution. I'd helped his sister save his life. And then, right after he got out of the hospital, he was back to dating someone else again. To make me jealous? As a decoy to make his parents think he was moving on?

Or maybe he really had given up on us and was moving on.

I stayed at the lake party for an hour, which was as long as I could stand to sit around forcing a smile. Then I made up an excuse about my dad being sick and needing to get home to take care of him. It was all I could do not to run to my truck and speed the whole way home.

Parked once more in the driveway, I took long, deep breaths and tried to think it through.

Okay. So he was dating someone else.

You knew this could happen. That it probably would happen, I thought, resting my forehead on the steering wheel as the heated air from the cab finally began to warm my clammy skin. Maybe I'd imagined hearing him at the dance because some instinct had made me realize he was in danger, and it just got all twisted and crazy for a few seconds. Then my abilities sorted themselves out, and I felt his physical pain instead.

If that was true, then he'd never done a spell to tell me to have hope that we'd find a way to be together again. He really had moved on.

There was zero reason for me to feel betrayed. I'd broken up with him, not once but twice. Now that he understood it was truly over, he was dating someone new, trying to find some happiness in life again.

And I would be happy for him. I *would*. Because it could be so much worse, couldn't it? Would I rather he be dead, or alive and happy with someone else?

When I texted Anne at church camp with the news, her reaction wasn't quite so nice. In fact, it was filled with a whole lot of four-letter words I was pretty darn sure the church camp counselors wouldn't be thrilled to see her typing if she got caught.

She was convinced he should never date again. She wanted him to spend the rest of his life moaning about the love he'd lost with me, and die a miserable and lonely old man.

While her staunch loyalty was appreciated and did make me smile, and maybe a teeny tiny part of me might agree with her, the larger part of me knew we were both being unreasonable.

Thankfully I had two and a half months to make my heart agree with my head before I would be forced to see him again at school.

Then I got a strange call that totally changed my summer plans.

"So how did your final exams and Charmers party go?" Mom asked when she called during the first week of summer.

"Um, okay I think."

Actually, I was finding out that this choosing to be grateful and happy business was a heck of a lot harder than it seemed in all the self-improvement books Mom had given me while we'd packed up Nanna's house.

Silence filled the phone. Finally Mom said, "Listen, you know that box of books I gave you?"

"Yeah. I'm working my way through them now. I'm about halfway through *Love Yourself and Change Your Life*." Not that it was helping any.

She cleared her throat. "Well, you might want to skip to the bottom of the stack. And do it when your dad's not around."

Okaaay. "Why?"

"There are a few of your grandma's books at the bottom."

Nanna's books? Nanna used to read all the time. Her favorites were celebrity biographies. She used to say their lives were far crazier than anything she'd ever had to live through, so they made her feel normal by comparison. Of course, none of them had died after being magically kidnapped and held hostage by a bunch of ticked-off descendants in the woods.

More silence from Mom.

"Okay, Mom, what's your point?"

"They're not...normal reading."

I was starting to get a funny feeling here. "You mean, they're like..."

"Something we shouldn't discuss by phone. And nothing your dad should ever see. Okay?"

I dug through the box, which was almost as high as my waist. At the bottom I found old leather books filled with hand-drawn sketches and handwriting. Spell books. I gasped.

"Mom! Why on earth would you—"

"She made me promise to give them to you if anything happened to her! She knew *I* never wanted the ability. So it's only right that they're passed down to you. Not that I'm condoning anything, or even want to know anything about what you do with them. I'm just keeping my promise to her. Oh, and she said to be sure to tell you that she and I made the promise to the Clann, but *you* never did."

Her words sent goose bumps racing down my arms. I'd thought the same thing two weeks ago after Tristan's wreck and the "chat" with Dylan at the Sonic.

She sighed. "Now maybe she'll stop showing up in my dreams every night and bugging me about this."

"Nanna's *haunting* you?"

"Well, maybe not her actual ghost. I don't know. The dreams are so real, it feels like I'm awake. Anyways, whatever it is, maybe it'll stop now that I've done the magic queen's bidding." Her tone was more than a little cranky.

Okay, this was getting beyond creepy.

After ending the conversation with Mom, I decided to put all of Nanna's spell books into a smaller box. Then I considered where to hide them. Under my bed? No, Dad might find them there if he ever got around to refinishing the hardwood flooring in here.

Dad wasn't home today. He'd gone to Tyler to pick up some crystal drops for a chandelier.

Before I could change my mind or lose my courage, I sent him a quick text saying I had to do some Charmers fund-raiser stuff and would be back later this evening.

Then I grabbed Nanna's box of contraband and carried it out to my truck.

As soon as I pulled into the pine-needle-covered driveway of Nanna's former house, so many emotions welled up within me…surprise at the lack of a rental sign out front, relief that it looked untouched, homesickness, sadness, and above all the guilt. It was worse than visiting Nanna's grave could ever be. The memories of Nanna weren't in some lifeless cemetery. She was here at the front stoop, watering her potted plants, now dying, that hung from hooks at the sides of the porch roof. She was in the front yard, fighting a futile and endless battle with a rake against the needles that fell constantly from the towering pines that both shaded and threatened the brick house with their leaning trunks and branches. The haunting memory of all I'd once known and called home reached out to me everywhere I turned.

Taking a deep breath, I grabbed the box of books and carried it around the side of the carport to the backyard. I set it on the metal stool I used to sit on and spin for hours as a little kid beneath the old pecan tree.

The garden was starting to go wild. Nanna used to work daily to keep it under control and tidy.

She should be here, sweating under the East Texas sun while Mom and I begged her to take it easy and come inside. She should be kneeling on that green spongy cushion she used to save her knees while she talked to the plants as if they were her children, making this little section of the world beautiful and useful and helpful to others with its produce of herbs and strawberries and pecans and peaches.

She would have been here still, if not for the Clann.

I ran a hand over the box lid, thinking about its precious contents. Contents created by Nanna's own hands, filled with her thoughts, and maybe those of other Evans before her.

If I tried very hard, I could almost hear Nanna now.

Okay, Savannah. You've had time to think it over, and you know just sitting back isn't working anymore. Those descendants have grown far too big for their britches. Now what are you going to do about it? Because we Evanses do not just sit around all helpless and moping when times get dangerous or hard, do we? Especially not when our loved ones might be in danger.

I eased the box lid up an inch.

I'd lost so much because of the Clann…Nanna, Mom, Tristan, my home. And now Dylan might be planning to go after Anne next year. Unless I stopped him.

I would have two and a half months to figure it out. The

question was…could I do it? I had no one to teach me other than the words written in this single box of books. No one to turn to if I got confused or frustrated or screwed up. Learning how to use power might even be dangerous, for all I knew.

But if I found a way to stand up to Dylan and the Brat Twins and the rest of the Clann and protect the people I cared about, the risk would be worth it.

Maybe my imagination was still running wild, but I almost could have sworn I felt Nanna's arm around my shoulders, reassuring me as I flipped the box lid open and took out the first book.

It was incredibly slow going. No wonder descendants started training early and practiced for years.

I'd expected to be able to do at least *something* that first day. But nothing happened, no matter how hard I tried. Maybe it was because I'd started with the first lesson in the book marked for beginners, which was on grounding. I didn't need to siphon off any extra energy. Unlike most descendants apparently, I was already tired all the time. I needed to gain energy, not ground it off.

The first day was a bit of a letdown. But I wasn't ready to give up. So the next day, I told Dad I had Charmers stuff to do every day of the week for a while. I was scared to death that he'd see the truth on my face, but he was too busy flipping through paint samples for the upstairs bathrooms. He simply made me promise to keep my phone with me at all times and to call him if I started to feel weird.

So I ended up spending the summer days at Nanna's. My key still worked on all the doors, and the house stayed empty. The company that had bought it didn't seem too anxious to rent it out anytime soon. They hadn't even put a sign out front to let people know it was available. And yet they'd kept the electricity and water on, so I was able to go inside for a drink from the kitchen faucet or use the bathroom if I needed to. I left the air conditioner off to avoid running up the new owner's electric bills, which might give my presence away. Plus, I enjoyed the heat from the greenhouse effect as it thawed out my muscles each day.

I felt like I was going camping, sneaking out rolls of toilet paper and a comforter to kick back on in the empty dining area for reading. It was the most fun I'd had in months.

And unlike at my new house with its many views of the Tomato Bowl where I'd watched Tristan play football, at Nanna's there were hardly any reminders of him, which was a huge relief.

But after the first month of reading spell books and practicing the exercises they recommended, the fun wore off. I was ready to do magic. *Now.*

Had I waited too long to try to develop my descendant side's abilities? Mom said doing magic was like using a muscle…if you didn't use it, it would atrophy. She'd purposely made hers weaker by refusing to do magic.

Maybe my vampire genes were just too strong?

A door slammed shut outside. Squeaking, I had just enough time to throw the comforter over the stack of books beside me on the dining room floor before Dad showed up in the backyard. He turned and peered at me through the patio glass door.

"Savannah? What on earth are you doing here? I thought you had Charmer things to do."

I jumped to my feet, opened the patio door and stepped outside. "Oh. Um, I was just…you know, hanging out. What are you doing here?"

"I wanted to check on the place to make sure it is still okay."

"Why?"

"Because you should always keep an eye on your property."

"You…own Nanna's house now?" Had he bought it from the new owners? That would explain why there was no rental sign outside.

"I own the company that purchased it from your mother. I knew the day would come when either you or your mother would grow homesick and want to revisit the house. It was also your mother's childhood home, you know."

Yeah, I knew that. "But you paid too much for it. If you'd just told us you wanted to buy it, we could have stopped the whole bidding war and let you have it way cheaper."

"I own both the companies that bid on it. And your mother never would have knowingly permitted me to purchase her childhood home."

He had to be kidding. "Why would you jack up the price like that?"

"Your mother told me many times how much she wanted to see the world in an RV, to have complete freedom to travel as much as she wanted. And of course I wanted to ensure that you would have adequate funds for any sort of college education that you might choose. But your mother's pride would not allow me to directly fund either of these goals."

"So you purposefully paid way too much for the house."

"Yes."

"And lied to Mom about where the money was really coming from."

"Actually, she never asked who owned either of the companies that bid on the house. So technically I never had to lie to her about my involvement."

Holy crap, he was devious. I couldn't tell if his actions were romantic or just really sneaky.

"You should be aware that the house has been set up to become yours when you turn eighteen," he added. "You may then do anything you choose with it…sell it, rent it out as an investment property, or even use it as your own home if you so choose. Until then it will remain empty and available for your use as needed."

Wow. I didn't know what to say to that. "Um, thanks."

"You are more than welcome."

"So, if I wanted to come here and hang out sometimes, it would be okay?"

He glanced past me at the comforter on the linoleum floor. "I cannot see the sleeping accommodations as being all that comfortable since there are no furnishings left. I would prefer you come home in the evenings to sleep. And it would also be safer if you only come here alone."

Meaning no secretly meeting Tristan here or throwing wild, unsupervised parties with my friends. "Sure." Like I would do any of that anyways.

I only wanted to come here to learn magic.

"Well, everything looks fine, so I had better get back to the renovation efforts. I will see you for dinner? Say eight o'clock?"

Raging guilt made me press my lips together and nod, afraid if I opened my mouth I might blurt out what I was really doing here.

Then he walked back around the house to his car and left, and I could breathe again.

I had to do this, I reminded myself. Dylan and the Brat Twins and the whole Clann's hatred toward me and anyone I called a friend had forced me to do whatever I could to protect my friends and myself. Even Nanna's ghost, if it was hanging around Mom, seemed to want me to learn how to do magic.

If I used magic only for protection, how could the Clann or the vamp council complain about that?

Sighing, I grabbed the beginner spell book and went out-side to sit in the cool dirt under the old tree at the center of the backyard. "Okay, Nanna. You wanted me to learn how to do this. How about a little help here?"

There had to be something in this book that I was missing. Tristan had told me once that descendants began training as soon as puberty hit, so I was definitely old enough. If a twelve-year-old could do basic magic, surely I could figure it out, too.

I flipped back to the very first lesson on grounding. I didn't need the effects from grounding, but it might be necessary to do every single lesson in order or something. Skipping ahead certainly hadn't worked so far.

Following the first lesson's instructions, I closed my eyes, pressed my palms flat against the grass, and tried to imagine pushing my energy out through my hands.

My palms tickled a little. Because the magic was finally starting to work, or because of the grass against my skin?

I tried again, determined not to leave this yard until I figured it out.

Sharp tingling spread across my palms, spreading to my fingers and making me gasp.

The grass was now darker in the exact shape of two handprints right where my hands had rested.

"It's working!" I squealed, then clapped a hand over my mouth. Nobody was outside in the only neighboring yard, but if I made too much noise and anyone was home, they might come out to investigate.

Okay, settle down, Sav, I told myself. *You've got the grounding down. Now let's do the next step.*

A flip of the spell book's page revealed the next lesson was to draw energy from the ground. So I just needed to reverse the process, right?

Closing my eyes, I pressed my hands to the ground again and tried to visualize the earth's energy entering my hands.

Nothing. No tingling, no warmth.

I reread the lesson's directions but didn't see anything that I'd missed. Grumbling, my back and head aching probably from sitting hunched over on the ground so long, I lay back on the sun-baked grass and tried again.

Come on, I thought, pressing my hands against the earth. *Give me some energy already!*

My hands grew warmer and tingled this time, and I sighed with relief. Finally, it was working. But when I tried to sit up, I couldn't move. It was like someone had parked a car on top of me.

Oh crap. What had I done?

I must have accidentally grounded off more energy instead of drawing it into me.

I opened my eyes in panic, opened my mouth to yell for help. But all that came out was a tiny squeak. And my phone was inside the house beyond my reach.

Okay, relax, Sav. You can do this. You figured out how to ground energy. Maybe too well. Now just chill out and do the opposite!

Less warmth in my hands this time, and my thoughts grew fuzzy.

The backyard seemed to grow dark. Was it time for the sun to set already?

I should feel cold, too, but I didn't. I didn't feel much of anything other than the need to sleep. Except a voice in the back of my mind said sleeping was a very bad idea. I should call someone.

I tried to roll toward the patio door. But I couldn't move any part of my body. Even breathing felt like an effort.

The yard was so quiet. I could hear the wind as it wove through the backyard, making the plants rustle and whisper.

If I could just find a way to tap into those plants' energy…

I should start watering everything. Nanna would have wanted that.

That was my last thought as even the tree branches over-head faded from view.

And suddenly I was free. I was floating above my body in the garden, held by only the thinnest of silver cords at my navel.

"Savannah, what on earth are you doing?" Nanna de-manded as she walked through the garden toward me, her feet not quite touching the ground.

"Nanna! How—"

"Child, you're in the in-between world. Which means you've gone and done something pretty dumb. They sent me to come and send you back where you belong."

When I frowned in confusion, she added, "You're dying, dear."

CHAPTER 13

TRISTAN

Three-quarters of the way through afternoon practice, I felt like I'd been steamrolled, and it wasn't from the defense or the hot July sun sizzling on my skin. It was like something had drained every bit of energy out of me till I could hardly breathe. Coach Parker pulled me off the field to rest on the bench, thinking I was overheated. But I knew it was something much more serious.

When I caught my breath again, I realized it wasn't my own exhaustion I was sensing. It was Savannah's.

Savannah was in trouble. I didn't know how I knew, maybe it was that connection spell still in effect, but I knew. I could feel her out there somewhere, slipping away.

But I had no idea where she was or what was wrong with her or even how to reach her.

I was forced to wait half an hour till practice ended before

I could get back to the field house and grab my phone in my locker to text her.

Sav, I know you don't want to talk to me, but I felt like you were in trouble just now. Are you okay? At least let me know that much.

SAVANNAH

"Well, crap," I muttered. Talk about a failed magic lesson. "I was trying to learn how to draw energy. But all I kept doing was grounding instead."

"Yes, well, do it again and you're going to end up *in* the ground," Nanna said.

"I probably shouldn't even be trying to do magic in the first place," I grumbled. "If the Clann or the council find out, they're going to go nuts."

"Pfft." She waved a hand with a scowl. "They're just afraid you'll give them a taste of their own medicine. Of course, you won't have to worry about them at all if we don't get you back into your body soon."

Maybe that wouldn't be such a bad thing. "It's nicer being like this. Being here, with you."

"I can't stay here, hon. And neither can you." Her voice was softer now, like a gentle hand coasting over my hair.

"Why not?" There was no pain here, no endless heartache or anger or loneliness or guilt. Just peace. I looked at her, re-memorizing the lines in her cheeks that showed how often she used to smile and squint in the sun. "I miss you, Nanna."

"I miss you, too, kiddo. But you have to go back. It's not time for you to cross over. God's got big plans for you yet."

"For the earth's biggest freak? Why?"

She made a hissing sound. "You are just as much His creation as every other living thing on earth. Who are you or me to ask why He chose any of us for anything? It is what it is. You've just got to learn to stop fighting everything."

"What do I fight against? All I do is put up with endless crap!"

"You're fighting what you are. Even when you start to give in and embrace your abilities, you still end up fighting them. Look at your body lying there in the dirt, dying. That's you fighting the energy."

"I was *trying* to let it in—"

"You don't understand the give-and-receive nature of energy. Right now, what you're doing is trying to reach out and grab the energy like it's this solid thing you can pick up, like a rock or a leaf. But it doesn't work that way."

She sighed, and it sounded like the wind in the trees. "It never should have been called drawing. There's no pulling to it. It should be called receiving, or accepting, because that's all you've got to do. Chasing after it doesn't make it come to you. You've got to step into the river and let it wash over and into you."

She moved closer then reached out and took my hand, and I was stunned by how solid and real she felt. "Can't you feel the energy already beneath your body, pulsing in the earth and grass and roots of all the plants around you?"

"How can I? My body doesn't feel anything right now."

"Hardheaded. Get back in your body. Then just relax and open up your senses. The world is your battery, hon. All you need to do is allow the energy to flow in."

I didn't see how I could get any more relaxed, seeing as how I was supposedly dying. Grumbling, I lay down in my body again, then gasped.

It was like resting on top of a wool blanket full of static electricity.

"I can feel it!" I said, and this time the words came out of my actual lips.

"Good! Now relax. Pretend you're lying in a shallow stream, and let that current flow over your skin."

My skin tingled on my hands, my forearms and my left ankle where my jeans had bunched up, allowing my bare skin to touch the ground.

"That's it, dear." Nanna's voice was fading.

"Wait! What about the rest of it? Which book should I work on next?" I had so many questions to ask her. But most of all, I didn't want her to leave.

"Your mother already told you. Most Clann spells just need willpower and focus. These books are just to give you ideas of what can be done with that focus and will."

"But what about the bloodlust-dampening spell?"

"Ah, now that is old magic better left alone, dear. It requires too much sacrifice to make it work. It's dangerous."

I hesitated, but I had to know the truth. "Nanna, did you… sacrifice your life for it?"

"In a way, I did. And that's why it's no longer taught. But you don't need it. The safer ways, the new ways, will give you almost everything you need."

Except Tristan.

If I could learn the old ways, I could do so much more. I could perform the bloodlust-dampening spell to make it safe for me to be around descendants like my mom and Tristan. Maybe I could even turn off my vamp side completely.

To be able to kiss him again without stealing his energy… To be able to dance before an audience again without fear of revealing my vamp strength and speed…

"You have enough self control over the bloodlust on your own, Savannah." Her voice was only a whisper now. "And all the sacrificial magic in the world still wouldn't stop the energy flow if you kiss Tristan. I'm sorry, but even magic has its limits. It can't change what you are, no matter how much you might wish it could."

She sounded like Sam Coleman in the Circle when I wanted him to bring her back to life without a soul. Frustrated, I rose up on an elbow, determined to learn how she'd performed the bloodlust-dampening spell even if it killed me.

But I was alone again in the bright afternoon sunlight.

A breeze picked up a strand of my hair, and I could swear I felt Nanna's hand brush it back. *I gave what I had to for you and your mother, and I have no regrets,* the wind whispered. *But nothing is worth sacrificing your life for. At least, not yet. You have so many great things left to do. So mind your grandma, stick with the safe magic, and go make me proud. I love you.*

"I love you, too, Nanna," I whispered, my throat so tight it was hard to swallow.

A tear slipped down my cheek. I didn't wipe it away. It helped to make this moment feel more real, less like the dream my rational brain kept saying it had been.

I needed to believe seeing Nanna, talking with her again, had really happened. That my stressed-out, overtired mind hadn't imagined that whole conversation on its own. That she really was somewhere out there, waiting to take me to the other side someday and watching over me in the meantime.

I flopped back on the ground, too tired to get up yet. Overhead the sun beamed at me through the mostly bare branches of the old pecan tree. Thin wisps of clouds stretched overhead like the thinnest froth over a perfect blue sky.

Could Nanna see that sky, those clouds, this yard with all her plants, from where she was now?

Closing my eyes, I relaxed and pretended a silver stream was washing over me. And again, that low level of electric current sent tingles racing over my skin everywhere it made contact with the dirt.

I smiled, a sense of peace stealing over me for the first time in too long to remember. I couldn't have dreamed that conversation with Nanna. The proof was in my ability to finally draw energy.

When I felt less like the living dead, I rolled to my feet, gathered all the spell books back into their box, and put them in the corner of the closet in Nanna's room. I hadn't been able to enter her room before, when Mom and I had been packing up the house. The room had felt too much like Nanna's private space, an area where I didn't belong. Now, the guilt wasn't quite so heavy in my chest, and it was simply an empty room.

Nanna said I didn't need spell books to do the new magic. So I was going to trust her on that and leave the books here. Bringing them home or carting them around in my car was asking for trouble if anyone discovered them. But they should be reasonably safe here, especially if this house was destined to stay empty till it became mine.

It was a shame that I couldn't pass the books on to my own child someday, not only as tools to learn from, but as part of my family's heritage. Now that my vamp side was taking over, Dad had said I would probably become infertile like all the other female vamps. I would be the last in the Evans line.

I shook off the old heaviness that tried to drape itself over my shoulders. I couldn't change my parents' choices or what I was becoming. All I could do was try to make the best of what I'd been given. And with Nanna's help, take back what the Clann had tried to steal from me...my heritage as an Evans witch.

My phone buzzed against the worn-out linoleum floor where I'd left it. I picked it up, checked my missed messages.

Tristan had texted me. His message confused then scared

me. How could he possibly have felt me almost die? His connection spell had stopped working the moment his heart had nearly stopped beating after his wreck. Unless it had kicked back into effect when Emily fixed him?

Swallowing hard, I texted back, I'm fine. Stop texting me. It's against the rules. Go text your new girlfriend instead.

A few seconds later, his reply arrived. Girlfriend???

Oh please. Did he really think everyone in Jacksonville hadn't heard about him and Bethany?

I was so irritated I didn't bother replying. If he wanted to lie and pretend he wasn't seeing someone, that was his choice. But I wasn't going to waste my time arguing with him about something that was already public knowledge. I had better things to do. Like practicing using my newfound powers.

I would need every hour available this summer to train for the upcoming school year. Now that I was finally learning to use magic, I had a lot of catching up to do.

Dylan and the Brat Twins were going to be in for a major surprise if they tried to mess with me or my friends this year.

Learning how to do magic gave me a sense of confidence I hadn't had in too long to remember. I no longer felt like the Clann's doormat, lying around waiting for them to step all over me.

I was ready to kick butt. Starting with Anne's birthday party in August, two weeks before school started. It seemed the perfect time to get a head start on my magical to-do list.

This year Anne was having her annual sleepover in the small hunting lodge her family had built out on a remote piece of land they owned in the country between Jacksonville and Rusk. Anne said it was where they liked to go deer hunting every fall. She had emailed me directions, which weren't too hard to follow, and soon my truck was kicking up a huge cloud of dust down a long dirt drive that cut through the front fenced-in fields to where a tiny pier and beam house was set in the middle of the property.

I'd arrived late on purpose. Since I was the last one there, everyone else's vehicles were already lined up outside, giving me the perfect opportunity to place a protection spell on the back bumpers.

Friends' cars protected? Check.

With the first phase of tonight's mission completed, I climbed the short wooden steps to the lodge's door and knocked. Anne answered, and the smell was the first thing that hit me when I entered the one-bedroom house. It was all I could do not to stagger from the stench and cover my nose with my hand.

"Savannah," Anne whispered as she gave me a quick hug at the door. "Have you eaten at all since school ended? You're a stick!"

"Thanks," I muttered, holding out her present. "It's great to see you again, too, birthday girl."

"Sav! Wow, you look great!" Michelle called from where she was laid out on the floor of the living room area on her stomach. "New diet?"

Forcing a smile, I ignored the question and walked over to sit beside her and Carrie, trying hard not to breathe too deeply. Something in the house smelled absolutely awful. It was making my stomach roll over with every breath I took.

Michelle held up her wrist. "Check out my new perfume! I picked it up when we went swimsuit shopping. Which you missed."

I took the quickest of sniffs. Superstrong flowers soaked in alcohol. It might make me sneeze soon, but it wasn't the source of the house's stench.

I refocused on what she'd said. "Oh come on, guys. Like

you really wanted to be blinded by the sight of me in a swimsuit."

Carrie snorted. "Yeah, about that. What have you been doing all summer, other than avoiding us? Obviously not tanning, by the looks of it. You know, just because it's recommended that you wear sunscreen to avoid getting burned doesn't mean you should live your whole life in a cave, either. Step out of the Addams family mansion every once in a while. A little sunlight is good for you. It gives you vitamin C and D."

I laughed. "Thanks, I'll try to keep that in mind." Then I remembered the small bundle in my pocket. "Oh, by the way, I made y'all something." I dug the bundle out, untangled it and held up the four bracelets I'd spent hours and checked out a book from the public library in order to make.

"Friendship bracelets!" Michelle squeaked, plucking one from my palm. "Awesome!"

Anne walked over from the kitchen to join us.

Carrie grinned and took a bracelet. "Nice. Thanks. Have we ever had these as a group?"

"No," Anne said as she leaned over my shoulder and snatched one for herself. "But we should have. Good idea, Sav. Here, tie mine on."

I tied hers around her wrist and tried not to feel guilty about the magical reason behind my gift. They were still given in the spirit of friendship. I was trying to protect my friends here. They just didn't need to know that part.

Once everyone's bracelets were on, Anne said, "So who's ready to party? Let's do cake so I can get to opening more presents!"

"Not so fast," Mrs. Albright said over her shoulder before turning away from the oven with a giant homemade pizza. She set the steaming meal on the tiny table, which was set and just large enough for four people. "You know the drill, Anne. Pizza first, then cake and presents."

My stomach knotted up, causing what felt like my entire esophagus to clench shut with it. Oh boy. I hadn't planned how to get out of eating tonight.

"Mrs. Albright, it's a work of art," Michelle whispered as we gathered around the table.

She wasn't kidding. Every single mushroom, pepperoni and sausage chunk was perfectly spaced in an uninterrupted circular pattern as if arranged there by a robot.

But the smell. Oh lord, I wanted to hurl.

We took our seats at the table, with Anne's parents choosing to stand behind their daughter due to the lack of chairs.

"Bow your heads," Mrs. Albright commanded.

We all bowed our heads for prayer, even Michelle, whose family didn't go to church. Silently, I added my own prayer that I would somehow get through this meal without spewing all over the table.

And then the ordeal began. I took the smallest nibbles I could manage under Mrs. Albright's eagle eyes, using my fingers to tear the slice into smaller pieces so hopefully it would look like I'd eaten something.

I glanced up and caught her frowning at me. "Does it taste all right?" she asked.

"Oh! Sure, it's great!" I pasted on a smile and forced myself to take a healthy bite, chew and swallow.

My prayer was answered…sort of. I didn't spew all over the table. But I should have asked not to be sick at all. I held it down as long as I could, then muttered an excuse about needing something out of my truck and all but ran out the door. Anne found me hunched over by my truck's tailgate under a lovely sunset, holding on to the ends of my ponytail with one hand and my nose with the other as I tried without success to puke as quietly as possible.

"I'm so sorry," I gasped in between retches. "Please tell your mom her cooking is fine. It's not…"

"Wow. You really can't eat food anymore, huh?"

Miserably I shook my head. "It sucks so bad. I used to *love* pizza!"

"Why are you holding your nose? I can't smell anything."

"So it doesn't come out my nose."

"Oh gross." She awkwardly patted my back. "Don't worry, I'll cover for you. I'll tell them you just came out here to help me get the four-wheelers ready."

"Four-wheelers?" I took the water bottle she offered and rinsed out my mouth as my stomach reluctantly settled down again.

"Yeah. You'll see. I'll be right back with the girls." Anne ducked inside the house. I had just enough time to move away a couple of yards and paste on a smile before she returned with Carrie and Michelle in tow.

"I thought you wanted to have cake and presents," her mother was loudly complaining.

"Later, Mom!" Anne yelled back before pulling the door shut behind her.

Great. I was screwing up her birthday. "Sorry," I muttered to her as Carrie and Michelle walked ahead of us toward the quartet of four-wheelers parked at the other end of the building.

Anne waved off my apology. "Aw, don't worry about it. We'll get to the cake and stuff later. Let's go have some fun first. Um, if your stomach's up for it, that is."

"It's fine." I refused to let this stupid vampire business mess up her party any more than it already had.

Michelle hung back and bumped her shoulder against mine. "New diet, huh?"

Before I could come up with an excuse, she said, "You know, you should never lose weight just to get a guy back. Not even for *him*."

"I didn't... I mean, I'm not dieting—"

Michelle continued as if I hadn't said anything. "Of course, the competition is pretty tough this time. Bethany's so tiny, and they've been seen together all summer now. And everyone says she's a shoo-in for Charmers captain next year, too."

He was still dating Bethany? My shoulders slumped. Before me, his longest relationship had lasted all of two months.

"But don't you worry about it, because obviously she's way too short for him," Michelle added with a wave of dismissal as she hopped onto a four-wheeler like a pro. "He'll get a backache having to bend over to kiss her all the time. He'll get tired of it in no time and see how perfect you two were."

At the thought of Tristan kissing Bethany, my stomach threatened to rebel again.

Anne stopped explaining how to start the four-wheeler to Carrie. "Michelle, don't be dumb. She's not on a diet. Especially not for Tristan Coleman!"

I was surprised how much hearing his name hurt. But I'd have to get used to it. I would hear his name all the time when school started back up.

Anne showed me how to start my four-wheeler and make it go and stop, which was all easy to do since it was an automatic. No shifting or clutch work required, just push the lever-type button under my thumb to go.

"Don't drive behind anyone," Anne warned us with a grin as she hopped onto her own four-wheeler. "These fields are filled with cow patties."

I drove slowly in the beginning, getting used to the sensation of driving across bumpy terrain on a machine with no protective windshield, seat belt or doors. The property was larger than I'd thought at first, giving us plenty of room to chase each other and make huge donuts in the fields. Then we found the field with the terraces, now grass covered to form long horizontal mini-hills.

And then the fun really began.

Anne started it, daring us to take the terraces a little faster each time. Before I knew it, my four-wheeler and I were airborne, the wind whipping wildly through my hair as a crazy shrieking sound mixed with laughter erupted out of me.

The faster I went, the more fun it was as the rush of the wind around me in the fading light filled up my lungs, cool and clean, my adrenaline-laced blood rushing through my body. This was what I'd needed—to let loose, to get away, to go where no one was sneaking looks at me to see if I was okay, like Dad did at home when he thought I wasn't watching. No phone calls or texts "just to see how I'm feeling" like I got twice a day from Mom. No more keeping secrets, at least not from Anne.

I never wanted it to end.

Unfortunately, Anne's parents had made her promise that we wouldn't ride the four-wheelers in the dark. So once the sun finished setting, the fun was over for the day. I was the last to follow her back to the lodge and park.

"Sav, you coming?" Anne called from the top of the steps. Carrie and Michelle were already inside.

Reluctantly I turned away from the four-wheeler and joined everyone in the lodge.

Mrs. Albright was just lighting the last candle on the cake. She glanced at me with a quick frown then pasted on a smile while we all sang "Happy Birthday" and Anne blew out the candles.

Then Mrs. Albright handed me a paper plate full of cake.

"Feeling better now?" Her tone made it more of a challenge than a sympathetic question.

"Uh, Mom, Sav's…on a special diet," Anne said. "Sorry, I totally forgot to tell you. She can't eat the cake or it might make her sick."

I flashed her a look of pure gratitude.

Mrs. Albright gasped and took a step back like I was Typhoid Mary. "You're sick, Savannah?"

"No, Mom," Anne quickly answered. "Not like with the flu or anything contagious. I said the cake will make her sick. She's on a healthy foods only diet."

The alarm slowly faded from the air around Mrs. Albright. "Oh. Well, that's certainly understandable. I keep trying to get Tom and Anne on a diet like that. But all Anne wants to eat is junk food." She waved at the now empty pizza pan in the sink as if to prove her point, though the pizza had been so nongreasy I could almost swear she must have wiped the cheesy surface dry after baking it.

"How about I break out the strawberries early?" Mr. Albright suggested, his voice low and kind, and I understood then why Anne never hesitated to proudly call herself a daddy's girl.

Mrs. Albright brought out a bowl of sliced strawberries from the fridge. Feeling everyone's eyes on me again, I quickly grabbed a strawberry slice and popped it into my mouth, thinking maybe my body could handle the plain fruit at least.

I nearly choked. They must have coated the strawberries in sugar or something. The darn thing was so sweet it literally made my jaw ache.

"It's…good," I managed to say as my jaw muscles did their best to lock up in protest. I chewed once, twice then gulped the bite down and arranged my face in a smile. "They're great. Thanks."

Mrs. Albright smiled and relaxed in the chair I'd vacated earlier. "You go right ahead and eat as many of them as you want."

Carrie shook her head and dug into her cake, one eyebrow raised as she watched me trying to find a way out of having to choke down more of the too-sweet fruit.

After Anne opened all of her gifts, her parents went to the lodge's only bedroom while the rest of us settled in for a movie fest on top of sleeping bags laid out in front of a small TV set. Watching the birthday girl's favorite movies was a tradition at all of our b-day sleepovers. In the DVD stack for tonight was an eclectic mix of Johnny Depp's movies, including all of the *Pirates of the Caribbean* movies and a really old one called *Cry Baby*.

She started with the first *Pirates* movie, but I didn't pay much attention to it. I kept getting distracted by the smells assaulting my nose from the kitchen just a few yards away. There were also a whole host of smells I couldn't identify, and those were the worst. But not because they smelled bad. Actually, they smelled...mouthwatering.

Why couldn't I have had the source of that scent for dinner? Had Mrs. Albright cooked something else earlier? Maybe Anne would let me have the leftovers if there were any.

There was a really distracting sound in the background, too. Maybe a movie Mr. and Mrs. Albright were watching in their room? The sound was like a low thumping, almost like a car outside with one of those loud stereo systems. Except this beat was out of rhythm, as if several drums were being played at once and out of sync.

Then I caught snatches of conversation coming through the bedroom door.

"Well, Savannah's always been weird," Mrs. Albright muttered. "But what can you expect, considering that family of hers? Joan was always more than a little strange in school, too."

I tensed up, then glanced at my friends. They were all glued to the TV. Apparently only I could hear the discussion in the other room.

"I heard Joan ran off after her mother's death and left Savannah on her own," Mr. Albright murmured. "Savannah's dad had to move here to take care of her. Perhaps we should feel sorry for the girl."

"You call her father's parenting style 'taking care of her'?" Mrs. Albright snapped. "What kind of parent buys a health hazard and makes his kid live in it? And on top of that, he's apparently too busy chasing after rats in their new house to bother with getting his daughter some new socks every now and then. Did you see the size of the hole in hers? She looks like a thrown-away orphan."

Still lying on my stomach on the sleeping bag, I glanced over my shoulder at my feet behind me. Sure enough, my left big toe peeked out past a ragged opening in the cotton. I hadn't even noticed when I'd pulled them on earlier. All I had cared about was that they were clean.

"Mmm, I know what you mean," Mr. Albright said. "It's no wonder the poor girl has developed an eating disorder, living with a father she doesn't even know in a deathtrap like that. I tried everything I could to talk Michael out of buying that house when he called me about home insurance. But he wouldn't hear of it. He called it a 'priceless piece of history.'" He snorted. "He's probably spent all his money trying to make it liveable and didn't have any left over to buy her new socks."

Nausea rose hard and fast, driving me to sit up. Anne looked at me.

"I need some air," I muttered, yanking on my sneakers over my holey socks and heading for the door.

"But you can't!" Michelle protested. "There are coyotes out there."

I managed a half smile. "Don't worry, I'll be fine."

As soon as I stepped out and shut the door behind me, the smells changed. Sun-warmed ragweed was the strongest. But then I heard something rustling through the surrounding pasture's tall yellow grass. At the same time, a breeze blew a new scent to me. Something warm and wild was out there.

Then the door opened behind me and Anne walked out. I froze as she came to stand beside me, bringing the delicious scent from inside the lodge outside with her.

That scent should be fading. But it wasn't. It was…

Oh no. This could not be happening. Not here. Not now, with my friends…

The bloodlust…for normal, nonmagical human blood. Dad had warned me that this would happen, but I hadn't believed him. I hadn't wanted to. I needed to believe that I could still be friends with humans and everything would be okay.

But it really, really wasn't. My teeth ached with the need to sink into something….

I clamped a hand over my mouth, my heart racing harder than it ever had before. I had to get out of here. Now. I made a beeline for my truck.

"Sav, what's wrong?" she asked, grabbing my shoulder to stop me and leaning closer to peer into my face.

I twisted away from her, silently cursing the full moon's brightness. She would be able to see my teeth.

My fangs.

Oh God. It was one thing for her to have to know what I was, and another to actually see it. Even *I* didn't want to see what I looked like right now.

"I've gotta go," I muttered, taking the last steps to my truck.

I opened my door, slid in behind the wheel and glanced up to make sure she wasn't too close to my truck.

Anne gasped. "Your eyes...they're silver..." She took a quick step back, her hands falling to her sides.

I froze, one hand on the steering wheel and the other on the handle of my still-open door, both hearing the fear in her voice and sensing it in the air.

My best friend was afraid of me.

I slammed my door shut, rocking the truck.

How had everything come crashing down again? I'd spent the last month feeling so great about myself for the first time in forever, like learning magic had given me back some control over my body and my life.

And now *this*.

"I'm sorry," I said through the open window, hoping my face told her just how much I did not want this to be happening.

Her gulp was loud in the dark silence. "It's okay. It's just another birthday. I have one every year, right?"

My eyes burned. I closed them, took a deep breath in an attempt to regain control over myself, smelled that delicious scent again and realized my mistake. There would be no regaining control, not here, not now.

I sucked as a best friend. "I...I'll see you at school, okay?"

As I drove away, tires churning on the dirt road, I tried to find some way to make the tight knot in my throat ease up.

Maybe I wasn't a complete failure as a friend. I had managed to distribute all the protection spells tonight.

Except Anne didn't know about them. So it couldn't really make up for my having to bail on her birthday party.

Then again, I would feel a heck of a lot more guilt if I stuck around and ended up attacking one of my friends tonight.

The burning in my eyes increased, making my eyes feel like they were being bathed in acid.

No, there was no way to lie even to myself about this. I really did suck as a friend.

Maybe I should have put vamp wards on those bracelets instead.

CHAPTER 14

I didn't realize I was crying until I walked into my house twenty minutes later and Dad leaped off the couch only to reappear beside me in the foyer.

"What happened?" he demanded.

"What?" I caught a glimpse of myself in the mirror over the side table. My cheeks glistened. I swiped them dry with my sleeves. "The pizza made me barf, and then the bloodlust showed up. You were right. Happy?"

"Why would your unhappiness ever make me happy?" He frowned. "Come with me. It is time you learned how to feed."

"No way. I am not sucking on someone's blood like some kind of..."

He turned to face me, and my throat closed up on the word *monster*.

"Perhaps you would prefer to return to the party then?" he said. "I am sure your friends would be only too happy to welcome you back."

I pictured being shut up inside that tiny hunting lodge with all those hearts pulsing around me, and my mouth watered.

And then I wanted to be sick. I closed my eyes. "I don't want to be…" My mind struggled for a word that wouldn't hurt his feelings. A bloodsucker. A leech. A danger to my friends and mother and every other human around me. "I don't want to be…*this!*"

"We are what we are, Savannah. You cannot stop the change. You can only decide either to take control of your new life or let it control you."

Control. That was such a thing of the past right now. "I don't want to kill anyone. Or hurt them, either."

"I would never allow you to kill anyone. And I have been told that feeding actually can be quite a pleasant experience for the humans if performed correctly."

Like that made preying on humans any better? "There's got to be some other way."

Silence. Finally he sighed. "I might be able to make a call or two and come up with another solution."

"Thank you." I nearly wilted from relief at the thought that I wouldn't be forced to go find someone to bite. "Can I go to bed now?"

He nodded, and I slunk upstairs to my room.

The next morning, we received a special delivery.

The doorbell rang a little after eight, right around the time our mail usually arrived. It was probably yet another shipment of some historically accurate doorknobs or something.

"Savannah, can you get that?" Dad called out over the ear-piercing sander from one of the guest bedrooms.

I went downstairs, opened the front door and froze. The delivery guy was hot, probably early twenties, with sandy hair cut short at the back and long enough in the front to have to be brushed sideways out of his eyes. He was definitely two yums up, as Michelle would say.

Then I noticed the color of his eyes…the same white/silver as mine and Dad's and every other vampire I'd ever met. He wasn't wearing a FedEx, UPS or postal worker uniform, either.

Smiling, he held up a small cooler and said, "Did someone around here order some blood?"

Speaking of blood…mine went decidedly cold.

"Um, hang on just a second," I mumbled. My heart pounding loud enough that he had to have heard it, I kept my gaze on him and yelled, "Dad!"

Dad appeared beside me a second later then froze. Silence. Then he smiled broadly. "Gowin! You did not say you would be coming by for a visit anytime soon. To what do we owe the pleasure of hosting a council member?"

Oh, so that's why he looked familiar. He had been one of the vamps at my "test" in France last spring.

"The council heard a rumor that our Savannah here is having some trouble adjusting to the new lifestyle." Gowin smiled. "And since I hadn't seen my own protégé in quite some time, and I was in the neighborhood anyway, I offered to make the first delivery myself and see how you were both doing."

It was like walking into class and hearing we were going to have a pop quiz. But worse. Way worse.

Wait. Protégé? "You're…my dad's maker?"

"The proper term is *sire*," Dad said. "And yes, he is."

I stared at Gowin, trying to see how someone who looked so young could possibly be older than my dad.

His grin widened under my scrutiny. He sighed and gestured at Dad. "These kids. They leave home, they never call or write or visit."

A smile formed before I could stop it.

Dad hesitated only a fraction of an instant before stepping back to let Gowin enter. "It is always good to see you again. Will you come in and see my latest project?"

Was he talking about the house or me?

Dad quickly sent the floor crew home early for the day, then we vamps gathered around the kitchen table.

I couldn't stop staring at our guest. Not because he was overwhelmingly gorgeous. Only Tristan's looks could really make me breathless. But it was strange to see a vamp who appeared so young yet had to be at least as many centuries old as my dad. Gowin was the first vamp I'd met who looked anywhere close to my age.

Appearances could be deceiving, though. I tried to remember that fact as Gowin and Dad talked. Gowin was such a contrast to my dad. Unlike Dad, who always seemed a little formal and old-fashioned, Gowin was completely relaxed both in how he talked and dressed. Right now, he was wearing a T-shirt tight enough to show off his well-defined biceps and trim waist, plus faded jeans and sneakers.

He could fit right in on any college campus. And yet, while he and Dad talked about the good ole days, I had to forcibly remind myself that those good old days were probably pre-American Revolution era. Gowin was anything but the harmless college kid he acted like.

He made that hard to remember though, especially when he told jokes.

"Hey, do you know how the Roman Empire was cut in half?" Gowin asked.

Startled from my thoughts, I joined Dad in shaking my head.

"With a pair of Caesars!" Gowin answered.

Dad and I both groaned.

"Missing your toga days, old man?" Dad teased.

"Ah, now *those* were the days." Gowin sighed and slouched back in his chair. "Talk about the perfect man fashions to show off these legs!" He stretched one leg out in my direction. "Now I have to wait for summer swimwear. And of course do the sunless tanning thing all the time so the ladies don't laugh me out of the pool."

My jaw dropped. "You were a Roman?" That would make him a couple thousand years old.

He grinned. "You are looking at one of the youngest senators Rome ever had. I had barely turned twenty-five when I joined the Senate."

"Gowin is also the third oldest vampire still existing," Dad murmured.

"And who are the oldest two?" I asked.

"Caravass is the second oldest," Dad said. "And the oldest is Lilith."

Gowin froze, his entire demeanor completely changing in a flash. Gone was the humanlike college kid, replaced in an instant with a too-still and very alien creature. "Don't speak her name, old friend, or you may not like the consequences."

Silence filled the kitchen before Dad said, "I am sorry. I forgot your beliefs."

"They're not just *my* beliefs," Gowin muttered. "Those who know of her also know that to speak her name is to invite her attention. And trust me, you don't want that."

"I thought she was sleeping under a desert or something," I said, wondering if maybe I should whisper. Half vamp or not, I was getting seriously creeped out. What was it about Lilith that could possibly make even the old and powerful vampires too scared to say her name?

"She may be physically asleep, but she's still always listening," Gowin said. "Saying her name, even here, is the same as standing outside someone's bedroom door and calling out to them. We're all her children through the blood, and as such, she's connected to us at all times. She has only to choose to wake up and she can be here in an instant in any form of her choosing."

Silence in the kitchen.

Clearing his throat, Gowin glanced out the kitchen window and put on a smile. "But enough about her for now. What time does the sun set around here?"

"Around eight or nine in the summer," Dad said.

Gowin checked the black sports watch at his wrist. "Plenty of time to see the local sights before our girl here has her first feeding. The drive in was quick and I didn't see much, but it seems like you might have chosen a lovely town to settle down in." He smiled at us. "I don't suppose it would be okay for Savannah to give me a short tour? Maybe check out the downtown shopping area while we're at it? I'm on the hunt for a particular little Queen Anne side table."

At my confused look, Dad said, "Gowin is a procurer of antique furnishings for some very illustrious clients."

Gowin smiled wider, and suddenly I had the impression of the Cheshire Cat from Alice in Wonderland. Warning rippled down my spine, reminding me yet again that Gowin was not what he seemed.

Which meant his wanting me to give him a "short tour" of Jacksonville wasn't going to really be about seeing the local sights.

He was a council member. And he was obviously here to check up on me, and maybe even interrogate me, without my dad around for protection.

After an awkward silence, Dad finally said, "Sure, why not? Savannah, do you mind giving him a quick tour?"

"Uh, sure." I tightened my cheek muscles, pulling the corners of my mouth up into a semblance of a smile.

There was no point in trying to avoid this. If I didn't agree, with one command Gowin could use his advantage as an older vamp to force my dad to go away.

Might as well play along with the pretense of politeness as long as it lasted.

We all got up from the table and headed for the door.

In the foyer, I slipped my phone into my pocket, making sure Dad saw the movement.

"I trust you will drive extra careful with a council member in the passenger seat," Dad said, his smile tight.

He knew I always drove carefully. So he must really be telling me not to forget who I was with and to watch every word that I said. I nodded to show I understood, and his smile seemed slightly less forced.

Gowin laughed and opened the door. "Ah, Michael, you worry too much. Even if she does wreck us, we're immortal, so we'll recover…eventually!"

Chuckling, Gowin stepped outside and led the way to my truck. After I got in and started the engine, I glanced back at the house. Dad was still on the porch, his casual pose of leaning against the carved posts failing to hide his underlying tension.

"So where to?" I asked.

"Oh I don't know. How about the downtown shops to start?"

"Okay." We crossed the railroad tracks ten yards from my house then parked in front of the Jaycee Community Center across from the Tomato Bowl fifteen seconds later. "We're here."

Gowin snorted. "You're kidding."

"Nope. Want to get out and walk?" I didn't like being cooped up in a vehicle with him and forced to pay attention to driving. It made it harder to focus on the conversation and choosing every word I said.

He got out first, and I joined him on the sidewalk.

He pointed at the Tomato Bowl, a brownstone open-air stadium with beautiful arches at the entrance, prominently situated on top of its hill. "Why is it called the Tomato Bowl?"

His question confused me. I'd thought for sure he would immediately begin the interrogation. Maybe the stalling tactic was because we were still within hearing distance of Dad?

"Um, Jacksonville used to be the tomato capital around here." Of course I couldn't remember even half of the local history taught to us in school, but I did my best to play along with the farce of a tour, answering the questions I could and confessing the stuff I didn't know as he led the way up the street past banks and shops and under the overpass with the thunder of the passing traffic's wheels rolling overhead. We continued on to the boutiques and stores that sold local artisans' crafts. Nanna used to sell her custom crocheted names and blankets in several of them.

As we walked, the emotions I sensed from him were even more confusing. He seemed genuinely curious. I was also picking up a certain kind of warmth from him, not so much that I thought he was romantically interested in me, but more that he wanted to like me in general. It was…strange. The council had seemed so scared of me at my trial, yet here was one of them walking and chatting with me as casually as if we were long-lost cousins getting reacquainted.

We paused by one shop, and he peered in through the window. "So I'm sure you're wondering why I asked you to give me this tour."

"Um, a little," I admitted. "I figured you wanted to soften me up before the interrogation began."

He laughed and looked at me, his eyebrows raised. "Interrogate you? Not hardly. Though I will confess that, like my fellow council members, I'm quite intrigued by you. You are such a wonder among our kind. A real miracle, if you will. I do have a thousand questions I'd love to throw at you, about your life, your abilities, and what this slow evolution into our world has been like so far for you. Obviously it hasn't been easy."

I lifted one shoulder in a half shrug, not trusting myself to start speaking yet. This was going way too easy so far. It made me even more nervous. "Maybe I have a few questions for you, too."

"Things you don't feel comfortable asking your father?" he said. "Ask away. That's part of the reason the council agreed that I should come see you."

"Okay. What's it like to be turned? I mean, through the normal way?"

"Well, I guess it's a little different for each of us. But in general, the vamp drains you then gives you his or her blood, and then it's fast and terrifying and exciting all at once. One minute you're a human, the next you wake up and you don't remember anything at all. Your memory eventually comes back to you, but slowly, usually days or even weeks later, mostly because you're too busy trying to absorb all the input from your newly heightened senses in the meantime."

"So everything seems different to you then?"

"Yes. It's a very big change. For us, at least. It's like going through life half blind, and suddenly putting on the perfect pair of glasses. The world around you seems more alive, beautiful and sharp and vivid. You get used to it after a while, even start to take your new senses for granted. Some of us forget how dull the world looked through our human eyes. And then there's your new speed and strength and reflexes... now those take a while to get used to, because your body is literally able to move faster than your mind can fully process in the beginning. That's the real danger for fledglings." He said the last in a low murmur, as if confiding a secret to me.

"I guess the bloodlust doesn't help, either," I said.

Gowin nodded. Shoving his hands into the back pockets of his jeans, he continued along the sidewalk. "For a fully turned fledgling, the urge to hunt any human they can smell is nearly overpowering within a few hours of being turned. And because they can move so fast, as soon as the impulse to attack hits them, they don't have the time to think it through before their bodies act on that urge."

Wow. No wonder Dad was nearly obsessive about making me practice tai chi every morning. "I guess that's why we need to learn how to slow ourselves down then?"

"Is your father teaching you tai chi yet?"

I nodded.

He grinned. "That's the method I used on him. It works, too." He let out a long sigh. "You're incredibly lucky, you know. So is your father. You both have so much time to ease you into this, to train you properly before it becomes a real problem."

I thought of the knob I'd ripped out of the bathroom door at the spring dance, and gulped. "What happens if you wait too late to train a…"

"Fledgling," Gowin supplied.

"Right."

"Well, they usually go on a killing spree, massacring humans right and left until we manage to catch them and put them under."

Put them under?

At my confused look, he added, "Stake them."

Oh.

We turned and headed back toward my truck, walking a little faster now that he'd seen it all. "So the council sent you to…what, make sure Dad's teaching me correctly?"

He nodded. "We want to be sure he isn't getting confused

by the fact that you're his biological daughter and neglecting his duty as your sire to train you properly."

"Any other reason the council sent you?"

He glanced around us as if to be sure we wouldn't be overheard. "There have been...stirrings of unrest in cities that are shared by both the Clann and vamps. The council wanted to be sure that unrest isn't spreading all the way to Clann headquarters, too."

I frowned at him. "What do you mean, unrest? I thought there was a peace treaty."

"Peace treaties are broken all the time, Savannah." He said it kindly, like a history teacher correcting his student. "The council needs to know if that is happening here."

"And how are you supposed to figure that out today?"

"Oh, I'm not going to be here for just a day. Your father needs help finding a long list of historically accurate items for his latest renovation project. Who better than me to find and deliver them in person?"

"And while you're making these deliveries, you'll be checking out the situation around here." Great. Just what we needed, council members dropping by Jacksonville on a regular basis. The Clann was going to *love* that. "You know if any of the Clann see you and learn you're a council member, they're going to have a hissy fit."

He grinned. "Then I guess you and your dad better not tell them who I am, huh?"

I scowled. "Trust me, telling them would only make my life around here way harder."

"Oh yeah? So I take it they're still none too pleased about your dating Tristan?"

"Yeah, they *really* loved that. Not that they liked me all that much before."

"And now that you two are broken up?"

I shrugged. "They're leaving me alone, at least."

"But they were bothering you before." He made it a statement not a question.

Uh-oh. I might have already said too much. "Not all of them, and nothing too serious. Mainly just calling me names."

Gowin hummed. "Sounds like the Clann could definitely use some supervision around here. Though I'll admit I'm a little surprised. Seems like they would be working harder to get you to side with them against us."

"They kicked my family out of the Clann before I was even born. I doubt they're all that interested in having me join their ranks now." We reached my truck, and I yanked open the driver's side door.

"Maybe." He opened the passenger's side door and got in. "But all the same, the council thinks they need to be watched a little more closely. Your father's not delivering the intel we need."

I froze in the act of inserting the key into the ignition. "You're saying the reason we're here is so he can spy on the Clann for you?"

He shrugged. "Spying. Checking in on them. You say tomato, I say tomahto. Whatever you want to call it, it's past time the council started keeping a better eye on things."

Scowling, I started the truck. "Well, I guess you and Dad have to do whatever you've got to do to keep the council happy. But I'd appreciate it if you could leave me out of it, all right? I kept my promise to the council. I broke up with Tristan. And that's the last of my involvement with the Clann from now on. All this political stuff is just messing with trouble."

Gowin stretched out in his seat as much as his long legs would allow. "Politics is the vampire's way of life. We've been at war with the Clann for centuries. It's only a matter of time before the current era of peace ends. Of course, with a super vamp like you on our side, perhaps the next go-round won't last so long."

"I never said I was on anyone's side."

"So you would remain neutral?" he continued. "Even though your vamp side is growing stronger by the day?"

"I don't see why there has to be any fighting in the first place. Both vamps and witches have to hide what they are from the world. Seems like that would give you a good reason to work together instead of against each other."

Gowin chuckled. "That is a unique point of view. Not sure anyone shares it, though, on either side. Ever heard that song 'Everybody Wants to Rule the World'?"

I clamped my lips shut. The less I said about the Clann around this council member, the better.

It only took half a minute to drive back across the railroad tracks and park in the driveway. But Gowin didn't seem ready to get out. Maybe the heated cab of the truck felt like a relief to his cold blood, too.

"How exactly did you get to be on the council?" Belatedly I realized how rude that was. "Sorry. I mean—"

He waved off the apology. "When a seat becomes available, the current council members tend to choose those they know and trust to fill it. Usually older vamps they personally sired."

"You said Lil—I mean, she who must not be named—was the oldest, and Caravass was the second oldest. What about all the other vamps she sired?"

Gowin's smile faded fast. "God killed them."

"Are you kidding?"

"Nope. It's believed that she was Adam's first wife, and when she got sick of his attitude, she ran off and started hanging out with demons instead. The story has it that she then became something of a demoness herself, or the very first vampire. I guess God could have handled that, until she decided to give in to that mothering urge and started making more like herself. That's when God put the proverbial hand down and began killing off one hundred of her children, or fledglings, a day. Of course, he probably had to just to keep the vamps from wiping out the entire human population back then. Rumor has it she went on kind of a tear and was turning out the vamps faster than the humans could procreate."

"So he killed all of them but Caravass?"

"Well, not completely. A good number of them got caught by human vigilantes over the years. That whole Spanish Inquisition took out hundreds all on its own, and the witch trials didn't help much, either."

I frowned. "Why didn't they just fight back and escape?"

"Between you and me, I think the old ones got tired of living and let themselves be taken. Maybe they were worried about their souls if they did themselves in, so they let the humans take their lives for them. Depression is a problem once you get older. At least, it was. Now that technology is advancing so rapidly, life has kind of gotten interesting again."

After a few seconds of silence, I was about to reach for my door handle when he said, "You know, I really am sorry you and the Coleman boy were forced apart. Not everyone on the council felt that was necessary. But we were overruled."

I froze. "Overruled?"

"By Caravass. The vote was divided, and in those rare cases the council leader can break the tie if he chooses."

So one vote had tipped it all the wrong way.

My throat tightened hard enough to choke me. I had to clear it before I could reply. "Well, it was probably the right vote anyways. I am a danger to him. If I'd remembered the whole draining through a kiss thing, I never would have dated him in the first place. Besides, you guys weren't the only ones who made me promise to break up with him. So even if y'all had voted differently, the breakup was still inevitable."

Propping an elbow on the edge of the door, Gowin rubbed a hand over his chin. "Yeah, your dad told me what the Clann did to your grandma in the woods. It's a sad part of any war. Innocents always get hurt in the process, no matter how hard everyone tries to protect them. But that doesn't make it any easier on the ones who face that loss." He rested a hand on mine on the seat between us, and our skin was the same temperature. It threw me off balance again. "I'm sorry about your grandmother. I heard she was a great woman."

I stared ahead at the windshield, now covered in drops of pinesap and dead bugs. "Thanks." It came out hoarse. I cleared my throat and had to blink fast a couple of times as my eyes began to sting.

"Your dad was impressed with her magical skills. Apparently she was the only witch to ever come up with a spell that could dampen the bloodlust without hurting or weakening us, even around the Clann."

"It was how my mom and dad could stay together for so long."

I glanced at him. He stared at me, going completely still like my dad did sometimes.

A quiet note of warning sounded somewhere in the back of my mind. "Too bad she didn't write the spell down anywhere or teach me or my mom how to do it."

"She didn't teach your mother, either?"

"No. Nanna said she had to turn to the old ways and they required too much sacrifice to make them safe for anyone else to use. Plus, Mom never wanted to be in the Clann, so she refused to develop her magical abilities. She used to throw plates around without touching them when she was mad, but that's about it. And I don't think she can even do that anymore."

He grinned. "She threw plates at your father with her mind?"

"So they say."

"Ah. So that's why she's not around now."

My mouth twitched with the quick urge to smile. "No, that's not it at all. We just didn't want to risk feeling the blood-lust around her now that Nanna's protective magic has died with her. It's safer for Mom to stay away."

Finally Gowin opened his door. We both got out and slowly headed up the lawn toward the house.

"I imagine losing your grandma, mother and true love all at once must be a terrible burden for you."

I stared straight ahead. "Or maybe it's just karma for breaking the rules."

"I don't believe in karma," he said as he stepped up onto the porch. "Only the destinies we create for ourselves. And I definitely do not believe that you deserve to have to endure so much pain at so young an age."

If he was trying to be sympathetic, he needed to stop, because his words were like physical slaps to my body. Every word left its own bruise.

"Karma, accident, whatever it was, you can tell the council that it's all been a lesson very well learned here."

He shot me one last look I couldn't decode, then we entered the house.

It turned out that the actual feeding itself wasn't too bad. Dad mixed the donor blood Gowin had brought with a bottle of V8 juice, which I chugged down so I wouldn't be able to detect the taste of the blood.

Then there was this flash before my eyes, and I stumbled. What the heck?

"Dad, I'm...seeing things," I muttered.

"Michael, you didn't warn her about the blood memories?" Gowin made a tsking sound.

"I did not expect her to guzzle down the drink so quickly. I thought I would explain as she fed slowly in a more mannerly fashion."

"Forget the lesson on manners. Someone tell me what's going on!" It was like someone had stuck some kind of movie headset over my eyes with wraparound vision…there was a scene playing out everywhere I looked with people I didn't recognize, calling me by somebody else's name, somewhere I'd never been. And yet in the background I could still hear Dad and Gowin's voices.

"The blood contains traces of its owner's memories," Dad said as someone took my elbow and guided me somewhere. "I am leading you to your room now. Take a step. And another. And another."

We made it up the stairs and to my room, where I fell onto my bed. Dad draped a comforter over me.

"How long will it last?" I said, even as the scene changed before my eyes to a birthday party and the sounds grew louder.

"A few hours. I am sorry I did not have time to explain more fully. Rest now, and try not to fight against the blood memories. They will pass in time."

"I have Charmers practice in the morning," I mumbled. "Seven o'clock."

There was a beeping noise to my left. "Your alarm is set. The blood memories should be gone by then. However, I will also check on you and make sure you wake in time just in case."

In case what? I never regained control over my own mind?

That was the last thought of my own that I had. And then I was lost to the real world, drowning in someone else's life.

CHAPTER 15

When I woke up the next morning, Dad said Gowin had stayed overnight to be sure I reacted well to the donor blood. He'd left early this morning, but he would be back; Gowin had rented an apartment in Tyler so he could visit anytime the council felt it was a good idea.

A council member was moving to East Texas. The Clann would be so thrilled.

I had a hunch exactly who they would blame when they found out, too.

I didn't bother to mention how much I did *not* enjoy the blood memories. I was pretty sure the look on my face said enough. Dad promised I should need to feed only once a week, which I would be allowed to do on weekends so I could recover from the blood memories by the start of each week.

Being forced to relive a confused jumble of moments from someone else's life was terrible. While it lasted, I was completely out of control of my own mind. But at least the donor blood meant I didn't have to go around biting people. Or deal with the bloodlust while at the Charmers boot camp, which lasted from seven till eleven every day for the last week of summer. The team used this week to bond with the Indies, or sophomores, who were just joining the team. The Braves, or juniors, seemed to enjoy no longer being the newbies on the team. But the Chiefs, or seniors, and the new captain and her lieutenant officers, definitely were having the most fun. They spent the week endlessly whipping the newbies into shape with laps around the track and push-ups and sit-ups, mixed in with actual dance practice as everyone learned the first new routines to be performed at the upcoming fall pep rallies and football games.

When I wasn't working the sound system on the practice field for the team, I was getting to know the new sophomore managers while we worked together to clean and organize Mrs. Daniels's office. It was hard not to smile when they whined about how hot it was on the third floor without any air conditioning, which wouldn't be turned on again until next week when school began. To me the heat felt good, thawing me out so my constantly tense muscles could finally relax.

On Wednesday several boxes of new poms came in, so we spent the entire morning crinkling each strand of every pom by hand so the metallic strands would be fuller and catch and throw more light when the Charmers danced with them. I tried not to think about how it would feel to dance with a pair of poms at a football game. That was a dead dream better left forgotten.

Other dreams were harder to forget while I took inventory of all the stage props and backdrops. More than once I caught myself lost in the memories, fingertips pressed to my lips as they tingled with the haunting sensation of the way he'd kissed me over and over here in the dark that last night before Dylan caught us together and it all started to fall apart.

It didn't help to know that the varsity Indians had their football practices at the same time as the Charmers in an attempt to avoid the rising heat of the day. Which meant Tristan was somewhere on this same campus every morning, probably getting all hot and sweaty in the back practice field with the other varsity players in a see-through practice jersey

Unfortunately Charmers boot camp in the mornings and magic practice in the afternoons didn't fill up my evenings. So I started doing tai chi in my room at night in an attempt to battle the rising tension that kept my muscles kinked in knots.

But it was increasingly hard to find any peace from my emotions. Maybe I wasn't trying hard enough, or focusing properly. Or maybe it was the fact that the new school year would begin in a few days, and I felt anything but ready for it.

The Friday night before the last weekend of the summer, Dad found me in my room trying as hard as I could to think of nothing beyond the next tai chi move.

At his knock, I called out, "Come in."

He opened his mouth as if to speak, then hesitated and stood there with a frown, watching me practice.

"What? Am I doing it wrong?" I asked, waving my hands like clouds passing across the sky as he'd taught me.

"No. But..." He studied me for a few more seconds. "You look miserable doing it."

"Gee, thanks," I muttered.

"It's supposed to bring you peace and tranquility."

"I know."

"Is it?"

I sighed and moved on to the next step. "I'm probably just not focusing enough."

"Maybe you should dance instead."

I froze, the anger a quick rush of heat blooming in my stomach. "Excuse me? I thought dancing was off-limits."

"In public. The council said nothing about dancing in the privacy of one's own home."

I took a long, slow breath for patience. "Well, they didn't say I could, either. So maybe I'd better just stick with the tai chi instead." At least until they banned that, too.

I restarted the routine from the beginning.

"But dancing made you happy, correct?"

I shrugged one shoulder. "It causes problems. Why push the issue?"

Besides, I didn't feel like dancing. I hadn't ever since Nanna died. Every time I tried to dance, I remembered how proud Nanna had looked, sitting in the audience of the local Lon Morris College's theater with my mom and dad at my first and only dance recital. And in the too short, too few weeks afterwards, how Nanna used to sit in a lawn chair in the backyard and loudly cheer me on while I practiced for my doomed Charmers team audition.

Tai chi was never going to help me relax as long as he was standing there critiquing me. I stopped and propped my hands on my hips. "Do you need something?"

Frowning, he strolled over to my closet and opened the door. "School starts on Monday."

"I know." *Believe me, I know.*

He lifted a sleeve on one of the button-up shirts I'd had for years. I had a quick flash memory of Tristan's hands gliding down my arms within those sleeves…. "I would have assumed that you would want or need to go shopping to prepare for the new school year."

"I will. I figured I'd go late tomorrow night to Walmart when the store's mostly empty and buy my school supplies then."

"What about your wardrobe?"

"What about it? I haven't grown any, so everything still fits."

"But this is not what the magazines show the teens to be wearing now."

"No one cares what I wear, Dad."

He turned to face me, arms crossed. "That is not a good strategy for blending in."

"Uh, actually it's a great one. No one's going to notice the wallflower with three-year-old clothing. Trust me, I'll be practically invisible."

"No, you will not. You will... How would your mother put it? Stick out like a..."

"A sore thumb?" I finished for him.

"Precisely."

I let my stare show him how much I agreed with him.

"Perhaps we should discuss this with your mother. Skype is showing her as online now if you would like to webcam with her."

Ha! Mom would totally side with me on this. She was all about the waste-not want-not mentality. "Fine." I sat down at my desk, booted up my laptop and logged into the program. Sure enough, as soon as I appeared online, Mom sent me a video chat request. Within seconds we were able to see each other onscreen.

She gasped.

"What's wrong?" I asked, half rising from my chair out of instinct, as if I could actually do anything to help her from here.

She gaped at me, leaning toward the screen and adjusting her laptop, judging by how the angle of my view of her changed.

"Is it weird lighting or...?" she asked.

"No, it is not," Dad said, standing behind me. "Which

brings us to why I suggested Savannah webcam with you this evening."

"I see what you mean," Mom muttered.

"What?" I asked, gripping the edge of my desk. "What's wrong?"

Mom made that face she always made when she was trying to choose her words carefully. "Well, dear, it's been a while since I've seen you, and you look so...different."

"Like a vampire," Dad said, his tone flat.

"Really?" I touched my cheeks with both hands. It felt the same to me. Of course, I hadn't taken a good look at my reflection in weeks, not since Anne's birthday. There hadn't been any reason to as I stayed at home all the time now and saw only Dad and Gowin.

"Perhaps it is due to the feedings," Dad murmured.

I glared at him over my shoulder. "I *told* you it was a bad idea!"

"Hon, it was necessary," Mom said. "None of us could stop the change. And it's not like you're ugly now. In fact, you've become quite...beautiful."

So why did her tone sound so weirded out about it?

"I have been trying to convince our daughter that she needs a new wardrobe this year," Dad said. "One that is fashionable enough to be a distraction."

"He means he wants to waste money on stupidly expensive clothes," I corrected. "All my old stuff still fits just fine. There's no point in spending a lot of money on a whole new wardrobe. Right, Mom?"

She cringed. "Well, sweetie, your dad might actually have a point this time."

Huh? Okay, maybe I was going deaf instead of developing better hearing. My penny-pinching, world's-most-frugal mother did not just say she agreed with her ex-husband about blowing a wad of cash on unnecessary clothing.

"Think of it as camouflage," Dad said. "Like birds. If you return to school wearing the same clothing you have always worn, everyone will have no choice but to notice every single change in your physical appearance. But if you show up wearing not only new clothing, but highly fashionable attire that most of the other teens will not have, their attention will be drawn to that instead. Then any physical changes they do notice will simply be written off as part of your makeover."

"This is so dumb," I muttered, flopping back in my chair and crossing my arms. I couldn't believe Mom had sided with Dad this time. They never agreed on anything!

"Oh come on, Sav," Mom teased. "Shopping is supposed to be fun, not torture."

I looked away as I confessed the truth. "But...I don't read magazines. I don't even know what's in fashion now." Heck, I didn't even know which fashion magazines were in fashion right now!

"Ah, but I do," Dad said with a smile.

I stared up at him with one eyebrow raised. He had to be kidding.

"What?" he asked. "It is important that vampires do not draw attention by being old-fashioned."

This coming from the guy who couldn't speak a contraction to save his life.

I squinted, studying him, wondering if maybe I could get away with a spell to change his mind. On second thought, knowing my luck, not only would Dad figure out I'd used magic on him, but Gowin would too and then the whole vamp council would have a major freak-out session over it.

"Hon, trust your father on this," Mom said. "When we used to go out together, the waitresses never noticed how pale he was, or how little he ate. All they saw were his nice suits and shoes."

"Thanks," Dad said somewhat dryly.

"He's actually pretty good with the whole fashion thing," Mom added with just a hint of reluctance. "In fact, I even used to let him pick out a few things for me sometimes."

"Only when I grew tired of your garage-sale consignment-shop bohemian look," Dad replied.

Sensing yet another of their infamous arguments brewing, I sat up. "Okay. Fine, buy whatever you think is necessary, Dad. Happy?"

"Oh, and let's do a fashion show Sunday night so I can see your new look!" Mom said, practically clapping her hands in anticipation.

"Sure Mom. Talk to you later." *And thanks for all the help with Dad.*

She blew me a kiss and we ended the webcam connection.

I turned my chair to face Dad, expecting him to still be standing behind me all smug about winning the debate. Instead he was already in my closet pawing through the clothes.

"Excuse me, but what are you doing?" Maybe it was time to set some boundaries here.

"Seeing if anything can be salvaged."

"Uh, just because I agreed to new school clothes doesn't mean we're throwing out all my old stuff. I still get to wear what I want around the house, right?"

He sighed heavily. "Fine. Be ready early tomorrow morning. I researched area stores and the Galleria in Houston appears to have the brands you need."

Me, at a mall with my dad? "No, thanks."

He stared at me with a frown. "You just agreed—"

"To wear whatever you pick out. But you don't need me there to weigh in on any of it. Just take down my sizes from

the perfectly good clothing I already have and use that." Whatever he chose I was bound to look ridiculous in. Everyone
knew I was clueless about fashion. Fashionably hopeless was
my *look* now. If he thought I'd actually help him turn me
into a fashionista wannabe, which everyone was going to see
right through within seconds and laugh in my face about, he
was nuts.

They'd probably even blame my new wardrobe on some
pathetic attempt to win Tristan back. I could practically hear
the Brat Twins teasing me about it now.

"Fine," he snapped. "Forgive me for assuming you might
want some input in this process."

"Well, I don't." I swiveled my chair away from him and
back toward my desk.

"Fine!"

"Great!" I snapped back. "And don't forget, I have the
Charmers slumber party tomorrow night." I threw that last
part over my shoulder at his retreating back as he headed out
the bedroom door.

He reappeared in the doorway. "I do *not* think you should
attend that."

"They have it every year. I have to be there. It's one of the
best parts of being on the team!"

He glared at me. "You will be locked within a room with
over forty humans. What if the bloodlust should join the party,
as your mother would say?"

I scowled. "I'll be fine. We're just going to play a bunch of
silly games and listen to music." And exchange our old team
bracelet charms for new ones while we learned the team motto
and theme song for the upcoming year. And this time I'd be
doing it all as the official head manager.

"I'll have my phone with me at all times," I promised, trying not to let a whine creep into my voice.

He stared at me.

"Please, Dad?" I said, giving up and letting the whine out.

Maybe I should use that mind-changing spell on him after all.

"In return, you swear you will wear whatever I choose for your school wardrobe this year? Including accessories *and* shoes?"

Okay, now this was starting to feel like a trap. "Well, within reason. I mean, it has to meet school dress code requirements or else they'll keep sending me home to change all the time."

He looked down his nose at me. "I have already consulted the school website for these dress codes and will keep them in mind while choosing your new attire."

"Fine. I'll wear whatever you pick out." *Please, do not let it be too revolting or make people laugh at me too loudly.*

"Fine. You may go to the Charmers slumber party tomorrow night. As long as you feed tonight."

I wanted to argue about that last part. But the look in his eyes said not to bother. And on second thought, maybe it was a good idea. Better safe than sorry, and if I fed now, hopefully the blood memories would have stopped by the time the party started at six tomorrow night.

"Okay," I grumbled.

He walked away with a satisfied air, and I got the distinct impression that I'd just been tricked somehow.

Whatever. At least I'd get to go to the party.

CHAPTER 16

Which turned out to be way harder than I'd expected, even though the blood memories had faded by the time I arrived at the school's main gym.

Last year's slumber party had been a blast. Of course, that was before I apparently looked like a cross between a human and a mannequin. By the end of the night I'd lost count of the times I had to explain why I was so pale and all my freckles had faded away ("the weird gym lighting"), or why I wasn't eating anything ("already ate").

And then there was the small fact that I could now hear everyone's thoughts.

When I'd first walked into the gym, I'd thought that the noise level seemed so loud because they had multiple jamboxes on somewhere, each one turned to a different radio talk show or something. It had taken me a few minutes to realize what I was really hearing. When I did figure it out, I'd had to duck into the girls' restroom in order to calm down. The stupid feeding must have caused it.

At least the bloodlust hadn't shown up, too.

"How did it go?" Dad called from the kitchen as I entered the house the next morning.

"Fine," I sighed, knowing he'd hear me even if I whispered no matter what room he was working in today.

I left it at that. No way was I going to tell him about the ESP ability. If I did, the council would know about it and try to recruit me as their newest spy or something.

I trudged up the steps to my room, kicked off my sneakers, went to stick them in my closet, and froze.

When I'd given Dad the go-ahead to buy new stuff, I thought he'd get a few things to supplement my wardrobe.

We really had to work on our communication skills.

"A skirt?" I muttered, holding up a clear-plastic-draped black-lace thing on a hanger. Next to it hung some kind of black-and-white dress. Hadn't he noticed that my closet featured only jeans? I didn't own dresses or skirts for a *reason*. Surely he didn't really expect me to wear this kind of stuff to school. Maybe the skirt and dress were for special occasions. Though what those would be, I had no idea. Maybe I could wear them for Christmas and the Charmers end of year banquet or something.

Then I spotted the shoe boxes. Holding my breath, I opened the first one, and the air whooshed out of my lungs in pure horror.

My phone rang in my pocket. I grabbed it, still staring at the new footwear as I answered.

"Hey, ready for school on Monday?" Anne said by way of a greeting. At least I couldn't hear her thoughts over the phone.

Then I realized what she'd said. Oh great. Tomorrow I'd have to deal with school, rumors about Tristan and me, gossip about Tristan and Bethany, who were still seeing each other, *and* hearing everyone's thoughts all day.

"Oh yay, I can hardly wait," I grumbled. "How'd your shopping go?" The girls had gotten together yesterday evening to take advantage of all the back-to-school sales in Tyler.

Anne launched into telling me all about it…where they'd shopped, the mountain of "crap," as she put it, that Michelle and Carrie had talked her into getting.

"I needed you there to keep them from ganging up on me!" she growled.

I smiled, realizing how much I missed my friends. At least there was one good thing about going back to school tomorrow. I'd get to see them all again in a nice, safe public setting.

"Sounds like you had fun." I flopped into the rolling chair at my desk. "My dad insisted on buying all new stuff for me to wear this year. Wait till you see what he picked out. You're going to fall over laughing."

"Total makeover, huh?"

"And then some. He went to the Galleria. And the stuff he picked out…dresses. And skirts. And *heels!*"

Anne snorted with laughter.

"I ask you, just how the heck am I supposed to walk across the practice fields and climb metal bleachers at Charmers practice in heels?" I asked.

After she stopped snickering, she said, "Well, you could always take a second outfit of normal clothes with you every day and change at school."

"Tempting. Except I promised I'd wear whatever he picked out."

"Why would you do that?"

"It was the only way he would let me go to the Charmers slumber party last night."

"Oh yeah? And was it worth it?"

"I wish I could say yes. But I ended up spending the whole

night lying about why I wasn't eating and why I'm so pale now."

"You've always been pale."

"Yeah, well, according to Mom I've reached whole new levels of pale lately." Ever since I started the dumb vamp feedings. But no way was I discussing *that* with Anne.

I sighed. "Hey, if we don't have any classes together before lunch tomorrow, save me a seat at our usual table, okay? I may not be able to eat, but at least we can all go over our class schedules together. And before you ask, yes, you have my permission to laugh as loudly as you want at the heels."

She snorted. "My grandma makes me wear heels to church. So I'll probably be feeling your pain too much to laugh."

"Thanks." I smiled.

"Good luck getting to school without breaking an ankle," she added with a snicker before ending the call.

I tossed my phone onto the bed while eyeing the remaining shoe boxes. I probably didn't even want to know what was in them.

Then again, I'd have to find out sooner or later.

Taking a deep breath for courage, I quickly bent over and flicked the lids off the rest of the boxes. And then I sighed.

Dad had gotten me ballet flats. Lots and lots of ballet flats in all kinds of colors and fabrics. And they were *cute.*

I sat down, pulled on a pair and had to bite my lower lip to hold back the urge to squee. Okay, now these just might make wearing the rest of the new stuff bearable.

Then I glanced up and saw the collection of notes, each stuffed within a clear sheet protector, which hung from a metal ring attached to the knob of my closet door. A quick flip through them showed countless suggested outfits, complete with recommended shoe and jewelry options, enough for at least a month. He'd even taken pictures of each outfit laid out on my bed so I couldn't get confused.

"Geez," I muttered, unsure whether to be alarmed or grateful.

Would I get this anally retentive when I was three hundred years old?

The next morning, I tried not to look in the mirror too closely as I got ready for school. I didn't want to dwell on how different I looked and whether anyone at school would get weirded out about it. I was nervous enough as it was.

Please don't let me run into Tristan, part of me prayed with every breath I inhaled.

And on the exhale of every breath, another part of me yearned for just one glimpse of him, just one more time to hear his voice, his laugh, or see his smile...

Dad was waiting by the front door as I came down the stairs.

"I see you found my notes." He nodded in approval as he assessed my outfit.

I bit the tip of my tongue to keep from telling him just what I thought of his "notes." When I thought of a more diplomatic reply, I said, "Thanks for the ballet flats. I really like them.'"

"And the rest of it?"

I went through three or four possible responses and chose the nicest of them. "I'm sure I'll learn to get used to them." I tacked on a teeth-baring attempt at a smile.

At least none of the new stuff was too wild or crazy or slutty.

His lips twitched.

"I want you to keep this with you at all times." He held out what looked like a short, fat black-and-gold pen. "Click it and it is a pen. Turn the clip sideways and it is an emergency stash of blood."

It was my turn to fight a smile. "Sort of like an epipen for vamps?"

"Exactly. It has extra anticoagulants to keep it from clotting, so it might taste strange. But if you reach the point where you have to take it, you will be beyond the point of caring about taste."

Yummy. "Thanks." I put it in my new Coach purse, feeling like the vampire version of James Bond.

"And I will have my cell phone with me at all times, of course," he added.

I couldn't help but smile now. "It's okay, Dad. Remember, I've done this whole starting school thing a few times. Same old school, same old people, same old town."

"But you are not the same."

Right. Good point. "I'll see you tonight, probably around five or so after Charmers practice." I tried to act cool and calm and completely confident as I waved goodbye.

Five minutes later, I parked in the front school lot in my same old spot. Then I got out and felt the breeze around my legs below the dress.

Okay, maybe this wasn't quite like all my other first days of school.

At least getting ready for the Charmers morning practice, which started early and continued through first period every day, was the same old routine. What wasn't part of the usual routine was the fact that I could now hear the director's thoughts before she said them, which was hard to hide. I had to watch her lips and wait until I saw their movement match the words in her head before I took notes on the clipboard.

The rest of first period was spent working the music and sending the sophomore managers off for bags of ice for two dancers who had knee trouble. By the time I carried the sound system back to Mrs. Daniels's office, the sameness of the general routine had almost lulled me into forgetting about all the other changes in my life. And because I'd chosen the black ballet flats instead of the heels as Dad's notes had suggested for this outfit, walking wasn't a problem.

At this point, my life was so cloudy I would take any silver lining I could get.

But when I went into the main hall for my second period class, it all came slamming back into me as the sound of everyone's thoughts filled my head with a low roar. By the time I nearly ran into the Brat Twins, I was tense and in real need of escaping the crowd.

Then I realized Vanessa and her sister Hope were carrying the exact same purse as me. The only difference was the color. Vanessa's was powder-blue, Hope's was hot-pink, and mine was black to match the black-and-white wraparound dress Dad's notes had suggested for today.

"Is that…" Hope began, staring at my purse. I had to read her lips in order to understand the words. Otherwise I never would have been able to hear her over everyone's thoughts.

"It's a knockoff." Vanessa reached out and twisted my purse on my forearm until she could see the metal label. As soon as she saw it, she froze. "Where did you get this?" She acted like I'd stolen it straight out of her closet.

"At the Galleria," I answered with a smile while trying not to laugh. Maybe the new wardrobe came with a few perks after all.

Vanessa eyed my dress, my necklace, my shoes. I managed to catch her fleeting thoughts as she considered grabbing my wrist to better inspect my bracelet then decided she didn't want to have skin contact.

"Is that a—" Hope gasped and did reach for the bracelet. Vanessa slapped her hand down. "Shut up, Hope. Come on, we'll be late for class." She yanked the purse off my forearm and tried to drop it on the ground.

I caught it before it fell more than a few inches. The move hadn't felt any different than anything else I'd ever done, but both twins shrieked and took off at a fast trot, looking back over their shoulders at me every few seconds.

Crap. Had I done a vamp blur thing?

I needed way more tai chi practice if I was ever going to blend in this year.

I slowly slid the purse onto my shoulder. Then I repositioned it on my forearm in the crook of my elbow. Well, crud. How was one supposed to carry a designer purse? Dad's notes hadn't included any tips about that, and I'd never carried even a normal purse, much less one that was nice enough to tick off the Brat Twins.

Giving up for now, I continued toward my second period class, trying to ignore that too familiar ache forming in my chest and stomach warning me that Tristan was nearby. He was tall enough to be visible even in a crowd. Since I couldn't see his head of golden hair standing out above everyone else's in the hall, he was probably already in his second period classroom somewhere in this building. Good. I really didn't want to have to run into him this morning if I could help it.

As the crowd parted for me, I caught bits of thoughts that stuck out from the jumble, several of them directed at me.

Is that a Coach bag?

Are those Jimmy Choos? No, they can't be. Everyone knows she's too poor to afford those. They're probably knockoffs.

How can she afford that? Oh, I know, it's her dad. He's probably a drug dealer. Or maybe he's in the mafia or something. Too bad they spent all their money on clothes instead of that run-down shack they're living in now.

Part of me wanted to run through the hall and escape as

fast as I could. Dad was half right. Everyone was looking at my clothing instead of me. But it obviously hadn't changed how people thought of me.

Somehow I resisted the urge to use my vamp speed and just blow through the crowd. Control. It was all about self-control. I forced my legs to move human slow, then slower, casually strolling into class just before the tardy bell rang.

I had been looking forward to this class. English was my best subject in school. But when I walked into the room and saw everyone still standing around holding their books, I let out a long sigh.

There was only one reason that my classmates wouldn't be seated already. The teacher must be getting ready to assign seats alphabetically.

I glanced around the room and locked gazes with Tristan. Everything inside me froze.

In that second, I knew just how wrong I had been to hope that my feelings for him had faded over the summer. Seeing him was like a physical blow as all the memories of our months together came crashing back over me, robbing me of breath and forcing me to acknowledge just how much I had missed seeing that face.

I still loved him as much as ever, if not more.

But now he was with Bethany.

And I would be stuck sitting near him again. With our last names of Coleman and Colbert and alphabetical seating, it was inevitable. For the first time, I found myself actually wishing the Clann's control really did reach all the way to the JHS computerized class scheduling system so I wouldn't have to share another class with him.

I tried to look away, really I did. I knew I was the one who had broken up with him and that it was flat-out rude to be staring at him now. But I couldn't seem to stop myself, even as the raw hurt in his eyes seemed to burn through me.

The teacher, Mrs. Knowles, pointed at the front-row desk closest to the door, said a name, and someone sat down in it. She repeated the process with the desk beside it. Apparently she was going to assign seats horizontally like Mr. Smythe liked to do with all of his history classes, instead of in vertical rows. Which meant this year Tristan would end up beside me instead of behind me. Great. I wouldn't be able to avoid seeing him out of the corner of my eye.

Maybe I should start wearing my hair down instead of in its usual ponytail, to block the view.

I tried to pay attention to Mrs. Knowles, but I couldn't hear her over the rising roar of thoughts from my classmates driving into my head like an iPod turned up full blast.

She moved on, pointing to the third desk in the front row. Tristan moved to sit there, and at last I was freed from his gaze. But that didn't lessen the volume of chaotic voices inside my head, or my racing pulse.

I couldn't do this. I could not make it through yet another year of being so close to Tristan every other day. Every time I came to this class, I would have to sit just inches away from him for a whole hour and a half. I'd managed to make it through the final few weeks of torture last year. But then I'd had a whole summer away from him. And though I'd missed him, it had also been a relief from the physical ache of being around him.

I didn't want to have to fight that battle yet again. Not this year. Not after all that we'd been through, the memories we'd made together, falling in love with him…

And the bloodlust.

Mrs. Knowles' helmet-shaped hair filled my vision. I blinked, looked around. Everyone was seated now, with only one desk left open. The second desk in the front row...beside Tristan.

Mrs. Knowles was saying something to me, but I couldn't hear her. I tried to read her lips and thought she was probably telling me to take my seat.

Since I had no way of telling how loud I actually was over the noise in my head, I tried whispering, "Um, couldn't we please choose our own seats?"

She frowned, her entire face pinching as if she'd just taken a bite of food and found a hair in it. She said a single word that looked like, "What?"

I tried again, repeating myself a little louder so she could hear me. But she spoke so fast I couldn't make out the words. Panicking, I tried again, loudly saying, "I would really like to choose my own desk please."

Her face turned white, and from everyone's shocked thoughts, I gathered that I'd just yelled at her. Crap.

CHAPTER 17

Whispering fast, I said, "I'm so sorry. I'm actually a little deaf right now from...from running music for Charmers practice last period."

She searched my face, the color slowly returning to her cheeks. Taking a long, slow breath, she pointed at the empty desk and said, "Go. Sit. Down. Now."

I didn't look at the other students as I sat down in the dreaded seat, my skin prickling all over with awareness of how close Tristan was. I could tell from everyone's thoughts exactly how crazy I looked. My fingernails bit into my palms as I sat as close to the edge of my seat away from Tristan as I could.

Inside my head, everyone's voices grew louder and louder.

Oh man, those two can't even look at each other!

Whoa. The veins in his neck are bulging. He looks mad enough to kill Savannah! What did she do to him last year?

Perfect shot! These pics are gonna get the gossips going on Facebook for sure.

I turned and caught some girl at the back of the room playing with her phone under her desk.

Drugs. She's definitely dealing drugs to have all that money all of a sudden. Unless maybe that grandma of hers left a bundle of insurance money and she blew it all on clothing. Typical white trash, she should've used it for college instead.

I was starting to miss the Brat Twins' daily insults. At least they said it all to my face.

Isn't she Anne's best friend? Yeah, I remember her sitting at their table every day. I wonder if she's seen Anne yet.

Relieved to have heard one halfway nice thing about me, I latched on to that person's train of thought, wondering who it came from. Then I snuck a peek at the desk to my left between me and the door. Ah, of course. Ron Abernathy, Anne's one and only ex.

Listening in on Ron's thoughts felt like an invasion of his privacy. But until I could figure out how to turn the ESP off, I was already invading everyone's privacy as it was. And at least listening to Ron was better than focusing on the seething pain Tristan was projecting at my other side. Maybe if I concentrated on hearing only one person at a time, I could manage not to go crazy today.

Interestingly enough, it seemed the strength of each person's "signal" was based on how strongly they felt about whatever they were thinking. Ron was pretty steady in his emotions when he thought about Anne, but since he wasn't obsessively thinking about her nonstop, I couldn't pick up every thought. Only the ones about Anne were loud enough for me to hear.

By the end of class, I was really starting to wonder what secrets Anne was keeping. It was obvious that Ron was still very much in love with her, and that Anne had been the one who had broken them up. Maybe it had something to do with

Ron's weird obsession about black cats? He thought about them almost as much as he thought about her.

In an effort to avoid as much of the foot traffic as possible, I was the first one out of my seat when the lunch bell rang. I gave in to the urge to walk at least human-fast down the main hall, slowing only after I was out the doors and on the cement, metal awning-covered catwalk that spanned the valley between the two hills the main building and math building rested on. I walked even slower down the ramp that led from the side of the catwalk to the valley floor where the cafeteria building was located. It was nice and quiet out here away from everyone's thoughts, and I was tempted to just stay. But my friends were waiting for me.

As soon as I opened the cafeteria doors, the tidal wave of thoughts hit me so hard that I actually stumbled back a couple of steps.

Whoa. If this ESP crap continued at this level, the gossips wouldn't have to lie about my going nuts in English class, because I really would go stark raving mad.

I staggered to my friends' usual table, grateful for a change that we sat right beside the center aisle that cut across the cylinder-shaped brick building. The girls must have gotten out a little early from second period; their stuff was already there and they were in line getting food.

I knew I should buy my usual chili cheese fries and a soda, or at least a salad to pretend to eat. But the thought of having to even fake eating was too much at this point. I buried my head in my hands, closed my eyes, and prayed everyone's thoughts would just shut up.

Last year when I'd started to sense the emotions around me, I'd learned that the ability grew worse when I was upset. Hearing everyone's actual thoughts was so much worse than sensing their emotions. But maybe the ESP worked the same way. I tried to calm down, focusing on my breathing as if I were doing tai chi. Slow breath in. Hold it. Slow breath out. I pictured myself back home doing tai chi in my room, how the controlled movements made me feel like water flowing in slow motion.

There. The voices were fading away now. I could handle this. I just needed to stay calm.

"There's our *Vogue* girl," Anne greeted me as my friends returned to our table.

They took their seats, each one setting down a stinking tray or carton or plastic bowl full of food. My eyes told me their food was perfectly fine and should smell good. But my nose and stomach screamed an entirely different story. It was like someone had just plunked me down in the middle of a landfill during the dead heat of summer. The stench of rotting things seemed to fill my nostrils, tempting me to gag.

I made myself smile for their benefit while I tried not to breathe through my nose.

Michelle squealed and reached across the table to grab my new bracelet. "Oh my God, did your dad get this for you?" She looked up, her eyes wide and bright. Then she spotted my purse on the table beside me. "No friggin' way. A Coach bag, too? Let me see!"

Dutifully I passed the purse over to her.

"And the heels?" Anne asked, her eyebrows arched.

Finally I could give a sincere smile. "After you and I got off the phone, I discovered Dad surprised me with some other shoe choices." I held up a foot so she could see my new ballet flats.

Anne made a face. "I might have had to stick with the heels. Those would look like fairy shoes on me."

Michelle ducked under the table to see, raised her head back up and squeaked, "Jimmy Choo doesn't make fairy shoes. Besides, those are black."

"So they're for goth fairies." Grinning, Anne cracked open her soda.

"Oh stop," I said with a laugh. "You're just jealous that my feet have been super comfy all morning, while you're stuck wearing those sweaty twenty-pound sneakers."

A clatter of plastic. I looked up in time to see Carrie take off.

"What's the matter with her?" I asked.

Michelle's face scrunched up. "She's probably upset about the poor children in Africa. At least I think it's Africa this time. She's probably wishing they all had cute shoes like that."

Anne leaned around the curved table and whispered, "I think it's more that Carrie's folks might be having trouble coming up with enough money for medical school."

Carrie had wanted to be a doctor for as long as I'd known her. But I'd never stopped and thought about how expensive it would be for her, or whether her parents could afford it. I'd always assumed, since they lived in a brick house by the lake, that they had plenty of money.

"What about scholarships and grants?" I said, accepting my purse back from Michelle and tucking it under the table in my lap.

Inside my head, everyone else's thoughts grew a little louder.

"She's going to try, but her grades this year and last year are going to factor in on what she gets," Anne said around a mouthful of food. She took a noisy slurp of soda. "And apparently they haven't been all straight A pluses like she wanted."

And here I'd been flaunting my dad's money like a complete idiot. It was just so weird to suddenly have money after never having enough all my life. But that was still no excuse.

"Wow. I didn't know. I'm sorry."

The voices ratcheted up a bit more in my head.

"If you'd stuck around a little longer at my party, you would have heard all about it," Anne muttered. She said it so quietly that she probably never intended for me to hear her. But I did, and it stung. She knew why I'd had to leave early.

"Are you feeling better now?" Michelle asked. "I know Anne said you were feeling sick and all, but you still could have said goodbye, you know."

The voices ramped up still louder. They were nearly at full blast now. I had to fight the urge to yell.

"I'm sorry I had to leave so quick. I…I've been having some…health problems. Headaches and stuff. Trouble hearing sometimes. Digestion issues. That kind of thing."

Michelle's eyebrows drew together. "Have you seen a doctor?"

"It's nothing serious, don't worry about it," I said, trying to focus on breathing slowly. I could do this. I just needed to calm down again, maybe think about something else for a while. "By the way, guess who I was assigned to sit beside in English last period? Ron Abernathy."

Anne thumped back in her chair as if I'd slapped her. She blinked once, twice, then shrugged. "So?"

I mimicked her shrug. "So he seems kind of…sad. Like maybe he hasn't gotten over you yet."

"Did he say something about me?" Anne stared at me.

"Not in so many words." I wished I could read her mind right now, but Michelle's eager need for answers was drowning out Anne's quieter thoughts.

Anne stared into the distance, too many emotions flickering across her face for me to read them.

"Well, if he's upset about the breakup, he can just get over it." Grabbing a plastic fork from the handful of extras Michelle had brought to the table, Anne stabbed her nachos so hard I thought the fork would break. "Because I am so not the right girl for him." She took a huge bite of food and said, "I don't want to talk about it anymore, okay?"

While she chewed, she gave her poor nachos a few more stabs to break up the chips. If she kept at it, she'd poke a hole through the bottom of the paper carton.

And since when had Anne ever used a fork to eat nachos anyways?

I leaned closer to her and murmured, "Anne, are you sure you don't want to talk about it?"

Longing shot out of her like a bolt, then faded. "No. It's over and done. Did you want to talk about you and Tris—"

"No, I don't."

A hint of smugness twisted her mouth and gave her chestnut ponytail back its usual swing. "Okay then."

Look at that freak over there. What will it take for her to get a clue that she doesn't belong here?

I wonder what I should wear for our first date on Friday?

I can't believe she thinks I don't know what she said about me behind my back! The next time I see Sally Parker, I swear....

The roar of voices in my head combined with my own frustration, driving me to say, "But, Anne, Ron seems so nice! And he's miserable without you, and you're obviously miserable without him—"

She threw down her fork and turned to glare at me. "If he's so great, why don't *you* date him?" *He's not what he seems,* she thought loud enough for me to finally pick up.

"Because I'm in love with—" I stopped myself just in time. "You know why."

Michelle's already large eyes opened wider as she looked at me, then Anne, then me again.

Anne took the longest drink I'd ever seen from her soda, as if she intended to down the entire can in one long slurp.

I pressed a shaky hand to my forehead. This wasn't working. At all. The voices weren't getting any quieter. If anything, they were at the screaming level now. As a result, I couldn't think straight.

Stupid ESP. At least for today, it was getting the upper hand. I needed to go somewhere quiet for a few minutes, take a quick break before third period, or my head was going to explode. "Um, listen, I think I'm getting a migraine right now."

"Do you want an aspirin?" Anne reached for her backpack.

"No, thanks," I mumbled. "I can't take it. I just need to go somewhere quiet—"

"The library's open during lunch if you can sneak by the librarian without a pass," Michelle suggested. "Or you could ask the nurse to let you lie down for a while."

"Thanks, I'll do that." I was already on my feet, fumbling for my duffel bag and purse. Should I duck into a bathroom and drink the emergency stash of blood? Somehow I didn't think that would help with the ESP. In fact, it might even make it worse by feeding the vamp side. And then of course I'd have to deal with the blood memories immediately afterwards….

Anne grabbed my wrist, the apology loud enough in her mind that I could finally hear her. She didn't want us to be fighting.

I forgot to wait for her to actually say it. "Don't worry. Everything's fine. We're fine. Don't worry about it. I shouldn't have asked again about him. It's just this…headache making me stupid. I'll call you tonight when my head's not trying to split itself in two, okay?"

I managed a wave goodbye then stumbled out of the cafeteria and up to the catwalk, its metal awning blocking out the bright sunlight.

The sudden and blessed quiet nearly made me sag with relief. But I couldn't stay here for the rest of the lunch period or some teacher would probably show up and tell me to go to class. No one was allowed to hang around beyond the cafeteria on our lunch breaks. I checked my watch and groaned. There were still twenty minutes left before third period. I could go to the nurse's station, but then I might have to answer a bunch of questions. And I definitely didn't want to have to hide out in the restroom that long.

The library was the best option. So I ducked into the main hall, walking slowly past the glass front wall of the office, then allowing myself to rush as fast as I wanted until I reached the double blue doors of the library.

I opened one door just enough to peek at the checkout desk. No librarian in sight. She was probably in her office eating lunch, judging by the putrid smell in the air. Good. If she saw me here without a library pass, she would kick me back out.

I slipped in then moved vampire fast along the carpeted aisles past the tall wooden bookcases, looking for a table out of view in case anyone else came in and tattled on me to the librarian. Spotting the edge of a table in the far back right corner, I hurried over to it.

And nearly shrieked out loud when I discovered someone already seated there.

CHAPTER 18

At the last second, I managed to swallow the gasp and whisper, "Sorry, didn't see you there."

Ron looked up from the book he'd been reading. "Oh, hey, Savannah." He was alarmingly loud.

Then I remembered how deaf I'd seemed in English. "Shh. I'm not deaf anymore. I can hear you now."

Smiling, he held out a hand toward the table. "Have a seat if you want."

I opened my mouth to say no thanks.

It'd be nice not to have to eat alone for once, he thought.

Well, he did have the only table out of view of the front desk.

And maybe if I sat here and listened to his thoughts long enough, I'd hear the truth about his breakup with Anne.

I took the creaky wooden chair opposite him and sat down.

"So what's a girl like you doing in a place like this?" he whispered with a lopsided grin. But underneath that, I heard him think, *Anne's best friend. Maybe she can tell me how to fix things with Anne. It's been months. This is getting ridiculous.*

"I could ask you the same thing," I whispered back. "I didn't realize jocks read."

He shrugged, his smile fading. "It's better than being in that jungle you call a cafeteria."

"That's for sure," I agreed without thinking. At his surprised look, I added, "It gets pretty noisy in there. It's much quieter in here."

"I thought you were deaf last period."

It was my turn to shrug. "Temporary hearing loss. It came back with a vengeance. So what's the deal with you and Anne?"

He froze. "Why? What did she tell you?"

"Nothing. That's what makes me wonder. All she said was that she's not the right girl for you. And that maybe you aren't what you seem." Or had Anne only thought that last part?

"Nobody's what they seem around here. Take you and Tristan, for instance. What's the story there? No one knew you two were even dating for months."

I so didn't want to talk about that. "Why don't you focus on telling me what's really going on between you and my best friend. Did you hurt Anne? Because if you did—"

"No way!" He grabbed the edge of the table. "I would never hurt her."

I searched his thoughts. He was too upset for me to pick out a single thought, his emotions swirling into a big tangle. But he was telling the truth. "You really cared about her."

He blinked once, twice, gave a short, sharp nod. "But now she won't see me, won't talk to me. I don't know what to do. I've tried to be patient, but she's driving me nuts here."

I crossed my arms over my chest. "Maybe she has a good reason."

"Or maybe she's just being pigheaded."

"Maybe. It is Anne we're talking about." We smiled at each other in understanding. "You'll just have to let her come around when she's ready. If she does. Or you could always move on, date somebody else."

He was cute in a boy-next-door kind of way. With that quick grin and those blue eyes under a flop of straight, light blond hair, he could easily find someone new. Last year before Anne snapped him up, he'd briefly dated Vanessa Faulkner, and she was notoriously picky about her arm candy.

He stared at me. "You act like moving on after getting dumped is no big deal."

"You moved on fast enough after Vanessa."

He rolled his eyes and leaned back in his chair. "I wouldn't count dating her as a real relationship. More like pretending to be a giant Ken doll for her to endlessly make over. Besides, I broke up with her, not the other way around." Seeing my eyebrows shoot up, he added, "Anne told me what you overheard her saying to her sister in history class. Did you guys think I'd just sit back and wait for Vanessa to dump me first?"

Interesting. My respect for him went up several notches.

"Speaking of getting dumped," he continued, "I heard what you did to Tristan. Rumor has it the event was brutal, even by high school standards. Did you really dump him in front of his entire family?"

I winced. No telling what version of the real story he'd heard.

I leaned back in my chair and crossed my arms. "I didn't *dump* Tristan."

"Really? Because that's not what I heard. Guess I should consider myself lucky Anne wasn't that harsh. All I got was a Dear John text."

"My breakup with Tristan isn't anything like your breakup

with Anne. Trust me." Why was he even comparing the two events?

"Oh yeah? How do you know?"

I snorted. Unless he was half Clann and half vamp and Anne had suddenly joined the Clann without telling me, there was no way their breakup was even remotely similar to mine. "Look, you don't know anything about us or what really happened—"

"And you don't know anything about me and Anne."

Only because she wouldn't tell me what happened. I gritted my teeth, searching for a retort.

The bell rang. He jumped up. "See you in English lit." He walked off, shoulders hunched, hands buried deep in his jeans pockets, his notebook and textbook somehow staying tucked between his left forearm and his body. Maybe from all that practice carrying the ball for a touchdown as our varsity Indians' best receiver.

I bent down to gather my things and noticed the book he'd left open on the table, cover side up. *Legends and Monsters of East Texas,* it proclaimed. What in the world? I flipped it over. A snarling black cat, almost as large as a tiger, took up half the left page, its claws reaching out as if to attack the villager in front of it.

Boys. They were into the weirdest stuff.

The next day, I discovered Ron and I shared second period chemistry class, too.

"Hey, want to be lab partners?" he leaned over and muttered after Mr. Knouse told everyone to partner up and choose lab tables.

I started to agree then hesitated, remembering yesterday's conversation in the library. Did I really want the added drama in my life?

Sighing, I went with my first instinct. "Sure, why not? Fair warning, though, I suck big-time at anything having to do with numbers. Science included."

One corner of his mouth slanted upward. "Then you're in luck. Science is my one area of expertise. Well, that and football."

I grinned as I followed him to a table. "That remains to be seen at this week's game. Isn't Texas High our biggest rival? If I remember correctly, they really stomped your butts last year."

"Please. That was just bad luck. Trust me, this year those Tigers will be nothing but kittens in need of a nap by the time we get done with them."

I dropped my bags to the floor and sat on one of the two stools at our table. When I rested my forearms on it, the contrast with the table's black surface made my forearms and hands blindingly white.

I hastily dropped my hands to my lap. "You know, if you're as good as you say you are, about chemistry I mean, I might be willing to do a trade. Help with our homework in here in exchange for tutoring in English lit? You're not the only one who picks up on the gossip every now and then, and rumor has it that English is definitely not one of your areas of expertise."

"Did Anne say that?" The poor boy actually looked hopeful, projecting shards of longing over my nerve endings, and a sympathetic ache welled up in my chest.

I tried to laugh it away. "She might have mentioned helping you a little last year. Which is really saying something, because it was *my* constant help that turned her C- into a B+."

Ron grinned. "That figures. I thought some of her explanations didn't sound right coming from her. English class was the only time I ever heard her use a four-syllable word."

"Yep, that's our girl."

While the teacher explained how to do our first lab experiment, I snuck a couple of glances at Ron's profile. Like Anne, his eyes, once shiny, now had a certain dullness to them, the skin tight around them as if ready to wince at any second.

As if he were in physical pain.

I thought about Anne's reactions yesterday at lunch, and that flash of longing that had escaped her for a second. Whatever her reasons for breaking up with him, she still deeply cared about him.

They were being so stupid! How could two people so in love refuse to be together? At least I had a solid reason not to be with Tristan. Anne and Ron, on the other hand, couldn't possibly have anything that bad keeping them apart. It might even be a simple misunderstanding. Maybe Anne had figured it out already, and that was the real reason she refused to talk about it. She knew she'd made a mistake, but her pride wouldn't let her admit it to anyone. Better to be in misery than for everyone to know she was wrong.

Well, I wasn't going to let her screw up her love life anymore.

I couldn't fix Tristan and me. But I could help Anne.

Ron had always been so quiet at our lunch table last year, so I didn't know him all that well. If I got to know him better this year, especially with the ESP, I ought to be able to figure out a way to help them fix their issues. They might not get back together. After all, Anne was the single most stubborn person I'd ever known, and I wasn't a miracle worker. But if I could at least get them to be friends again, it would be better than seeing them stuck in all this endless misery. Then, if they decided not to get romantically involved again, that would be their choice and I would at least have the satisfaction of knowing I had done everything I could to help.

Happy with my new goal, I focused on the teacher as Mr.

Knouse finished going over the lab instructions. Then Ron and I got started on our first lab experiment.

I watched Ron measure out blue liquid from one beaker into another using a giant dropper, eager to hear his thoughts and hopefully pick up a few clues.

Too bad there was nothing but science stuff in his head at the moment.

He noticed my stare. "What? Am I doing it wrong?"

"You tell me. You're supposed to be the science expert here." I smiled. "Actually, I was just trying to figure out why Anne broke up with you."

He frowned, possibly in concentration, and added another measure of blue liquid to the beaker. "I told her…something. Something about my family." Something about black cats running around in the woods, according to his thoughts. "She said she didn't care, that she was okay with it. But then she got really quiet, and the next thing I knew, every time I called her cell phone she wouldn't pick up, and every time I called her at home her mom answered and said she either wasn't home or was in the shower. And then she sent me a text message the following Monday saying she didn't want to see me anymore and that it just wasn't working out. And ever since, she won't talk to me about it."

That didn't sound like Anne at all. She had always been the blunt, take-no-prisoners type. "What the heck did you tell her that freaked her out so badly?"

I caught only one thought from his mind. *Keepers. But Mom said Savannah doesn't know, so…* He shook his head. "I really can't talk about that. It's private family stuff. But it's nothing that would hurt Anne or anything like that."

Silently he started humming a song in his head, blocking me from picking up any other thoughts.

He said the Keepers, whatever they were, weren't dangerous to Anne. If that was true, then why would she break up with him over it?

And why had he discussed these Keepers and me with his mom?

Should I know what Keepers were for some reason?

By the end of second period, Ron had silently hummed that same darn song over and over so many times I had it stuck in my head too now. And I still didn't have any possible answers about his breakup with Anne.

What could he possibly be hiding about his family that would freak Anne out? She was one of the toughest, bravest people I knew. Look how well she'd reacted to the news that I was half vamp and half witch. She hadn't acted scared at all until the night of her birthday when the bloodlust had started messing with me and made me all vampy. What could be worse than that?

Maybe it had something to do with the black cats he'd been thinking and reading about in the library yesterday.

Were Ron's family cat wranglers or something? Maybe they bred exotic cats and sold them on the internet?

Or maybe it was some weird religious belief or something, like the Abernathys worshipped black cats?

Nah, that couldn't be it. There had to be some other reason, something big for Anne to run away from the relationship like that. But try as I might, I couldn't come up with anything.

When the dismissal bell rang, we gathered our books and headed out the door, Ron directly behind me. When the chaotic noise of the main hall slammed over me and I stopped in surprise, he stepped on my heels.

I hadn't realized till now just how peaceful chemistry class had been.

"Sorry. Headed to the jungle?" Ron asked, nearly having to shout to be heard over the stampede.

"Um, I don't know." There didn't seem much point in going to the cafeteria when I no longer ate human food, other than getting to see my friends since we didn't have any classes together this year.

On the other hand, considering what a mess of things the stupid ESP had helped me make yesterday, maybe Carrie and Anne would be happier if I wasn't there today.

"You headed to the library again?" I asked him.

He nodded. "Figured I could get a head start on my homework. I'm pretty tired after football practice, and my mom likes to do supper early every evening. By the time we get done eating, all I want to do is crash."

I could empathize with that. I was trying to drink as little blood each week as I could get away with in an effort to reduce the flood of the donor's memories. Which meant I was exhausted almost all the time lately.

And then there was the near nightly issue of having nightmares about Tristan and Nanna.

As if my thoughts had conjured him up, I felt my chest and stomach ache, as well as pinpricks race along my neck and down my arms. Two signs that Tristan was nearby and ticked off. I looked to my left down the main hall, and there he was.

Tristan crossed to the other side of the hall before passing by, not looking my way in the process.

Gritting my teeth, I headed for my locker a few yards away. Ron walked with me, his mouth moving as he talked about something, but I couldn't hear him with everyone's thoughts screaming inside my head. At my locker, I nodded like I could hear every word he said while I spun through my locker's combination lock then yanked the metal latch to open it.

Something sticky coated the latch, and now my hand, too.

"Oh ew!" Nose wrinkled, I glanced at my hand, then

stopped breathing. It was dark red and looked an awful lot like…

Blood.

"Hey, are you okay?" Ron grabbed my hand. "You're bleeding!"

"No, it's not me. It was on my locker." I couldn't seem to look away from my hand. My mouth watered, and I had to swallow a few times.

Ron studied my locker's latch. "Aw, now that's just nasty. Who would…" He looked at me, confusion turning into annoyance on his face. "The Clann."

The hall was starting to clear out as everyone hurried to class or the cafeteria. But I couldn't seem to move.

"Okay, why don't you go wash up in the bathroom while I get something to clean this up?" Ron said, firmly grabbing my shoulders and steering me to the door of the nearest girl's restroom.

I stumbled into the bathroom and over to the sink. My arms and legs didn't want to respond to my brain, their movements slow and jerky. I turned the water on with my clean hand, started to stick my other hand under the faucet, then hesitated.

The blood…I could smell it. Blood used to smell sharp and metallic to me. But that was before I'd first felt the bloodlust.

Now, it was different.

I lifted those red fingers to my nose and inhaled deeply, closing my eyes as a hundred different scents filled my head.

Something about the blood was familiar. As a whole, it was new, unique. But underneath ran this thread of…

Temptation. Perfection. Like chocolate, edible and completely divine.

Déjà vu swamped me, and I knew where I'd smelled that underlying scent before.

This was Clann blood.

CHAPTER 19

The blood wasn't Tristan's, or I would have recognized it instantly. But this blood definitely had a strong common thread. It had to be descendant blood. No donor blood ever smelled quite this irresistible.

Pain exploded in my mouth. Whimpering, I opened it and checked my reflection in the mirror.

My incisors were longer and sharper than before.

Holy crap. Fangs again.

I had to get rid of the Clann blood.

I tried to scrub the blood off. The soap dispensers were all empty, so I was stuck using plain water and my hands to get it off, feeling like Lady Macbeth in Shakespeare's *Macbeth,* which we'd studied last year in English. Out, damned spot, out I say! The blood was stubborn, refusing to come off at first. Had Dylan or the Brat Twins put some kind of spell on it to make it stain my hand?

By the time I finally got my skin clean, I was breathing fast and on the edge of true panic. The Clann was darn lucky there was a peace treaty between them and the vamps, or I would have hunted them down for this.

If they kept this up, I'd have no choice but to put a protection spell on everything I came into contact with.

And maybe hex them with a wart or zit curse or something while I was at it.

Ron was waiting by my locker. "Hey. I found a janitor to help me clean it up. It took a bit of work, but I think we got it all."

I let out the breath I hadn't realized I'd been holding. "Thanks, Ron."

He lifted one shoulder in a half shrug. "Somebody really ought to put those descendants in their place."

Exactly what I was thinking.

Distracted, I nodded and headed for the library doors. "Too bad they run half the friggin' world."

"And all of East Texas," he added.

I returned his grin. "Yeah."

In the library, we sat at the same corner table as before, taking seats opposite each other. Which reminded me...

"By the way, you left that book here yesterday. You know, the one about the East Texas myths and legends?"

He shrugged. "I've read it so much I've just about memorized it anyways."

"You're into that stuff?"

"Sure. Some of it's actually true. Or pretty close to it."

I snorted. "Oh yeah, like what?"

He leaned back in his chair, and I caught the thought, *Maybe Mom's wrong and she knows after all. Her mom still could have told her.* "Well, for instance, they got some of the facts right about the monster black cats that run around in the woods outside Palestine."

"Monster black cats. Here in East Texas? Yeah, right. Panthers are jungle animals, aren't they?"

"Not this kind. They came over hundreds of years ago with the Irish and Scottish settlers."

Okay, now I flat-out knew he was joking. "And why would the settlers have great big exotic cats for pets?"

"Not for pets. For protection. Originally, Scottish and Irish lords relied on them to guard their castles from attack and to battle at their side against the English and other enemies. By the time they came to America to settle the new land, it was only natural to bring those protectors with them for defense against bears and other predators in this area."

"And now they run around wild in the woods." I didn't bother trying to hide my lingering skepticism in my voice.

He nodded, returning my stare. "Over the last century, those settlers turned to technology and weapons for protection instead."

After a long moment of silence, I shook my head. "I've lived here my whole life and never heard about these so-called monster cats. Why didn't we ever talk about them in history class?" Growing up, we'd had to take Texas history not once but twice in elementary school. The teachers had covered the Alamo, Davy Crockett and Sam Houston, bluebonnets, mockingbirds and the yellow rose. We'd even had to learn how to sing "The Yellow Rose of Texas" and recite the pledge of allegiance to the Texas flag. But not once were any legendary black cats mentioned.

Nope, Mom's right, he thought. *She doesn't know.*

I wanted to growl in frustration. *What* didn't I know?

"Not everyone knows about them. The cats prefer to stay deep in the woods out of sight. But some people have seen them while out hunting. Including me."

"Seriously?"

He grinned. "Yep. In broad daylight, not twenty yards away from me. It was huge, at least six feet from head to butt, and massive."

I leaned forward. "What did you do?"

"Nothing. It didn't come after me or anything. It seemed kind of nice, actually."

"Were you deer hunting at the time?"

"Yeah, why?"

"If you used that deer pee hunters around here like to use, you probably stunk too bad to eat."

Ron threw his head back and laughed. "How do you know about deer pee? You go hunting, too?" His eyebrows rose in obvious doubt as his gaze slid down to check out the heels Dad had finally talked me into wearing today.

"No. Anne mentioned it. She goes hunting with her Uncle Danny every year…."

He winced, and I could have bitten off my tongue.

"Sorry," I mumbled.

He looked down at the table. "We should get to work. Lunch break's almost over."

"Right." Clearing my throat, I reached for my bag.

Someone walked over to our table. It was the librarian. Crap.

Ron reacted first. "Oh hey, Mom."

The librarian was Ron's mother? No wonder he could get away with being in here every day without a teacher's pass.

"Hi, son. Getting your homework done?" Her eyebrows rose, and I could see the family resemblance between them. Ron had her eyes and hair color.

"Yeah," he replied, cheeks turning red. "Oh, sorry, this is—"

"Savannah Colbert. Yes, I know," Mrs. Abernathy finished for him. Her tone was solemn.

I searched her face, still surprised she knew who I was. But I couldn't pick up her thoughts for some reason. All I could hear was her humming an unrecognizable tune in her head.

Had the Clann been talking about me around town or something? Maybe she'd heard the rumors about me and Tristan that were still spreading throughout the school like trash blowing on the wind?

"It's nice to finally meet you," she said. "You're welcome to come here on your lunch breaks any time you need to." Smiling, she reached out to ruffle Ron's hair before walking away.

After she was out of hearing range, I leaned forward and whispered, "How does she know who I am?"

"Mom's the head of the local genealogical society. She knows who all the descendants are."

Heart racing, I froze in my seat, the wooden edge digging into the back of my thighs. *Descendants.* He'd said that word before, back in the hall by my locker today. At the time, I'd been too freaked out over the blood to pay attention.

"How do you know they're called descendants? Is your family in the Clann?" Only descendants knew to call themselves that. If Ron was a descendant, the Clann could consider my being alone with him as possibly breaking the rules.

"No. But my family's heard a lot about them."

Why hasn't her family told her about the Keepers? he thought.

I yearned to ask him what the Keepers were. But then that would reveal that I could read his mind sometimes. And I couldn't think of any other way to bring them up casually.

"We'd better get to work," he muttered, pulling his chemistry book over and opening it to today's lesson. When I didn't move, he glanced up at me. "Do you want help with this stuff or not?"

He didn't seem angry, and his thoughts were entirely focused on the homework now. But he was definitely acting different.

Sighing, I gave in for the moment and reached for my chemistry book.

The next day, I thought I might find a way to somehow bring up the Keepers during study time. But while on my way to second period English lit, I ran into Michelle in the main hall as she was leaving the office.

"Hey, we missed you at lunch yesterday," she said. "You'll be there today, right?"

"Um, sure. Of course." Maybe I should try to eat in the cafeteria again, face my growing fear of crowded places and see if I could learn how to control the ESP. I sure hadn't mastered it in any of my classes yet. If it weren't for the occasional lecture notes displayed on the overhead projector in each class plus textbooks and Ron's help in chemistry class, I would be in serious trouble already. Hearing the teachers' oral lectures was going to remain impossible until I found a way to turn down the noise of everyone's thoughts in the room with me.

"Good! We'll see you then." Grinning, Michelle waved before turning down a side hall toward her second period class.

With a sigh, I went to English class.

It was hard not to fidget and sneak peeks at Tristan while the teacher's lecture droned on and on. Tristan stayed slouched down in his desk, legs stretched out before him and crossed at the ankles, his arms crossed over his broad chest. A lovely frown completed the look.

He hadn't moved from that position since I'd first entered the class, as if he couldn't care less that I was there.

Unlike me. The more I thought about him, the louder everyone's thoughts became inside my head. I needed to calm down, think about something else. So I closed my eyes and imagined I was on a sunny hillside somewhere doing tai chi, a cool breeze caressing my skin…

"Miss Colbert."

My eyes snapped open. Mrs. Knowles was staring at me from where she stood at the dry-erase board.

"Could you kindly try to stay awake while you are in my class?"

Someone giggled at the back of the room. But at least the ESP had finally turned down enough for me to actually hear the teacher for a change.

"Yes, ma'am. Sorry," I mumbled.

"Thank you. Now as I was saying…" Mrs. Knowles returned to her lecture and writing notes on the board.

Unfortunately, turning down the noise of everyone's thoughts only seemed to increase my ability to sense Tristan's emotions. And the emotions pouring off him now were anything but sunshine and rainbows.

The anger and hurt were nearly overwhelming, rolling from him in dark waves that I could practically see if I had dared to look at him.

Maybe his wounded pride hadn't gotten over us quite as fully as everyone thought.

I was surprised when the bell rang for lunch. Tristan was slow to leave, so I hurried to gather my books and escape first so we wouldn't have to walk near each other out of class.

"Hey." A male voice near my left ear made me jump just outside the classroom door.

I froze and looked up. It was Ron.

"Oh. Hi, Ron." We left the alcove that the two English classrooms emptied into, merging with the traffic already flowing through the main hall.

"Are we meeting for lunch again?" he asked.

"Oh, um, actually I promised Michelle this morning that I'd eat with the girls today. Can we meet tomorrow instead?"

A low level of disappointment flashed from Ron, along with the chorus from Celine Dion's "All By Myself" in his thoughts, which nearly made me laugh out loud. I only managed to hold it in by biting my lower lip.

He gave a lopsided smile and a half shrug anyway. "Sure, no problem. See you then."

With a wave he strolled toward the library.

Giving in to the urge to smile now, I watched him head for the library alone. If not Ron, then somebody in his family sure was a Celine Dion fan. His thoughts were harder to hear under the crowded hall's collection of brain waves. But I could still just barely make out him humming the rest of the tune in his mind.

He seemed like such a nice guy. Why didn't he have any friends? Shouldn't he at least eat with the other football jocks at lunch?

Needle pricks of pain stabbed over my arms and the back of my neck as Tristan walked past, his long legs helping him put distance between us faster than some shorter people could manage at a jog.

The sensation on my skin faded, taking my good mood with it. But the knowledge of its meaning refused to go away as quickly. Tristan was furious. At me? At the Clann and the council?

Probably all of the above.

Tears sprang to my eyes, burning them and forcing me to blink fast before the tears could run down my cheeks. He knew I had only done what I'd had to for his protection. Did he think I actually *liked* to feel miserable without him all the time?

Besides, he had Bethany now to keep him happy.

He joined the crowd exiting the far end of the main hall, and I could move again. Still, I took my time in getting to the cafeteria.

As soon as I entered, the whole room morphed into some weird version of an audience at a tennis match, almost everyone's heads turning to look from me to where Tristan was seated at the Charmers table beside Bethany.

My stomach lurched.

I sat down beside Anne and opened a book. Feeling my friends staring, I forced a smile and glanced at them over the top of the pages. "What?"

"Are you going to actually eat?" Carrie asked.

"Um, not right now, no. I'm not really hungry."

"Told you so," Carrie grumbled to no one in particular. *Eating disorder, plain as day,* her thoughts added.

Michelle leaned forward. "Savannah, is there anything you want to talk about with us? I mean, you know we're here for you, right? We know things have been kind of tough for you lately, what with your grandma dying and moving into a haunted house with your dad, and the whole thing with Tris— I mean, other stuff. But none of that is because of you or how you look or whatever."

I stared at her, completely lost. "Yes, I know you guys are here for me. Thanks."

"Does your dad know that you're anorexic?" Carrie blurted out, her hands clasped together on the table before her.

Oh wow. So that's what this was. I sighed, propping my forehead in my hand. "You guys can stop the intervention. I'm not anorexic."

"Told you so," Anne said, her tone more than a little exasperated.

"He probably doesn't care enough to notice," Carrie said.

"Huh?" I said. "My dad cares about me." A little too much

at times, in fact, what with his constant warnings and less-than-subtle questions about how I was feeling every other minute I was home.

Carrie acted like I hadn't said anything. "Even if your dad doesn't notice or care that you're slowly killing yourself, we do. And you need to get some help."

I leaned back in my chair. This was going to be such a long lunch break. "I don't have an eating disorder. I'm just on a new—"

"A new diet? Please, we've already heard that one," Carrie snapped. "How stupid do you really think we are? It's obvious you've got a problem. Why else would you bail on Anne's birthday party? And you skipped lunch yesterday, and you didn't eat anything the day before, either. And now you're not eating again today."

I didn't know whether to be thrilled that they cared so much, irritated that they couldn't just believe me, or worried that I had no plan for how to lessen their concerns. If I ate anything, it would just come right back up and worry them even more.

I tried one more time. "Guys, I swear I'm not trying to lose weight here. I've just been having trouble eating stuff like I used to."

"Like I said." Anne turned to face me. "I told them you were just having stomach problems. But Miss Future Doctor of the World over there's convinced otherwise."

Michelle's head whipped from side to side like she was watching a tennis match. "I always thought you had a cast-iron stomach, Sav. Was it eating all those chili cheese French fries last year that hurt you?"

"Well, actually," Carrie began, her tone more than a little reluctant now. "People *can* develop digestive problems after experiencing prolonged periods of stress. I guess she could be suffering from an ulcer, which would make it hard for her to eat much for a while until her stomach lining heals."

"And she's definitely been stressed out lately." Michelle shot me a sympathetic smile.

"So why'd you miss lunch yesterday?" Anne asked.

"Um, about that," I began. "I've been meaning to tell you... you'll never guess who I have both chemistry and English lit with."

"Ron Abernathy?" Anne asked drily.

"Yep. And he needs help in English, and I'm clueless in chem. So we agreed to help each other out with our homework during lunch sometimes in the library."

Anne stared at me. "In the library, huh?"

"Because it's quiet there," I added. "And his mom's the librarian, so she lets us work there without requiring a teacher's pass."

"Makes sense," Anne muttered, as if it were no big deal.

However, the flashes of heat from her told a different story, almost as if...

She was jealous.

"Anne, it's really not like that," I said, feeling like I was suddenly facing a wild animal that needed soothing with an extra calm voice. "I would never, ever go after your ex. Plus he's not my type."

"Really? Because your type isn't the tall, blond earnest-eyed football player?" Carrie said.

I could have almost laughed if it weren't so insulting. "Ron's nothing at all like...you know who."

Carrie glared at me, while Anne pretended to be very interested in her soda.

I touched Anne's shoulder. "Come on, Anne. You know me. You know I would never go after anyone you cared about. And I know you still care about Ron. Even if you didn't, I still wouldn't date him." After my last two dating attempts, I definitely would not be trying it again. Two total disasters were enough for one lifetime.

"I know that," Anne mumbled, but it didn't sound like she believed it. She looked up at me, sighed and said more firmly, "I do know that. I know you'd never date Ron."

"Still, he could have asked someone else for help," Carrie muttered.

"Does he have any friends?" I asked, curious now.

Shrugs and a head shake were the general consensus.

I turned to Anne again. "Is there a reason that I shouldn't at least be nice and help him pass English lit?"

"You mean besides the fact that he's your best friend's ex?" Carrie said.

"Anne dumped *him,* not the other way around," Michelle argued.

Silence from Anne.

"Anne, you decide," I said. "Say the word, and I'll find a different lab partner and tell Ron to wing it on his own in English lit."

If it made her that uncomfortable, maybe I shouldn't try to help patch up their issues after all.

"You don't have to tell me what happened between you two," I added. "But at least tell me this…should I go kick his butt for you? Because if so, I'll do it. I'll go right now and give him a good ole smack-down in the library. Just say the word, and I'll bury him in the heaviest hardbacks I can find."

Michelle snickered. Even Carrie's lips twitched at that.

Anne gave a reluctant smile. "No, don't kick his butt. You'd only end up snapping those puny arms of yours like pretzels. You're right. I did break up with him, not the other way around. And…I guess it's not really his fault, either. I mean, it wasn't something he actually did. It was just something I had to do."

A glimpse of black kitty cats running through Anne's mind this time. What was with the black cats already?

"So it's okay if I meet with him for tutoring during lunch every other day?"

She rolled her eyes and sighed loudly. "Well, *I'm* certainly not around to help him anymore. And the boy is an idiot at English stuff. If you don't help him, he'll probably wind up flunking and missing out on playing football. And heaven help *that* from ever happening."

Carrie snorted.

"So by all means, help the big lug with his English, I guess." Anne grabbed her soda, trying to act like the whole conversation was no big deal now.

But I saw through her act. The flares of emotion coming from her told the real story...she was still crazy about Ron and desperately wishing she were the one meeting with him at lunch instead of me.

Which meant there was still hope for the two of them.

Smiling, I leaned sideways to bump shoulders with her. "Deep down, you are such a softie."

She choked on her soda. "Don't ever say that again!" She glanced around us, making a show out of being horrified. "I've got a *rep* to maintain here!"

The next day during chem lab, I said, "I told Anne about our tutoring exchange."

Ron's hand froze in the act of reaching for a glass dropper. "What'd she say?"

"She wasn't thrilled about it, but she said it was okay."

"She wasn't happy about it?"

"I think her exact words were something along the lines of

'well, I'm not going to help him, and he is an idiot in English class, so somebody better help him pass.'"

He smiled at the beaker as its green contents began to bubble.

I wrote down the chemical reaction as the teacher had instructed earlier. "Ron, be honest. You're not having me help you with your homework just to make Anne jealous, are you?"

He scowled. "What? No way! It was your idea in the first place. And besides, why would I need to try to make her jealous? She already knows how I feel about her." He measured two drops of water then added them to the beaker, and the contents turned blue. "She knows if she changes her mind, all she has to do is tell me."

"And you'd take her back? Just like that? Even after she dumped you?"

He shrugged. "Pride just gets in the way in life. The less pride you have, the easier it is to have what you want."

"Huh. Ever told Anne that?"

He frowned at his lab directions. "I'm hoping she'll figure it out someday."

"You do remember how hardheaded she is, right?"

He grinned. "It's one of the things I miss the most about her." After adding two more drops of water to the beaker, he glanced at me and said, "You know, I could ask you the same question. Are *you* working with me to make a certain guy jealous?"

It was my turn to scowl. "No. Why would I? I broke up with him."

"I heard he and a certain Charmer have turned into a real couple lately."

I swallowed hard and focused on taking notes in my notebook. "Good for him. He deserves to be happy."

He was safe. It was all that mattered.

"With someone else?"

"If she makes him happy."

"That's big of you. Not sure I could say the same." He leaned back on his stool, making the metal legs squeak.

I forced one corner of my lips up into a half smile. "Trust me, it's a daily effort."

Over the next few weeks, my life slipped into a routine that, while not exactly always happy, was at least comfortable. Mostly. Except for English class, I found ways to stay focused on other things...helping the Charmers at practices, pep rallies and games...helping my friends with their homework and listening to the latest gossip from Michelle at lunch every other day...working and joking around with Ron in chemistry class and our lunchtime tutoring sessions...practicing tai chi with Dad and Gowin when he was visiting in the evenings before doing my homework and then falling into bed. And of course finding ways to sneak out to Nanna's for magic practice every spare moment I could. The only problem was I couldn't seem to tap into my Clann side in the first two or three days after feeding. My current theory was that feeding empowered the vamp side too much to allow my descendant abilities to work. Either that, or filling my body with human blood made me temporarily too human and not witchy enough.

English class and the weekends after feeding were the bad times when I couldn't pretend everything was okay.

Every Friday night after the football games, no matter how late I was in coming home, both Dad and Gowin were always waiting in the kitchen with a vial of donated blood for me. Not drinking it wasn't an option. I'd already tried every excuse I could think of to get out of it without success.

"Eventually you'll come to enjoy the blood memories," Gowin had promised one time when he found me sitting on my bedroom floor drenched in sweat and holding my head in my hands as the images whirled past inside my mind.

"How could anyone possibly enjoy this?" I'd managed to gasp.

"Think of it like a mini vacation from your life. You get to be someone else for a while."

"But nothing I'm seeing makes any sense! I don't know who these people are, who I'm supposed to be in the memories."

"So think of it like one of those artsy-fartsy films instead, where you're not supposed to understand. Does your own life always make sense? Does the world around us make sense? Of course not. And it's not supposed to. Real life is chaos, sweetheart, not order. It's only humans and the lingering humanity within vampires that drives any of us to try and make sense out of it."

But I hated the chaos. I hated being so totally out of control over my own mind. And I definitely resented anything that prevented me from regaining my magical birthright.

English wasn't much better. In every other class, I'd managed to master the ESP enough to turn down the volume of thoughts. But that only allowed me to better tune in to Tristan. And now I was starting to pick up the occasional thought from his mind.

Hearing Tristan's thoughts was both a pleasure and a torment. In those moments when I could hear him speaking within my mind without censorship, I felt closer to him than I ever had before.

But that only made it harder to control my feelings for him.

Especially now that everyone was getting ready for the upcoming annual Charmers masq ball, our biggest fund-raiser of the year. During practice, it took constant effort to block out Bethany's excited mental chatter as she pondered what matching costumes she and Tristan should wear to the dance. Apparently he'd agreed to wear whatever she picked out.

Last year, he had been the one to insist that we secretly dress as a couple, he as a knight and me as an angel, like Leonard DiCaprio and Claire Danes in the movie *Romeo + Juliet*. And then Bethany had shown up that night dressed as Guinevere, making everyone think Tristan was actually dressed as her Lancelot.

Even then, Bethany had managed to look like the perfect girl for him.

This year, she could openly choose any matching set of his-and-hers costumes that she wanted. She would be hanging on his arm all night long, just like she'd done during the homecoming dance in September.

And of course kissing him as much as she wanted to without any danger of killing him.

At the masq ball, they would be able to flaunt just how perfect a couple they were. And, as usual, I would be relegated to cooking and serving food and drinks in the concession stand where half our money was made.

While she danced the night away in Tristan's arms, I would be sweating it out over a big Crockpot full of cheese sauce and a plastic jar of pickles.

I was so ready for Halloween to be over. Too bad it was still weeks away.

CHAPTER 20

TRISTAN

I had a real love/hate thing going on with English lit this year. Sometimes I was grateful just for the chance to sit beside Savannah and sneak glances at her when she was busy reading or writing something.

But she wasn't exactly making it easy for me to forget about her when she showed up wearing skirts and heels that showed off her awesome long legs.

Was she trying to torture me now? I'd never thought of her as the sadistic type. Maybe it was a sign of her vampire side taking over.

She uncrossed her feet and tucked them under her desk, making little stones on her heels wink and shine.

Geez. I'd never even paid attention to girls' shoes before. Sav was turning me into some kind of a shoe freak.

Savannah's feet twitched.

A coincidence that I'd just been thinking about them. Right?

I looked at her directly, checking to see if she was looking my way. She turned the opposite direction, bending down to search her Charmers bag for something. An excuse to avoid eye contact? Probably.

Maybe I should try to talk to her after class, see how she reacted.

She jumped then froze in her seat, her shoulders hunching up. Almost as if she'd heard me.

No, she couldn't have. Everyone knew vampires and witches couldn't read each others' minds. It was a basic survival mechanism that both our species had evolved over the centuries to protect ourselves from each other.

So if I grabbed my book and dropped it on the floor...

I started to pick up my textbook from my desktop, and her entire body flinched as if I'd already dropped the book.

Slowly she sat back up in her seat and appeared to be copying notes from the classroom board again.

Very carefully, I thought, *Savannah. Can you hear me?*

Her writing hand jerked, her pen making a slash of blue across her paper.

I waited for her to look at me. Instead, she went back to her note taking, her mouth tightening. It was the first sign of emotion I'd seen on her face in months, since our argument at Charmers practice last year. I'd begun to wonder if her face had become permanently frozen in that Ice Queen mask I was really beginning to hate. She used to be so easy to read, every emotion plain as daylight both on her face and in the way her eyes changed colors to match her moods.

Lately, all those irises had displayed was that same icy silver-gray.

On purpose now, I remembered the last time I'd held her

in the council's jet…the way she'd sat in my lap, her head on my shoulder, her arms around me. Her fingertips slowly rubbing tiny circles on my shirt. The lavender scent of her hair beneath my chin. The way it had felt to kiss her…

She sighed. But that could have been another coincidence.

So I tried another tactic that would hopefully get a more obvious reaction from her. I pictured myself kissing Bethany under the bleachers at the practice field. We'd never actually done this. I'd been careful not to lead Bethany on and only kissed her cheek goodbye sometimes. We probably hung out together too much as it was, but Bethany was a good friend.

But I didn't think about the facts now. I imagined holding Bethany in my arms, stroking her back, my hands tangling in her hair…

Savannah's pen snapped in half, spilling ink all over her writing hand and notes. Jaw clenched, she got up to throw both in the trash by the classroom door then asked permission from the teacher to wash up in the restroom.

Oh yeah, Savannah could definitely hear my thoughts.

The only question was whether I could hear hers, too, if I tried.

I kicked back in my seat and pretended to be focused on taking notes along with everyone else. When Savannah returned, I didn't look up. I waited until she was back in her seat and writing again. Then I willed myself to hear her mind, which was all it usually took unless the target was a descendant trained to block their thoughts from others.

I picked up nothing. Not even a stray word or image from her thoughts. No static or music or any hint that she was actively trying to block me out.

I tried harder, staring straight at her now, focusing all my energy on the effort.

She sucked in air through her nose and rubbed her forearms as goose bumps appeared all over her skin.

Crap. I'd forgotten to keep my energy under control.

Sorry, I thought, pulling the energy level back down.

"It's okay," she replied, then froze, her eyes wide.

"What's okay?" the teacher asked from her desk two yards away.

"Oh. I, um…" Savannah began.

"I was apologizing to her for forgetting our study session," Ron said.

Which was total bull. Savannah hadn't even been looking at him.

Ron was covering for her. But why?

She had been going to the library with him during lunch a lot lately. To study together?

Why not study together in the cafeteria instead where everyone could see them?

Ron went out with Anne last year. Maybe Sav was dating him now and trying to hide it from Anne?

No, Savannah wouldn't do that. She would never hurt her best friend by sneaking around with Anne's ex.

Then again, Savannah had spent months secretly dating me last year. Maybe she'd grown to like that kind of thing.

When the lunch bell rang, I took my time grabbing my stuff so Ron and Savannah could leave first. Then I followed them into the main hall. I stopped by my locker, pretending to need to switch out books while watching them walk together down the hall. Ron must have said something funny, because Savannah laughed. She bumped shoulders with him. Then he stopped and opened the library door, holding it so she could go in first.

I stood there, frozen, while the only girl I'd ever loved disappeared into the library for a lunchtime date with someone else. But this time, watching her with another guy was way worse than when she'd dated Greg the soccer jerk. Because this time, I knew what it felt like to hold her, kiss her, see her blush and know I'd caused it. This time, her being with someone else meant I'd truly lost her.

Savannah had moved on.

That afternoon at football practice, I watched Ron. The guy actually had the nerve to nod hello at me as we headed out to the back practice field.

I didn't nod back.

Ron was a running back, and I was an offensive lineman. Technically my job was to help him catch or carry the ball for a touchdown. I'd worked my butt off for months to earn my spot back on the team after missing half of last year.

But even the risk of ticking off the coach couldn't help me resist the urge to miss a few key blocks that were supposed to clear Ron's path. As a result, Ron got creamed several times. After the fourth time, Ron finally got a clue.

"What's the deal, man?" he growled as he yanked chunks of grass and mud from his face mask.

"Whoops. I just keep on forgetting that darn play. Is it sweep right, or sweep left?" I said with the fakest smile I could manage.

He stared at me for a few seconds then stomped off.

When practice ended, he didn't nod goodbye as we headed out the field house exit at the same time.

I was so focused on resisting the urge to magically smack him in the back that I nearly ran over Bethany waiting outside the door.

"Oh. Hey." Confused, I stared down at her. Had we agreed to meet up and I'd forgotten? It wouldn't be the first time I'd told her something then spaced out on it later. Why she never got angry was beyond me.

"Hi." Smiling, she tucked her hair behind her ear. "Um, I'm sorry to have to ask, but could you give me a ride home? My car won't start."

"Yeah, sure." A ride home was the least I could do for her after she'd helped me so much all summer, first in bringing my homework to me and prepping me for last year's final exams while I was in the hospital after my wreck, and then taking me to physical training sessions for weeks afterward. I couldn't even count the hours she'd spent cheering me through the sometimes painful recovery.

"Thanks." Her smile turned from embarrassed and hesitant to grateful.

We walked together through the coaches' lot to the parking lot by the sports and arts building where I'd started parking lately.

"Everyone else gone for the day already?" I asked just for something to say. Bethany never seemed to mind the frequent bouts of silence between us, but I did. Savannah and I had never had a problem finding stuff to talk about. The silences with Bethany were my fault. I didn't pay close enough attention to think up stuff to say.

"Yeah. Savannah's still here somewhere, though. I was going to try and find her if you were gone already."

My feet slowed like they had a mind of their own. I glanced toward the front parking lot partially visible between the cafeteria and math buildings. Sure enough, Sav's small primergray pickup truck was still there, the only vehicle in the lot's growing gloom. Which meant its owner was probably up on the third floor of the sports and arts building, locking up the dance rooms. Alone.

Unless Ron was with her…

At my truck now, I unlocked the driver's side door, tried to hit the electric button on the inside handle to unlock the passenger side for Bethany, then remembered. My new truck was actually an older used vehicle and didn't have quite the number of upgrades my previous one had, including power locks.

Sighing, I leaned across the single cab's bench-style seat and jerked up the lock so Bethany could get in. While she did, I glanced around us.

Ron's stupid black Mustang was already gone. Which meant Sav really was all alone on campus.

I shouldn't care anymore. She'd dumped me. Twice, even though I'd all but begged her not to. And she had a new boyfriend. I should let him worry about her now. She'd made it more than clear that I was the only one still hung up on the past.

Not to mention she was a vampire. They could handle themselves. Supposedly. Heck, she was practically the enemy now, one of the only monsters on the planet that I was supposed to fear.

All of that made for a long list of good reasons that I should drive out of here without a single look back.

Except I couldn't do it.

Cursing under my breath, I threw my door open.

"Tristan?"

Crap. I'd forgotten about Bethany. "Uh, I forgot something. Lock the doors. I'll be right back." I started the truck and turned on the heater. Then I headed back to the field house, taking my time and keeping one eye on the sports and arts building's foyer doors where Sav would have to exit when she left.

At the field house, I realized I didn't have a single reason to be there. So I pretended to look for something in my locker for a few minutes. Then I headed back, taking my time crossing through the back lot. At the corner of the girls' gym, I paused, feeling like an idiot, hands shoved inside my wool letterman jacket as the early evening steadily grew cooler now that the sun had finished setting.

Mercifully, I didn't have to wait long, as Sav emerged a couple of minutes later.

I took my time returning to my truck as Sav headed down the cement ramp that led away from the building's foyer doors. We had to be at least a hundred yards or more away from each other, the lot barely lit by a couple of lights. And yet she still looked right at me. She hesitated at the end of the ramp for a second, like she didn't know what to do. And even knowing she didn't care anymore couldn't stop my heart from taking off like a jackhammer.

Her hands fisted around the shoulder strap of her duffel bag as she turned in the opposite direction and walked across the grass past the math and cafeteria buildings.

I returned to my truck, and Bethany leaned over to unlock the door for me.

"Did you find it?" she asked as I slid in behind the wheel.

"Find what?" I put on my seat belt, fiddled with the heater and the radio. Finally, headlights shone from the front parking lot then swung away.

I shifted my truck into gear and followed those taillights at a distance.

"Whatever you were looking for. Did you find it?" Bethany patiently repeated.

"No, I didn't."

CHAPTER 21

SAVANNAH

The look on Tristan's face was burned into my mind. The memory of it kept flashing before me when I least expected it. He'd looked so…hurt. And angry.

I'd thought he had moved on. He'd been dating Bethany for months. How could he still be mad at me for making the right call and keeping him safe?

Maybe it was the fact that I was one of the few girls who had broken up with him, instead of the other way around. Maybe it was just his ego that was hurting and not his heart.

Whatever the reason for his anger, now that he'd figured out I could read his mind, he seemed bent on using it to punish me every chance he got.

By the second week of being loudly tortured by his never-ending variety of mental imagery, which ranged from memories of him and me together to memories of him with Bethany, I'd lost all sympathy for his side of the situation. He was acting like a spoiled brat. If he kept this crap up, I would have to call Emily and beg her to make me a memory confusion charm or whatever it was Tristan used against my gaze daze stalkers last year to keep them away from me.

And then if he ended up flunking English and getting benched from the football games because of it, well, that would serve him right for being such a horse's rear!

Worse, Bethany's car was still in the shop, so now I couldn't even escape seeing him at Charmers practice. Every morning and afternoon, there he was, the golden prince of Jacksonville, sweetly walking Bethany to and from the edge of the track that circled the practice field where the dancers practiced all football season when the weather allowed it. And on days when rain drove us inside to practice in the girls' gym in the basement level of the sports and arts building, Tristan was even closer, walking Bethany right up to the gym doorway just yards away from where I was setting up the sound system.

If he'd used the same torture strategy every time, maybe I could have learned to ignore him. But Tristan was diabolically creative. Knowing me as well as he did no doubt helped. He knew that just seeing Bethany hanging on his arm was enough to set my teeth on edge. So he saved the mental imagery for English class, and simply let me "listen" in on their conversations at Charmers practice.

I'd given up on ever getting the ink stains off my writing hand. I'd broken six pens in English class. Thankfully two of the perks of my vampire genes were speed-reading and a nearly photographic memory, so I could read from the textbook what I missed in the class lectures.

That didn't exactly help my steadily rising stress levels, though.

The week of Halloween, I decided to get smart about English class. On Tuesday, I started taking notes with a pencil instead. Every time Tristan's thoughts managed to make me lose control and break it, I simply used a sharpener I'd also brought so I could keep using the broken pieces to write with.

By the time class was nearly over, my pencil was down to only two inches. Which Tristan of course found vastly amusing.

Boy, you vamps really have anger management issues, he thought, lounging in his desk with his arms crossed over his chest and his long legs stretched out in front of him.

If only the ESP was a two-way thing, the piece of my mind that I would give him...

Do y'all have a group for that? he thought, one corner of his full lips kicking up. *A vampire therapist could make some serious dough teaching that. If he survived the sessions with his clients, that is.*

Okay, now that made me smile a little. Maybe that was a good career option for me. Vampire therapist, specializing in anger management issues. If I could learn to control my own temper first, that is.

How would a vampire therapist go about advertising her services? Probably by word of mouth. Maybe I could take referrals from the council, offer counseling to help rehab rogue vamps who lost their cool in public...

Of course, maybe I should sign up for a few sessions myself, he thought, the words quieter now in his mind. Was he still "talking" to me? *Man, the other day when I learned about you and Ron, I wanted to...* The words faded away, replaced by vivid images of Tristan pummeling the crap out of Ron's face.

I didn't know what was more shocking...that he thought Ron and I were dating and was upset about it, or how quickly my own fury rose up and out of control.

"Do it and I'll—" I snarled, leaning over the armrest of my desktop, my nails digging into the wood.

"You'll what?" Tristan murmured, barely turning his head

to look at me with raised eyebrows. *What would you do to pro-tect your precious boy toy?*

Someone was grabbing my shoulders from behind, but I couldn't see them. All I could see was the way Tristan's eyes crackled with heat like twin emeralds held before a roaring fireplace. Eyes I wanted to poke out right now.

"Savannah, chill out," someone murmured against my ear. Ron leaning across the aisle at my left. But that wasn't what finally brought me back to earth. Nor was it Mrs. Knowles standing at my side, also demanding that I calm down.

It was the two fangs pricking at the inside of my lower lip. That sensation alone sent a cold wash of fear cascading down my entire body, effectively drowning the fury. And right on its heels came the stupid tears to fill and burn my eyes like poison my body refused to process. They spilled out and down my cheeks faster than I could wipe them away with my hands.

Furious embarrassment over crying in front of Tristan only made the tears fall faster.

"Why don't you take a bathroom break and cool off," Mrs. Knowles said, her tone making it more an order than a sug-gestion.

My fangs still hadn't retracted, so I opted for nodding si-lently and making the fastest exit I could while still hopefully appearing human.

In the restroom, I used toilet paper to mop up the mascara tracks on my face. Then I just stood there gripping the edges of the porcelain sink.

How did Tristan do this to me? Nobody on this planet could make me laugh or cry as easily as he could. One minute he had me trying not to burst out in laughter during class. The next second, I was ready to choke him with my bare hands! Even Dylan and the Brat Twins couldn't drive me as crazy as Tristan could.

Which made me wonder if the evil trio would soon be back in business, too. Other than the blood on my locker, they hadn't bothered me in quite a while. Were they tired of messing with me? Had their parents told them to leave me alone?

Maybe they knew Tristan had taken up their cause for them.

If so, they couldn't have chosen better. No matter how I tried to steel myself against him, Tristan kept finding ways to get around my defenses.

And what was with all the references to "me and Ron" and Ron being my "boy toy"? He was acting like he thought Ron and I were dating or something.

Even if Ron and I had been dating, why would Tristan care?

He had Bethany now, and it was clear to every single person on this campus that she was beyond in love with him. Why couldn't he just be happy with her and stop punishing me already? We'd broken up months ago. And obviously he didn't love me anymore, judging by the way he seemed bound and determined to make me miserable.

Whatever the reason behind his attitude, the torture had to stop. My showing fangs in class definitely wouldn't make the vamp council or the Clann happy. If Tristan kept pushing me like this, either I would have to use a spell on him or I'd have to start homeschooling. I couldn't take much more.

I waited till the dismissal bell rang then returned to English class, expecting the room to be empty. It wasn't. Both Ron and Tristan were waiting for me.

"Sorry, Sav," Tristan muttered. He was standing in the aisle between our desks, leaning forward, his hands braced on the backs of our chairs. He wouldn't look at me. And I couldn't hear his thoughts for a change.

My fangs had retracted in the restroom. Still, I thought it was a good idea to stick with a short nod before I gathered up my books and bag and left with Ron. If I spoke one word to Tristan right now, I was pretty sure it wouldn't be anything nice.

Grateful that it was a tutorial day, I retreated to the sanctuary of the library with Ron. My hands shook as I flipped through the English lit textbook, my eyes unable to focus enough to make sense of the words running across the pages.

Tristan had gone way too far this time. His fighting Dylan and Greg had made at least a little sense each time. But to want to hit Ron just because Tristan thought I was dating him?

And where had he gotten that idea anyway? Everyone else knew Ron and I were just friends, nothing more. Couldn't Tristan be bothered to ask around instead of jumping to conclusions? Heck, he might as well be jealous of Anne, Carrie and Michelle while he was at it!

The whole thing was ridiculous. Tristan was being completely unreasonable.

"Want to talk about it?" Ron asked, making me jump.

"About what?"

"Oh, I don't know. How about whatever Tristan thought back there to make you lose it like that in class?"

"It's… Hang on, what do you mean, 'whatever Tristan *thought?*'"

"It's rumored that descendants can still hear each others' thoughts. Since he didn't say anything out loud today, I assumed you two must be doing the ESP thing instead."

My eyes narrowed. "How do you know so much about descendants?"

Ron shrugged. "I grew up hearing stories about them. Everyone in my family did."

Just what the heck were they discussing in his mother's genealogical society meetings?

"I'm pretty sure I'm not supposed to talk about Clann abilities to an outsider," I mumbled, feeling awkward now.

He leaned forward and grinned. "But you *can* hear his thoughts, right?"

In the background, I heard his mother at the front desk, her voice rising enough to carry down the entire length of the library. Whoever she was on the phone with was getting an earful.

"What's up with your mom?"

"Aw, she's just ticked off 'cause some punks broke into the genealogical society office and trashed the place."

"Whoa. How bad was it?"

"They busted the locks off the filing cabinets and threw a bunch of paperwork all over the place. Probably bored and stupid with nothing better to do. Don't worry, she'll get over it once she gets tired of hearing the detectives tell her there're no new clues to follow."

Though beautiful, Jacksonville was a little short on teen-aged entertainment, other than the movie theater and annual festivals and rodeo. For an average weekend when nothing was on the local calendar, most people drove the half hour to Tyler or even farther to Dallas or Houston.

Still, who would want to break into a genealogical society's office?

"Now quit avoiding the subject," Ron said. "That's why you went berserk today, isn't it? Because you can read Tristan's mind. He's been driving you nuts with his thoughts, hasn't he?"

Ugh. Ron had a pit bull's gleam in his eyes. He wasn't going to let this go.

I sighed, exhausted by all the secrets everyone expected me to keep. "Yes, I can. And yes, he's driving me insane. When he's not drudging up our past, he's picturing making out with Bethany."

"What a jerk."

The overly sympathetic tone made me smile. "Yeah, lately he is."

I glanced down at the textbook, realized it was turned to completely the wrong lesson, and found the right page. "What did you say to him after I left today? He was awfully quick to apologize when I got back."

His face became the image of innocence. "Nothing."

I grinned. "Yeah, right. What'd you do, threaten to beat him up or something?"

Now there was a fight I definitely wouldn't want to see. Both guys were around the six-foot mark in height, both broad-shouldered, muscular and fast from all their football training. They were evenly matched physically. The only way Tristan could gain the upper hand in a fight with Ron was to resort to magic.

Before today, I would have said Tristan would never stoop that low in a fight with someone who wasn't a descendant. But after today, I had to wonder.

"No, I swear, we didn't say a word to each other," Ron said. I stared at him, but he didn't blink. "Maybe he just felt bad about making you cry."

My throat tightened, making my voice come out raspy. "He hasn't done that in a long, long time."

Ron reached across the table and patted my shoulder. "Want me to beat him up for you?"

A laugh burst out of me. "I made that same offer to Anne about you."

His eyebrows shot up. "I take it she turned you down?"

Smiling, I went back to reading the lesson I'd missed this morning. "Maybe she didn't. Maybe she requested a surprise attack."

He snorted. "I wouldn't put it past her. When that girl gets ticked off…"

"Yeah, she's a true warrior. Get her mad enough and she'll fight just about anybody who's doing wrong in her eyes."

"Which is how I know she'd never ask you to try and beat me up for her."

I laughed. "Of course not. She'd rather do it herself."

CHAPTER 22

TRISTAN

I'd made Savannah cry today.

I'd seen her close to tears before, and red-eyed and red-nosed from crying about Greg Stanwick once just before their breakup. I'd seen her kneeling in the rain as her grandma died, and the drops running down her face probably had been a mixture of rain and tears.

But today, there hadn't been a shred of doubt about what had happened in English lit. Savannah had burst into tears. Because of me.

Which made me the biggest jerk in East Texas.

What was wrong with me lately? I was just so dang ticked off all the time! And nothing seemed to make it go away, not even playing football.

"Tristan?"

"Hmm?" I answered out of habit.

"Have you heard a word I've said?" Bethany's tone finally got my attention. She actually sounded a little irritated.

"Oh. Sorry. What'd you say?"

She said something about costumes.

"Great," I murmured.

Was Ron hugging Savannah now, even kissing her in the library to comfort her? Probably. At least, that's what I would have done. She sure as heck wasn't here in the cafeteria. Where would she be if not in the library with him?

Bethany was rattling on about costumes for the dance, which I'd agreed to take her to. She'd complained about not having a date, and offering to take her had seemed the friendly thing to do.

Last year, Savannah and I had spent days trying to choose costumes that would secretly match each other, teasing and tormenting each other in the process. It was during one of those costume tryouts that I'd first blurted out *I love you*. Man, I'd been a nervous wreck for a couple of minutes, waiting for her reaction.

And then she'd said those three little words back, looking up at me with that sweet, beautiful smile of hers....

A pause. The silence made me glance at Bethany. She was glaring at me.

"What?" I asked.

"I said that I had our costumes overnighted. So when yours arrives today or tomorrow, could you please remember to try it on and let me know if it fits?"

"Sure," I agreed, taking a long chug of soda.

I glanced across the cafeteria to where Savannah should be sitting with her friends. The empty seat beside Anne was like a punch to the gut.

Anne was laughing about something with the other girls at their table. Must be nice to be that clueless.

How could Anne not know what was going on between her best friend and her ex?

Bethany said something about a game.

"What about the game?" I muttered, staring at that empty seat across the cafeteria.

Bethany huffed, which finally got my attention. I gave her a sheepish smile and she calmed down.

"I asked you if we're still on for you to give me a ride home after the game this Friday," she said.

"Oh. Sure." It was an away game this week, Pine Tree maybe. Whoever it was, we'd have to ride the buses with our teams back to the campus. But from there, Bethany would need a ride home, which I must have offered her at some point earlier in the week.

The bell rang. She smiled and gave me a peck on the cheek goodbye before racing off for her next class.

I walked more slowly to mine. Would it be wrong of me to put an anti-love spell on Sav to make her forget about Ron? Dating him was obviously a sign that she'd lost her mind. Maybe if I broke them up before Anne found out, I could save Sav and Anne's friendship.

I entered the main hall and blew out a long breath. No, I'd better stay out of her mess of a love life. If she wanted to turn all self-destructive with her friendships, there wasn't much I could do about it.

SAVANNAH

Usually I could write off the feeling that everyone was watching me as vampire paranoia. But Wednesday morning at Charmers practice and then again in second period chemistry class, everyone really did seem to be staring at me and whispering. Apparently the grapevine had caught word of my blowup in English lit yesterday. Which meant I would have to work extra hard to tune out everyone for the next few days.

During chem lab, Ron leaned over and murmured, "Is it just me, or does it seem like everyone's talking about us today?"

I shook my head, my jaw clenched. "It's not you. I think they heard about yesterday."

His eyebrows shot up. "And they care because…?"

"Anything having to do with you-know-who seems to interest them. Because obviously they need to *get a life*." Anger made those last words come out a little louder than I'd intended.

Someone giggled, and the whispers ratcheted up another notch, making me want to cover my ears with my hands. But that would probably only fuel the gossip even more.

Sighing, I said, "Just ignore them. Now what are we not supposed to blow up in here today?"

By the end of Charmers practice, I was exhausted. It had taken way too much energy to block out thoughts, thanks to the little scene Tristan and I had enacted yesterday in English lit.

I trudged across the parking lot, my Charmers duffel bag banging against my hip hard enough to make my bones rattle, only to discover a very unwelcome visitor waiting for me at my truck.

"Get lost, Williams," I said as I unlocked the driver's side door and tossed in my duffel bag so I wouldn't be tempted to hit Dylan over the head with it instead. I was so not in the mood to deal with him today. And I really didn't appreciate the way he was leaning against my truck as if he owned it.

"Heard about you and Tristan in English yesterday." Rolling off my truck, Dylan tossed his long blond bangs out of his eyes and moved closer to me.

I refused to move back, even though he was definitely in my space now. "Give me a break, Dylan. We were fighting, not getting back together."

"Really? Because what I heard was that you two were creating sparks hot enough to set off a bonfire."

I sighed, and it felt like the last remaining drop of my energy seeped out with it. "What do you want from me? I broke up with him months ago, and we're not going to get back together."

I want you.

I blinked fast several times, sure I'd heard his thought wrong.

He hesitated before replying. "I'm here to warn you. Don't think the Clann's stopped watching you, because we haven't. We know that Tristan's coming around the Charmers practices again. And we know about your ability to lure victims in with those freaky eyes of yours." I noticed he was extra careful not to make eye contact with me, his gaze hovering somewhere in the vicinity of my mouth instead.

His fear of being gaze dazed would have been amusing if his warning wasn't so dang annoying. "Well, if you're really doing such a good job as the Clann's little spy, then you should already know that the only reason Tristan's at Charmers practices lately is to pick up and drop off Bethany Brookes."

"Maybe. Or maybe that's just an excuse to see you again."

The door between us groaned, and I realized I needed to ease up on my grip. "Or maybe *you're* just paranoid and delusional. Tristan hates me now thanks to you and your stupid Clann."

The corners of his mouth twitched. "Do you really expect any of us to believe that scene you two clearly staged?"

Now he was just boring me. "This argument's getting old. I'm going home now, Williams. Nice chatting with you again, as always." I slid behind the wheel of my truck.

He smiled, peering at me through his bangs. "Have a safe trip home." Turning away, he strolled toward the back parking lot, where I could only hope someone would run over him with their car.

Seconds later, a black muscle car came tearing around from the back parking lot. It screeched to a halt beside me, sliding a bit on the asphalt. The driver's side window was already rolled down, revealing a panicked-looking Ron.

"Hey, are you okay?" he asked as he threw the car into Park and got out.

"Uh, yeah, why?" I could not wait to get home. I was going to take the longest, hottest shower on the planet, put on my softest, comfiest nightgown, maybe do some homework in bed, and then sleep like the dead.

I slid the key into the ignition.

"I heard Dylan was going to do something to make sure you and Tristan weren't working out your issues, or something like that."

I waved a hand in the air. "I'm fine."

Then I turned the key to start my truck.

Nothing. Not even the stutter of a dead battery. I tried again, then rested my forehead against the wheel. "Great. Now my truck won't start."

"Pop the hood."

I pulled the release for the hood. It popped up a couple of inches, and Ron hit the catch underneath to raise it the rest of the way. I was tempted to get out and look for myself, but I was exhausted and it would be wasted effort anyways. I didn't know the first thing about engines.

"Uh, I think I see the problem," Ron said.

"Yeah? Is it fixable with some duct tape and baling wire?" Anne was always joking about the southern male's top two tools of choice.

"Even a mechanic with a shop full of tools couldn't fix your truck, at least not without a heck of a lot of replacement parts. Come and see for yourself."

Sighing, I got out of the truck. As soon as I got within sight of the exposed engine, I could see the problem, too.

My engine was a colorful rainbow of melted red, blue, white and green everywhere. "Uh, is that normal? Because I don't remember it looking this...rainbowlicious the last time Dad and I took it in for an oil change."

"No, this is definitely not normal. All the wiring has been melted."

Huh? In October? Even East Texas wasn't *that* hot in the fall.

"Now how the heck did that..." Oh. Of course. My stomach sank. "Dylan."

"Yep, probably so. Looks like he melted every wire in your truck."

I sniffed the air, realizing it smelled pretty awful, too. I'd been too tired and focused on getting rid of Dylan to notice it earlier.

"Come on, I'll give you a ride home." Ron folded down the rod and let the hood drop with a crash that made me jump. "I hate to say it, but you're probably going to need a new vehicle."

"Seriously?" It came out as a squeak. "Can't the wiring be replaced?"

"Well, I guess it could. But I help out at my uncle's shop in Palestine on weekends sometimes, and for something like this, he'd usually say it would cost more to put in a whole new electrical system than it would to just buy another used car. Especially this one." He glanced at me. "No offense."

"None taken. My parents got it for me last year for my sixteenth birthday. Mom couldn't afford much, and she wouldn't let Dad spend much on it, either."

But it had been a good little truck, dependable, always starting rain or shine. It had never once had a problem. Until Dylan murdered it.

Teeth clenched, I leaned across the seat, grabbed my bags, then shut the door. As I got into the front passenger seat of Ron's car, I tried not to stare at my destroyed truck. But as we pulled away, I couldn't help but watch it shrink from view in the side mirror.

"I can't believe he did that," I said as Ron navigated us through the neighborhoods that bordered the JHS campus. "How did you know what Dylan was planning?"

"I didn't. I mean, I didn't know exactly what he was going to do, just that he was going to do something. I'm sorry I didn't get there in time. Coach Parker made me run lines because I wasn't paying enough attention in practice. Otherwise I would've gotten there sooner, maybe early enough to stop him. Did he do anything else?" He gave me a nervous sideways glance.

"No, just harassed me with some paranoid crap about my trying to get back with Tristan."

And I was going to try and forget the part where I thought I heard him think that he wanted me. Just the idea made me shudder.

"So, where to?" he asked a few minutes later.

"Home," I said on a sigh.

I gave him directions, then leaned my head back and closed my eyes.

A few minutes later, I felt the car jerk to a stop.

"Looks like someone's having a party," Ron muttered.

I raised my head and opened my eyes. My driveway was filled with familiar cars and trucks and one large RV. Not only had my mom come to visit for the first time, but it looked like Anne, Carrie and Michelle had all decided to stop by my house for the first time ever, too. What the heck?

And then it clicked. "Oh my lord. I actually forgot my own birthday."

"It's your birthday today?" Ron asked, his eyebrows raised.

I nodded. With all the chaos and mess going on, I'd completely forgotten what day of the month today was. As of 4:22 p.m. this afternoon, I was seventeen.

And apparently everyone had decided to throw me a party.

My first reaction was, *Awww, that's so sweet of them!* I'd never had a surprise birthday party before.

And then I felt the tightness in my shoulders and neck and realized how dog-tired I was. After battling not to hear the riled-up grapevine's thoughts about me and Tristan all day, on top of the dead truck, all I wanted was to crawl up the stairs to my room and fall into bed. Trying to force a smile and act happy for a whole bunch of people was the *last* thing I felt like doing. Everyone inside that house genuinely cared about me. They always knew in an instant when I faked a smile. They were all the people in my life whom I loved and cared about, the ones I didn't want to hurt or upset.

And no matter how tired I was, how little I felt like being at a party right now, this was my house and I wouldn't be able to make my apologies and escape early like I might have if this were a public place.

On top of that, my mom and dad would be in the same room together again for the first time since Nanna's death, which would be awkward as always while they less-than-subtly forced themselves to be polite and get along with each other for their daughter's sake.

And it would be my first birthday without Nanna around.

"Well, hey, happy birthday!"

"Thanks. And thanks for the ride home." I opened the passenger door, started to get out, then froze with one foot on the curb. Ron was my friend now, too. He would be hurt if I didn't invite him in.

But Anne was in there, and she definitely wouldn't be happy to be stuck at a party with Ron.

Oh please stake me now.

Anne might take care of that for me later after she saw who I'd just brought home.

"Want to come inside? I'm sure there will be plenty of cake and pizza to go around." I looked back over my shoulder.

He was staring at her truck. "I probably shouldn't."

I took a deep breath. "Yeah, you should. Anne can get over it. She told me she broke up with you and you didn't really do anything wrong. She knows we're friends. And it's *my* birthday, not hers. I should be allowed to have all my friends at my own dang party."

Ron blinked a few times, eyebrows raised. "Well, since you put it like that."

We both got out of the car and headed across the lawn for the porch.

At the front door, I paused, took a deep breath to brace myself for the next few hours, plastered on a smile and checked my reflection in the stained glass. Party mask in place? Check.

"Here we go," I muttered. Then I opened the door to an explosion of "happy birthday!" and hooting on party horns.

Someone hit the play button on the stereo's remote in the newly refinished living room to our left, cuing the beginning drumbeat of "We Are Young."

"You guys!" I shouted over the sound, my smile a little easier to hold in place. "Aww, you shouldn't have!"

Anne was tooting on a horn when she saw Ron enter the

foyer after me. She stared at him, her horn blast dying away like the air escaping an inflated, untied balloon set free.

"I had a little car trouble," I explained to everyone. "Ron was nice enough to give me a ride home."

Sorry, I silently mouthed to Anne when her gaze finally darted back to me.

She looked at him again. Then her chin rose. "Well, that sucks. About your truck, I mean. But hey, we've got cake and presents, so it's all good, right?"

"You poor baby," Mom said, squeezing through the tightly packed foyer until she'd reached my side for a hug. "And on your birthday, too!"

Thank you, I mouthed to Anne as Mom dragged me past my friends and dad to the kitchen, which had been decorated with huge draping swoops of curled crepe paper, hologram foil Happy Birthday banners, and balloons taped to every vertical surface imaginable, including the brand-new cabinets' handles.

In the center of the built-in banquet, which Dad had custom built to fit in the corner of the now-cavernous kitchen, sat the strangest birthday cake I'd ever seen. If you could even call it a cake.

Mom used a long fireplace lighter to light its precariously placed candles, which were in the shape of a one and a seven and in true danger of falling off the back side.

"It's a fruit Jell-O mold!" Michelle said with a grin, her hands waving artfully around the wiggling, whip-cream-frosted mass as if she were a game show girl displaying a prize.

I looked at Michelle, unable to stop a blank face of confusion from forming. Fruit Jell-O?

"You know, since you liked the fruit dessert at Anne's party," Michelle added, her eyebrows pinching with worry.

Standing behind her, Anne and Carrie both pointed silent fingers at Michelle's back. Anne mouthed, "Sorry, we couldn't stop her."

I had to press my lips together to stop a laugh from slipping out so Michelle wouldn't think I was laughing at her. When the urge had safely passed, I gave Michelle the first fully genuine smile I'd managed to make all day. "Thank you so much. This is brilliant!"

Even if I still couldn't eat it, just the idea that Michelle cared enough to try and make a unique cake I might like brought quick tears to my eyes.

"Aww, don't cry, Sav." Michelle circled the table to give me a sideways squeeze. "I promise it only took me like an hour last night to make it. But we should probably sing Happy Birthday quick before the heat of the candles melts it."

Everyone took that as their cue to start singing at the top of their lungs.

Standing in the back corner of the room by the kitchen cabinets, Dad watched me with a funny twitching smile, as if trying not to laugh. I didn't want to see the humor in this mess of a birthday party for a half vamp who probably couldn't even age. But laughter bubbled up out of me all the same.

Maybe a party was what I needed after all.

When the song ended, Michelle said, "Hurry, make a wish!"

And that's when the brief moment of happiness came sinking back down.

I knew exactly what I wanted.

I wanted to be with Tristan again, but for it to be okay. To be openly dating him, no secrecy or hiding how we felt. Walking together in the halls between classes. Holding hands. Kissing in public. Going out to eat together without cowering in a corner booth and praying the entire time that no one would recognize us.

And I wanted Nanna to be alive again.

I couldn't have any of that. So what was the point in wishing for it?

Closing my eyes, I blew out the candles without making any wish at all.

CHAPTER 23

Mom dished up bowls of the Jell-O "cake" to everyone. She made my portion half the size of everyone else's, sneaking me a knowing smile and a wink as she set it on the table before me.

"Ready for your presents, birthday girl?" she said.

Michelle and Carrie jumped up and started passing me gifts. Usually I liked to take my time opening presents, enjoying the suspense. But this time I ripped through the packages, pretending to be too busy opening them to eat. The mound of gift wrap grew before me, covering my untouched bowl, which Mom carefully made sure to take away along with the paper later and sneak into the trash.

Dad's creative excuse for not eating was that he'd eaten earlier and was still full. He kept busy by taking photos of the entire event with Mom's camera, which I later realized also gave him the perfect excuse to avoid appearing in any of the photos.

Maybe I should have been taking notes. Watching him at this event was like sitting in on a demonstration in Sneaky Vampire 101.

I could tell from everyone's thoughts that Dad had already given Mom and the girls a tour of the place before my arrival. They were bowled over by how much nicer the house was compared to their expectations. Anne had told Carrie and Michelle that she'd nearly gotten into a fight with her mother just to get permission to enter the "lead-filled rat's nest" tonight. Now they were all having the opposite problem, trying not to show how intimidated they were by Dad's newest showcase while worrying that I'd become too rich to want to hang out with them anymore.

I tried not to laugh out loud, but it took some real effort. If they only knew how much I feared they wouldn't want to be my friend anymore because of my family secrets...

To help set them at ease, after the presents, I talked Michelle, Carrie, and Mom into joining me in the newly refinished parlor to sing on the karaoke machine Michelle had brought over. We went through several songs from our favorite movie and TV soundtracks, as well as my favorite, "Raise Your Glass," which I threw myself into at the top of my totally untalented lungs. Like riding four-wheelers at Anne's party, it was a much-needed chance to forget myself for a while, and it helped everyone else relax and loosen up.

Well, everyone but my dad, Anne and Ron, that is.

At some point, Mom left to join Dad in cleaning up the kitchen, and I noticed Anne and Ron were missing. Movement outside the parlor windows drew my eye to the front porch. They were out there talking, the streetlights turning them into featureless silhouettes as Ron braced his hands against the front railing and Anne paced. Unfortunately the windows and front door were all closed, blocking me from hearing their voices or their thoughts.

What was going on? Were they finally working through their issues?

Part of me wanted to go outside, see if they needed a mediator. Especially with Anne's hotheaded temper.

"Oooh, let's do this one!" Michelle jabbed a finger at the back of a CD case in Carrie's hand.

"What do you say?" Carrie asked, turning to me with a smile. "Ready for one last number before we have to leave?"

"Leave?" Michelle whined. "But…"

Carrie held up a hand. "Don't even start! You know I've got to study for that test, and you promised you'd help me with the flash cards."

Grumbling, Michelle bent over to start the new song.

This time, I had to force myself to go through the motions of singing with them. Halfway through the song, the shadows at the window disappeared, and seconds later Anne and Ron came back inside, Ron staying back to shut the door.

"What's up?" I whispered to her.

She shook her head, her lips pressed together, her arms hugging herself for either warmth or comfort. She entered the parlor but didn't join us at the karaoke machine, choosing to flop into an armchair by the window across from us instead.

Ron hovered in the parlor's arched doorway, leaning against the shiny white molding with the worst frown I'd ever seen on his face.

I focused on Anne's thoughts. She was already replaying the tail end of the conversation and regretting it.

You can't be serious! she'd snapped at him then instantly wished she'd said it in a nicer tone. *Savannah doesn't need to know this stuff any more than I did.*

Well, my parents and I all think you're wrong, Miss Know It All, he'd said. *They gave me permission to tell her. And I think it would help her feel a lot better about herself.*

And just when and where do you plan on springing this crap on her?

I don't know. Maybe tomorrow where I always go? Why?

So I know when to expect her totally ticked off phone call, of course!

Anne… He'd reached out to her, touched her bare arm, made her shiver before she'd turned away from both his touch and that yearning in his voice.

Just stop. It's never going to work between us, and you know it. I was never the right girl for you. You should…you should be with someone like you. One of your own kind.

And though Anne hadn't said it out loud to him, she'd thought to herself, *someone who isn't so plain and boring and hopelessly clueless about all of this stuff. Someone who could possibly be interesting enough to keep you from getting bored with her.*

And that's when she'd headed inside with Ron on her heels.

Oh Anne, I thought, shaking my head and wishing I could admit I'd heard her thoughts so I could cross the room and give the both of them a hug.

Why were they so determined to be stubborn?

And what the heck was Ron planning on telling me that worried Anne so much?

Ron slipped away to the kitchen. I heard him murmuring something to my mom, but they were too far away for me to pick up their thoughts.

"Okay, that's it, pack it up," Carrie ordered Michelle when the song ended a few seconds later. "Study time."

Grumbling, Michelle took the CD out of the karaoke machine and returned it to its case.

The machine seemed heavy, judging by the grunt Carrie made when she tried to lift it by its handle. Smiling, I said, "Here, let me. You guys get the CDs and the mike."

Carrie rolled up the microphone's cord while Michelle collected the CDs. Then we lugged our respective loads toward the foyer.

"Don't mind us doing all the heavy lifting here," Carrie called out to Anne as we passed her.

Lost in thought, Anne muttered, "Okay."

Carrie, Michelle and I looked at each other, eyebrows raised, then continued on through the foyer and out to Michelle's car. I thanked them for everything, watched them leave, then headed back inside just as Ron was leaving the kitchen.

"See you tomorrow," he murmured to me while glancing through the parlor doorway at Anne. "And, uh, happy birthday."

"Thanks. Bye."

Rubbing the back of his neck, he left through the front door.

Anne twisted in her chair in time to watch him through the window. I waited till the throaty rumble of his car had faded away before saying her name.

She jerked back to face me with a scowl. "Crap, you scared the crap out of me!"

"Well, crap, sorry about that," I teased, hands on my hips. "And sorry about the unexpected guest."

She shrugged one shoulder, her fingers drumming on the arm of the chair. "It's fine. Sooner or later we would have been stuck in the same room together anyways."

"Are you okay?" I murmured.

"Sure," she answered automatically. "Why wouldn't I be?"

I didn't have to read her mind again to know that was a lie. But I didn't press her.

After a minute of silence, she sighed and seemed to realize where she was again. "Hey, where'd Carrie and Michelle go?"

"They left to go study for Carrie's next big test."

She frowned. "Oh. Guess I didn't hear them leave." She rolled up to her feet. "Well, happy birthday."

"Thanks."

I walked with her to the front door. She paused at the

threshold, turning back with her mouth parted as if to say something.

"Yes?" I prompted her. She looked like a robot that had run out of batteries.

"Um, nothing. G'night. See you tomorrow." With a little wave over her shoulder that reminded me of Ron, she slowly walked out to her truck.

Several minutes after she'd climbed into the cab, Anne's truck finally backed out of the driveway into the street, the back right tire running up over the curb before she pulled forward toward her home.

Wow. That was the most distracted I'd ever seen her. Whatever was going on between her and Ron was really messing with Anne's mind.

Blowing out a long and loud breath, I went back inside the house to see what emotional destruction my parents might be wreaking upon each other in the kitchen.

They were sitting at the banquet opposite each other. And they looked…peaceful.

It was way more shocking than if I had walked in on Mom throwing plates at Dad again.

"Er, what's up?" I asked them, searching Mom's face then Dad's, unsure I dared to go a step further and check their thoughts. I might not like whatever I'd find there.

"Hmm?" Mom asked. "Oh, nothing dear. Just reminiscing about the day you were born."

Dad smiled. "You were so beautiful, so…"

"Amazing," they both said at the same time, then grinned at each other.

Okay. "That's…nice. Um, Mom, shouldn't you be…?" I jerked my head in the direction of her RV.

"Oh! Right. That reminds me, we have one more present for you!"

A creak of the front door was our only warning before we heard Gowin call out from the foyer, "Hey, did I miss the party?"

Dad and I exchanged horrified looks.

"Mom, you should go," I hissed. "Out the back. Quick!"

Too late. Footsteps announced Gowin's arrival in the kitchen. I turned to face him, my heart hammering like mad in my chest.

Two vamps, one half vamp, and a descendant all in a room that suddenly felt way too small.

It was like the beginning of a bad joke. Unfortunately, this was no laughing matter.

"Oh, I interrupted a family moment!" Gowin rocked back on his heels, fidgeting with a silver-and-pink-wrapped present he'd brought in. "My apologies. I just wanted to drop this off for Savannah."

He held out the present, staying where he was in the doorway.

I crossed the room to him and put on a smile. "Thanks. You shouldn't have."

He shot me a quick grin. "It's the latest tablet. I figured you could use it for doing homework or tweeting or something."

"Oh. Great! Thanks." I sounded like an idiot. Or a cheerleader robot. But it was all I could do not to throw myself in front of my mother for protection. Not that doing any such thing would save her if Gowin lost control.

Mom rose to her feet. "Wow. That was very generous of you," she murmured as she crossed the room with her right hand extended. "I'm Joan Evans, Savannah's mother. You must be…"

Oh geez, she had to be Miss Manners *now*?

Visions of Gowin lunging for Mom's throat, followed by Dad either trying to fight him off or else joining in on the bloodbath, robbed me of the ability to breathe. Mom couldn't do magic, so she'd be completely vulnerable. And even if Dad tried to step in and save Mom, Gowin could simply order him to stop and Dad would be helpless not to obey the older vamp's command. Which would leave one wimpy half vamp with only minimal magic skills as Mom's sole protector.

Dad was at her side in the same instant Gowin accepted her hand between both of his. "This is Gowin. My sire, and currently a council member."

Mom froze. "Oh! Uh…it's nice to meet you, Gowin."

"I have heard so much about you," Gowin said, his voice soft and low.

Was that the faintest bit of a wolfish gleam in his eyes, or was it my imagination?

Gowin turned to me, but I noticed he still held Mom's hand captive between his. "I thought I might be still early for the party since your truck isn't outside. Did your father gift you with a new car?"

"Um, not exactly," I said. "My truck died. My friend took a look at the engine and said the electrical system is fried. He had to give me a ride home."

Gowin made a face. "Now that stinks. And on your birthday, too."

Mom smiled, but it looked a good deal less warm this time. "That's what I told her earlier. Well, no worries, I'm sure your father can have it towed to a repair shop tomorrow."

"Or to a junkyard," Dad muttered.

Mom scowled. "Don't start, Michael. It's a perfectly decent first vehicle for any teen."

"It was a rust bucket long overdue for retirement," Dad replied. "And I for one am glad its life span has finally reached its conclusion. It makes the perfect opportunity to get her a proper vehicle. Perhaps one of her own choosing this time?"

"That is so like you," Mom snapped. "Why fix something perfectly good when you can simply throw it away?"

Dad stared at her. "I believe that is more your usual method, actually."

Silence filled the room as Mom's face turned bright red and she glared at him. I was blocking all three of their thoughts as hard as I could right now.

After a long moment, she said, "Fine. You're in charge now. Do whatever you want. But no motorcycles. At least give me that much. She doesn't have a license for them. And she's only seventeen."

Dad nodded as formally as if this were some kind of major vamp/Clann negotiation. "Agreed. No motorcycles."

I took a deep breath then let it out slowly. And my friends wondered why I didn't want my parents to get back together. If I had to deal with this kind of crap on a daily basis, I'd have to run away from home!

I cleared my throat. "Um, thanks for the gift, Gowin. Mom was just headed out. She has to get on the road for a sales meeting early in the morning. Right, Mom?"

She glanced at me, then Gowin, then my dad. "Right. Sav, will you come with me for that one last present I promised? It's in the RV."

"Sure!" I tried not to wince at how overly bright and chirpy that came out.

"It was a pleasure to meet you." Gowin gave my mother's hand a quick squeeze then released it. Finally! I thought he was going to chop it off and keep it as a souvenir or something.

"And the same to you," she said. She looked at Dad, and a wave of sadness and regret projected from her to add its weight to my shoulders. "Good to see you again, Michael."

"You, too," Dad murmured, his eyes warm. Then he stepped aside so we could pass between him and Gowin.

As Mom and I headed for the foyer, I glanced back at the kitchen. The vamps were still facing off in the doorway. Were they about to fight like territorial animals?

My rising panic allowed the vamps' thoughts to slip through.

Still in love with what you can't have, old friend? Gowin thought with a smile and a shake of his head. *You always were a bit of a masochist.*

Dad sighed. *Do not worry, I have learned my lesson amply. I will not risk giving in to the bloodlust around Joan. And with her mother gone and all traces of her bloodlust dampening spell along with her...*

Mmm, Gowin thought in sympathetic regret. *Such a loss, that one.*

I hustled Mom out the front door and down the porch steps.

As Mom stepped onto the lawn, she hesitated, and I caught her thought. *I'm in the dark alone with a new vamp and no protective charms.*

I froze, glad she couldn't read my mind or see my face as the hurt from her fear slammed through me.

No, she decided a second later. *She is my daughter, Michael said she has good control, and I will trust them both.*

She continued across the lawn and up the steps of her camper trailer, pausing at the door to look back at me in confusion. "You coming, kiddo?"

Smiling, I made sure I walked human-slow across the lawn to join her.

As soon as we entered the RV, I heard the yapping. "Is that...a dog?"

Mom's face turned mischievous. "That, sweetie, is the surprise." She hurried past the wall containing an electric fireplace and flat screen TV combo to the master bedroom, scooping up a furry brown-and-black miniature missile as it attempted to career past her feet toward me. "Meet Lucy, your birthday gift!"

The dog wouldn't stop barking. I worried Mom's arms were in danger while holding it, but the thing seemed to want to eat only me for now. "Wow. You, um, shouldn't have."

Mom grinned down at the dog, stroking the long glossy hair at the back of its head. In an apparent attempt to make the thing cute, a pink-and-brown polka-dotted bow held up a tuft of hair between its pointy ears. The bow was now in danger of falling off due to the energy the dog was throwing into its every bark.

"She just needs to get used to you," Mom said, raising her voice to be heard over the barking. "She's usually a real sweetheart! Your dad and I went halvsies on the fee for her, but I picked her out myself at the breeders'. She's a purebred Yorkie."

More like a purebred demon spawn from Hell. "That's great."

"Want to hold her?"

Which was like saying Do you want to have your fingers chewed off?

"Um, maybe we should let her settle down first."

"Okay." Mom moved to sit on the couch. Holding the dog to her chest with one arm, she freed the other to pat the seat beside her. "Come catch me up on everything. Feels like I haven't seen you in forever!"

Keeping an eye on the dog as its beady black eyes watched my every move, I sat down across from Mom.

The demon dog switched from barking to snarling. "She's really lovely."

"Isn't she the best?" Mom beamed down at the dog, raising it up to her face. My heart stopped as visions of the thing gnawing off her nose raced through my mind. But it only licked her cheek, then returned to growling at me. "She's such a good protector. And a great little friend to have around, too. I've gotta admit, I'm going to miss her company. But at least I can always come for a visit with both my girls, right?"

"Right." I tried to imagine that furry thing in my house. It would probably either claim the underside of the couch as its own, biting the ankles of all who passed by, or else it would wait under my bed like an assassin, waiting for me to enter my bedroom unsuspecting.

Of course, there was always that face-eating option when I was asleep and at my most vulnerable, too.

"So whose idea was it?" I asked.

"Your father's. He called me a couple of days ago and asked if I could pick out a toy-size dog for you. He let me choose the breed and everything!"

Dad had suggested they get me a dog? That must mean vamps didn't terrify all dogs. Just this one. Either that, or there was something else specifically about me that it hated.

"You should hold out a hand, let her get used to your smell," Mom said.

Everything inside me said, *Oh heck no!*

"Go on," Mom said.

Holding my breath, I slowly inched a hand out toward them, Mom all encouraging smiles, the dog all bared teeth and eyes full of don't you dare. When my hand was inches away, the dog tried to lunge out of Mom's arms and bite me. Only my vamp reflexes saved me from losing who knew how many fingers.

Holy crap.

Mom frowned and tapped the dog's nose with her finger, which I guessed passed for punishment. "Lucy, no! You have to be nice to your new mommy so she'll love you."

"Er, Mom, I was thinking…I'm so busy with homework and Charmers and tai chi training, I wouldn't really have time for a pet right now. I mean, she's cute and all…" The demon dog growled louder. "But she'd be alone most of the time. Maybe you could keep her for me, just for a while till my schedule settles down?"

"Oh, sort of like Grandma babysitting her grandbaby?" Mom looked down at the furball and crooned, "Would you like to stay with your meemaw? Would you?" It licked the end of her nose several times, and I tried not to barf. "You would, wouldn't you? Aww, Lucy loves her meemaw!" Mom raised her head, all smiles. "I think that's a great idea! She can keep me company, and the minute you're ready for her, you just give me a call and we'll be here in a flash."

Right. Don't hold your breath for that one. "Thanks, Mom." I started to lean forward and hug her, nearly forgetting the demon dog. It snapped a reminder at me, and I darted back.

She put the dog in her bedroom again so we could talk in relative peace, though it kept yapping from behind the closed door. We talked for an hour, getting caught up on Mom's work gossip and what little news I could pass on about Anne and Ron's breakup, which Mom had been following like a soap opera via updates from me every time she called.

"That Ron Abernathy boy...he's a good friend to you?" she asked oh-so-casually.

Misunderstanding her tone, I laughed. "I have no interest in dating Anne's ex. He and I are friends and study buddies for chem and English lit, but that's all."

"Ah. So you're pretty good friends then."

I shrugged. "Mostly we talk about homework and chem labs and Anne. He's still in love with her, I think. And she's definitely still hung up on him, though she'd rather die than admit it. I'm hoping they'll get back together eventually."

"Well, he's a pretty good friend for you to have around." Her tone was all approval. "I'm glad you reached out to him."

Whatever. I still wasn't going to date him, no matter how much Mom not-so-subtly nudged me in that direction.

When it got late, I reluctantly hugged Mom goodbye, thanked her for "watching my gift," then headed back into the house. Gowin had left. I found Dad alone in the kitchen taking down the decorations.

I jumped in to help, and he tried to wave me off. "It is a school night. You should get some rest."

"It's not that late. And the least I can do is help the host clean up after my surprise party. Thanks for throwing it, by the way."

He nodded and smiled. "I am glad I could finally be a part of your birthday party celebrations. So how did you like your surprise gift?"

Knowing he expected the truth and wouldn't get offended, I didn't hesitate to answer. "Oh lord. Dad, that thing is a demon dog. It hates me!" Hastily I added, "But don't tell Mom, okay? She thinks I'm letting her keep it because my schedule's too busy for a pet."

One corner of Dad's mouth twitched. "I thought that might happen."

"Really? Why?"

"You are half vampire. Animals do not generally take to us all that well. They sense the predator within us."

"And yet you suggested Mom get me a dog." Then I read the truth in his mind. "It was never really for me, was it?"

Dad shrugged. "Your mother has always wanted a little dog. But her pride has never allowed her to buy one. She felt having one would be too much of a personal indulgence. However, her tone when she calls you has held a certain note of loneliness of late, and she is in need of some protection while on the road. A small dog seemed the perfect solution. So I simply…manufactured an opportunity for her to finally have one at half the cost."

"Why not just buy her one and be upfront about it?"

"She would never accept such a gift from me. She would not even allow me to pay for the dog outright when it was supposed to be your gift."

"Yeah, she mentioned you two went in on it together." Leaning a hip on the counter, I crossed my arms and studied him. "You still love her, don't you?"

He did not look at me, intently focused on taking down the crepe paper looped through the antique chandelier over the banquet. "Love does not necessarily die just because the other person involved no longer wishes to be with you."

A wave of longing swept over me, so intense I couldn't tell if it was my father's heartbreak or my own I was feeling.

Swallowing hard, I said, "You know, I think I'm tired after all. I'm going to bed."

"Good night, Savannah. And happy birthday."

On the way out of the kitchen, I spotted Gowin's gift on the counter, still gleaming in its silver-and-pink wrapping. After a couple seconds' hesitation, I grabbed the box of high-tech gear and took it upstairs. At least I had one birthday gift that wouldn't try to eat me.

As soon as my dreams began later that night, I found myself in Tristan's backyard.

I looked around, knowing he had to be here somewhere. The dream felt too real, too sharp and vivid to be anything other than a connected dream. I could practically feel his presence on my skin.

But even though I could feel him watching me, Tristan was nowhere in sight. I sat down on the grass, pulled up my knees to my chest under my long nightgown, and used my legs as a pillow for my cheek. I closed my eyes, wondering how long it would take for him to lose his patience and show himself.

A mouthwatering smell drove my dream self's eyelids open again in fear. Descendant blood?

Nope. It turned out to be a birthday cake, round and several layers thick, sitting on a silver platter to my left in the perfectly trimmed grass. And I knew just what kind of cake it would be.

I poked a finger into the top layer, scooping out a little. Red velvet cake with vanilla frosting. My favorite. Tristan had remembered.

But he obviously hadn't remembered something else…I was a vampire now. I couldn't eat this stuff anymore without barfing it back up.

Except…in real life my birthday cake had smelled awful.

Hesitant, I took a small taste and moaned. Just the way red velvet cake was supposed to taste.

I imagined a fork, and one appeared on the plate's rim. "Thanks Tristan," I whispered to the cake's creator before digging in.

On Thursday at lunch, Anne was acting weird. I put it down to her argument with Ron at my party last night. Tempted as I was to read her mind for confirmation, I resisted the urge. My patience was partially rewarded when she walked out with me at the end of the break.

As soon as we reached the catwalk, she grabbed my elbow to stop me. "Listen, there's something I've got to tell you. Or at least I want to, but I can't. See, it's someone else's secret, and I promised I'd keep it…."

Pinpricks of pain erupted along my neck and arms, and Anne's voice faded away from my mind. Tristan must be around somewhere.

I half turned in time to see Dylan start up the ramp that led from the cafeteria's sidewalk up to the catwalk where we were standing not ten yards away. Great.

Instinctively my shoulders began to hunch up toward my ears. I forced them down, lifted my chin, and worked to stay calm.

He stopped not six inches away from me, his height forcing me to crane my head back to look up at him. On Tristan, the height difference was nice, making me feel protected, sheltered. With Dylan, it was the definition of looming. He towered over me, he knew it set me on edge, and he liked it.

"I guess I should say thanks," I said, keeping my voice even though it wanted to shake.

He grinned. "Oh yeah? What for?"

"My truck's electrical system is fried."

"Aw, that's too bad. Do you need a ride to school? I could swing by your crypt in the mornings for you."

"That won't be necessary. My dad's getting me a brand-new car to replace it." I let the acid drip into my tone now. "Which is why I should thank you. If not for your…help… yesterday, I might still be stuck driving that old truck instead of a sleek, custom new ride soon."

Dylan's smile faded, and mine grew.

He leaned over me. "Stick around, and your electrical system won't be the only thing that gets fried around here."

Yawning, I pretended to study my nails. "You've really got to get a new routine. This one's beyond boring."

His eyes flared then narrowed. "I keep repeating myself because you're not hearing me. Why can't you get a clue? Nobody wants you here. Get out of Jacksonville."

Spit flew from his mouth and landed on my cheek, and everything inside me wanted to take a step away from him. But I was sick of running and hiding, and I'd trained for months for this moment. So I calmly wiped my cheek, lifted my chin and dared him to make eye contact with me.

"This is my hometown, Williams. I like it here. I'm not going anywhere." *So what are you going to do about it?*

He stared down at my mouth, and the darkness within him ramped up several notches. But underneath it, the driving emotion was fear. He was...afraid. Of me? I dug deeper into his mind. No, his dad. He was afraid of what his dad would do to him if he couldn't find a way to push me hard enough.

But his dad didn't really want me to leave town. That was Dylan's wish, and the reasons behind it were too jumbled to make out. His dad wanted...something else. Something bigger. Something too complex for me to understand from the too-brief images and snatches of conversation swirling within Dylan's mind.

"What does he really want?" I murmured. As I leaned in close to him, I heard his heart beat faster. "Tell me, Dylan. What does your dad really want?"

Fear swamped him. "You can read Clann minds now? What did you hear?"

Before I could react, Dylan's hand shot out and clamped around my throat, lifting me onto my toes as I gasped for air. He backed me up until I was pressed against the metal railing of the catwalk.

"Get out of my head!" he shouted, his eyes wild. "Do you hear me? Stay out of my head!"

But I could barely hear him over the noise of his thoughts, ramped up to full volume apparently by the contact of his skin at my neck.

In his memory, Dylan screamed, his body on fire from head to toe, as his father stood over him shouting.

Why haven't you done what I asked?

I tried! Dylan said. *But they're too smart. Savannah's never going to let him break the rules again.*

You will find a way, son, or so help me...

Anne hissed out a curse at my side. Then there was a loud thunk as a small, tanned fist crossed my field of vision and connected with Dylan's nose, followed by a crunching sound.

Shock filled his eyes a split second before the pain registered, driving him to release me. Dropping his books, Dylan bent over with a groan and held his nose with both hands.

But he wasn't the only one in pain.

Anne had turned the other way, hunched over at the waist, cradling her right wrist against her body as she moaned.

"Anne!" I tried to touch her wrist to see how badly it was hurt.

"Oh ow! Stop!" she cried out. "Oh God, I think it's broken."

Behind us I heard movement. I looked back. Dylan had straightened up. He held his nose between both of his flattened palms and made a shifting motion. There was another crunching sound that made my stomach roll over as he realigned his nose.

Then needles of pain jabbed at the back of my neck and arms.

The trickle of blood beneath his nose stopped, reversed direction then disappeared.

The stabbing sensation all over my skin stopped, and Dylan sneered.

"There. It's good as new already," he said.

Anne tried to stand up straight, but the pain kept her hunched over. She glowered at him over her shoulder.

He laughed. "Looks like you might have broken your hand there, Albright. Let's see how you finish the volleyball season like that."

Still laughing, Dylan gathered up his books and sauntered off down the catwalk toward the main hall.

As soon as he was gone, Anne collapsed onto the cement, rocking and cursing. "Sav, my wrist…I think it really is broken!" She looked up at me, her face stark with fear and pain. "What do I do?"

I looked at it. Unless Anne had developed amazing flexibility in her wrist that allowed her thumb to naturally rest a mere inch away from her forearm, it was definitely broken.

"We have to get you to the nurse," I said, grabbing her shoulders and trying to help her up to her feet.

"No! I'll miss the tournament tomorrow."

She'd be missing way more games than that. She'd be out of commission for the rest of the year.

"Can't you do something to fix it?" she pleaded, shocking me.

"Like what?"

"You know, something witchy." She hissed that last part as if afraid others would hear us despite the fact that we were the only people on the catwalk.

I glanced at my watch, my heart racing even faster. We had only minutes till the bell, and the cafeteria would be emptying a flood of people soon. Including a lot of descendants. Already students were trickling in singles and pairs through its various exits, though most were passing below us to the other ground level areas of the campus.

Oh boy. Was I ready for this? Could I even fix it? What if I made it worse?

"Please," she whimpered.

Anne never whimpered. Or moaned. Or begged.

She'd broken her wrist and jeopardized the rest of her volleyball season for me. The least I could do was try.

"If this doesn't work, swear to me that you'll go to the nurse," I told her.

She nodded. "I swear."

"Hold out both wrists."

She did, and I carefully laid a palm on both of them, memorizing the shape and feel of her uninjured wrist so I could have some idea of what I was aiming for. Carrie, with all her medical studies and desire to be a doctor, would have been so much better prepared for this.

If I did this wrong, or somehow set the bones back incorrectly...

No. I would not paralyze my best friend. Anne was counting on me, and I would get this right. I had to. Besides, Nanna said all magic was created from my will and my intentions. And I intended to do this right.

I closed my eyes, focused on her broken wrist and envisioned the snapped bones within it realigning to match the good wrist. She started to cry out, then pressed her lips together so it became a whimper instead.

"Sorry, almost done," I muttered.

I told the bones, now realigned, to knit together, putting all of my will and determination into it. I imagined my energy flowing out of my left hand into her broken wrist.

"It's getting warm," she whispered. "And it's stopped throbbing. I think it's working!"

I nodded but kept my eyes closed, continuing to send my will and energy into the broken bones.

Then the bell rang and the cafeteria doors burst open. Time was up.

"How does it feel?" I asked.

"Better. Still hurts, but not as bad."

"Try not to use it," I said.

"For how long?"

"I don't know, I'm not a doctor!" I muttered, grabbing her books from where she'd dropped them on the cement. "Anne, are you *sure* you don't want to go to the nurse? I really think you should have it looked at. What if I set it wrong, or—"

Slowly she circled her right hand, then looked up at me. "I think it's okay."

I blew out a long breath and shook my head. "If it starts to hurt again, or feels weird or—"

"Yes, Dr. Sav, I will get it checked out by a professional," she said in an ultra deep and somber tone, one corner of her mouth twitching. She reached for her books.

"Use the other hand!" I blurted out.

But if Anne was joking around again, she must be feeling better.

"Yes ma'am!" She used her right hand to salute me. Then she grinned and relaxed. "And thanks, Sav. You just saved my volleyball career."

"No. Thank you for that awesome right hook."

"I can't believe he actually tried to choke you," she muttered as we walked along the catwalk. "Maybe I should make an anonymous tip to the principal or something. Then again, his dad's on the school board, so unless Sav agrees to press charges..."

Staring straight ahead of us, I clenched my back teeth. "At this very second, I would love nothing more than to press charges against Dylan. But then Tristan would hear about it and do something stupid, and that's what Dylan's dad wants. We can't give them what they want. So no anonymous tips, okay?"

I wasn't letting the fact that his father was abusing him with magic sway my emotions. Really I wasn't. Just because Dylan's dad was a magical bully didn't mean Dylan had the right to ever touch a female, much less choke one.

But I also refused to let my anger sway me into making the exact tactical error they wanted me to.

She stopped beside me. "Excuse me? I didn't say anything."

I stopped, too. "Yes, you did. You were going on and on about making anonymous tips and—"

"No, I didn't. I thought it, but I didn't say it." Her eyes narrowed. "You can read minds now, can't you! That's why he was so freaked out."

I gave her a sheepish smile. "Um, surprise?"

Growling, she started walking again. "If you hadn't just fixed my wrist, I swear… How long have you been able to read minds?"

I shrugged one shoulder. "A few months, I think?"

She growled. "And all you can say is 'surprise.' You know, I'm going to remember tonight that you said that. Oh, by the way, Ron said he'll be giving you a ride home after practice. He said he already worked it out with your parents last night at the party. He has something to tell you in private."

"Ron does?" I pretended confusion as I opened the heavy metal and glass main building's rear exit doors for her then followed her inside to the main hall. "About what?"

"You'll find out." With a dark, smug grin, she gave me a wave over her shoulder with her right hand. "See you later."

About time. This should be interesting.

CHAPTER 24

The fall sun was already slipping below the pines that wove throughout Jacksonville when Charmer practice ended that afternoon. As I walked through the fast-growing gloom down the hill toward the practice field's chain-link gated exit, I saw a familiar black muscle car purring at the curb.

I tilted my head and looked through the open passenger's side window.

"Hey!" Ron said, his smile tight at the corners and not quite reaching his eyes for once. "Anne said she talked to you at lunch. Ready to go?"

Okay.

A few minutes later, I was settled in the passenger seat and we were on our way up the hill and off campus.

"So Anne said you needed to tell me something?" I said.

"Yeah. Well, that and show you something."

We drove past the turn that would have led toward my house, instead heading out of town. "Where are we going?"

"Somewhere a little more private."

My imagination tried to cue the creepy horror movie picture at this point. But this was Ron, and both Anne and my parents and his supposedly knew about this roadtrip. So I forced myself to relax back in the seat.

"Are we going to Palestine?" He had just turned onto Highway 79, which led to the next town over. Palestine was also where Ron's family had moved from when we were in the ninth grade.

Behind us, the town's lights faded from view as the sun finished setting and left us to zoom through the cold in the dark.

"No, not that far. Just another mile or so." The dashboard lights turned Ron's face green as he glanced at me with a smile. "I'm taking you to this spot I like to go to where I can be alone and…think."

His expression looked the same as always, with that lopsided boy-next-door smile, and the emotions he was projecting were a little on edge but mostly…hopeful. Nothing about him said he intended to kill me in a ditch somewhere.

Besides, I was half vamp and half witch. I could take care of myself now.

I searched for something to talk about so I wouldn't feel so weird. "What's this band?" I gestured at the radio, which was turned down low.

"You like it? They're called Flogging Molly."

"Sounds Irish."

He nodded. "Yeah. They're awesome. Oh here, listen to this one. It's my favorite." He cranked up the volume and hit the forward button to play the next track.

I picked up the plastic case wedged into the space between our seats and read the back listing of songs. We were listening to "If I Ever Leave This World Alive."

Because we're about to die? my stupid imagination wondered before I told it to shut up. Other than creeping me out with the lyrics, I liked the music and let my head bob in time with the beat.

After ten minutes, Ron slowed the car then turned onto a black top road that quickly changed to dirt.

The headlights flashed on a familiar green Ford F150 parked at the side of the road ahead.

"That looks like—" I began.

"Yeah, Anne's truck. But what the heck is she doing here?" He didn't sound thrilled.

"You two didn't plan this?"

He shook his head as he parked a few yards behind her. He didn't shut off the headlights, though.

Anne slid out of the driver's side of the truck, her face set in a scowl. She moved to the back end and dropped the tailgate with a loud clang that made me jump.

Ron and I got out of the car. He was projecting every bit as much confusion as I was feeling.

"Anne, what are you—" he muttered.

"Hog hunting, of course," she said. "Brought my bow and everything. Uncle Danny couldn't come with me this time, though, so I thought I'd just go out on my own for a few hours."

Ron glared at her. "Alone? You were going to hunt *alone?* Are you *crazy?* You could get killed!"

Eyebrows raised, she gave her best innocent face. "Well, sure. Why not? You do it all the time. And besides, everyone knows the wild hog population's getting out of control around here. Halloween's tomorrow. All those trick-or-treaters are going to be in danger if we don't cull the hog population as much as possible before then."

"No." He took a step toward her. "Absolutely not. There's no way I'm gonna let you go out there alone—"

Her mouth twisted into a dark smirk. "Oh please. Give it

a rest, Neanderthal. I was just joking. I'd never actually be that stupid. I only came because you said you'd be bringing Savannah here for the talk."

He rocked back on his heels, and she barked out a short, humorless laugh. "You really thought I'd let you just drop a bomb on my best friend without me here for emotional support? I don't think so." She hopped up to sit on the tailgate then patted the metal beside her. "Come on, Sav. Better get comfy for storytelling time. Ron tends to ramble."

I had no idea what was going on and wasn't sure I wanted to dip into their thoughts for clarity. Even though we were outside, the air between them was way too heavy.

Still, for the sake of keeping what little peace remained, I sat beside her then waited for Ron.

He sighed, rubbed the back of his neck, and stared at the dirt lit up by his car's headlights. After a hesitation, he began. "Okay, Savannah, do you remember the day we talked about that library book I was reading? The one about the East Texas myths and legends?"

I nodded.

"And do you remember what I told you about the black panthers that the Irish settlers brought over with them?"

"Sure," I said. "They helped protect their owners' castles in the old country and their homesteads here in America until their owners set them loose in the wild."

He winced. "Well, first off, the settlers weren't their owners. Secondly, those big 'cats' are actually the Keepers, and they were once allies with the Irish settlers until their help was no longer needed. And third, those settlers weren't just any Irish immigrants. They were the Clann."

Why did it always have to come back to the Clann? "So that's why you thought I'd already know about the Keepers. Because my family used to be in the Clann."

He nodded. "But there's another crucial detail to this story that I had to leave out before since you didn't already know about the Keepers and I wasn't sure my parents would let me tell you. The Clann actually *created* the Keepers."

"You mean they bred the cats?"

Anne snickered. Ron frowned at her, and she raised her hands in surrender. He looked at me again. "No, they didn't breed them. They created them using one of the biggest group spells the Clann has probably ever done. They cast that spell, though some prefer to call it a curse, on a select few human families. In return, those families promised their aid anytime the Clann needed it."

Whoa. No wonder some people called it a curse. I couldn't even imagine how miserable I'd be if a bunch of witches turned me into a cat.

"Okay, so there are a bunch of humans running around out here ticked off at the Clann because they were turned into giant cats then abandoned," I said. "And...what, you want me to change them back? Because regardless of what Anne might have told you, I'm really and truly not that good yet. I've only been practicing how to use power for a few months now. She's just lucky I could fix her wrist."

Ron froze, then took a huge step forward and grabbed both of Anne's hands.

"Hey!" she said. "What do you think you're doing? Hands off!"

He turned her hands over, running his fingers over her wrists despite her struggling. "What happened?" He searched her face, both of them eye level due to her sitting on the tailgate. "Why didn't you tell me you got hurt?"

"I didn't tell you because, one, it's none of your business anymore, and two, because I'm not hurt anymore. Sav fixed me with her hoodoo voodoo." She jerked her hands free and gave me the evil eye. "Which, by the way, I did *not* spill the secret about, thank you very much!"

He looked to me now for answers, his eyebrows pinched. "Savannah?"

Her eyes widened then narrowed in an unspoken warning not to tell him. But she hadn't made me promise not to. And diehard romantic that I was, I couldn't help but be moved by the anxiety and confusion pouring off her ex.

"We...uh, had a little encounter with Dylan Williams at lunch today," I said.

"Sav, seriously, it's none of his business," she hissed.

"Yeah, it really is," Ron said. "What'd he do?"

"He went after Sav, so I went after him," Anne said. "End of story."

He ignored her, staring at me, wanting more details. I gave in. "Well, yeah, it's basically like she said. He figured out I could read his mind and flipped out. When he went after me, Anne hurt her wrist while trying to put the hurt on his nose."

"Which totally would have worked if the jackass hadn't been able to fix it immediately afterwards," she said. "But then Sav healed my wrist, too, so we were basically even. And now you know everything. Happy?"

The muscles in his jaw worked for several seconds. Finally, he stepped back, arms crossed. I expected him to throw a million questions at me about my spell-making abilities. Instead, gratitude radiated from him. "Then I guess I need to thank you, Savannah."

I shrugged. "It was no big deal. She wouldn't have gotten hurt if not for trying to protect me."

Why wasn't he curious about my ability to heal Anne?

I snuck a peek at his thoughts and got the answer. "Your mom told you about me, didn't she?"

He nodded. "And why your family was kicked out of the Clann and why you didn't know about the Keepers."

So he knew I was half vamp and half witch. And yet he didn't seem scared. "How long have you known?"

"Since that day I told you about the panthers of East Texas."

I thought back over the weeks and months since then. How he'd guessed that I could read Tristan's mind and didn't seem bothered by it. The way he'd acted so quickly to help me when Dylan left his blood on my locker.

And how he hadn't once been afraid to be alone with me in the library. My throat got a little tight at that.

"Thanks for not freaking out about it," I said.

Smiling, Ron shrugged. "It's no big deal."

So now two normal people knew all about me and were fine with it.

I took a deep breath. "Okay, but none of this explains why we're out here tonight. I mean, I feel bad for the Keepers. Believe me, I've had more than my fair share of crap from the Clann, too. But what do you want me to do about it? Even if we could find and catch one of those poor creatures, I'd never be able to change it back to human. Especially if it took a whole group of descendants to do the spell in the first place. I'm not that strong, and I wouldn't even know where to begin."

One side of Anne's mouth hitched. "Oh, we don't have to hunt down a Keeper. They're much easier to find than you think. In fact, I bet if we sit here for a few minutes, Ron can go find us a Keeper, can't you?" She looked at him, eyebrows raised with a weird twisted sort of smile.

He made a face back at her. "Sure. I'll be right back." And then he took off into the woods.

Whoa. Was he suicidal? "I thought you said these woods were filled with wild hogs. Isn't it dangerous for him to—"

"He's fine. Trust me. The hogs will be more afraid of him than the other way around. You'll see."

Silence as Ron's footsteps faded.

"So why'd you think I'd need emotional support for this Keeper stuff?" I asked. "Or was it really that you just wanted an excuse to see a certain tall, blond and handsome guy?" Grinning, I bumped a shoulder against hers.

"Puh-lease. Actually, I just wanted to save time by being here so you wouldn't have to call or text me later all ticked off because I didn't tell you myself."

"How in the world are the Keepers going to make me mad at you?"

"Because it's a secret I swore to keep, even from you." There was something in her tone, a note of pain that combined with a strange sense of loss she was projecting. It socked me in the chest and squeezed my lungs.

How could she not want to do whatever it took to stop that pain and get Ron back?

"Does this Keeper stuff have anything to do with why you two broke up?" Maybe Ron was so obsessed with finding a way to end the Keepers' curse that Anne had gotten tired of it and broken up with him?

No, that couldn't be the reason. Anne was just as obsessed with perfecting her overhand volleyball serve and her skills as the junior varsity Maidens' star setter.

She surprised me by nodding and swallowing so hard I heard the gulp in her throat.

So that was it? She'd broken up with Ron over his Keepers obsession?

I searched for something to say to make her feel better. "Well, you know, nobody's perfect. Everyone's got a weird hang-up or two. Have you tried searching for Keepers with him? You never know, it could turn out to be a bonding hobby or something."

Lips pressed together, she shook her head. "I already told you, we don't have to hunt for them. And trust me, this is not the sort of thing you 'take up as a hobby.'"

Fine. I was just trying to help.

Irritated now, I stayed quiet, listening to the nighttime sounds of the forest…an owl hooting somewhere off in the distance, the slight breeze rustling through the pine trees all around us. That cool wind brought with it the familiar scents of pine and dirt and unfamiliar smells of the wild things that lived in these woods.

I heard the breathing first, loud and heavy, almost like a warning. I froze.

"Anne, did you hear that?"

She looked at me. "Hear what?"

"Breathing. Loud, like something big's coming—"

And then I saw it, its black fur catching and rippling in the edges of the car's headlights as it padded out of the woods on silent paws that were as big as my hands. Its yellow eyes, their pupils vertical slits instead of rounded, watched us as it slunk ever closer.

Holy crap.

The last time my heart had raced this fast, Nanna had been hanging in midair, held captive by the power of the Clann in the Circle.

Tonight had to end better than that. I would do whatever it took to make sure of it. Dad said vampires were immortal unless we were staked through the heart, decapitated, or set on fire. As long as I kept my neck clear of that thing's claws, I should be all right. Anne, on the other hand, was all too human. I had to get her somewhere safe.

The inside of the truck cab. Surely it couldn't get through the windows or windshield.

Scared to make any sudden movements, I eased a hand out to touch Anne's shoulder, hoping this would keep her calm. "Anne? I don't want you to freak or jump or anything. But listen to me very carefully. I swear to you on Nanna's grave that there is a huge animal over there."

She glanced in the right direction. "Mmm-hmm, I see it."

"Okay. Here's what we're going to do. I want you to very carefully ease your feet up onto the truck. Move super slow and quiet, and maybe it won't attack. I want you to head for the back sliding-glass window and see if you can get it open."

"It's already unlatched. I thought I might need fast access to my bow and arrows—"

Was she thinking about *shooting* it? "Forget about the bow and arrows for now. I do not want you to play the hero. I want you to get inside the cab of your truck so it can't get to you."

She turned to me with a half smile. "Oh yeah? And what about you?"

Frowning, I kept staring at the monstrous beast. It had stopped at the opposite side of the road a few yards away. No telling how far it could leap, maybe right into the back of the truck with us. "I'll be okay. Don't worry about me. I'm a vamp, remember? As long as it doesn't cut my head off—"

"Oh, don't be ridiculous. Just let me get my bow and arrows and I'll take care of it." Anne hopped up to her feet, moving way too fast.

I hissed, "I said move *slowly!* And you will *not* get your bow and arrows. Just get inside and…" A whooshing sound behind me signaled she'd opened the back glass window. I risked a glance over my shoulder. She had thrust her arm and shoulder inside, but the rest of her body was still vulnerable outside the cab. "What's the matter? Are you stuck?"

"Nope, I'm good." She spoke at a normal volume.

"Keep your voice down!" Geez, did she *want* to provoke the thing to attack us?

She stood up, and I wanted to throttle her. She was holding a compound bow with arrows attached and a weird plastic hook thing strapped to her right wrist. "Dang it, Anne, I said no! Just get inside where you'll be safe."

But even as I spoke, she was inserting an arrow into the bow then hooking it with the wrist thing.

"Anne, don't!" What if she missed? It might make the beast run away. Or it might make it come after us for sure.

"Don't worry so much," she said, drawing the arrow and one of the three strings back to her jaw, resting the tip of her nose against the string with a smile. "I've got this. Ready? On three. One, two…"

Her right index moved forward and pressed the trigger of the hook attached to her wrist. The hook released the arrow. It went wide, missing the monster to the right by at least a foot.

The cat reached up and caught the arrow as easily as if it were a kitten grabbing a bird out of the air.

My jaw dropped. No normal panther would have done that. It must be a Keeper. We were *so* in trouble here.

Anne chuckled. "Good catch! But don't you dare mark it up with those teeth or claws. Just leave it on the ground and I'll get it later."

Male laughter sounded, not nearby, but closer, as if I were listening to it through headphones. As if it were in my mind.

And it sounded familiar. "Ron?" I called out in a stage whisper, daring to look around us and trusting Anne would keep an eye on the panther. Ron had to be close by if I could hear him laughing.

Yeah? Definitely Ron's voice. Was he up in one of these trees?

"Where are you? Stay away! There's a—"

A giant black cat staring at you? Yeah, I know. He sounded ready to laugh at me.

Had everyone gone nuts around here?

"Yeah, well, this cat's definitely not normal. Where are you? Can you get into your car safely? If you can't, stay where you are and we'll try to get inside Anne's truck and come and get you."

Anne laughed. "Yeah, Ron. We'll come save you." She laughed harder.

I scowled at her. "What is *wrong* with you? Can't you see that huge black animal over there ready to tear our throats out?"

"Hickeys on the neck, yes. But he's not going to hurt us." Lifting her chin, she called out, "Ron, are you done playing with her yet?"

The panther eased closer. And closer. It was beside the truck now. Throwing caution to the wind, I jumped to my feet and darted in front of Anne, using my body for protection.

Whew, you're fast! Ron said.

The panther leaped onto the tailgate, and the entire back end of the truck dipped under the panther's weight. Despite my clenched back teeth, a shriek escaped through my nose. It had to be at least six feet long from head to butt.

"Get inside the freaking truck!" I yelled at Anne, moving to stand between her and the monstrous cat. I had no idea how I would fight it off. I would have to pray my vamp strength would be enough against its huge size and weight. Was there enough of a human mind caged within that furry body to be reasoned with? Maybe if I apologized for Anne's shooting at it...

"Dude, easy on my truck," Anne said over my shoulder to the cat.

The panther sat on its haunches and made a sneezing motion with its head.

Give me a break, Ron said. *She carts around dead hogs back here but tells* me *to be gentle with her truck?*

For the first time since the panther's arrival, I stopped trying to figure out how to save Anne and fully focused on Ron's voice.

"Ron?" I said.

Yep.

The panther tilted its head, its tail slowly sweeping the tailgate.

"Where are you? Wave a hand or something so I can see you."

The panther slowly lifted a paw in the air.

No flipping way… My mind locked up.

"Yes, you were funny," Anne said, sounding bored now. "But I'm still not giving you a high five when you look like that."

"That's— The Keepers are—" I stuttered.

"Shapeshifters," Anne said, playing with her compound bow.

Right. Of course they were. Because if the world could actually contain witches and vampires, then why not shapeshifting kitty cats?

"So this is a Keeper," I said.

"Yep," Anne said.

One of them, at least, Ron said.

"Are there more like you?"

Oh yeah. Too many, in fact. It's why my family had to leave Palestine. The Keepers are overrunning the woods there and need to start spreading out before we attract more notice than we've already gotten. Heck, we've already been seen so many times in the area over the years that they named one of the high school mascots after us!

I frowned at the panther. No, at *Ron.* "Why can I hear your voice inside my head?"

Part of the Clann's original spell, he answered. *It allows us to communicate with descendants, or in your case partial descendants, when we're in panther form. Very handy in times of war, I guess. Not that any descendants have bothered to include us in anything they've been up to for the last hundred years. And it works both ways, by the way. I can hear your thoughts too right now.*

Oh yeah? I thought, testing him.

Yeah, he answered, and I could hear the smile in his tone. *Cool.*

"Okay, this is boring," Anne said. "Can we all go home now?"

Fine, Ron said, lightly leaping down off the tailgate.

"Sav's riding with me," Anne called out to his retreating furry backside, stuffing her bow and wrist device in the backseat of her truck again before hopping down over the side of the truck.

I climbed into the front passengar side of her truck in silence, still trying to absorb the whole Keeper revelation. What the Clann had done to those families—putting a spell on their very DNA that continued to work on their descendants throughout the centuries—was some seriously hardcore old magic. Talk about fundamentally affecting someone! I could see why the Clann had done it, too. The Keepers would make amazing allies during a battle. So why had the Clann let that alliance fade?

Ego, I finally decided. The Clann had gotten cocky, arrogantly believing their magic was more than enough in the modern world.

What a shame, too. Now the Keepers were stuck with what they were, whether they were needed or not.

"So what do you think?" Anne blurted out when she couldn't take the silence anymore.

"Um, I think...*wow* would be the word I'm looking for."

"Yeah. It's definitely some heavy stuff. I tried to talk Ron out of telling you, but he was convinced it would make you feel less alone or something." She rolled her eyes.

"No, I'm glad he did. He's right, in a weird way it does make me feel better." I snuck a glance at her. "So I guess this is why you broke up with him?"

She nodded, her mouth tightening at the corners. "I've had time to get used to the idea now. Especially after knowing about your...stuff. But when he first told me..." She shook her head, staring at the road through the windshield, the approaching lights of Jacksonville lighting up her face. "It was just way, way too much info to handle all at once. What kind of guy drops a bomb like that on a girl he's only been dating for a few months?"

"Weren't you two together for like eight months or something?"

"The key word being *months*. He wasn't even supposed to tell me about the Keepers, much less show me! No one outside the Clann or the Keepers is supposed to know about it. But there he went, blabbing his mouth to me last year. Was it any wonder I freaked out?" Her eyes looked wild in the streetlights as we reentered the city limits and the pines were replaced with buildings again.

"So you dumped him because he was different."

"No, of course not! You know I'm not like that. It wasn't the whole shifter business itself that bugged me. It was the fact that he was dumping this major huge family secret on me! I mean, what if I'd taken it into my head to shoot a video of him shifting with my phone when he didn't know it or something, and I put it on YouTube?"

"Oh Anne. You wouldn't do that."

"But I *could* have, for all he knew! Not to mention he was my first boyfriend and I was all of sixteen when he showed me. That is just *way* too heavy for a girl's very first relationship. For all I knew, he was planning on proposing the week after that!"

"So you broke up with him. Because he trusted you with his deepest, darkest secret."

Silence as we pulled up to a stoplight and waited for the light to turn green. More silence as we took off again.

"You know, I'm kind of surprised you decided to stay friends with me after I told you about my family's secrets."

"That's different and you know it. I'm not dating you. And you and I have been best friends for years. Ron is just some guy I dated for a few months."

She was so full of crap. "You're reaching."

"What?"

"You heard me. You're reaching for excuses. You know good and well that you never should have broken up with him. But you can't admit it because then you'd be admitting you were wrong."

"I was *not* wrong! Ron was pushing too hard too fast. What did he expect me to do with that kind of info? And that, by the way, was before my best friend told me vampires and witches actually exist, too. By the time you dropped your little bombshell on me, I'd had months to get used to the crazy crap that's out there."

I would not get offended by that. She was panicking at the truth right before her face, and she was lashing out like a cornered animal.

But it was time for her to wake up and see reality, whether she thought she was ready for it or not. Losing Nanna and Tristan had taught me life could be incredibly short and love could end at the drop of a hat. She needed to figure that out, too.

"You're scared."

"Excuse me?"

"You're running scared. You realized you love Ron. You could have handled a one-sided love, but then he showed just how much he loved you back by telling you all this. So you ran away."

"I'm not scared," she hissed. At the next intersection, she ignored the yellow light and plowed through without slowing down. "I go hog hunting all the time. Some of those boars are six hundred pounds! Scared little girls don't go hunting animals five times their size."

"So what? Maybe you're not scared to go hunting. But you're definitely scared of love. And do not run that red light."

She screeched on the brakes, the front tires stopping inches from entering the crosswalk area.

"That's ridiculous! I love my parents, my aunts and uncles, even my pain in the butt cousins—"

"Not the same thing and you know it."

Silence filled the cab as we waited for the light to change. When it did, she turned left without using a blinker, and I sent up a prayer of thanks that there wasn't any oncoming traffic.

She stomped on the gas as we passed the Tomato Bowl, and we hit the railroad tracks fast enough to get an inch or two of air between our butts and the seat before the curve in my street forced her to slow down. The tires squealed as she slammed on the brakes at the curb before my house, rocking both of us forward then back. I sighed in relief as she shoved the gearshift into Park then killed the engine.

The silence grew, the ticking of the cooling engine the only sound inside the cab. I could have gotten out, let her run away from the conversation. But I refused. Not this time. She needed to see what she was doing to herself and Ron.

"You know, I'm not the only one who's scared around here," she muttered. "What about you and Tristan?"

"What about him?"

"You come up with all these reasons why the two of you can't be together. But let's face it. If you really wanted to still be with him, you'd make it happen and to heck with the consequences. Just like when you first decided to start dating him."

"That was a dumb decision I made last year. I had no idea my grandma would pay for it. Once the consequences of what we were doing became clear…"

"That's a load of crap and you know it. You decided to break up with him hours before your grandma died. Remember? You said you promised the vamp council that you would break things off with him *back in France*."

"Because I found out my kisses were killing him!" Okay, now she was going too far. I tried to twist sideways to face her head on. The seat belt bit into me. Growling, I wrestled with the buckle till it finally snapped free. "So, what, I should just not even care if I accidentally kill him? To heck with risking his life, as long as *I'm* happy?"

She hesitated, and I heard her think, *Well, no, but…* "You could find a way. What about turning him?"

She sounded like Tristan. This was an old argument I shouldn't have to rehash with my so-called best friend. "I can't. For one thing, I'm not even a full vamp. And even if my vamp genes were strong enough to take hold, he'd still die from the process. Every descendant who's ever tried to turn died."

She looked away. "Sounds like a cop-out to me."

"No, what it sounds like to me is that right here, right now, you're *still* running away! Why face the harsh reality of your own mistakes when you can try to turn the tables and make your best friend feel bad about what she can't have instead?" I grabbed my door handle, gave it a jerk, thrust open the door and slid out. "If I could be with Tristan without risking his life, you'd better believe I'd do it. But there isn't a way. I can't turn off what I am. You, on the other hand, are miserable simply because you're acting like a spineless idiot!"

Her jaw dropped. "I am not a spineless idiot!"

"That's right. You're not. Which is why I said you're *acting* like one. And now that you know it, and I know it, and Ron sure as heck knows it, would you please do us all a huge favor and pull your head out of your butt already? Call him. Tell him you made a mistake and you're sorry. I swear to you, if he doesn't take you back and forgive you immediately, I'll… I'll…" I was so mad I couldn't even think of a good promise to offer. "I'll go hog hunting with you!" There!

I slammed the door, rocking the truck but thankfully not denting the metal, then gave in to the urge and did a vamp blur across the lawn up to the porch. Inside, it was all I could do not to slam the front door too and break its custom stained-glass design.

Outside, Anne started her truck, cranked up the radio to blaring, and took off with a roar of the engine.

"Have an educational outing in the woods with the Abernathy boy?" Dad greeted me from where he was reading the newspaper on the living room couch.

"Oh yeah," I snapped. "Very illuminating."

Stupid humans! Anne had a chance at love, maybe even true love, that I would never have again, and she was throwing it away! She had no idea what I would give to have Tristan back in my life.

"I'm going to bed," I said before blurring up the stairs and down the hall to my room.

By my bed, I flipped on my MP3 player's docking station, kicked off my shoes, then put on Kelly Clarkson's "What Doesn't Kill You." I listened to the words for a minute, my feet tapping the hardwood floor to the beat. Then my head started bobbing along. The next thing I knew, my body was whirling and punching and jabbing to the rhythm, and it felt *good*. Good enough to stop me from calling Anne and giving her another piece of my mind.

A minute later, something wet slid down the side of my nose. It wasn't a tear. Vampires didn't cry. Keeping my eyes closed, I brushed it away with the back of my hand.

But then another rolled down my cheek, and another, and suddenly my lungs and throat were burning like they used to when I was still fully human and tried to run for more than thirty seconds.

Even singing a song about feeling stronger felt like lying to myself.

I slumped onto the edge of my bed and held my head in my hands. I had been such an idiot, trying to fix my best friend's love life. How could I have possibly ever thought I could fix someone else's problems when I couldn't even fix myself?

CHAPTER 25

TRISTAN

The velvet cake wasn't just a birthday present. It was also my peace offering. I didn't want to fight with Savannah anymore, even if I was still hurt and frustrated that she wouldn't fight for what we once had. She'd moved on. She had Ron now. It was time I found a way to move on, too.

The Indians fought a good battle on our home turf Friday night. But even the hard workout on the field hadn't managed to take the edge off my restlessness. I felt...off, like I couldn't find my balance.

And Bethany's constant chatter with everyone in sight on the front lawn at the Tomato Bowl's entrance after the game wasn't calming me down any.

A hand slapped my back, rocking me forward onto the balls of my feet. "Son, that was a fine game you played back there!"

Dad and Mom. I forced a smile for them. "Thanks."

Silence grew within our group, contrasting sharply with the noise of everyone else's talking and laughter.

"It's good to see you again," Mom said to Bethany. She gave me a meaningful smile and a nod of approval, then looked up at Dad. "You know, I think I'm in the mood for a little ice cream. What do you think, hon? Did you save any room after those four hot dogs?"

Dad grinned and stroked his beard, pretending to consider it. "Hmm, I think I might have a little room left in the ole tank." He patted his gut. "I guess it depends on what kind of ice cream. Are we talking Coke floats? Or brownie sundaes?" On that last part, his thick eyebrows dipped and wiggled.

Mom laughed, a delicate hand rising to smooth back non-existent wisps of hair at the side of her bun. "Oh, I'm definitely thinking brownie sundaes."

Dad turned his grin on me. "Don't come home too soon, son. In fact, maybe you should take your girl here out for her own brownie sundae." He leaned close to me and stage-whispered, "Women like chocolate. Remember that. It'll make your life a whole lot brighter if you do."

Bethany giggled as my parents walked with their arms linked down the cement steps, stopping every few feet to say hello to at least half the crowd on the way.

"Your parents are so cute."

I looked away from them. "Yeah. They're adorable."

Her smile wobbled. "Is something wrong?"

"Nope. Everything's just perfect." According to my parents.

A breeze kicked up, brisk with the first snap of true fall. I tilted my head back and stared up at the sky, trying to see the constellations. But the lights of the stadium were too bright, blocking my view.

I was still hot from the game, and I'd overdressed for the weather. Too many layers, and my varsity jacket was tight, making it hard to breathe. I unsnapped its metal buttons, and the wind snuck in past the open edges like familiar hands to soothe my burning skin. Better. I sighed, remembering another crisp October night like this one under the stars, and how a certain girl's always-cool hands had rested at the back of my neck while we danced....

"Tristan? Hello, earth to my little brother." A small hand waved before my face, making me blink. It was Emily.

"Hey, sis! What are you doing here?" I bent over and gave her a quick hug.

"What, I can't come home to see my baby brother shining on the battlefield?"

I smiled. "I take it college life isn't all you thought it would be?"

"Of course it is! I just missed seeing you play."

Uh-huh. Then why did her smile look just a little too bright?

She sighed. "Okay, you caught me. I also wanted to check in on my old cheer squad and see how my replacement's doing."

"And how is she doing?" Bethany asked.

Emily made a face. "Well, you know Sally Parker."

Bethany laughed. "Don't we all." She glanced over her shoulder. "Oh, there's Jill! I need to get a pair of shoes back from her." She leaned in toward us and whispered, "She's the worst shoe klepto! She borrowed my favorite pair of sneakers over a month ago and keeps claiming she meant to return them but 'forgot' them in her car." She made air quotes with her fingers. "I'll be right back!"

As soon as she was gone, Emily's bright smile disappeared. "Tristan, there might be a small problem. I listened in on Sally's thoughts a few minutes ago, trying to see how she's really doing with the cheer squad, and learned she overheard the Faulkner twins planning to crash Savannah's Halloween party tonight."

I glanced in the direction I'd tried to avoid all night, across the railroad tracks to a certain house. Unlike the last time I'd visited, the Victorian was all lit up, with cars filling its driveway and lining its curb. It looked like the party was already underway.

I scanned the stadium's front lawn.

"I already checked," Emily said. "I don't see the twins anywhere. Think they've already—"

I nodded. "We should go over there and take a look around. Just to be sure."

She stopped me with a hand on my upper arm. "Okay, but Tristan? Promise me you won't do anything stupid if you see her."

Her meaning Sav.

I scowled. "I'm good, sis."

We headed down the grassy slope to the street, dodging and weaving in between cars filled with local football fans hooting and hollering out open windows.

Our final approach across the railroad tracks was too conspicuous under a bright streetlight, but there wasn't much we could do about it. Thankfully the twins were too busy huddling behind a tree trunk near the curb and giggling as they fiddled with something they were holding together.

"Dylan's going to love this!" Vanessa said, making Hope giggle again.

I realized what the object was as they threw it.

"Hey!" Emily said, showing off her cheer yell.

I didn't have time to say anything. I was too busy jumping over the curb onto the lawn while using magic to stop the object in midair.

"What do you think you're doing?" Emily yelled at the girls at the top of her lungs.

Squealing in fear, the twins took off at a run back toward the lights of the Tomato Bowl.

Either Emily's yelling or the twins' squeals brought the party spilling out onto the front porch to see what was going on. I hastily let the object fall to the grass, then walked over and picked it up. Lights from the house's front windows lit up the brick. The twins had used a blue-and-gold cloth hairband to hold a piece of paper in place around the brick.

"A scrunchie? How decorative," Emily muttered as I unwrapped the note and read it.

Get out of town monsters!

"And their creativity just keeps on going," I said, showing her the note.

The party poured onto the front lawn as people asked what was going on.

"Just some punks trying to ruin a perfectly good party," I told them with a smile, showing the brick but hiding the note.

Several people made tsking sounds of disappointment. Then somebody shouted, "Good job stopping them, kids! Y'all should come in and have a drink. It's all nonalcoholic, of course."

Several people seconded the idea.

"Oh, we really should be getting home," Emily said in her most mature and polite tone.

"Aw, sis, we can stay for a few minutes, can't we?" I'd have to be crazy to pass up the chance to see the changes to Sav's house when half the rest of the town had already gotten the full tour of the place. "We wouldn't want to be rude, would we?"

Emily flashed a glare at me before turning to the crowd

with a big smile. "Well, I guess we could stay for a *few* minutes."

And inside we all went.

Always the mingler, Emily had no trouble finding a conversation to join in, leaving me to walk around and admire the house on my own.

Mr. Colbert had put a lot of work into the place. The last time I'd been here, every room had been dark and gloomy, full of peeling flowery wallpaper and wood so dirty it had looked black. Now the rooms were brightly lit with wall sconces, smaller chandeliers in the two front rooms, and a huge chandelier over the open staircase that caught the eye and pulled it up to the stained-glass window in the ceiling two stories up. He'd replaced all the wallpaper with fresh paint, and the wooden wainscoting, trim and floors, all now several shades lighter, gleamed. The furnishings were nice, too, not too stuffy or cluttered, so a guy could move around without knocking something over. There was plenty of room for the hundred or so people who had crammed in here tonight to check out the old place and probably its new owner, too.

Mr. Colbert had made a lot of smart choices with the house, not just in its renovation, but in opting to hold a Halloween party here open to the public. Right or wrong, the residents of Jacksonville put a lot of stock in a person's home. They would be less likely to make up negative stories about Mr. Colbert and his daughter after seeing what he had done with a building everyone else had wanted to bulldoze.

And then I realized...this wasn't just Mr. Colbert's latest project. It was also Savannah's *home*. A small fact I hadn't given much thought to during my last visit here.

I tried to picture Savannah hanging out in the front rooms on either side of the entrance area, maybe running down the stairs in the mornings on her way to school, that curly red ponytail of hers swinging along the way. Something tightened in my chest, making it tough to take a deep breath.

The staircase led to a balcony that ran the length of the second floor, which must have been filled with more than a few bedrooms and baths considering the number of doors up there. One of them was Savannah's room, where she lived and read and slept every night, and probably where she danced, too. She used to love to dance, though not when anyone was watching. I caught her at it many times in the Charmers' dance room after school when she didn't know I was there, and even a couple of times in our connected dreams before she knew I'd joined her.

The moment she came home, I felt it. I found a corner by the stairs below the balcony, out of the way of all the other guests, so I could watch Savannah enter the house. God, she was gorgeous, even just with her hair in a ponytail and wearing her blue-and-gold Charmers windsuit.

Then she tugged the band from her hair, letting it fall to her shoulders.

More noise as Ron came in behind her. He tugged on a piece of her hair, and she turned to smile at him and say something that was lost beneath the thumping beat of the music. A few seconds later, Anne, Carrie and Michelle joined them in the entrance area, followed by a handful of trick-or-treaters. Savannah grabbed a big orange plastic bowl from the side table and held it out so the kids could take handfuls of candy. She put the bowl back on the side table, said something to her friends and boyfriend, and they all went in separate directions.

Alone at the front door, Savannah started to drop her bag by the side table, then froze, her eyes widening.

I'd seen her freeze like that countless times before. It meant she knew I was here somewhere.

She looked to the left, scanning the packed room then the

equally stuffed room to her right. Frowning, she toed off her sneakers and carried them with her as she ran up the stairs and down the landing toward the right. She opened the last door, ducked inside and shut it.

I should go. She was probably hiding now that she knew I was here. Besides, Emily would be looking for me soon.

I stood there for several minutes, torn between what I should do and what I needed.

Eventually my feet carried me up the stairs and down the landing to her door.

At my knock, there was a long hesitation before she called out, "Yes?"

I opened the door and stepped inside.

Seated in front of a vanity, Savannah's hand froze in the act of brushing her hair. "Tristan. What are you doing here?"

"Sorry. Thought this was the bathroom." I didn't bother trying to sound convincing.

"What are you doing at my house? Are you crazy?" she muttered. "There's a vamp council member here tonight. If he sees you…"

I shoved my hands in my pockets. "Does he regularly come up to inspect your room?"

She made a face. "No."

"Then how will he know I'm in here with you?" She opened her mouth to argue. "And don't even say vamp hearing, because there's no way he can hear us over all the noise downstairs."

She sighed.

I slowly walked around the room, looking at the shelf filled with glass ballerinas and pictures of her friends and the Charmers. No pictures of me anywhere, of course. Then I saw the snow globe I'd given her last year for Christmas and had to keep my back turned to hide my smile.

Yeah, she still thought about me.

I looked down at my feet. "Nice hardwood. Pretty good for dancing?"

"I don't dance anymore."

"Since when?"

Shrugging, she finished pulling her hair up into a bun. She'd changed into a pink leotard and tights with a glittery blue tutu.

I stated the obvious. "You don't dance anymore, but you're going as a ballerina this year?"

"No. A fairy. Just gotta add these." She picked up a set of see-through, glittery wings I hadn't noticed from her bed and crisscrossed the ribbons over her chest then down and back. But the ribbons weren't long enough to wrap all the way around her back and to the front again to be tied. She must have planned on having Anne help her tie them. Or maybe Ron.

"Here." I closed the distance between us, took the ribbons from her shaking fingertips and tied the satin at her back. I was tempted to let my fingers touch her skin, but I didn't. It was a miracle that she hadn't kicked me out of her room as it was.

"Thanks," she murmured. She sat down on the bed to pull on her slippers, glancing up at me in the process. "So what's with you crashing the party? Curious to see how the local vamps are living nowadays?"

I stared at her, silently letting her know how much I didn't appreciate the vamp humor. She knew better than to believe I would ever think that way about her.

She ducked her head to focus on tying the ribbons from her slippers around her calves.

"So I've been hearing some interesting things about you and your new boyfriend." Crap. I hadn't meant to bring him up.

"Who?"

"Ron Abernathy."

She made a face and stood up to check herself in the full-length mirror that hung on the wall beside her open closet door. "I'm not dating him. He's Anne's ex."

"And yet you're still seeing him. Does Anne know about the two of you?"

She sighed. "Whatever you think you heard about us, you heard wrong. Ron and I are just study partners. I would never date my best friend's ex." She glanced at me with one eyebrow raised as if to say I ought to know that.

Except I didn't. I felt like I didn't know her at all lately. And it was killing me. "Well, if you don't want people getting the wrong idea about you two, maybe you shouldn't be sneaking off to meet him in the library all the time."

She turned and scowled at me with her hands on her hips. "I'm not sneaking anywhere. Anne even gave me permission to help him with English lit in return for his help with chemistry class. And it's really none of your business anymore. Why are you even here tonight? Shouldn't you be with your girlfriend?"

"Who?"

She stared at me like I'd gone insane. "Bethany Brookes. You know, the girl you've been seeing for months? Where is she, anyways? Did you leave her downstairs at the punch bowl so you could come up here and lecture me?"

Oh crap. Bethany. She was still at the Tomato Bowl. I'd forgotten to give her a ride home. I snuck a glimpse at my watch. "She probably caught a ride home with another Charmer or her parents." I hoped. "And besides, she's not my girlfriend. She's just a friend."

"Uh, you might want to tell her that, because she's under the impression that you two have been a couple ever since you and I broke up."

"You mean after you dumped me." Twice.

"I did not dump you. I saved you."

I blew out a long breath. "That is such crap and you know it, Sav. You didn't save me. You just chickened out. And I've never dated Bethany."

She flinched, opened her mouth, closed it, then tilted her head to the side. "You've never dated Bethany."

"Nope."

"And all those images in your mind of the two of you kissing under the practice field bleachers and outside the gym and just about every other place possible on campus?"

I grinned. "What can I say? I have a great imagination."

She stared at me then shook her head, her cheeks turning pink.

She knew she had just sounded jealous.

Did she have any idea how cute she looked when she was jealous?

I walked over to her. When we were only a few inches away, her eyes widened. She looked around the room like a bird searching for somewhere to fly off to.

She disappeared then reappeared at the bedroom door, bending over to grab her sneakers from where she'd dropped them. She disappeared again, reappearing at her closet, where she tossed the shoes inside. She slapped the closet's folding door, apparently trying to shut it. But she only succeeded in knocking it out of its track at the top, and she was too short to pop its plastic wheel back in, though she rose up on tiptoe to try.

Moving slower now so I wouldn't startle her, I closed the distance between us then reached over her head to fix the door.

"Do you really think I could move on that easily after losing you?" I said.

She looked everywhere but at me for several long seconds. Then she finally dared to make eye contact. "I've heard Bethany's thoughts. If you're not really dating her, then you've been lying to two girls. She truly believes the two of you are a couple."

"I haven't lied to her. Maybe she just got the wrong idea. Kind of like I did about you."

She frowned. "What are you talking about? I never lied to you."

"What about all those times you said you loved me?"

Her breath caught and held. When she spoke again, it was in a whisper. "I wasn't lying."

"Then why? Why break us up? Why throw it all away? Why didn't you help me fight them?" I was hissing out the words without meaning to, all the anger I'd been pushing down for months rising up and out of me. I wanted to grab her, shake her, but I kept my hands clenched in fists at my sides.

"I did the right thing," she snapped back at me. "I made a promise, to the council and the Clann, and I've kept it. I did what I had to in order to keep you safe. And someday you'll thank me for it."

"You really expect me to thank you for ripping out my heart and stomping all over it?"

"Yes, I do! Someday, when you're not being stupid and hardheaded about it."

"Stupid and hard—"

She held up a hand. We were standing so close it would have been easier for her to just rest the hand on my chest. I noticed she was careful not to touch me, though. "I really don't want to argue with you anymore, Tristan. What's done is done."

"You know, I'm not too crazy about arguing with you all the time, either!"

"Then don't!"

"You started it."

"Who came into whose room and started this whole conversation?"

She had a point. "Well, how else can I get you to talk to me? You run out of English lit so fast I can't even say two words to you."

"Please. You have all the time in the world to shout anything you want to me without interruption for an hour and a half before I ever leave. English lit is nothing *but* having to sit through your monologing."

"Believe me, I'd much rather hear your thoughts." What I wouldn't give to have her ability, to be able to hear her uncensored thoughts for a change.

She drew in a sharp breath, and as I watched, her eyes turned from green to silver-white. "Tristan, step away."

"Or what? You'll bite me?"

Unable to resist any longer, I stroked a fingertip along the curve of her cheek. Though her impossibly smooth and poreless skin was cold, strangely my finger felt warmer where it had touched her, as if my skin were having some kind of chemical reaction to the contact.

Her chin trembled. "Please. Don't do this."

I wanted to hold her, kiss her just one more time. But even that wouldn't be enough. One kiss would only lead to more, and we were indoors away from the ground where I could draw replacement energy. The second she felt my energy level weakening, it would be all over. She'd go right back to blaming herself for what she couldn't stop or change, and using that excuse to add to the walls between us.

Sighing, I stepped back toward the bedroom door, hating every inch of space that grew between us.

Someone knocked on the door, making Savannah jump.

Anne popped her head in. "Oh, sorry." She started to duck back out.

"I was just leaving," I muttered. I hesitated, waiting for Savannah to say something. To tell me not to go. To say she was wrong and we never should have broken up.

But she didn't say anything at all.

Anne stared at us, her eyebrows raised.

"Have a fun party," I told Savannah before leaving the room.

My steps were heavy as I slowly headed down the stairs. Every time I came to this house I left in defeat.

No matter what I said or did, no matter how jealous I managed to make her, no matter how much I argued with her, I couldn't change Savannah's mind. The fact that I'd convinced her to give us a chance once seemed like a miracle now. Because she loved me, there was nothing I could do to make her risk my life.

If it weren't making both of us miserable, I could almost admire that unbreakable will of hers.

I reached the entrance area just as Emily stepped through the living room's archway. She didn't notice me at first, too busy laughing at something some guy at her side was saying. Trust Emily to find the only frat boy in the place to flirt with.

Finally she looked up and saw me. "Tristan, there you are! We've been looking all over for you."

Sure she had.

Overhead, a movement of glitter caught my eye as Savannah stepped out onto the balcony with Anne. Savannah stopped there, returning my stare.

Emily followed my line of sight. "Uh-oh, time to go."

"Call me," the guy said as Emily and I left the party.

"That was the best party I've ever crashed!" Emily gushed as we crossed the lawn toward her car.

Yeah. Too bad we couldn't stay longer.

At home, I'd just toed off my shoes in my bedroom and was getting ready to fall into bed when I heard a thud across the hall.

I glanced out through my open door in time to see my sister closing hers and throwing a quick glance in the direction of our parents' room.

Emily was definitely up to something.

I darted out in time to beat her to the top of the stairs. "Hey sis. I thought you'd be headed back to your dorm by now."

"Shh," she hissed, glancing over her shoulder at our parents' closed door again.

Oh, naughty, naughty sister.

"Sneaking out?" I grinned.

"I'm not sneaking out," she said, still keeping her voice at a whisper. "I'm headed to a friend's house. Mom knows."

Liar. "Girl friend or guy friend?"

Her face went carefully blank. "Why would you ask that?"

"Oh, I don't know. Maybe it's the short skirt you're wearing, or the extra makeup and perfume? You sure it's not another Halloween party you're off to instead?"

She hesitated a fraction of a section, then rolled her eyes, pressed a finger to her lips in warning to be quiet, then waved me after her down the stairs and into the kitchen.

Leaning a hip against the island, she crossed her arms and scowled at me. "Fine, you caught me. Happy? I'm going to a party. But don't tell Mom or Dad or they'll kill me, okay?"

I let the silence grow, pretending to consider it while I moved past her to the fridge and dug through the shelves full of plastic containers in search of leftovers.

Finally I sighed loudly. "Okay. But you'll owe me one. Why all the secrecy, though? You're in college now. So what if you go to a party? Why not just tell them the truth?"

"Mom was acting weird after we got home. She said Aunt Cynthia called her while Dad and her were out getting ice cream. Aunt Cynthia said she thought she and Uncle James were being stalked or something. Said they both kept feeling

like they were being watched wherever they went. They were
wondering if anything like that was going on with any other
descendants. So now Mom's doing her whole overprotective
thing. It was her idea that I stay here tonight so I wouldn't
have to walk across the campus in the dark."

Aunt Cynthia was Mom's sister. We went to visit Uncle
James, Aunt Cynthia and their two kids Kristie and Katie in
New York City every year, usually for New Year's Eve.

I spotted a clear plastic container full of shrimp etouffee.
Mom had been experimenting with her book of Paula Deen
recipes again. I stuck the container into the microwave and
hit the auto reheat button. "Huh. Aunt Cynthia's not usually
the paranoid type. Did Mom say anything more specific?"

"No." Circling the island, Emily stopped the microwave,
opened one corner of the container's red lid, then restarted
the microwave. "Anyways, I'll be home long before they wake
up, so don't wait up, okay?"

"Have fun. Call me if you need a safe ride home."

"Thanks, little brother. But I don't plan on drinking tonight. Which means I'll probably wind up as everyone else's
designated driver." She stopped the microwave two seconds
before it could ding, covering her tracks as always in case our
parents heard us down here and came to investigate.

"Keep the top down. They can barf over the side instead
of on the floorboards," I joked, grabbing a spoon to stir my
now steaming food.

"Gross. But good idea." Nose wrinkled in disgust, she
grinned and waggled her fingers over her shoulder as she
snuck out the kitchen door to the garage. A minute later, the
garage door creaked its way up. I grinned, imagining my sister silently cursing the noise as she tried to make her getaway.

I grabbed a can of soda and the food, burning my fingertips

on the container's hot bottom, and ran up to my room to wolf down my snack while watching an old episode of *South Park*.

But something was wrong, and for a change it wasn't just my relationship with Savannah.

Something about that whole conversation with Emily seemed…off. Her smile after being caught had been a little too sheepish. And she'd totally dodged answering the question of whether her friend was male or female. And then there was that hesitation and the way her eyes had flashed before her confession, and how she'd neatly brought up family gossip as a distraction.

She was lying.

I'd seen her do it to our parents too many times to mistake it tonight. But why would she lie to me? She'd never lied to me, at least not that I knew about.

I'd have to see what clues I could get out of her tomorrow over breakfast.

By the time I made it downstairs the next morning, Emily had already gone back to college. Mom said Emily had claimed she had a ton of homework and studying to catch up on.

Yeah right. She knew I was on to her and was running off to hide out at school.

I tried calling her a couple of times later in the weekend, but apparently she wasn't taking any calls from suspicious brothers.

She was definitely up to something. The question was what?

SAVANNAH

After Tristan left my bedroom, I went downstairs and made the required rounds through Dad's party, smiling and pretending I was having a great time. But the minute the guests began to leave, I headed right for the kitchen fridge then my room, blood-laced juice in hand.

It was the first time I actually appreciated the escape that the blood memories offered.

The next day, Dad let me sleep in, deciding we could go car shopping on Sunday instead. After forcing my body through a half hour of tai chi and a shower, Dad let me take his car over to the Junior Livestock Barn at the edge of town to help the other Charmers get everything ready for our annual masq ball fund-raiser for that night. Since I would only get dirty and no one cared what I wore anyways, I'd decided to go as my own scary self this year and wear my Charmers windsuit. Somehow the thought of putting on last night's fairy costume and fixing my hair in a bun again didn't seem like a lot of fun.

At the huge barn, I threw myself into scrubbing the cor-rugated metal walls and cement floors free of dust and cob-webs, refusing to think about how a certain boy dressed in plastic shining armor had once caught me as I fell off the rickety ladder. We spent several hours decorating and setting up folding tables for the desserts the Charmers had brought to be given out as prizes for costumes and musical chairs. It took another hour to unload and prepare all the snacks, candy and sodas I would be supervising the sale of in the conces-sion stand all night.

And then all too soon it was time to open the front door and let the dancers in.

When Tristan and Bethany arrived, I made sure I was too busy stirring a Crockpot full of cheese sauce to look up. I didn't need to see how perfectly matched their costumes would be, or how happy Bethany probably looked on his arm.

Later Carrie, Michelle and Anne showed up and stopped by the concession stand to say hello. By the looks of their wildly varying costumes, Carrie and Anne had managed to talk Mi-chelle out of her idea for them to all dress alike.

"Why don't you two go on in and I'll catch up?" Anne

suggested to the girls, and they took off for the dance room. Anne turned back to me. "Look, about our argument the other night…I didn't get a chance to apologize at your party last night, what with a certain Clann boy showing up and all, but I wanted to say I'm sorry. Maybe you're right, and this whole thing with Ron does have me a little too weirded out."

"Have you called him yet?" I asked.

Her gaze darted from one side of the snack lineup to the other, like she was pretending to shop. But I knew her better than that. She was avoiding making eye contact.

"Anne," I said on a sigh.

"I'm working on what I'm going to say, okay?"

My, but someone was feeling snippy tonight. Because she knew I was right. "Fine. But when you do call him and he does take you back right away, remember, I told you so."

She snorted. "Yeah, well, just remember what you promised if he doesn't."

A hog hunt. "Never going to happen. Now hurry up and call him already."

She drummed her fingers on the countertop. "Aw, why bother when he'll probably show up here tonight anyways? I can just talk to him then."

"Unless you chicken out again," I murmured with a smile.

"I'm not chicken," Anne muttered.

The front door opened to admit a new arrival. It was Ron.

"I'd better go find the girls," Anne said, turning the other way and pretending she hadn't seen him.

I made chicken sounds at her as she all but ran into the dance room. She didn't look back during her escape.

Ron sauntered up to the counter, dressed as a giant black cat, swinging his fake tail like a propeller. Apparently I wasn't the only one who had decided to go as themselves tonight. "What bee flew up her butt?"

I choked down the laughter. "Oh, she'll probably tell you about it later."

"Hmm, maybe I should go hunt her down and say hi."

"What a great idea! Tell me how it goes, and good luck."

He headed for the doorway that connected the foyer with the larger back room, waving a paw goodbye over his shoulder.

I fell into a rhythm then of taking orders and dishing them out to the customers. The work was a good distraction, keeping me on my toes and moving without thinking about anything personal for a few blessed hours.

Until Bethany showed up to work her shift at the concession stand.

The room behind the open window was small, made even harder to move around in by the folding table full of food and the numerous stacks of sodas and ice chests full of drinks. She was avoiding making eye contact with me tonight for some reason, but that was just fine by me since I didn't know what to say to her, either.

Did she really not know that Tristan thought they were just friends?

Part of me wanted to warn her. But what good would that do? Everyone knew she was crazy about him. She was headed for heartache no matter what, and she might not believe me or appreciate it if I said anything anyways.

So I stayed out of it. It was Tristan's mess to clean up, not mine.

But I felt sorry for Bethany all the same. What girl could resist those smiles of his, the way he laughed or touched the small of your back while leading you into a room, how he tilted his head down closer to you when you talked to him...

When the dance was nearly over, I told her I was going to go start the cleanup process in the dance room. She nodded without speaking to me, busy screwing the lid back onto a giant plastic tub of pickles.

The cavernous back room was dimly lit by only strobing, color-changing lights on the stage. A fog machine working overtime in one corner to fill the dance floor with billowing clouds of smoke that clung to my ankles as I skirted the dancers. Even at a distance I could tell the dessert table by the wall was a wreck, littered with empty soda cans and food cartons. Might as well start cleaning there now and get a jump on things so we could all go home quicker after the dance ended.

But before I could reach the table, my friends spotted me and grabbed my arms.

"One dance!" Carrie yelled over the near deafening music and the crowd. "It won't kill you!"

They tugged me into the center of the dance floor as a song was ending, and I wondered where Ron was. Then a fast-paced country song began, one that I recognized as Anne's favorite, and we shared a grin. The lyrics were infectious as the male singer sang about life going from bad to worse and walking through Hell. All four of us wound up singing the song at the top of our lungs while shaking our butts to the beat.

For three brief minutes, I let it all go…the stress, the sadness, the loneliness and missing Tristan all the time. I pushed it all to the side and pretended I was just a normal girl jumping around and singing at the top of my lungs with my best friends in a barn in the middle of nowhere.

And man, it felt good.

But all too soon, the DJ announced the last song of the night, and it was a slow one full of heartbreak and longing. My cue to beat a hasty retreat.

I moved over to the dessert table by the wall to do my job, grateful there was always work to turn to for a distraction. But then out of the corner of my eye I saw Ron walk over and ask Anne to dance. She agreed, and I couldn't help but stop cleaning and watch them. They were so completely and thrillingly *cute* together. It was like watching a romantic movie, only more intense because they were both my friends and I so desperately wanted them to be happy together.

Then I saw Tristan and Bethany swaying together, her cheek pressed to his chest, his chin resting on top of her head.

The same way he used to hold me.

As if he could feel my stare, Tristan looked at me, squinting under the moving lights over the dance area. Despite the darkness of the area where I stood frozen, our eyes met.

TRISTAN

The collar of my prince costume tightened like a noose around my neck, and my hands were sweating inside the too-tight gloves. Why had I ever agreed to wear this thing?

I jerked the gloves off behind Bethany's back and stuffed them into a pocket in my slacks, then unbuttoned my collar one-handed. But I still felt like I was choking.

I couldn't do this anymore.

That look in Savannah's eyes, so filled with accusation, was like being slapped awake.

Not to mention Bethany had her arms wrapped around my waist tightly enough to squeeze the air from my lungs.

What was I doing?

All these months, all the signs had been there, and I'd been too messed up over getting my heart ripped to shreds by Savannah to see how I was breaking someone else's.

Bethany was head over heels for me.

I'd believed we were just friends and that Bethany understood that, too. I should have broken my personal rule about reading others' thoughts and checked hers to be sure we were on the same page right from the start.

Both Emily and Savannah were right. They'd tried to warn me, and like an idiot I hadn't listened.

Bethany was a great girl and a good friend. But I could never feel for her the way I still felt about Savannah, even if trying to fight the Clann and the council was hopeless.

Even if we could never be together again, Savannah was the one. She always had been, and she always would be.

I looked down and found Bethany staring up at me, her eyes shiny with tears.

She knew. Somehow, tonight, she'd figured it out. All night, she'd been quiet and unsmiling, completely unlike herself.

I had to find a way to fix this. "Maybe we should go somewhere and talk."

Her eyes rounded, and she shook her head fast. "No. Let's just stay here and keep dancing. Everything's fine—"

"No, it's not." I stopped dancing, my hands resting on her shoulders left bare by her pale blue Cinderella gown. "I think you might have gotten the wrong idea about you and me. It's my fault. I haven't been thinking right for months. I thought you understood we were just friends. But I should have explained things to you that first day you showed up at the hospital." I took a deep breath. "I can't be the guy you need, Bethany. I'm still trying to get over someone else."

"You mean Savannah."

I hesitated then nodded, hating how the truth was hurting her, wishing I'd told her the truth from the start and avoided all of this.

A tear slipped down her cheek. She reached up and wiped it away with a shaky hand. "You still love her. That's why you're always staring at her. I heard you were at her house last night, that you and your sister stopped someone from throwing a brick through her window. That's where you ran off to, isn't it?"

"Yeah, but I didn't go over there to see her." At least not at first.

"Did I do something wrong? Did I talk too much, or not enough, or—"

My gut clenched. "No. You didn't do anything wrong."

"But I'm not the right girl. I'm not Savannah."

I nodded. God, I'd screwed this up. "I'm sorry—"

She stepped back, her chin quivering. Looking away, she blinked fast a few times then shook her head. "I've got to go."

"Bethany—" What could I say to make this right?

Obviously nothing she wanted to hear. Turning, she gathered up her long skirt and walked away, pushing through the crowd at the edge of the dance floor so she could escape to the foyer and her friends.

CHAPTER 26

The Monday after the masq ball was a long day thanks to all the ticked-off Charmers who had sided with Bethany and believed I was the worst jerk on the planet. Since they were probably right, I didn't bother to try and defend myself when they huddled in glaring, whispering groups in the halls and cafeteria. I just kept my head down, sat outside at my old grounding tree during lunch, and waited for the backlash to blow over.

At the end of the day, I was only too happy to go home. All I wanted was to eat, tackle a little homework and then crash.

After parking inside my family's four-car garage, I got out of my truck and crossed the dim space toward the door leading into the kitchen.

Halfway across the garage, I heard it…the worst kind of wailing I'd ever heard.

I ran the rest of the way to the steps and threw open the door, sure I would find someone on the floor bleeding to death or something.

Instead I found Dad standing with one arm around Mom

while his free hand furiously dialed numbers on his cell phone. What the…

He looked up as I opened the kitchen door, relief the barest flicker in his eyes. "Tristan, you're home. Good. Call your sister for me, will you?"

He tossed me his phone. I caught it out of reflex.

"What's—" I started to ask.

"They're dead!" Mom cried out, her bony fingers clutching Dad's beefy arms like claws. "Cynthia, James, the girls. They were slaughtered like animals by those murderous undead filth. I'll *kill* them. I'll kill them all!"

Dad shushed her, hugging her to him and rubbing a big hand across her back. After a few seconds, he looked over her head at me, his expression intense.

"The police found Cynthia and James and your cousins dead at their home. It appears they were murdered—"

"By vampires," Mom hissed, spit flying from her mouth, her eyes round and rolling wildly. I'd never seen her like this. She looked unhinged. And dangerous.

Then their words fully registered and I had to grab the doorjamb for support.

My aunt and uncle and cousins were all dead. Maybe from a vampire attack.

We saw them once a year, so I wasn't that close to them. But still, they were family….

I pictured Katie and Kristie the way I'd seen them the New Year's Eve before last, all smiles and freckles and bouncy blonde curls and giggles.

They would have been ten this year.

"Are you sure it was…"

Dad nodded. "When your mother couldn't reach Aunt Cynthia all day, she asked one of the other New York descendants to go check on them at their apartment. They found them, called 911—"

Mom wailed again.

"Come on, honey, let's go upstairs for a while," Dad said, trying to steer Mom toward the hallway.

"I want to go to New York," she said. "I have to see them."

Dad and I shared a look. Mom leaving Jacksonville like this was a bad idea. Mom was almost equal to Dad in magical abilities, if not stronger in some areas. That made her a loaded gun nearly impossible to disarm. Normally her sense of propriety and desire to protect the Clann's secrets held her abilities in check.

But now her only sister's family had been murdered by a vampire. I couldn't see how anything could possibly keep her from literally going nuclear all over New York.

Dad was going to have his hands full this week keeping Mom's temper reined in and under control.

"I'll call Emily and let her know," I said to Dad's back as he led Mom upstairs.

Emily picked up on the second ring. "What's up?"

"Uh, I've got some bad news. Aunt Cynthia and Uncle James and their girls..." My throat convulsed and I had to clear it before I could finish. "They're...they're gone, Em."

"What? What happened?" she gasped.

"They think it was a vampire attack." Just saying the words made me feel sick. I braced a hand against the cold granite island, dropping my head.

"Oh my God," Emily whispered. "Are they sure?"

"Dad says they're pretty sure. A descendant found them first."

"Could it have just been made to look like a vamp attack?" In the background, horns blared then quickly faded. Emily must be driving through Tyler like even more of a maniac than usual.

"Maybe. Are you coming home?"

"Yeah. I should be there soon."

"Okay." I started to hang up, hesitated. "Listen, drive careful, okay? I don't think Mom could handle you getting into a wreck right now."

"Yeah, yeah. I'll be home in thirty." With a sniffle, she ended the call.

I dropped down onto a barstool at the island and rested my head in my hands.

This couldn't be happening. As far as I'd heard, the Clann hadn't had anyone die in a vamp attack in decades. How could a vamp have taken out an entire family of descendants like that? And especially my aunt and uncle. Aunt Cynthia and Uncle James were almost as powerful as my parents.

Twenty-three minutes later, Emily's car roared up the driveway and into the garage. She must have broken the speed limits and then some to get here that fast. Seconds later she burst into the kitchen, giving me a quick, hard hug before heading upstairs at a jog.

"Emily," Mom wailed as my sister opened our parents' bedroom door. "They're gone!"

Emily murmured something, followed by our mom's sobs before someone shut the bedroom door again.

A few minutes later, Dad came back downstairs. He dropped onto the barstool beside me, his heavy frame making the metal creak in protest.

"Well, looks like we'll be going to New York." He sighed. "There's no talking her out of it, not with the state she's in."

"You'd better at least keep her drugged or something then," I said, not joking in the least. "Otherwise there's no telling what might happen."

"I know. I'll take some sleeping pills with us. While we're gone, Emily will stay here—"

"Dad, come on. I'm seventeen. I don't need a babysitter."

"No arguments, Tristan. It's the only way your mom and I are going to let you stay here. Your mom would already prefer you and Emily come with us. But to be honest, I don't think you two need to be anywhere near New York. If there's a rogue vamp in that area, the farther you two are from it the better. Furthermore, an adult descendant will be coming to stay here with you."

"Are you serious? I'm probably more advanced than any of them now!" That wasn't cockiness, either, and we both knew it. Dad had been training me to become the fifth generation Coleman to lead the Clann someday, and the weekly practice sessions over the last couple of years had taught me almost everything he knew about magic. Even Dad sometimes had trouble blocking my practice spells.

Not that he seemed to remember that right now.

"Son, do you have any idea how serious this situation is? We're talking about a possible total breakdown of the peace treaty if we don't get a hold on this thing right away. The Clann leader's in-laws were just taken out by one or more vamps in direct violation of the treaty. We've got to find out what's really going on before the Clann makes up its own mind and starts calling for another war."

War? We hadn't had a battle with the vamps in decades.

I searched his face, gauging the hard glint in his eyes and the grim set of his mouth. He was serious.

"You don't think it was just some random vamp who accidentally lost control?"

Dad shook his head. "I wish I could believe that. But you know how big New York is. What are the odds that a vamp would lose control in a city of that size and only go after your mother's family? Plus, it was too clean a hit. They were attacked at home with no witnesses and no sign of a break in."

He scrubbed both hands over his face, his palms rasping over his beard. "Your mother's convinced it's a message, that they're all but openly declaring war on us."

"What do you think?"

"I think it was planned ahead of time. Beyond that, I don't know. We've got to find out if this was a rogue attack or a council-sanctioned hit. And we've got to do it fast before mass hysteria breaks out within the Clann."

He stared ahead at the kitchen without seeming to see anything. "I spent my whole life, and my father half of his, working with the council to create that peace treaty. There's no way I'm going to make any rash decisions to destroy all that hard work without knowing exactly what's going on and seeing if we can stop this train from going off a cliff."

"Can you talk to the council?"

"I'm going to try to reach out to them. But with your mom around, it's not going to be easy. She doesn't want to hear anything short of an immediate declaration of war on all vamps."

I blew out a long breath, running a hand through my hair. This was getting crazy fast. "You've got to calm her down, Dad. And everyone else, too."

"I know. Our cell phone provider's gonna love us this month." One corner of his mouth hitched in a halfhearted attempt at a smile. "In the meantime, I need to know you and your sister will be protected. So do you think you could help your old man out and put up with a babysitter just for a few days till I get back?"

"Yeah, okay." If it made him feel better so he could focus on his job in New York, I guessed I could put up with a babysitter. I just wished he'd change his mind and let me come with him to help him get some answers.

Emily returned downstairs, joining us at the island, her face pale and splotchy beneath its usual tan. "Mom said to call the airlines. She's already packing."

Dad nodded. "I'd better grab the Clann address book while I'm at it." He headed down the hallway off the kitchen toward his study.

"Don't forget your phone's charger cord, too," Emily called out.

"Right. Thanks, Em!" he yelled back.

In the kitchen's silence, Emily and I stared at each other without having to say a thing. She couldn't believe this was happening any more than I could.

Emily sighed. "I'd better go check on Mom, make sure she's packing clothes instead of weapons or something."

She trudged back up the stairs, not bothering to keep her footsteps light and graceful like she usually did.

Unsure what to do, I headed upstairs to my room, opting to lie on my bed and stare at the ceiling. Like everyone else in the house, I left my door open. As a result, my parents' unguarded thoughts drifted throughout the house like radios left on in other rooms They must have been pretty upset to let their mental guards down so completely, even at home. Usually they tried to protect Emily and me more.

I couldn't hear Emily's thoughts, though. Apparently she'd learned how to keep her mental guard up no matter what. Probably because she didn't want our parents to ever learn just what their perfect princess really had been up to over the years.

I wouldn't be surprised if she'd found a way to keep her mental guard up even during her sleep.

Between our parents, Mom's thoughts were the most unguarded and definitely the loudest, her mind a painful mix of wondering how soon she and Dad could get to New York, how she might track down the killer, memories of growing up with Aunt Cynthia.

And surprisingly, memories of an old farmhouse in the middle of nowhere that Mom seemed scared to death to enter.

Later Mom came into my room like a small tornado, her ebony hair once again secured in a harsh bun low at the back of her neck, her outfit all black.

The wrist cuff she carried was also black leather and stamped with a Celtic border along both its edges. In the center was stamped some kind of circular Celtic knot.

"Give me your hand," she demanded, her eyes and cheeks dry now, her lips set into thin lines.

Sitting up, I held out my left arm.

She wrapped the cuff around my wrist and snapped its buttons closed to secure it.

"What is it?" I turned it around so I could see the Celtic knot. On closer inspection, it looked more like some kind of crest.

The Clann's group crest. I recognized it from the same design that had been carved into the back of the stone throne Dad sat in for all the Clann gatherings in the woods.

"It's a vamp ward," she explained.

CHAPTER 27

I reached for the snaps to take it off. No way was I wearing this thing.

Her hand darted out to clamp over mine. "You *will* wear this, Tristan. Do not make me add a locking spell to it. I *will* have you safe."

She stared at me, her fingers digging into the back of my hand. She looked right on the edge of crazy.

"Okay, Mom. If it makes you feel better, I'll wear it. But you have to promise me something in return. Don't do anything crazy in New York."

Mom scowled. "Oh please. Do be sensible. Do you think your father lasted this long as Clann leader by having a stupid wife?"

Right. "Be careful."

At that, her scowl faded. "You, too, dear." She bent over to press a cold-lipped peck on my cheek, then turned and walked out of the room, her heels clacking on the hardwood. A few minutes later, Dad and Mom exited the house, the wheels on the suitcases adding to the clattering of Mom's heels before being cut off by the closing kitchen door.

Emily came in and sat on the edge of the bed, her face drawn. "Can you believe this is really happening?"

"Yeah, I know. Feels like a bad dream." I hesitated. "Dad said Mom thinks this means war with the vamps again. Is she mental or...?"

"I don't know. Let's hope she's just overreacting. I heard things got really scary before the peace treaty was signed. At the very least, I'd guess vamp wards will become the new fashion accessory again, at least for a little while." Staring at the open doorway, she didn't seem to notice as her left hand grabbed a tiny section of my bed's black satin comforter and rubbed it between her thumb and fingertips.

She caught me staring at her hand. "What?"

I nodded at her fidgeting hand. "I haven't seen you do that since we were little."

Smiling crookedly, she let go of the comforter and clasped her hands tightly in her lap. "I haven't been this worried in a while."

My smile faded. So it really was that bad. "Did Mom ever tell you anything about an old farmhouse?" At her confused look, I added, "I saw Mom thinking about it tonight. She seemed absolutely terrified of it for some reason."

"I don't remember her telling me anything about that. But you really shouldn't have listened in on her thoughts."

"I couldn't help it. She was practically yelling. And you know how loud she can yell when she gets riled up."

Emily sighed. "Yeah, I guess I see your point. I couldn't fully block her out tonight, either."

"Oh, but you could block her out a little more than me, huh?"

She gave a half smile and shrugged. "Don't hate me because I'm the gifted one."

Downstairs the front doorbell rang, interrupting the great comeback I was about to deliver.

Emily stood up. "That'll be Mrs. Faulkner come to stay with us for the week." She glanced down at me. "Dad did tell you, right?"

"He told me someone was coming, but not who. Why the heck did he ask *her?*" Mrs. Faulkner was a polished Texas trophy wife on the outside. But on the inside, she could give the Wicked Witches of the East and West a run for their money. She'd taught the Brat Twins everything they knew about bigotry and then some.

"Dad didn't. It was Mom's idea. She was the one who called and asked Mrs. Faulkner to stay with us."

The doorbell rang again. This time Mrs. Faulkner laid on it so that the chimes kept pealing.

"Better answer that before she wears it out," I muttered then rolled away to face the far wall.

"You're not coming down to say hi?"

"No way. Make any excuse you want."

As soon as Emily was gone, I yanked off the cuff then slipped downstairs and out the back patio door to the Circle. The clearing's magic buffering wards would prevent Mrs. Faulkner from sensing me while I worked a little late-night magic. If Dad was right, then the Clann kids would be on the warpath tomorrow.

Time to make a few protective charms for Savannah again.

The next morning, I made the mistake of stopping by the kitchen for a bowl of cereal, figuring I'd be out the door long before either of the females in the house woke up.

But apparently Mrs. Faulkner was an early riser. She was

waiting for me at the island in the predawn light, a steaming mug of coffee already in hand like she owned the place.

I switched directions, aiming for the door to the garage instead. No way was I having breakfast with a grown-up version of the Brat Twins.

"And where are you going?"

Oh man, she even had the same high-pitched, sugar-sweet voice as her daughters. The sound of it was way worse than fingernails down a chalkboard.

"Football practice. We start early in the mornings." I answered her without turning to face her, my hand on the doorknob to freedom now.

"Not without your mother's vamp ward, you're not. She warned me that you might try sneaking out without it."

I faced her now, my teeth clenched. "I don't need it."

She smiled sweetly. In combination with her overtanned leathery skin, she reminded me of an alligator. "She feels you do."

"Well, she's not here."

"No, but I am." She took a slow sip of coffee, her eyes never leaving mine.

I actually caught myself considering using magic on her. But then my mother would really blow a gasket.

Letting out a long, slow breath, I headed back upstairs to grab the wrist cuff then stomped downstairs again.

"Put it on, please," she said.

I stared at the door, so close to escape. From my own home. "You know I'm supposed to be the next Clann leader, right?"

"Yes, well, until that day comes, you are still expected to obey your elders. And your mother gave you a direct order to wear that ward."

Working hard to keep my energy level under control, I

slapped the leather shackle around my left wrist then snapped its buttons. "Happy? Can I go now?"

"Drive safely. We wouldn't want you to get into another wreck on my watch, either."

Implying what, that she thought she had the power to make me want to drive off a cliff?

Royally ticked off, I headed for school, hoping *she'd* find a cliff to drive off before I returned home tonight.

Along the way, I stopped and flash burned the cuff on the side of the road before continuing on to school.

I'd texted Savannah to ask her to stay home from school till things calmed down, but got no response, and she didn't answer when I tried calling her, either. I was hoping that, after talking to my dad, the vamp council would order Savannah to lay low. But just in case they didn't, or she decided to come to school today anyways, I was packing some pretty ingenious charms.

I waited till the end of first period football practice then made sure I was the first one out of the field house so I could get to the main hall before Savannah. As I entered through the main hall's rear doors, I spit out the charmed piece of gum I'd just chewed and slapped it onto the brick wall just above the doorframe. Then, instead of going straight to second period English lit, I went to the other end of the hall, pretended to exit the front doors, and slapped another chewed-up piece of gum above them.

I headed for class, figuring I could tag the cafeteria exits at lunchtime and the sports and arts building after school when no one would be there.

SAVANNAH

"You are not going," Dad said Tuesday morning. "I forbid it. They will most likely be wearing wards in full force."

"I have to, Dad." I tried to keep my voice calm as I stood in the foyer, Charmers duffel bag's strap gripped in one hand, the keys to my brand-new, just-delivered-last-night car in the other. "You don't understand. I may have never physically fought back, but at least I've never run away from a descendant. If I don't go to school—not just this week but *today*—they'll think they've won. They'll be even worse. They'll think they can run me out of school permanently. And then where would it end? Next thing you know, I won't be able to go to the store because some descendant might be there wearing a ward. And then they'll run me out of town or else make me a prisoner in my own house."

Dad stared at me, his silence proof that I had a point.

"I *have* to do this."

"I do not like this."

"And you think I do? I didn't say I *wanted* to go. But I have to, or they'll never stop. I just have to prove I'm tough enough to wait them out until Tristan's dad gets back and yanks them all into line again."

Dad sighed but stepped out of the way. "Call me if you need me to come get you."

"Right. Thanks, Dad." But of course I had zero intention of actually calling him. Not today. No way was the Clann going to get the upper hand, not now that I'd finally come into my own magical skills and had a sleek new mode of transport.

We'd bought me a new car Sunday morning. Well, new to me, at least. News of the silver 1971 Corvette Stingray hadn't made Mom too happy when she heard about it by video chat. She didn't like how fast it could go or that its body was made of fiberglass instead of steel. But the moment I'd seen its gleaming curves out on the car lot, every cell in my body had yearned to make it mine.

To appease Mom, Dad had had a protective roll cage installed, paying a local body shop an insane amount of money so it would be done and delivered to our house by this morning. He'd also had them put in a new stereo system, though I hadn't thought to ask for one, with a jack where I could plug in my MP3 player and listen to all my favorite music while I drove.

As a result, driving my new car to school for the first time was a real kick, and it was hard to resist the urge to floor the gas pedal just to hear the engine growl. The only thing that kept me at the speed limit was the fact that, despite my show of confidence with Dad, I really wasn't looking forward to school. I had no doubt he was right and the Clann kids would be at their nastiest.

When I pulled onto the JHS campus and parked in my usual spot in the front lot, I had to literally force myself to get out of my car and leave it behind. It was going to be such a long day.

At least I'd have a sweet new ride to look forward to driving home at the end of it all.

If I survived the day.

CHAPTER 28

TRISTAN

Savannah came to school after all. It took everything I had to block my ticked off thoughts from her. Obviously she was ignoring the danger of the situation, and anything I tried to tell her at this point would only make her more stubborn about it. So I sat back in my seat and tried not to think at all, even as a slow burn rolled in my stomach. I just had to pray that the protective charms I'd put up earlier would work like I hoped.

The charms got their first test at the end of English lit. Just before the bell, both Savannah's and my arms broke out in goosebumps as pinpricks of pain briefly exploded across my skin. Someone was using power on campus.

Drawing in a sharp breath through her nose, Savannah looked at me in question.

Not me this time, I silently told her.

A second, brief but intense explosion of pain jabbed across my neck and arms. What the heck was going on out there?

Her gaze flicked to the small windows on the far wall, which were too high up to give a view of anything but the sky. Her eyebrows pinched together into a worried scowl as she quickly gathered her things.

When the dismissal bell rang, as usual, Savannah was the first one out of her desk. I took my time stuffing papers into my notebook, hanging back on purpose with the plan to follow her at a distance and make sure no one's vamp wards were hurting her in the main hall.

She didn't make it that far.

The Brat Twins were waiting for her in the alcove shared by the two neighboring English rooms. They used the alcove like a choke point, letting everyone but her past.

"You," Vanessa hissed as soon as she saw Savannah. Vanessa raised her hands in the air, palm out. They were covered in what looked like red paint. "You did this!"

"Make her take it off," Hope whined behind her sister while furiously rubbing one red palm against the other.

A quick peek into their thoughts revealed the twins had been up to a new twist on their usual nastiness. During second period, they'd met up with Dylan in the front parking lot and tried to throw magic-laced paint on Sav's new car. That was probably the two uses of power Sav and I had just sensed. But somehow their spell had backfired and the paint had ended up on the twins' own hands instead.

I ignored the part where Vanessa believed Savannah had put a repelling spell on her car. Obviously that was pure Clann paranoia. What I couldn't figure out was why the twins weren't at least smart enough to cancel their own spell so the paint would wash off.

"What's the matter?" Savannah murmured. "Did you get paint on yourselves?" One corner of her mouth twitched.

"You b—" Choking, Vanessa took a step forward, drawing back a hand as if to slap Savannah.

More pinpricks of pain erupted over my skin.

The twins were using power? Here, on Savannah and in front of everyone? They must have lost their minds.

"Hey!" I lunged out of my desk, ignoring the paperwork sliding onto the floor along with my books.

Savannah glanced over her shoulder at me. The pain stopped.

"Later, girls," she said to the twins. Then she took off down the main hall.

"What do you two think you're doing?" I demanded, wishing the twins were guys instead of girls so I could take them outside and throw them up against a brick wall.

"It wasn't us!" Vanessa stuttered, her eyes wider than I'd ever seen them. Both girls were pale beneath their spray on tans. "I swear it, Tristan. It was her! She's learned how to use power."

I didn't bother to reply to that.

Stepping around them, I searched the hall. There. Savannah was leaning against a wall of lockers fifty yards away.

I recognized a too-familiar head of shaggy blond hair inches away from her. A shift of bodies in the crowded hall let me see that Dylan was actually holding Savannah trapped against the lockers, his hands braced at either side of her head.

On each wrist, he wore a leather cuff. Vamp wards. That's where the most recent needles of pain had come from. He was trying to either knock her out or kill her, but the charms I'd put up before second period were blocking his wards.

"It's Dylan," I told the twins cowering behind me while keeping my eyes locked on him. "He's the one you're sensing."

Grinding my teeth, I moved down the hall at a near jog, elbowing people out of my way and trying to decide where to hit Dylan first. Thank God for my vamp ward blocks. If not for them, Savannah would be on the floor unconscious or possibly even dead right now. Dylan's wards were only inches from her cheeks.

He frowned at those cuffs now, obviously wondering why the wards weren't affecting Savannah.

A second later, his back slammed to the lockers where Savannah had just been. Except it wasn't because of me. I'd planned to play by the Clann rules, skip the magic and just punch him, but I was still yards away.

More pain stabbed into life over my skin.

Somehow their positions had become reversed, and it was Savannah who held Dylan prisoner now, though she didn't touch him in any way, her hands at her sides palm out, fingers spread.

As if she really were using power to pin him there.

No way. Not possible. Except…the proof was right there for me to both see and feel. Somehow, Savannah had learned to use power. And judging by how Dylan struggled yet couldn't get free, she was way past the beginner level. She must have been developing her skills for months. But how? And who would have been crazy enough to teach her?

Leaning toward Dylan, Savannah tilted her head back and to the side in a way that reminded me of a curious lioness playing with its prey. She smiled and licked her lips, holding his gaze with her own.

"Dylan, Dylan, Dylan," she said. "You tried to fry my brand-new car, didn't you? You already took out my truck. What are you trying to do, force me to fly around like a bat instead?" She grinned at him, ignoring me though she must have felt me approach just like I could always sense when she was near.

I stopped two feet short of them, the needles of pain on

my skin screaming for attention now. God, she was a strong witch, almost half as strong as Emily already. I resisted the urge to rub my skin, focusing on her instead.

For the first time, she didn't look like my Savannah. She didn't look like she belonged to anyone at all. She had become a creature completely alien to our planet, her eyes gone a silver so light it was one shade short of white, her impossibly smooth and poreless skin a sharp and unnatural contrast to the bloodred of her hair.

She was vamping out.

Her gaze dropped to his neck, her lips moving as she murmured something to him too low for me to hear, and Dylan's eyes widened.

In his shock and fear, Dylan's mental guard dropped, letting me hear his every thought.

Oh God, she's going to do it, he thought. *She's going to kill me right here in front of everyone. Look at her! She doesn't even care if anyone sees.*

I glanced around, worried we were drawing an audience. Thankfully no one cared what Dylan seemed to be doing with his latest prize against the lockers. They were all too busy trying to get to class or lunch before the tardy bell rang.

"Maybe I should give you what you want after all." She eased in closer to him, peering into his eyes. "That's what you want, isn't it? For me to lose control and bite you? The thing is, I can't figure out if your daddy put you up to it, or if this one's all your idea."

Feeling her breath on his cheek, Dylan moaned, his knees bending.

"Ah, ah, ah, we're not done talking yet," Savannah said, and the pain stabbed harder at my skin as she ramped up the power to hold him upright. "Now what was I saying? Oh yeah, we were discussing how much you want me to bite you right now."

Yes, do it, Dylan thought, and I rocked back on my heels. *Sink your teeth into me!*

Whoa. He really wanted her to lose control.

"But you didn't answer my question," she said. "Do you want me to bite you because it'll help your dad become Clann leader, so he'll stop using magic to punish you? Or is it because you've got a thing for vamps?"

"I don't know what you're talking about, freak," Dylan pushed out through gritted teeth.

But he couldn't stop his mind from revealing the truth.

Both. I want to know how it feels, and it'll make Dad stop.

And then I saw his memories, thousands of them, flashing through his mind, his body twisting with pain as his father hit him with power over and over, using magic instead of his fists because the power didn't leave marks.

My gut twisted. Oh man. "Dylan, why didn't you say something?"

Realizing for the first time that I was there, Dylan's gaze darted sideways since Savannah wouldn't let his head turn.

"Tristan! She's using power, man!"

The tardy bell rang, emptying the hall around us. I looked behind me. Even the Brat Twins had scattered, probably in fear that Savannah would go after them once she was done with Dylan. It was just the three of us now. Time to twist this mess into something else so the Clann spy wouldn't go running off to gather up a lynch mob for Savannah.

In the sudden silence, I risked stepping closer to Sav and resting a hand on her shoulder.

"Dylan, you're imagining things. Savannah would never risk starting a war, especially right now when things are already tense between everybody. She knows the rules. She would never learn to use power."

"She's doing it *right now!*" he insisted, his face contorting with pain.

"He wants me to bite him, Tristan," she murmured. "Is it really breaking the rules if he begs for it?"

I squeezed her shoulder. *Don't, Sav. I know you can hear me. Now please trust me. You've scared the crap out of him. It's enough for today. Any more use of power and the adult descendants are going to come running, if they aren't already.*

She frowned at me, hesitating but at least listening to me.

Can you trust me to take over and get us out of this? I silently asked her.

One corner of her mouth tightened as if in disappointment. But she sighed and gave the tiniest nod.

As she pulled back her magic, I ramped up my own, using my power now to hold Dylan in place.

"Dylan, don't be an idiot," I said out loud. "I'm the only one using power here. And before you even think about going to the elders to complain, you'd better remember who started this. They told everyone to leave her alone. How do you think they're gonna react if they find out you're messing with a vamp and trying to destroy the peace treaty?"

He opened his mouth to argue.

I leaned in closer, getting in his face. "More importantly, I told you to leave her alone. What did you expect me to do when you refused? You should be grateful this is all I'm doing to you."

She's not the one...? he wondered, squinting as he looked from Savannah to me again. *It's a trick! It's all a setup to mess with my mind. She was just pretending she was the one using power on me. And her car...Tristan put a protective spell on it, didn't he?*

She probably went whining to him about her truck last week, and he just couldn't resist riding in to the rescue again.

"Let me go." He glared at me now, the terror in his voice turning to fury as he fell for the lie.

"Are you going to stop messing with her and learn to play nice?" I said.

He hesitated, considering.

I ratcheted my energy level up yet another notch, and beads of sweat formed on his forehead and upper lip. Savannah twitched under my hand.

Sorry, I told her. *Hang in there just a little longer.*

"Fine," Dylan mumbled.

"What's that?" I pretended I couldn't hear him.

"I said okay, I'll leave her alone." He looked away as sweat rolled down past his eyes.

I leaned back. Then on second thought, I reached down and ripped one of the cuffs off his wrist. While he watched, I flash burned the ward until it was reduced to a tiny indoor snowstorm of ashes falling to the polished vinyl floor.

"One ward's enough," I told him. "Two's an attack. Next time I see you wearing more than one ward, I'll burn it while it's still on you."

I stepped back, and Dylan slunk off down the hall toward the cafeteria. I didn't move until he was through the exit doors and out of sight.

Savannah sighed loudly and leaned against the lockers. Then she started to slide down toward the floor.

"Whoa, I've got you, Rocky." I wrapped an arm around her waist to hold her up.

She gave me a weak grin. "Thanks. No one ever warned me how exhausting this stuff is."

"It takes energy to use energy." I slung her closest arm over my shoulders so she could hang on. "You need to refuel. Do you have some bl—"

"I've got an emergency stash. But if I use it, I have to go home. There are…complications. I could draw energy, though. Just help me get outside?"

"Or you could kiss—"

"Don't start, Tristan." She tried to pull away.

"Okay, okay. I was just joking." Sort of.

We headed out the front doors, turning left past the entrance toward a small courtyard where we sat on a blue metal bench, Savannah at the end closest to the grass. She kicked off her shoes and angled her legs so she could rest her bare feet on the grass, then closed her eyes and sighed.

Needles arced over my skin, but I ignored them, too caught up in watching the play of emotions on her face.

After a few seconds, she opened her eyes, glanced down at the goose bumps on my hands, and smiled. "Guess it's my turn to apologize and tell you it'll be over in just another minute?"

"Don't worry about it. It doesn't hurt that bad. It's just… weird." At her raised eyebrow, I added, "I mean, that you're doing it."

I leaned forward, bracing my elbows on my knees. "For a beginner you're sure progressing fast. Is someone helping you or…?"

"Not really."

I frowned. "Working without a teacher is dangerous, Sav."

She laughed. "No kidding. I passed out the first time I tried to draw energy. I kept grounding by accident."

I froze. "This summer?"

She nodded. "The day you texted me, actually."

So that's what I felt. "Did you sleep it off?"

"No. Nanna showed up and told me what to do."

She had talked with her dead grandma. Which meant she

must have been really far gone. Fear mixed with fury, pushing me to my feet. I stood in front of her so I could see her
face clearly.

"Are you crazy? You almost died, didn't you?"

"I had to do something. Dylan was threatening to hurt
Anne. What would you have done?"

"You should have come to me for help."

She sighed. "I'm tired of always having to ask someone else
for help. It was time for me to grow up, take care of my own
problems for a change."

She wrapped her arms around her waist and looked away.

How could she be half vamp and supposedly dangerous to
me and any other descendant, yet seem so fragile?

My gut knotted. I wanted to hold her, tell her she wasn't
alone, that I was right here for her. But she didn't want to
hear any of that.

We stayed there for a moment, the heated air between us
quickly cooling and turning awkward.

"What you did today was reckless," I said.

Shoving her feet back into her shoes, she stood up and
headed for the entrance doors. "You just can't help but try to
boss me around, can you?"

I followed her back into the main hall. "I'm serious, Sav.
Now that descendants have died, things are going to get even
more tense. If you scare Dylan too much, there's no telling
what you might set off."

"No kidding." Her cheeks turned pink.

Remembering Dylan's twisted thoughts about her today,
it was my turn to look away now. I couldn't believe he was
that messed up.

"Did you know about…his dad? That he's using magic to
abuse him?"

I shook my head. "I swear, he never told me." I wished he

had, though. The Clann could have stepped in, either forced Mr. Williams to stop or maybe even taken Dylan away from all of that.

"I feel sorry for him. His dad's the reason he keeps going after us. The Williamses want to make you break the rules bad enough to force your dad into a decision between protecting you or upholding the Clann rules. They figure he'd choose you over the Clann, and then they could push for a change in leadership."

I shook my head. "What his dad is doing is wrong. But don't make excuses for Dylan. He still makes his own decisions. He doesn't have to play into his dad's political games."

At the main hall's exit, I pushed the heavy metal door open, holding it for her so she could go through first.

Scowling, she ducked under my arm and outside. "Oh, so he should just refuse to obey his parents and take the constant punishment instead?"

"No, of course not. He needs to either stand up to his dad or else leave home."

"What if he can't? What if his dad's too strong and he doesn't have anywhere to go? You know, not everyone has gobs of money and power at their disposal." She walked faster, arms crossed, headed for the catwalk.

Easily keeping pace with her, I ignored the jab about money. "Dylan's a descendant. He has the entire Clann to turn to for help. All he has to do is ask."

Not to mention he could have talked to me about it instead of stabbing me in the back.

She shook her head in silent disagreement.

"What, you think the Clann wouldn't help him? Come on, Sav, they're flawed but they're not that bad."

She shrugged and turned onto the ramp leading down to

the cafeteria's sidewalk. "They didn't seem to have a problem kidnapping and torturing my grandma."

"That was a mistake. My parents were desperate and freaking out and weren't thinking straight. Otherwise my dad never would have allowed that to happen."

Pressing her lips together, she walked down the ramp in silence.

Though I had no intention of eating lunch today and having to deal with the ticked off hordes of Charmers and descendants, I followed Savannah to the sidewalk, wanting this conversation with her to last as long as possible even if it wasn't the happiest of discussions. If fighting with her was all I could get, I would take it.

As we circled the cafeteria's brick exterior to the nearest entrance, I couldn't resist saying, "Speaking of mistakes, do you want to talk about how you nearly vamped out and bit Dylan?"

She rolled her eyes. "I was just messing with him. I never would have bitten him. I don't do that."

"Ever?"

"Never."

"You've never bitten anyone."

"No!"

We stopped at the doors. "And yet I never see you eat anything in there." I jerked a thumb at the cafeteria.

"My dad gets me donated blood once a week. I just go to lunch every other day to see my friends since we don't have any classes together this year."

"Donated blood? I guess that's not so bad." Maybe being a vamp was a lot easier nowadays than her dad had made it out to be. They might even have their own blood bank system by now, complete with delivery boys. Ordering blood was probably as simple as calling out for a pizza.

She snorted. "It's still bad, Tristan. Living off of other peoples' blood comes with a lot of complications."

"Yeah? Like what, deciding which blood type tastes best?"

"No, more like the fact that every time I feed, I take in that person's memories. Good, bad, crazy, boring, all of it hits me like a flood, and I can't control it for hours. It's definitely nothing I would ever wish on anybody. Even Dylan."

"Or me?"

"Especially not you," she whispered.

"Shouldn't you let me make that decision?"

Her chin lifted. "No. Because even if by some miracle the turning process actually worked for you, you couldn't possibly understand the consequences of that choice until after it's too late. No matter how much you might regret it later, you can't undo this."

"I would never regret getting to spend forever with you."

Swallowing hard, she looked away. After a minute of silence, she finally made eye contact again only to change the subject. "I heard about you and Bethany. Sorry it didn't work out."

"I thought you didn't want me to lead her on anymore."

"I wanted you to be *happy* with her. And honest with her if you couldn't be."

I gave in to the urge to study her face, rememorizing every curve, the wispy curls at the edges of her forehead, the new pearl-like gleam to her skin. "You were right. I was leading her on, though I swear I didn't know it. And when I finally did, I told her the truth."

One corner of her mouth deepened. "From the Charmers' reaction, I take it that didn't go over well with her."

"Yeah, not so much." I gave her a sheepish smile, appreciating the sympathy even if I didn't deserve it.

She opened the door, and I grabbed the edge of it to hold it for her, taking one last chance to be close to her.

"Hey, Sav?"

She stopped, turned back, looked up at me and was close enough to kiss.

"Be careful, okay?" My hand ached to touch her cheek. "Dylan and the twins are going to be suspicious now, no matter what I tell them. They might try to push you again just to prove to the adults that you're breaking the rules. Don't let them make you lose control again. You're stronger than that, stronger than them."

She searched my eyes, a faint smile curving her lips. "Thanks, Tristan."

Still wearing that trace of a smile, she entered the cafeteria, letting the doors drop closed between us.

Taking a deep breath, I reached for another charmed stick of gum in my pocket.

CHAPTER 29

It was a long week. Mom and Dad took turns shouting and threatening me over the phone about the burned vamp ward. But I flat-out refused to wear one and risk hurting Savannah. I told them I didn't care if they grounded me again, flew home and ordered me to, or had Emily and Mrs. Faulkner beat on my bedroom door and yell about it for days. It wasn't happening, and that was all there was to it.

Mom nearly went ballistic. Dad promised we'd have a talk when they got home next week. And that was the end of the discussion for now.

I stayed busy all week, using every bit of spare time to make replacement vamp ward blocks. Along with the other descendants on campus, Dylan and the twins stuck to wearing only one ward each, but even those few wards were enough to wear out my blocking charms on a daily basis. Even with drawing energy, I was distracted and played lousy during Friday night's away game. Coach Parker ended up benching me for most of the game in disgust.

I used the weekend to draw energy and worry about Savannah. Would she listen to my warning to be careful? Or was she still practicing using power without supervision? How often did she practice? She would have to go somewhere away from her dad to keep it a secret; there was no way the vamp council was knowingly allowing her to develop her skills. Was she outside in the cold?

Short of calling her and demanding that she let me supervise her practice sessions, there wasn't much I could do to keep her safe. And it made for a lot of sleepless nights.

She was at school on Monday, though, so I could relax while at school. That afternoon after football practice, I headed home and was surprised to find Dad's car already in the garage. They'd gotten home late last night, Mom sleeping in this morning and Dad off to work long before breakfast. I checked my watch. It was only five-thirty, hours before I'd figured he would come home tonight since he probably had a ton of work to get caught up on.

Hoping he was tired and comatose on the living room couch, I walked softly down the hall between there and the kitchen to check on him.

Halfway down the hall, I passed his open study door and discovered him on the phone behind his desk.

Great. Maybe he'd be too busy working from home to give me that "talk" he'd promised.

I turned toward the foyer, but I wasn't quick enough. A sharp snap of fingers commanded me to turn around again and join him in his study.

I eased down into the creaky leather armchair across from him. This was not going to be good.

My left knee bounced as I stared at my hands. Then I began to actually listen to what he was saying.

"No, you don't want to do that, and here's why. We don't

know for sure that vampires are the killers in the first place. Yes, I'm serious! Two holes in the neck does not automatically equal a vamp killing." He paused. "Yes, that's true, their bodies were drained. But they could have just as easily been bled out somewhere else then dumped where they'd be found fast. Think about it. Anybody under the sun could be behind it. If we start jumping to conclusions, we could be playing right into their hands. That's why for now I'm asking everyone to stay calm, lay low, wear a ward and let me and the vamp council do the investigating. I guarantee you, we will find out who's behind these murders, and they will be made to pay for it." Another pause. "Yes, I said the vamp council. No, I already told you, these are not council-sanctioned attacks." One last pause. "You be safe, too, and be sure to stay in regular contact with other descendants, at least once a day or so. Okay? Yep, you, too."

He hung up, ran a hand over his receding silver hair, then sighed loudly. "And that's the life of the Clann leader in a nutshell. Putting out brush fires one call at a time."

"We should get a website or something so we can release one mass statement to all the descendants at the same time."

Dad grinned. "You know, that's not a bad idea. We could use a little more organization around here."

The tension in my shoulders eased. Maybe he wasn't planning on punishing me after all.

I looked at his desk, which appeared to have been barfed on by a paper monster, and laughed. "Yeah, because obviously being organized is a major focus in this house."

He chuckled.

"But seriously, Dad, how do you do it? How do you say the same things over and over without going nuts?"

"That's the life of any leader worth a dime. You've got to have patience."

"Even with the prejudiced idiots?"

"Even them. We're only the Clann leader till death or revolt."

"I heard you warning them to wear their wards. Which is what I kind of needed to talk to you about."

"Mmm-hmm. I've been meaning to talk to you about it, too."

Uh-oh. Here it came. "I'm sorry I refused to wear the ward."

Silence. His eyebrows shot up, and he leaned back in his chair and clasped his thick fingers over his gut. "But?"

"But I couldn't do it. Not with a half vamp with no immunity to the wards on campus. She can't help what she is any more than I can. Why should she pay for something that's going on halfway across the country?"

Dad's mouth turned down. He rubbed his chin through his beard. "You know, your momma's really sore about it. She made that ward herself."

"Yeah, I know she was mad. But it just wasn't right. And it's not like I don't have other ways to protect myself."

He nodded slowly. "That's what I told your mom when she was sobbing about her poor, unprotected little boy and nearly making herself sick over it."

I tried not to roll my eyes at the less-than-subtle guilt trip attempt.

He sighed. "She's mad, but she'll get over it. Did anything else happen while we were gone?"

I rocked back in the chair. He sounded like he was asking for a report or something. "Um, not really. Well, there was a small problem with Dylan showing up at school wearing two wards. But I had a talk with him about it."

"Oh yeah? What kind of talk?" He grinned, leaning forward in his chair.

"I, uh, might have flash burned one of his wards." Seeing his eyes widen, I added, "But I ripped it off his wrist first. And I made sure no one else was around to see."

"So I should be expecting a whining call from his father any second now?"

"Maybe." In fact, I was surprised Mr. Williams hadn't already called. "He might not have told his dad about it, though. It happened while Dylan and I had a little face-off about Dylan wrecking Savannah's truck a couple of weeks ago, and then his working with the Faulkner twins today to try and wreck her new car."

Dad grumbled a swear word. "Okay, I'll handle it."

I hesitated. "If Mr. Williams does call you, you might want to ask him about how he's using power to punish Dylan. He's forcing his son to try and come up with ways to make me break the rules so you'll do something dumb. They want to make you look weak and biased toward protecting your family instead of upholding Clann law so they can push for new leadership. And when Dylan's less than successful at ticking me or Sav off…"

Dad's eyes flared then narrowed to dangerous slits. "You're kidding. He's using power on his own son for punishment?"

I nodded. "It doesn't leave a mark, so there's no proof of the abuse."

Dad swore again. "I'll have a talk with the elders. We'll figure something out to stop it. It would serve Mr. Williams right if his plan backfired and we banned him from the Clann."

Something tight in my chest loosened, making me realize just how much I'd worried that the Clann might not do the right thing to help Dylan after all.

"Thanks, Dad." I started to get up.

"Hey, tell me how the game went. Your mom and I were sorry we couldn't be there."

Well, maybe Dad had been. We both knew how Mom felt about descendants playing sports that might reveal their extra abilities. "You didn't miss much. I played like crap. With everything that's going on…"

"Tough to keep your head in the game?"

I nodded.

"Well, hopefully we'll find some answers soon that'll satisfy everyone and let this whole situation blow over."

"Did you mean what you said on the phone about how the deaths could be a fake vamp attack?"

Dad's big shoulders rose and fell. "It's always possible someone's playing on old fears. It could have even been a descendant behind it, for all we know right now. I went to the morgue with your mother. I saw the bodies and…" He swallowed hard, cleared his throat and continued. "Well, let's just say I've got a feeling the situation's not nearly as clear cut as your mother wants it to be."

"You know, I get that vamps are dangerous to us. But what I don't get is why all the hatred…people don't sit around hating lions or tigers for doing what comes naturally to them. And we're just as dangerous to the vamps, too."

Dad propped an elbow on the desk and slowly rubbed the back of his neck. Finally he muttered, "Don't let your mother know I told you, but…she lost both sets of her grandparents in the last war with the vamps. Her parents' families were poor folks with neighboring farms. After her parents got married, when times got too hard to afford both places, their families decided to move in together and work as a team to try and save one of the farms. One night she and her sister and parents went into town. When they got back home, they found everyone else dead. The vamps must have hit their house as a group. She says she can still remember how it looked."

Dad sighed and scrubbed a hand over his eyes, which had

more than a few bags under them. "It must have been a pretty bad sight to see, especially as a little kid. She still has night-mares about it sometimes."

The farmhouse from Mom's thoughts last week, the one she was afraid to enter...

I tried to imagine coming home and finding my family murdered like that, and the rage I might feel afterwards. "Oh man."

He nodded. "And she's not the only one with memories and loss like that. Most of us lost at least one or two loved ones. It left a lot of scar tissue. So you see how it might take more than a few talks to convince everyone to settle down and forget the past."

After about a minute of silence, I got up and headed for the door.

"Oh, by the way." Dad's voice stopped me in the door-way. "Your momma's off to Tyler to pick up your sister and bring her home."

"Why?" Couldn't Emily drive herself? Had her car broken down or something?

"Emily came down with a nasty case of the flu. Can't seem to stop puking. So you might want to drink extra orange juice this week and avoid your sister's room."

"Right. Thanks for the warning." I went upstairs to my room to chill out on my bed with my MP3 player for a while. But my mind wouldn't turn off.

It seemed being the Clann leader was a lot different than I'd thought. I'd always assumed that Dad had total power and could just make an order, and the Clann had to follow it. But he made it sound like he was some ordinary elected official who had to convince people to do what was needed.

Definitely not a job I was looking forward to taking over anytime soon.

He really should consider giving the role to Emily. She had always had the ability to sway people into seeing things from her point of view. She could convince you so well that within half an hour she'd have you believing it was your idea in the first place. And that was without using a spell.

Maybe I could talk him into seriously considering it.

I heard a racket on the stairs and stuck my head out the bedroom door just as Mom and Emily reached the second-floor landing.

"Hey, sis. Sorry you're so sick. Need any help or…?"

"No, thanks," she grumbled as she shuffled into her bedroom and flopped onto her bed.

"She'll be fine," Mom said, bringing up the rear with a glass full of murky greenish-brown fluid that could only be some terrible mix of herbs and spells. "We just need to get this down her, and keep it down long enough for it to kick in."

Emily croaked, "Honestly, Mom, I'm not that sick."

Yeah, right. She just didn't want to drink that nasty crap Mom always shoved down our throats every time we got a sniffle.

"Oh please, you've been barfing for hours," Mom argued. "Now hush up and let your mother take care of you for a while."

I shut my door, grateful not to be Emily right now. I didn't know what would be worse…alone in a dorm room with the flu, or suffering from Mom's herbal drinks. But at least one good thing should come out of it. Mom would probably be too busy taking care of Emily for a few days to stir up any more anti-vamp attitudes within the various branches of the Clann. That ought to give Dad a chance to calm everyone down.

I tried to picture Mom on the phone with all of the descendants and cringed. Now that would be bad. Mom could stir up World War III in a matter of hours. As smart as Emily was, I wouldn't put it past her to be faking the flu just to keep Mom too busy to nag Dad endlessly for a crackdown on vamps' rights.

Later that night, I went to Emily's door to check on her.

It sounded like she was barfing up everything and the kitchen sink in her adjoining bathroom.

I cracked her door open and called out, "Sis, do you—"

"Go away," she moaned.

I eased the door shut and carefully stepped away from her room. I should have remembered how cranky she got when she was sick.

There was a girl who would never go down without a fight.

CHAPTER 30

The rest of the week was relatively peaceful, at least at school. Either Dad or Savannah must have put the fear into Dylan and the twins, because they left her alone.

On the home front, though, things were decidedly less than calm. Not only were Mom's herbal drinks not working, but Emily and Mom were now arguing on a daily basis about sending Emily to the hospital or at least to Dr. Faulkner for a checkup. Apparently she wasn't able to keep much down. Knowing how much Emily hated needles, I wasn't surprised that she was refusing to go for a checkup. She would probably cave eventually; nobody stood up to Mom for long except maybe Dad. Then again, knowing Emily's pride, she was more than likely already wanting to see a doctor and just refusing to go in order to show Mom she was in charge of her own life now.

This wasn't the first time Emily and Mom had butted heads, and it wouldn't be the last. The safest course of action for Dad and me and any other innocent bystanders was to stay out of the war zone as much as possible until either a winner or a truce was declared.

But on Friday afternoon when I came home and heard her sobbing in her room, I couldn't stand it anymore.

I knocked on her door. She sniffled and said, "What, Tristan?"

I opened the door an inch. "How did you know it was me?"

"Because Mom just barges in, and Dad's too scared to cross the battle line."

I opened the door a little wider. "How are you feeling? Can I get you anything? The latest *Cosmo* issue, one of those eye mask thingies, some nasal spray?" She looked beyond bad, her face swollen so much I could barely see her eyes. Her nose was painfully red, as if she'd blown it so many times she'd rubbed off the top layer of skin.

She rolled her eyes and sighed. "I know, I look like crap."

"Not to side with Mom here, but maybe you should go see a doctor." Mom's herbal drinks, nasty as they were, had never once failed to cure us of any illness within a day or two.

"I know. I should have gone yesterday." She stared out the window on the wall opposite her bed. "I just...really don't want to see that smug look of Mom's if I give in."

I tried not to smile. "So in the meantime you're miserable. Very mature of you."

She tossed a pillow at me. It went wide, harmlessly bouncing off the wall.

Her cell phone beeped on the nightstand. She grabbed it and froze while reading the screen.

"Your college buddies worrying about you?" I asked, nodding at her phone when she looked up with her eyebrows drawn in confusion.

"Oh. Yeah. I posted how sick I was on Facebook just so no one would think I was dead yet. Getting texts about it now."

"Well, cheer up, kid. The flu usually only lasts a few days. You should be getting better soon."

Tears filled her eyes. "Right. I know that." She groped for a tissue, missing the box by six inches. I held the box closer to her. Her "thanks" came out muffled through a wad of Kleenex.

I was going to sit on the edge of her bed to talk and picked up her phone to move it out of the way.

She snatched it back and stuffed it under the covers.

"Paranoid much?" I asked. "I wasn't going to read it."

"No, I know that." She wouldn't look at me. "I just…have friends Mom probably wouldn't like, and the less you know about them, the less she can pick the info out of your brain."

"What kind of friends are we talking about here?" I'd heard of college students getting into drugs and stuff while away from home, but Emily had never seemed the type to do any of that. She valued her intelligence too much to risk the brain damage.

"Oh you know. Rockers. Computer geeks. Hardcore video gamers. Anyone who's not 'cool' enough in her book."

Mom was a little obsessed with our family image. Sometimes I got the feeling that she must have been a social misfit while growing up and was trying to live through her kids.

"Still running a fever?" I felt her forehead like Mom used to do for me on the rare occasion that I caught a virus. "Yeah, you feel warm. I'll grab you some meds."

I got up but she waved off the offer. "Don't bother. They make me too queasy. It'll all come right back up."

"How often are you barfing?"

She rested her head against her pillows and closed her eyes. "I've lost count. Pretty much all day and night with some naps in between. I've thrown up so much my abs are killing me. I could have sworn I was working out enough before now!"

Starting to feel useless, I refilled her water glass with fresh water from the bathroom. "Hey, how about some of that drinkable flu medicine stuff? I think Dad got some the last time he got sick and didn't want Mom to know." Even Dad hated the herbal drinks.

She made a face. "We can try it. But I'll probably barf it up, too."

I ran downstairs to the kitchen and found the medicine hidden behind Dad's stash of junk food in the cabinet over the fridge that Mom was too short to reach. After nuking a mug of water and stirring in the meds as directed, I brought the drink back upstairs to Emily.

"Mom left a note on the fridge. Apparently she's going to try some new herbs on you. She said she was going into town for supplies."

"Great." Emily was texting again, her face set in the darkest scowl I'd ever seen.

"Man, you are addicted to that thing," I joked.

She grunted in response, barely even glancing my way as I set the steaming mug on the nightstand.

"Anything else I can fetch for the flu princess?" I asked.

"No. Thanks, Tristan." She smiled at me, which would have looked normal on her any other week but this one. Today it looked forced. "Maybe later I'll go outside and get some fresh air."

"If you do, bundle up and don't go too far," I warned. "It's like fifty degrees out there."

Not that Mom would let her out the door anyways once she got home.

"You going to be around later?" she mumbled, her thumbs flying over her phone's keypad.

"I don't know. Why?"

She lifted a shoulder an inch in a weak half shrug. "It's Friday. I'm just worried about your nonexistent social life since you got dumped. Twice."

Ouch. "You know, that case of flu you've got really brings out the mean in your eyes."

She sighed. "Sorry. I just meant you should go out and do something. Football and Sav aren't the end-all and be-all of life."

It was my turn to grunt in response. "Quit worrying about me and get some rest."

Later Mom came home and went to check on Emily. I could hear their conversation from across the hall.

"Oh, Emily," Mom sighed. "I just came home from the store. Why didn't you tell me you needed more Sprite and crackers then?"

"Because I didn't know I needed them then," Emily said. "I just read where someone suggested it on Facebook. They said it was the cure-all for any kind of queasiness. Well, except for food poisoning, I guess. They promised it might settle my stomach till the virus has run its course."

Mom stood in the open doorway to Emily's room. "I just don't understand why the healing drinks aren't working this time."

"I don't think I'm really sick anymore. I actually feel much better overall. It's just my stomach that's irritated now."

Apparently the drinkable flu medicine was working. Dad would love hearing that his choice of meds was better than Mom's herbs and magic.

"Hmm. Maybe you got your father's nervous stomach after all," Mom muttered. "I swear that man eats antacids like candy lately." She sighed, rubbing a thin hand across her forehead. "Okay, I'll go back to the store and get you some Sprite and crackers."

"Saltines, they said," Emily added.

"Right. Saltine crackers. Got it. I guess I'll call your father on the way and see if he needs anything else, too."

"Thanks, Mom."

My door opened and Mom poked her head in. "I'm going to the grocery store. Do you want to come?"

"Sure." It wasn't like I had a hot date planned. Or much of anything else now that football season was over. A guy could only work out or listen to so much music.

I yanked on my boots and tied them, called out a quick goodbye to Emily, then jogged downstairs and out the kitchen door to the garage.

But as I opened the passenger door of Mom's car, I realized there was no way I could go with my mother to the grocery store on a Friday night. It was one thing to take a break from dating and another to purposefully commit social suicide without a cause.

"Uh, on second thought," I told Mom through the open door. "I think I'll stay. You know, in case Emily needs something. She probably shouldn't be alone and sick."

Mom frowned, then her lips twitched. "Oh. Right. Friday night. No, we wouldn't want anyone to see you buying groceries with your mom tonight."

Smiling a sheepish apology, I shut the passenger door so she could leave. Then I tried to figure out something to do with my evening.

My truck. It could use some serious TLC. Usually I cleaned it every couple of weeks, but lately I'd been too busy. Might as well tackle it now.

I was bent over wiping down the dusty dashboard when movement outside the garage door windows caught my eye. It was Emily. Apparently she felt well enough to get some fresh air like she'd mentioned wanting to do earlier.

She was wearing socks, house shoes, her long wool coat and a scarf. Satisfied she was dressed warm enough, I started to look away.

Then some guy came around the side of the house toward her on foot. He looked like he might be around Emily's age, dressed nice in slacks, loafers and a long wool coat and plaid scarf. He seemed vaguely familiar, but wasn't anyone we'd gone to school with. One of Emily's friends from the local colleges? Jacksonville had two junior colleges plus a seminary school. He could be a student at any of them, or a classmate with her in Tyler.

Whoever he was, Emily seemed to know him. She gave him a hug then stood talking with him, her hands resting in her coat pockets, the occasional smile showing on her face. She wouldn't have looked quite so relaxed around a stranger.

Dad pulled up in his car and parked to the side of the garage, probably so Mom could have the only open bay left to unload the groceries from. I figured he'd go inside the house, but he stayed to talk to Emily and the stranger. After a couple of minutes, all three of them began to stroll around the backyard.

Huh. Okay, maybe the guy was some business associate of Dad's.

Thankfully no one seemed to notice me inside my truck in the garage, so I wasn't obligated to go out and make small talk. I could still go back inside and up to my room without being missed.

My plan worked. I was in my room for two hours zoning out with the TV before I finally heard Emily come upstairs and go to her room. Within two minutes, the peace of the second floor was shattered by her snoring.

The fresh air must have really worn her out. Someday I ought to record her snoring. The blackmail possibilities would be endless.

Grinning, I turned my TV up a little louder to block out the log sawing across the hall.

Half an hour later, Mom came home. Bored, I decided to go down and see if she'd bought anything other than meds and stuff for Emily. Sometimes I got lucky and Dad would request junk food. He was the only one in the house who could get her to actually buy the stuff, but at least he took pity on his kids and shared his stash with us.

"Oh good," Mom said, her hands filled with the straps of multiple plastic bags. "You can help me unload."

"I thought you were just going for Sprite and crackers."

"In this household? Impossible!"

I went to the car and grabbed the remaining six bags from the trunk, using my elbow to slam the lid shut before I hauled the load to the kitchen.

"Your father," Mom muttered as she put away the new food. "He gave me the *longest* list of junk he wanted. Look at this! Cupcakes, oatmeal cookies, crème pies. I swear, if he keeps eating like this, he's going to die of a heart attack before he's sixty!"

"Nah. Dad'll never die. He's going to be the first descendant who lives forever." Grinning, I handed her more boxes to put away. "But if you're worried, you could always try putting him on another diet."

"Ha! Like that ever works. You know how pigheaded he is. He'll just sneak in more stuff and hide it in his desk in the study where he thinks I won't know about it." She glanced at her watch and frowned. "It's getting late. I'd better start on dinner. Go ask your father what he wants to have with pork chops."

"Okay." I went down the hall to Dad's study and knocked on the closed door. No answer. Just to be sure, I opened the door and checked. No lights on, and no Dad after I turned them on.

I went down the hall and looked in the living room. Everything was quiet, the TV off, the lights off. I turned on a lamp just to make sure Dad hadn't fallen asleep on the couch like he did sometimes on the weekends.

No Dad in sight.

Maybe he'd gone upstairs to change. I ran up, knocked on my parents' door, checked inside. Again, Dad was nowhere to be found.

I went back downstairs to the kitchen. "I can't find him. Was he still outside when you got home?"

"No. It's forty-five degrees outside. Why would he be out there?"

I shrugged. "Earlier I saw him talking with Emily and some guy. I thought maybe he was a business buddy of Dad's or something. Emily seemed to know him, too."

"Well, there was no one out there a few minutes ago. Just your father's car."

I opened the kitchen door and looked out through the garage door windows. Dad's car was still visible in the lights from the garage. "His car's still here. Maybe he went somewhere with that guy?"

"And not call me and let me know he'd be late for dinner? He knows better than that." Sighing, Mom grabbed the cordless kitchen phone from the wall and dialed. After a moment, her frown deepened. "Samuel Coleman, that phone of yours better be dead. And if you don't either call me back or get home right now, you're gonna be! Where are you?" She hung up, paused then snapped her fingers. The sound was like twigs breaking. "Grab a flashlight and your coat and go check the clearing. I'll bet he's out there."

I glanced at my watch. "Kind of late for spell work, isn't

it?" I pulled on my coat and a pair of Dad's boots he'd left in the garage.

"Oh, you know your father. He likes to go out there and practice his boardroom speeches. Says the pine scent helps him think clearer. Maybe he lost track of time."

And the clearing was notorious for killing all incoming cell phone signals. "Right. Be back in a minute."

"Hurry up. And don't forget the flashlight. Wait! You need a vamp ward."

Sighing, she took hers off.

"Mom, I'll be fine." The only part of our property not protected by vamp wards was the backyard, which took all of ten seconds to cross at a walk.

"Put it on. Your father is safe enough out there, especially with all the wards around that clearing, but you won't be until you reach the clearing. And I know you think you're just as tough as your father, but you're still learning. So wear it and quit arguing and go find your father please." She huffed out that last part all in one breath, not even trying to hide the snap in her voice.

I took the stupid cuff and snapped it around my wrist, then went out back, stopping to open one of the garage doors before jogging across the backyard. Once I hit the edge of the woods, I slowed down and turned on the flashlight. Usually enough moonlight trickled down through the pine branches to light the path. But tonight there was no moon at all to see by.

Which was why I nearly stepped on his hand.

CHAPTER 31

He was lying across the path just inside the clearing. I could have pictured him maybe sitting down on a rock or something, but never lying flat on his back like that. Not even in the clearing.

"Dad!" I crouched down, shook his shoulder. His head rolled toward me, his eyes wide open and flat with no shine, no hint of that spark I was so used to seeing in them.

"Dad?" Holding my breath, I laid a hand on his chest.

Nothing. No rise and fall from breathing. No heartbeat. And he was cold.

Not wanting to believe it yet, I checked his neck. No pulse.

"Dad!" I placed both hands on his chest and hit him with a jolt of energy like I'd seen Dr. Faulkner do for Savannah's grandmother last spring. But the attempt to restart his heart didn't do anything. I tried again, willing him to blink, breath, gasp, anything. Deep down, though, I already knew it was too late. But I still had to try.

I lost count of the number of times I tried to restart his heart, until finally I stopped. He was gone.

Then I saw the punctures in his neck, and I knew, but I didn't want to believe that, either.

No way could my dad, the fourth-generation leader of the Clann, be taken out by a vamp. It wasn't possible. Especially here in the clearing, where he would have been surrounded by some of the most powerful wards in the world. This place was magically designed to protect hundreds of descendants at a time. No vamp could have gotten past the edge of the clearing without a descendant present and consciously allowing them in, the way I had Sav's dad when we'd returned from France. And even if the wards had failed somehow, Dad was too strong, too skilled with magic. He would have fought, and Emily and I both would have felt that use of power and been able to come help him.

It had to have been a setup.

Even as I stared down at his body, at those unblinking eyes, I couldn't believe he was gone. My eyes burned, my chest so tight I couldn't catch a deep breath. He was supposed to live forever, or at least until he was eighty or ninety years old. I was supposed to have decades still to learn from him. He was invincible, the single most powerful and magically gifted descendant in the Clann.

Even though I knew he was gone and couldn't be saved, I didn't want to leave him there. But I had to. I hadn't brought a phone with me, and Dad's was nowhere in sight. I had to go back to the house and tell Mom.

Mom.

I remembered her reaction to the death of her sister. There was no way she was going to be able to handle losing Dad. Once the shock wore off, I didn't know how *I* was going to deal with it. It wasn't real to me yet. I didn't want it to be real yet.

I walked back down the path toward the house, across the back yard, the grass crunchy beneath my feet from frozen frost. Too soon, I was on the steps leading up to the kitchen, and then inside.

"Hey, did you—" At the stove, Mom turned toward me, a metal spatula in one hand, a glass of red wine in the other.

She took one look at my face, reading the thoughts I was too freaked out to hide.

She shook her head. "No. He's too strong."

"Mom," I choked out, slowly crossing the kitchen, the words lodged in my throat and refusing to come out.

"No," she whispered, the glass of wine hitting the floor, shattering, spilling red fluid like a crime scene all over us and the tiles and cabinets.

I tried to hug her, to offer some kind of comfort, knowing she needed me to be strong for her like Dad had been at her sister's funeral last weekend. But she shoved past me and out the kitchen door, not even taking a coat or the flashlight.

I had to run after her. She didn't even slow down when she reached the dark woods. She tripped over a branch on the path halfway to the clearing, would have fallen if I hadn't grabbed her elbow to steady her. She didn't say anything to me, just wrenched her arm free and took off running again.

I shined the light ahead of us just in time before she would have tripped over him.

She stood there for a few seconds, then a high-pitched wail tore its way out of her throat.

If the old stories about banshees had ever been true, this is what they would have sounded like.

She fell to her knees beside him, and it was like reliving that nightmarish day Savannah's grandmother died in her arms.

Once again, I was helpless, useless, without the right words to make this easier for any of us.

I went to my mother, tried to hug her shoulders, but she shoved me away.

"He's not gone," she growled, sounding like something wild, completely unlike the mother I'd known. My mother had often been scary during my life, especially when I'd done something wrong. But she'd never sounded this inhuman before.

She tried spell after spell on Dad's body, lighting up the surrounding woods and the clearing with her magic and her will.

"Mom, he's gone," I said.

"No, he's not! I just need the right spell. Your father's too strong to die. He's still in there. If I can find the right spell, I can bring him back."

But no one knew the old Clann ways that had once affected things on the DNA level, and the ability to bring someone back from the dead was lost to us now. No one could bring Dad back.

If only one of us had gone to check on him hours ago...

If I had only gone out to talk to him and Emily and that stranger...

Emily. She didn't know.

"Mom, we need to tell Emily."

"No, we're not telling her anything because he's not gone."

I touched her shoulder, trying to bring her back to reality. She hissed at me and slapped my hand away. "Leave us!" She leaned over Dad's body, whispering, "Come back to me, Samuel. I'm here now. I won't leave you. I know you can still hear me. Come back to me now."

I couldn't leave her here. Whoever—or whatever—had killed Dad could still be around. But I also knew I had to get Emily. She would never forgive us for taking even this long to tell her. She would be furious, sure that, like Mom, she could have done something to save him.

And the Clann. I would have to call the elders, tell them we were leaderless now that Dad was gone...

My dad was gone...I debated picking Mom up and carrying her back to the house. She was tiny enough. But she would fight me.

She pounded on Dad's chest with the heels of her fists now, and I couldn't watch. It wasn't right, her beating Dad's body and trying to bring him back like this. Anyone else could tell he was gone.

"Mom, it's too late," I tried to tell her again.

She shoved me with both hands, and I had to grab a nearby tree trunk to stay on my feet. It was like she was possessed. There was no reasoning with her, no calming her. And there would be no removing her from here, at least not by me. Not without force.

I couldn't do that to her on top of everything else. I couldn't just throw my own mother, as temporarily nuts as she was, over my shoulder like some kind of Neanderthal.

I would have to make a run for it, call Dr. Faulkner, try to yell for Emily and get her to come back with me to the woods, all as quickly as I could.

I took Mom's ward from my wrist and carefully snapped it around Mom's. Not that it would do any good. If a vampire truly had killed my dad, he had done it in spite of the wards around the clearing. But I had to at least try to offer her what protection I could. I also left the flashlight with her, keeping it on and on the ground pointed away from Dad down the path toward the house. It might help her, and it would help the descendants find her.

Then I ran as fast as I could, faster than I ever had in any football game, back to the house, stopping only when I reached

Dad's desk so I could hunt through the drawers for the black spiral-bound leather notebook that contained all the descendants' names, addresses, and phone numbers.

Dr. Faulkner answered quickly. He was silent after I told him about Dad. Then, "I'm on my way. Have you called anyone else?"

"No. I need to get back to the clearing. Mom wouldn't leave...Dad."

"Good. I'll call everyone soon enough. Just take care of your mother and sister till we can get there."

I hung up Dad's office phone, then ran out of the study to the base of the stairs, yelling for Emily.

No response. She probably couldn't hear me over her own snoring. She'd always been a heavy sleeper anyways.

Should I run upstairs and tell her?

No, I needed to go keep Mom safe.

But then Emily would be here in the house alone. What if Dad's attacker came in here and went after Emily?

Cursing, I ran up the stairs two at a time then burst into her room and shook her awake.

"Wha..." she muttered groggily, raising up on an elbow and rubbing her eyes.

"Emily, wake up. It's Dad."

She frowned, blinking a little faster now. "What? What's going on? Is he home now? Tell Mom I'm really not hungry, okay?"

What was she talking about? She knew he was home. I'd seen her outside talking to him.

She had to be still half asleep or something. "Emily, you've got to wake up, get up and get dressed. The Clann's on their way, but I've got to get back to the clearing to protect Mom until they get here. And that means you have to come with me. I can't protect the both of you any other way."

Stumbling to her feet, she wrapped a fleece robe around herself. "Tristan, I swear, if this is a prank I will k—"

"Don't say it," I muttered. "This is for real. Dad's out there in the clearing. He's... He's..." I took a deep breath, pushed away my own emotions for the moment. "He's gone, Em. He's really gone."

Her eyes widened and she flew past me down the staircase and into the kitchen. I helped her balance while she shoved her feet into a pair of rubber boots in the garage. Then we were stumbling and jogging as fast as her too-big footwear would allow.

When she saw Mom with Dad's body, she gasped and fell to her knees beside our parents. And finally Mom allowed someone to hug her, burying her face in my sister's shoulder.

Dr. Faulkner found us first, with Officer Talbot right on his heels. They checked Dad, confirmed that he had been dead for hours probably, stayed with us as an ambulance showed up to take Dad's body away. Only then was Emily able to do what the rest of us couldn't, prying Mom away from Dad and walking her back to the house where she gave Mom a sleeping pill and helped her to bed. The sleeping pill was probably unnecessary, though...Mom had exhausted herself trying to bring Dad back.

While Emily got Mom settled for the night, Officer Talbot and Dr. Faulkner asked me questions in the kitchen. Their tone was calm, but they kept asking the same questions over and over.

And I kept telling them the same answers.

"I don't know who the guy was. He was dressed nice, slacks, shiny black loafers, long black wool coat. I never saw his car—he must have parked in front and walked around back. Emily seemed to know him. She hugged him hello. You should ask her who he is. I never heard them talking. I don't know what he wanted. He showed up around five or so."

At some point, Emily came back downstairs and Officer Talbot pulled her aside in the foyer. But I could hear her replies.

"I'm telling you, there was no one here. I never saw Dad come home," she insisted. "I've been in my room sick and asleep all day. Ask my mom, she'll tell you."

I'd known Emily was good, but this was a whole new level of lying. After several minutes of listening to it, I was ready to strangle her.

"Cut the crap, Emily." I wove around Dr. Faulkner into the foyer. "Just tell them the truth. This is our dad we're talking about here. You and that guy were the last ones to see Dad alive. So tell them the truth!"

Her eyes welled up with tears, her eyebrows drawn together. "But I am telling you the truth! I remember Mom going to get groceries, and you were going with her. I fell back asleep, and the next thing I know, you're shaking me awake and telling me about Dad—"

"You're saying you don't remember anything about putting on your coat and house shoes and scarf and going outside to talk to Dad and some stranger for nearly two hours?"

"No."

"No, you don't remember doing that, or no, you didn't do it?" I tried reading her mind, but it was a locked vault as always.

Could she have been sleepwalking? She'd never done it before that I knew about. But she was pretty exhausted. Maybe the flu meds or Mom's herbal drinks or the combination of them had somehow messed with Emily's mind or something?

"Does your sister have a history of sleepwalking?" Officer Talbot asked.

At the same time, Dr. Faulkner began checking Emily's pupils with a penlight he'd pulled from his pocket. "Emily, do you often lose track of time or hear about things others have seen you do that you have no memory of?"

"No." The tears ran freely down her face now. "And I think I'd remember my own dad being hurt by someone."

"Look, I'm telling you what I saw and everything I know," I said. "Maybe something or someone's messed with her memory. But I was wide awake, I haven't been sick or taken any kind of meds or drank anything, and I know what I saw. He was youngish, maybe early twenties, with light brown hair, short on the sides and back, kind of long on top. He was about Emily's height, maybe a few inches taller."

Emily frowned. She knew something.

"Who do you know that looks like that?" I asked her.

She shook her head. "Nobody." But there was something in her voice, deep down, the tiniest hint of uncertainty so faint no one but family would have caught it. And again when I tried to read her mind, her thoughts were barred to me.

"And you said you didn't get his license plate number?" Officer Talbot asked me.

"No, I said I never saw his vehicle at all."

"Did you hear him arrive?"

"No. I just saw him walk around the side of the house to the backyard."

Officer Talbot and Dr. Faulkner shared a look.

"What?" I asked.

"If he was a vamp, he could have walked in from anywhere," Officer Talbot said.

Except that didn't seem right. "A vamp would have had a hard time getting past the vamp wards in the clearing without a descendant's help, wouldn't he?"

"Unless your father was attacked outside of the clearing and then crawled within the wards' protection just before dying," Officer Talbot said.

"I don't know." I shook my head. "Something about this just doesn't seem right. Dad should have fought back, whether his attacker was human or vamp. He would have read a human's thoughts in advance and been able to stop them. And he never would have let a vampire get that close."

"Not even if he knew and trusted that vamp?" Officer Talbot asked, and I didn't like the way his eyes narrowed. He had someone specific in mind.

"Like who?"

"Oh, I don't know…how about our local resident vamps?"

CHAPTER 32

"Savannah and her dad? No way would they have hurt my dad, or helped anyone else to do it, either." I didn't know what had happened to Dad, but *this* much I knew for sure.

"All the same, I think I'd better pay them a visit, see where they were this evening," Officer Talbot muttered, his hand moving to rest on the butt of his gun at his waist.

"She had nothing to do with it," I growled. "She wasn't even here. Read my mind, see for yourself." I forced my mind to stay open to them so they could see the truth in my thoughts.

"How would you know if she was here?" Officer Talbot said.

"Because I would have sensed her," I snapped, completely out of patience now. If this prejudiced idiot couldn't get over his stupid hang-ups, he would miss following the real clues and the true killer would continue to get away with murder.

"How do you sense her?" Dr. Faulkner asked.

"It's like a punch to the chest or gut."

"Does this happen only when you see her?" Officer Talbot asked.

"No. She can be anywhere within a few hundred yards and I'll know it."

"Interesting," Dr. Faulkner murmured. "Could be a heightened survival mechanism of sorts."

"Or something else." Officer Talbot's mouth slowly stretched into a smirk.

"Hey, unlike some people, I'm not letting my emotions color the situation," I said. "Whether you like it or not, I've told you the truth. I would have known if Savannah was anywhere around here. And her dad would never go after mine, either. He's a former council member. He values the peace treaty too much to risk another war."

"He's still a vamp," Officer Talbot spat out. "Which means older vamps could order him to kill and he wouldn't be able to stop himself."

This was ridiculous. I grabbed the house phone off the kitchen wall and dialed Savannah's number from memory, hoping she hadn't changed it since our breakup.

She answered on the fourth ring with a hesitant "Hello?"

"Sav—" I started to say.

Officer Talbot grabbed the phone from me. "Where were you and your father tonight between 5:00 and 7:00 p.m.?"

"Who is this?" she asked, her tone firmer now.

"Just answer the question, please," Officer Talbot said.

"We were home. Why? Who is this?"

Officer Talbot ended the call. "I still think we should bring them in for questioning."

"Look, either you can waste time and explain yourselves to my mother tomorrow, or you can try to find whoever really did this. Now, the guy looked college-aged, so maybe you could start with the local colleges and seminary—"

"And tell them what, son?" Dr. Faulkner said. "We've got nothing to go on. No name, no vehicle description or license plate number. He could have been from anywhere. And bringing in a sketch artist would only open this can of worms up to the public and the national media. It'll be hard enough to keep it contained as it is, what with Sam's standing as a local figure and a nationally recognized businessman. Not to mention your parents' reputations among the charity crowds."

"But—"

"Why don't you walk with me a bit." Dr. Faulkner went out the front door. Following him through it felt weird to me because my family never used it. We always used the garage entrance in the kitchen.

Outside, he turned to face me. "I know you want to catch your father's killer. Believe me, we all do. And the Clann's going to be out for blood even more once they learn their leader's been murdered. But if the media gets wind that your father was murdered by someone even pretending to be a vampire, every descendant alive will go off looking for the nearest vamp to stake or set on fire. Your father was greatly loved, and he's going to be sorely missed. But you've got to let the Clann handle this discreetly or that peace treaty your grandpa and dad spent most of their lives working to bring about and maintain will be gone in an instant."

"So exactly what do you want me to do then?" Surely he didn't expect me to just sit around like a dumb little kid waiting for all the grown-ups to handle this.

"I'm saying let us figure this out as quietly as we can. We're going to catch the killer, have no doubt about that. We have to, or they'll never stop and none of us will ever be safe again. But let's keep the situation among our own kind and the vamps and keep the media and everyone else out of it."

"What about Savannah and her father? Talbot sounds like

he wants to go interrogate them. You know the vamp council won't react well to that."

"Let me handle him. I'll get him sniffing down the right track in no time."

I sighed, feeling tired and suddenly way older than seventeen. "What do we do about Dad?" My voice grew hoarse at the end, and I had to clear my throat. "I don't think Mom can handle arranging another funeral so soon. And I've got no clue what he would have..." My tongue stumbled over the words, and I had to try again. "What he would have wanted."

Dr. Faulkner clapped a hand on my shoulder. "Don't worry. The Clann will follow tradition and we'll get all the arrangements set up. We can hold the funeral this Saturday. And then we'll need to hold the elections that night while everyone's still in town—"

"Elections? For what?"

He blinked at me behind his glasses like a dazed owl caught in the spotlights that had just shown up at the front of my family's home. "For the new Clann leader, of course. With all the recent murders, the Clann can't afford to be leaderless for longer than a week at best. Wait any longer than that, and you'll have pure chaos on your hands."

This was one too many surprises to deal with in one night. "I never realized the leader was actually elected." Colemans had been leading the Clann for the past four generations. My dad had already been the leader before I was born, so I'd never seen a new leader take over.

"Usually it's just a formality because everyone expects the next generation of male Colemans to step into the role. But this time, things are quite different, what with the unexpected loss of your father, your being underage—"

"The leader has to be eighteen?"

"Yes, in order to officially lead."

"Is there an actual rule against females being the leader?" Emily was already old enough.

"No, not officially. But there's never been a female Clann leader in the Clann's history—"

"Why not?" Some kind of desperation was pushing the words out of my mouth as soon as I thought them. "Emily's old enough. And she's definitely got the skills to lead."

Dr. Faulkner hesitated, cleared his throat, hesitated again. "The Clann is founded on ancient traditions—"

"Which are obviously in need of an overhaul."

He stared at me for a long minute. "To be honest, son, your sister as Clann leader would be a tough sell even under the best of circumstances. But considering the situation as it is, with her loss of memory, her refusal to let others read her mind, and all the unanswered questions regarding her whereabouts at the time of your father's death, no one's going to vote for her. I'm sorry, but that's the sad truth of it."

"Because she could know something about Dad's death."

"Or worse."

I stared at him, my mind refusing to even go down that road. "She's my *sister.* She loved our father. She never would have—"

"I'm not saying she did. I've known that child since she was born. I'm her godfather, for heaven's sake. I know she had nothing to do with it. But not everyone knows her as well as we do, and you've got to consider how others might view it. The facts are that you saw her and a stranger with your father just before his death, and everyone can see your memories and verify this. But Emily claims to have no memory of it yet either she can't or won't let anyone read her mind to see if she's telling the truth."

"Can't? What do you mean?"

"Well, there have been cases where a descendant has practiced blocking their thoughts so much that they actually forget how to lower the barrier again."

That was possible. "I can't remember a time when she wasn't blocking her thoughts, even from me," I admitted.

"Okay, then let's assume she is telling the truth and doesn't remember. Then we've got a situation where something's going on with her mind to make it unstable. And no one's going to want someone like that for their leader."

I sighed. "She could get her memory back."

"Sure she could. But until then, Emily is not a viable candidate as Clann leader. Which brings us back to you. Now ordinarily the Clann would overlook the next few months until you come of age, allowing your mother to serve as temporary leader until your eighteenth birthday, at which time she could step down from the role. But this time, there is the added issue of an actual contender for the vote—Jim Williams."

Dylan's father. Of course.

If Dylan's father took over the Clann, not only would we be at war with the vamps in no time, but Mr. Williams wouldn't rest until every single vampire was staked or burned out of existence.

"Dad always acted like it was a done deal that I would be the next leader," I murmured. Now that the shock and anger were wearing off, I was starting to have a tough time staying upright and on my feet. I didn't want to deal with all this political crap right now. I just wanted to fall into bed.

"If he'd lived even one more year, it probably would have been."

But he hadn't. And now everything Grandpa and Dad had believed in and worked so hard for was about to fall apart.

"Do you really think a vampire killed my dad?"

Dr. Faulkner paused, considering. "Well, it's certainly possible to fake a vampire bite with prosthetic fangs or even those plastic fangs you see everywhere at Halloween time. And he could have been drained elsewhere then brought back to the clearing. I'd have to do some tests to be sure, though, like checking the wound for saliva and running a pretty covert DNA test on whatever I find. I couldn't go through the normal channels, of course, so it would take longer to get the results."

"I'd appreciate it if you would." Maybe a DNA test would prove it wasn't a vamp bite at all. Or at least it could help match Dad's killer with whoever had killed my aunt and uncle and cousins.

"Do you think the vamp council keeps DNA records on all the known vamps?" I asked.

"I highly doubt it. The security risk in maintaining such a database would be astronomical. But it couldn't hurt to ask them. You know, your dad wasn't lying to everyone when he said he was working with the vamp council to investigate the descendant murders. Now that he's gone, and especially with the Clann reaction that's sure to come, maintaining contact with the council is going to become more crucial than ever. If you were to reach out to the council personally, that could help preserve the peace treaty a little longer until we can catch the killer. Not to mention adding some important credibility to your bid for Clann leadership."

I opened my mouth to tell him the truth, that I'd never really wanted to be Clann leader. That it was my parents' dream, a dream that wasn't ever going to take place because my dad was going to live forever. And that I would probably fail miserably at trying to lead a bunch of people spread out all over the world, most of whom I didn't even know.

But then I thought about what would happen if I didn't step into Dad's shoes… How disappointed Dad and Grandpa would have been, not to mention Mom… What the Clann could turn into with vampire haters like the Williams family running things.

And what that would mean for Savannah.

I took a deep breath. "You're right. I'll see what I can do to make contact with the council. Savannah's father is a former council member. I'll talk to him and see if he can set up a line of communication for us."

Dr. Faulkner stared at me, a strange look on his face. After a long moment, he said, "Your dad would be incredibly proud of you tonight."

My chest tightened to the point where it was almost a struggle to breathe. "Thanks."

"Get some rest if you can. Tomorrow we rally the allies and start pushing for the vote. The sooner we can get everyone thinking of you as the natural and best choice for leader, the harder it'll be for Williams to gain support."

I saw his point. It also made me think of something I'd heard in world history class, how when a king died people would cry, "The king is dead. Long live the king!" I'd never understood what they meant before. Now I was starting to get it.

It didn't make it seem any more right, though. Politics just plain turned my stomach. It didn't take into account stuff like pain or loss or needing time to grieve, or shock or fears and doubts.

Would I even make a decent leader? I'd assumed I would have decades to learn from Dad. Had he had enough time to teach me what I needed to know to carry on his dream?

I said goodbye to Dr. Faulkner then trudged back inside the house. Officer Talbot was gone, Emily already in her room, Mom moaning in her sleep.

I locked the front door, reset the alarm system, went upstairs to my room and toed off my shoes. Across the hall, Emily's sobs were muffled by her closed door.

Part of me wanted to knock on her door, offer her a hug, pull together like we always had in times of trouble. No matter how different our opinions had been on any one subject, we'd always stuck together. I'd always been able to count on Emily to figure out a game plan if I didn't already have one.

But after watching her either lie or at least hide something about Dad's death, the greater part of me held back from reaching out to her. There were too many unanswered questions, too many secrets she was keeping. Even a tiny clue might lead us to the murderer. Until she opened up and told me what she knew, I just couldn't trust her like I used to.

So I shut my bedroom door and lay down on my bed in the dark. And tried to forget the image of Dad's unseeing eyes staring blankly up at me, until exhaustion pulled me under.

CHAPTER 33

I had always believed it was my mother who had placed the charm on my bedroom to keep me from dream connecting with Savannah all these years. But it turned out that my dad was the one who had actually created and maintained the charms at Mom's request. And with his death, the last bit of his magic in the already weakened charm on my bedroom died, too.

I learned this when my subconscious reached out to Savannah's that night, connecting our minds in our sleep as easily as if we'd never stopped.

"Tristan!" She hurried across the dimly lit yard toward me. "What's going on?"

I was sitting in the grass of my backyard, with no energy or will to get up. I waited till she was standing right beside me before I told her. "My dad's dead."

She drew in a long breath through her nose then dropped to her knees beside me. "Oh my God. Tristan, I'm so sorry. What happened?"

"Someone killed him in the clearing." The clearing where so much had happened: where Savannah and I had pretended to play together in our connected dreams in the fourth grade, and again where we'd kissed and danced and talked for hours while dream connecting last year. And where her grandmother had died.

Now I understood how a real-life memory could poison even the dream version of a place. I would never be able to step into those woods, or even look at them, without remembering Dad's lifeless, cold body lying there on the path.

"He died alone, Sav. In the cold. In the dark. He didn't have a flashlight with him. He didn't even look like he fought back! Why wouldn't he fight back?" I was shouting, my fingers clawing up chunks of dirt and grass at either side of me. I had to get control of myself. I couldn't let Savannah see me go nuts like this.

"Shh," she whispered, wrapping her arms around me.

I couldn't hold her at first, scared if I reached out for her I would lose it. But then I found myself turning in her arms, holding on to her, and it was there in that moment that it finally, truly sank in.

I would never see my dad again, never talk to him or have the chance to ask him anything about how to lead or what to do. He would never be able to teach me anything new about magic or football or the best way to deal with my neurotic, controlling mother in any situation.

"He's gone, Sav. He's really gone." I buried my face in the curve where her neck and shoulder met, my arms around her waist, grateful for once that she was so strong and I didn't have to worry that I might break her. The rage and pain rose up, trying to drown me from the inside out, but she was my anchor, saving me, grounding me, holding me together, her hands stroking my back in soothing motions that gradually tugged me away from the darkness.

She knew how I felt right now. She'd gone through it, too, after her Nanna's death.

I hadn't known then, couldn't possibly relate. This level of pain and loss was something that had to be personally felt in order to be understood.

"I know," she murmured. "It feels like someone's ripped out your insides, doesn't it?"

I nodded, unsure I could even speak. I'd lost all control, even wet her shirt with childish tears. She was the last person I'd ever wanted to see me like this.

I dragged my sleeves over my face before leaning back to search her eyes, wondering if she thought I was weak. But all I saw was…love. It shone out of her gaze, warm, without judgment, telling me we were still the same. Vampire or witch, right or wrong in everyone else's eyes, when I looked at Savannah, I saw beyond the exterior to the person she was deep down, and I recognized the one person on this planet who made me more, who matched me so completely she left me breathless and lost in wonder. She didn't complete me, or fill some stupid, imaginary hole inside me. And it was way bigger and more important than our being two puzzle pieces made to fit together. It was something for which I had no words, only an undeniable feeling of everything being right when we were together and wrong when we were apart.

"I don't know who I am without you," I murmured, cupping her face, needing her to stay and hear me and not run away like she always seemed to be doing lately. "I don't like who I am without you in my life. Without you, everything is just wrong."

Tears shimmered in her eyes then slipped over the edges and fell down her cheeks. "I know."

I took a deep breath, hoping she would hear and believe me. "Things are going to be seriously bad for a while."

She nodded.

"No. I mean it, Sav. You've got to really hear me this time, okay? With Dad gone, the Clann's going to be leaderless until Saturday. That means there will be no one to stop any descendant from doing whatever they want. So you need to leave Jacksonville for a while."

She ignored that last point, setting my gut to churning with fear that she wasn't taking me seriously. "What happens on Saturday?"

"The Clann will elect a new leader after Dad's funeral."

"And that's when you'll officially become the leader." I could see her pulling away from me. The growing distance was there in her eyes.

"Not necessarily. Dylan's dad wants the job."

Her eyes widened. "Then you'd better get the majority vote. If you don't…"

"Yeah. We'll be dragged into another war for sure."

She swallowed hard, and though she didn't pull free from my hands where they still framed her face, she looked down at her lap.

"Then I guess I'd better wish you good luck for Saturday."

"I don't want to be Clann leader, Sav. But we need this."

"I know."

"Then what's wrong? What's going on inside that mind of yours?"

She bit her lower lip for a few torturous seconds then forced a smile that didn't reach her eyes as she looked up. "I'm sure you'll still be chosen. The Williams family is too annoying and unlikable to vote for. And once you're Clann leader, my dad and I will be safe, right?"

"Right. Once I'm leader, everything will be better. I'll

make sure the peace treaty stays in place. And I think in time I can maybe even teach the descendants not to hate the vamps. Well, maybe. Some of their issues run pretty deep. But we'll work on it. In time, they'll come around."

"That would be nice."

But she was still holding back.

"What is it?" I sighed. "You know becoming more of a vamp hasn't made you any better at lying to me."

She shook her head and looked away, her pale fingers plucking up bits of grass to shred. "I'm happy for you, Tristan. Really, I am. You're going to do what your parents always dreamed for you. What you were *born* to do. And that's the important thing. So let's just leave it at that, okay?" She leaned forward, pressed a hand to one side of my face and slowly, gently kissed my cheek. It felt like a kiss goodbye. "You're going to be a great leader for the Clann. Your dad would be really proud of you. And I am, too. You need to do this. The descendants need a leader with a good heart like yours."

I caught her chin when she tried to look away again. "Then why does it sound more like you're begging me not to do it?"

"I'm not. I'm telling you that you *should*."

"Liar."

She shifted her feet under her like she was going to get up. But she'd forgotten, in our connected dreams she didn't have the physical upper hand. I moved faster, leaning forward until she was lying on her back in the grass and I half covered her.

"Stop running away," I growled, nuzzling the curve of her neck, testing her. If she had tensed up beneath me, if she had given me one sign that she didn't want to be close to me, I would have moved away again. Instead, her hands crept up to circle my waist.

Resting most of my upper body weight on my elbows at

either side of her head, with our faces only inches apart, she had to know she couldn't possibly hide anything from me.

"Tell me you don't miss what we had," I whispered into her hair, daring her to try and lie to me now.

"I do."

"Tell me you don't think about us every day and regret breaking up with me."

Her hair fanned out in the grass around her head, begging to be touched. I buried my nose in it, filling my lungs with that warm lavender scent that I missed every waking second now.

My chest expanded with the deep breath, pressing against her, and she shivered.

"I do think about it. And I wish I hadn't had to break up with you."

"Tell me you don't love me." I stared into her eyes now, frustrated, hurting, missing her so much it formed its own kind of physical pain that burned my lungs and throat. "Because I've tried, Sav. I've really tried not to be in love with you, even to the point of hurting others along the way. But I can't make myself stop loving you. So if you've figured it out, if you've found some spell or something that will end my feelings for you, I'm all ears here."

She closed her eyes, covered her face with her hands and sobbed, her shoulders shaking. "I can't! I wish I could. I wish every day that I could find a way not to love you. But I still do. I—"

It was all I needed to hear. I covered her lips with mine, careful to also press a palm to the ground and draw energy.

Then I remembered. I'd fallen asleep indoors in my room tonight. There was no real ground beneath me to draw energy from.

So I kissed her cheeks instead, her nose, her wet eyelids, her throat, the ridge of her collarbone.

"It's going to be all right," I promised her over and over in between kisses. "I'll be Clann leader soon, and then no one can tell us that we can't be together."

Her hands froze in their journey from my hair to my shoulders.

Too caught up in the moment, it took several seconds for me to notice how tense she'd become beneath me.

"Sav?" I lifted my head to look at her.

Her expression was unreadable for a change. "Are you sleeping outside tonight?"

"No, I'm in my room—"

She twisted her head to look down at my right hand cupping her shoulder. My hand was shaking.

Suddenly she scooted up and away before I could stop her.

"Oh come on, Sav!" I sat back on my knees. "You're driving me nuts here."

"You don't get it! Nothing's changed between us. Learning how to do magic hasn't made me suddenly not a vampire anymore. I'm still draining you when we kiss, still psychically draining you with a kiss even in our dreams together. I haven't learned a single thing about how to turn it off. And you becoming Clann leader? That doesn't change anything, either. In fact, it just makes it more impossible for us to be together." She scrambled to her feet.

I stood up as well. "Fine. I won't become leader."

She rolled her eyes. "Don't be ridiculous. We've already covered all the reasons why you need to. You have to, Tristan. This isn't about you and me or what we want anymore. It's way, way bigger than that now."

I closed the distance between us. "We can make this work. We're good together."

She took a deep breath then looked up at me, letting me see the tears in her eyes. "How? Are we going to live in a tent with a hole in the floor so you can draw energy every time we kiss?"

"I'll find a way to make the vamp turning process work on me. Then we'll be the same again, two vamps who can't hurt each other."

Her jaw clenched. "And then the Clann will choose Dylan's dad to be their leader. And then what will our life be like together while all the descendants and vamps and innocent humans die in another pointless war?"

I opened my mouth to argue. She shut me up the only really effective way that she could.

"Goodbye, Tristan. And good luck on Saturday."

Then she kissed me, psychically draining me despite the physical distance separating our actual bodies, until I didn't have enough energy left to keep the dream connection going.

I woke up in my room. Yelling out a curse, I rolled over and punched the mattress beneath me.

CHAPTER 34

SAVANNAH

The next morning, as soon as I ended the dream with Tristan I ran downstairs, found Dad in the living room reading a newspaper and told him what had happened to Tristan's father.

He jumped to his feet then froze, losing the few humanlike traits he had. Finally he breathed and blinked again. "This is…quite disturbing news."

"Has the council made any headway in tracking down the New York Clann killer?" Restless and needing something to focus on, I started looking around for the paperback I'd dropped here last night when Tristan called.

"They have Gowin working on it."

That explained why I hadn't seen him around much lately.

"I do not believe they have any new clues," Dad continued. "I have not spoken with him in some time, though, so I am not sure. He has been quite busy with the investigation and reporting to the council. Whom I must now call with this news regarding the Clann's leader."

"Um, while you have them on the phone, maybe you could see if they want to keep in contact with Tristan, just in case he gets chosen as the new leader?" I dropped down onto my knees and peered under the couch. No paperback book. "It might be a good idea for them to start working on some kind of friendship. Or maybe the council has an official ambassador or something who could represent them in talking with the Clann?"

I stood up again in time to catch Dad's frown. "No, we do not have anything like that. Peace was created only a few decades ago."

He was kidding, right? I rested a hand on one hip. "Okay, I know you're hundreds of years old, so to you maybe a few decades doesn't seem that long. But to a descendant, that could literally be over half a lifetime. You really need some kind of official rep who can meet with the Clann elders every so often to make sure everything's all good between the groups."

He continued to frown at me. "We always assumed any vampire who attempted to make contact with the Clann leader would be set on fire or staked."

What a drama vamp. "I'm pretty sure the tradition of killing the messenger went out of style a few centuries ago."

"You would be surprised."

"Well, I'm just saying Tristan might become the new Clann leader in a week, and it would be smart if the council made some kind of official outreach effort to him. His dad was just murdered by what looks to be a vamp attack. Not to mention the tiny fact that the council *kidnapped* Tristan last spring. They haven't exactly made the best of first impressions on him and his family, you know."

Dad had covered the couch with pages of newspaper, making it impossible to sit down anywhere. I began gathering it up.

After a minute, I heard him say, "Perhaps *you* would make the ideal ambassador."

I whirled around in horror. "Me? No way. Leave me out of it. I hate that vampire politics crap—"

"Though I did not actually speak those words, that is indeed what I was thinking," Dad muttered, his face darkening into a scowl.

Oh crap. I'd read his mind. Not good. And now he knew it, and soon the vamp council would too...

There went any hope of a normal life I might have ever had.

"Forget it, Dad. I don't care what the council says or demands." I shook a handful of wadded-up newspaper at him. "I'm *not* going to spy on the Clann for you guys. And I'm not going to be any ambassador, either. I mean, come on! Besides the fact that I'm only seventeen and completely clueless about playing the political game, I want to have a life of my own. A normal life, or at least as normal as possible. Playing peace ambassador doesn't fit in with that." Seeing how I'd mangled one sheet of the newspaper already, I gave up trying to refold the rest of it and settled for tossing the whole stack onto the coffee table so I could check under the sofa cushions for my book.

"At least consider it." Dad remained standing, staring down at me. "Now that you quite obviously can read vampire— and I assume Clann—minds, you are uniquely positioned to always be able to discern the truth from the lies that either side might attempt to employ. And you already have a...connection to the descendant who, as you pointed out, may very well become the next Clann leader. The...friendship has already been forged."

"Your...pauses already point out why that's a bad idea." Aha! There it was, under some papers on the floor under the coffee table. I snatched up the paperback and tried to figure out which page I'd stopped at last night.

"Or a very good one. He listens to you, values your opinion."

"I'm not using my history with Tristan to push the council's agendas."

"You are seeing it from the wrong angle. I am merely suggesting that, rather than having to get to know some strange and as you would say 'ancient' vampire, Tristan already knows one who is his age. Someone he trusts and is capable of having logical discussions with. Someone who also happens to be the daughter of a former councilman who—"

"Who clearly is still looking for a way back onto the council," I grumbled.

"—who still converses regularly with the council and could easily pass on any of Tristan's concerns or requests," he finished with a glare.

I really hated to see his point. But I did. Still, it seemed an invitation to trouble at the same time. And then I had the perfect argument.

"The council will never go for it. Remember? They made me promise to stay away from him."

One thick black eyebrow arched. "They have also been known to change their collective minds when it suits their needs."

Whatever. They would still never choose me as vamp ambassador. Not as long as Tristan was my contact with the Clann and there was any risk that my feelings for him might overwhelm my reasoning and cause me to lose control and kill him. Dad was just trying to lose the argument gracefully. I flipped through the pages until I found the spot where I'd last read.

"Also, you are not going to school this week," he ordered, walking from living room to kitchen to parlor to living room and back. *Where is that blasted cell phone? And why must the makers forever insist on making them smaller and smaller?*

He'd managed to lose his cell phone somewhere in this house yet again. What was this, the seventeenth time? Or the twentieth?

"Fine. Want me to call it?"

"Call what?"

"Your phone. That's what you're looking for, right?"

Pulling himself up straight, he puffed out his chest and scowled. "Stop reading my mind, please. It is rude. And I am a vampire. I do not lose things."

"I can't help the mind-reading thing any more than you can help overhearing my phone conversations when I'm in my room. It doesn't have an on/off switch. And even vamps can lose itty bitty phones that tend to fall out of the pocket of their slacks every time they sit down to read the newspaper." On a hunch, I dug in between the cushions and the back of the couch to my left, then held up his phone.

"Hmpf." He took the phone and flipped it open, then paused. "Now about your missing school this week—"

"Are you going to call the school, or should I?"

He stared at me through narrowed eyes. "You are not arguing with me about it?"

"Nope. Why would I want to be anywhere near that campus this week? Do you have any idea how bad the descendants will be now that their leader's been killed? Besides, it's exhausting dealing with them all the time as it is."

And now with Tristan gone all week… He would be preparing for his dad's funeral. And becoming even more out of my reach as a boyfriend.

The memory of his breaking down in front of me last night jolted through me. I'd never seen him like that. At first, I hadn't realized he was even crying while I held him. He had been so quiet. It was only when he leaned away and I felt the dampness on my shoulder that I'd understood my shirt was wet from his tears.

He'd always been so…strong. So confident and sure and capable of handling absolutely anything.

Every time I thought about how much he must trust me in order to lose control in front of me like that, I got choked up and teary-eyed.

"I am glad you see this my way," Dad said. Then he circled around in front of me and frowned. He tilted my book so he could read the title on the cover. "*The Art of War* makes you tearful?"

I sighed and rubbed the back of a hand over my cheeks. "I'm not seeing it your way. It's just common sense. Sun Tzu says you have to pick your battles, so that's what I'm doing. And don't worry about the tears. I was just…remembering something sad."

"Other than the constant tears, which were also an unfortunate habit of your mother's, your mother was never this easy to deal with." He searched my face as if he thought I was plotting to sneak out the first chance I got.

I resisted the urge to read his mind for confirmation. "Mom isn't a vampire."

"Hmm. Yes, there is the blessing of my genes to factor in. Now, do I want to know why you are reading Sun Tzu?"

"School assignment," I lied without even looking up. Actually, I had started reading it thinking it would help me pick and choose my battles with the Clann. Now that Tristan might become Clann leader, I wanted to read it today in case he ever needed some leadership advice. But Dad didn't need to know that.

Maybe this was how vamps got to be good at lying. They were forced to do it so much that it became second nature.

"*Hmpf.*" He dialed a series of numbers on his phone so fast that even I couldn't make out which buttons he pushed. Into the phone he said something in another language that sounded vaguely like French at super high speed. After a few seconds, he walked away, speaking in English to Caravass about Tristan's dad and the elections.

Alone in the living room, I tried to read. But every few seconds, I caught my attention drifting. I was too restless. My body didn't want to sit still. I needed something more physical to do. Maybe some tai chi? Sighing, I tossed the book onto the coffee table and returned to my room.

I turned on my MP3's docking station, scrolled past all the songs I usually listened to, and found one I hadn't heard in a while.

Soon Florence and the Machine was thumping out a catchy beat. Even the lyrics about shaking off regret called to me.

It seemed I'd felt guilty and full of regret for so long for so many things…for breaking the rules and causing Nanna's death, for what I was and how I endangered Tristan's life with our every kiss, for the secrets I was forced to keep, even for my birth and all that it had cost my parents.

What was that saying about hindsight being 20/20? It was so easy to judge myself looking back at those decisions now. And yet, at the time of each choice, I had thought I was making the right one.

Tell me you don't think about us every day and regret breaking up with me.

I had told Tristan the truth last night. I did wish we could still be together. But I didn't regret doing what was needed to protect him. And I never would.

It was the one path I'd taken so far that had left me completely regret free.

And that was why, when I woke up this morning, I hadn't

cried. Seeing him, talking to him, being held and kissed by him last night, had been painful to lose at the dream's end. But I had been able to face the day strong this time because I knew all the way to my core that I was *right*. He had to become the new Clann leader for the sake of so many people. It was his destiny, and our being together would endanger that. Only he could help teach all the descendants to let go of their fear.

I thought of the Brat Twins and Dylan, trained for years to fear me and all vampires. I used to wonder why they couldn't just let go of that fear.

But maybe, if it was so easy to let go of a negative emotion, then I could have let go of my own guilt and regrets by now.

Maybe it took conscious effort to let it go. And in my case forgiveness, not for others' mistakes, but for my own. I had to find a way to forgive myself for not being perfect, for screwing up even when I tried my hardest not to. For not being able to foresee the future and the consequences of every action I took.

I set the song to loop, then walked over to the vanity, my footsteps instinctively matching the beat. Leaning over, I looked at my reflection in the mirror. The outside seemed so perfect, made flawless by the vamp genes. But the inside was full of flaws.

"I forgive you," I whispered, smiling because it felt a little silly.

I forgive you, I told myself again, silently this time.

The smile went away. This was starting to feel not so easy now.

I tried it again. *I forgive you, Savannah Colbert. I forgive you for not being perfect. For being only half a vampire and half a witch and probably a horrible failure at both. And for having to drink human blood once a week.*

I hesitated then dived into the toughest part, determined to finish it. Staring into my reflection's eyes, I thought, *I forgive you for falling in love with Tristan, and for dating him in spite of the rules. And most of all, I forgive you for causing your grandma's death and for taking away your mother's mother before any of us were ready.*

Now the tears came, rushing over onto my cheeks. But this time it was okay, and I didn't curse myself for being weak and crying. Because I forgave myself for that, too.

I'm not perfect. And I don't have to be. I can figure it out as I go, and as long as I do the best I can, it's okay if I still screw up.

Closing my eyes, I took a deep breath, then let it out slowly. I felt...lighter. Better. Like maybe, just maybe, some of the guilt weighing me down was gone.

I gave in to the urge to sway with the music, letting it wash over and through me.

Then, for the first time in months, I truly danced again.

CHAPTER 35

TRISTAN

It had been the week from hell. Mom had self-medicated through the weekend, but on Monday she came back to life with a vengeance. Every time I walked into the kitchen past Dad's open office door, there she was in Dad's chair behind his desk on his phone with the descendants, destroying all of Dad's and Grandpa's hard work on the peace treaty.

Not that she saw it that way.

"Listen, Beth, you've got it all wrong," she snapped, her voice carrying down the hall to where I was digging through the fridge for a snack. "The vamps absolutely can not be trusted, and Tristan knows it better than anyone else. He's anything *but* a vamp lover! He made the mistake of falling for that little vamp's innocent façade, only to be tricked into being kidnapped by her and her father then drugged and carted off to the vamp council like some kind of trophy, where they tortured him and tried to get him to spill everything he knew about us. But Tristan is a Coleman, and four generations of Colemans haven't led our people for nothing. He was strong, just like his father. He withstood everything they put him through, and then some. My son has been to war, he's been in the trenches as deep behind enemy lines as you can get, and he survived. If that alone doesn't make him worthy to be our next leader, I don't know what does!"

A long pause before she replied, "So I can count on your family's vote for Tristan this Saturday? Excellent! I look forward to seeing you and John then."

I walked down the hallway, coming to a stop in the office doorway as she hung up the phone and made a note in the Clann address book.

She glanced up with a tight smile. "Got another family's vote for you. Honestly, son, I think we just might have this in the bag."

Yeah, but at what cost? "You know, the peace treaty was really important to Dad. It took both Grandpa and Dad's entire lives to get it instated and keep it going."

Her eyes narrowed. "Yes, well, your grandpa was delusional, and your father led a sheltered life. Sam had no clue what the vamps are really like, nor did he want to see the truth. I tried to tell him. Now look what his naive optimism has gotten him. But don't you worry, son. I will see to it that his murder is avenged. Starting with securing your leadership. Then we'll turn our sights toward making every last vamp pay."

I opened my mouth to tell her I had no intention of ever becoming a vamp hater like her. But then I shut my mouth and walked away. What would be the point of arguing with her now? She had just lost the love of her life. There would be no reasoning with her for a while. And who knows? Maybe if I had seen what she'd seen, lost as many loved ones as she had to vampires, maybe I would be just as filled with rage.

I only hoped I could undo whatever damage she might cause this week. If I got the majority vote.

I didn't see much of Emily all week. Mostly she kept to her room. The few times I did see her emerge from her room, we didn't have anything to say to each other. I wanted to forgive her for her "memory loss," but I just couldn't. Not yet. Every day that she couldn't remember or wouldn't tell the truth was one more day the trail of clues was allowed to fade away.

The funeral Saturday morning was a total circus. I'd expected a pretty big turnout as hundreds of descendants from all over the world flew in to honor the loss of our leader. What I hadn't prepared for was all the non-Clann people and media who showed up. People who had worked at Dad's manufacturing plant, local politicians, and local media mixed with recognizable celebrities in the business world and national media.

I'd had no idea Dad was so well known and loved outside the Clann. Realizing it made me miss him all the more.

I had to read a speech, which had taken me days to try and get just right. Afterward, I couldn't even remember giving it. All I remembered was the sight of that coffin with Dad closed up inside it, hidden from view so no one would see the supposed fang marks high on his neck.

After the funeral, Mom held a Clann-only gathering at the country club, where descendant after descendant got up to talk about Dad. I didn't remember much of it, either. I was too busy worrying.

Because now that it was real, now that I had seen my father buried in the ground, the upcoming vote was also all too real. And so were the possible consequences.

Savannah was right. I had to become the next Clann leader, for her sake, for her dad's, for the safety of all these men, women and children gathered today in the banquet room.

If the Williams family took control of the Clann, no one

here would be safe. Once they started another war, it wouldn't be just a single, organized battle: It would be ongoing and everywhere...in public places and private, spilling over into Clann homes and businesses. They would make sure it was as dirty a war as possible, and no one would be spared, not even the kids. And it wouldn't just affect the Clann and the vamps. Ordinary humans would also get caught in the crossfire.

I'd done my research this week, talking with Dr. Faulkner by phone so I could get caught up on the details of the Clann's history with the vamps. The last war had been fought on and off for hundreds of years, with historians mistaking it for all kinds of world wars and plagues and mob-related violence. Thousands had died on both sides, including ordinary people recruited to help each side.

We couldn't let another war begin. *I* couldn't, not if I could do something to stop it. Savannah was right. There was no way to run from my responsibilities. If I was selfish, if I turned away from the Clann, she and I would never be safe again anywhere on this planet.

I *had* to become the next Clann leader.

Maybe then, with enough time and effort and reasoning, I could bring the Clann around. I could help them see that we could coexist with the vamps, not just under an uneasy peace treaty, but with a better understanding for both sides. We didn't have to live our lives in fear like this.

Dad was right. Someone was behind the Clann killings, and there was no way it was just some rogue vamp. It couldn't be a coincidence that both the Clann's leader and extended family had been targeted. The obvious reason for the connection was that there was some kind of political agenda behind it.

Someone wanted another war. But who? Who had the most to gain from such a war?

Figuring that out would be my first and most important goal as Clann leader.

Savannah's dad had put me in touch with Caravass, the council leader for the vamps. I'd spoken to him several times this week, and though neither of us had any updates to share, we'd both agreed that someone must be trying to play off our groups' fears and mistrust. I couldn't be sure yet that Caravass was trustworthy, other than my instincts, which Dad had always told me to pay attention to. Only time would really tell. But for now, my gut said he was a necessary ally, and I was hopeful we could work together to put an end to the killings.

I just had to secure the majority vote tonight. Which was why, when I spotted Mom mingling throughout the banquet like the First Lady working for last-minute votes during a presidential election, I didn't try to stop her. Her methods might be crappy and cause me more work to have to undo later, but if they got me in as Clann leader, so be it.

I was starting to understand why politicians all had a certain underlying ruthlessness to them. In order to do good, it seemed like a whole lot of compromise and strategic maneuvering was required first.

I just hoped, a year from now, I could still stand to look at myself in the mirror.

By the time the banquet broke up and everyone prepared to head out to the Circle for the vote, I was strung tight and having a hard time not showing it.

Unlike Mr. Williams. He stood on the opposite side of the clearing's stone chair that had been my family's all the way back to my great-great-grandpa, and he should have looked nervous. Instead, Mr. Williams was nothing but cool, calm and confident. Where I felt like a kid playing pretend in my suit, he looked ready to become the next U.S. president, never mind leader of the Clann.

For the first time in my life, I hated being young. If I were a couple of years older, he wouldn't look so smug.

The stone chalice was passed throughout the crowd. You had to be eighteen to vote, which was probably a major point in my favor since it meant Dylan and the Brat Twins couldn't vote yet. The teenaged descendants had been allowed to attend, though, while younger descendants had been excluded from the gathering in order to keep the event as orderly and formal as possible. The vote itself was a magic-based process. Mom had explained it to me this afternoon. Descendants had to use power to make their mark on the ballots, ensuring that each vote's maker could be traced, thus preventing any ballot stuffing.

Finally Dr. Faulkner brought the chalice to rest on the seat of the stone chair.

He tapped the chalice once, twice, three times, and a fourth, each time at a different compass point on its rim. Then he turned to face the gathering.

"And now for the results of the vote!"

SAVANNAH

It had been the single longest week of my life, made complete by the longest day today. I hadn't been able to sit still. Dancing for hours hadn't helped, though it had taken the edge off and kept me loose and warm. As a last resort, I'd even tried grounding in the woods behind my house. But all that did was leave me panicky that I wouldn't have enough energy in case the vote went wrong and Mr. Williams's first act as the Clann's new leader would be to come after Dad and me. So I ended up drawing more energy instead until I felt like a cup ready to overflow.

Listening in on Dad hadn't helped, either. He'd been on the phone speaking in French to someone all day. The problem was, he was also thinking in French. Since I'd taken Spanish instead of French in school, I was beyond lost as to what he was up to.

At six o'clock, my phone rang and I nearly jumped out of my skin. Was this it? Had they voted already, and Tristan was calling to let me know?

"Hey, how you holding up?" Anne asked.

The breath whooshed from my lungs. "Um, fine, I guess. Kind of nervous. Sick to my stomach. Can't sit still." I'd told Anne about the Clann's vote earlier in the week.

"Want to come outside and kill time for a while? I'm in your driveway."

"Why didn't you just knock on the door?"

"Because your dad's home and he's got that whole mind-reading thing going on, too, and I'm pretty sure I'm not supposed to know about him and the Clann and the Keepers and the vote, and yet it's all I can think about today!"

Oh. Right. "Okay, I'm coming out."

I ran downstairs and told Dad I would be in the front yard talking with Anne. He waved and nodded, then went right back to arguing with someone in French.

Ron was sitting on the far side of Anne on the tailgate of her truck when I joined them.

"Having car problems?" I joked.

"Nah," he said with a grin. "We just needed the truck to go hog hunting earlier."

"Without me?" I gave Anne a pointed look. Did this mean she'd finally taken my advice and called him to apologize, and I had been right?

Anne cleared her throat, her cheeks turning pink beneath their tan. "I needed a safety buddy, and I didn't think you'd be up for it. But don't think you're getting out of that hunt you promised me. You owe me one."

Oh. So he hadn't taken her back immediately.

I read her thoughts. *Yes, I finally got the nerve to call him and apologize. But he insisted we meet and talk about it some more face-to-face over lunch the next day. So technically he didn't accept my apology until a day later.*

"Ah," I said. "Then I guess I do owe you a hunt."

She grinned. "That you do." *And by the way, thanks for helping me yank my head out of my butt.*

I returned her grin. "Anytime." I sighed, happy that at least someone around here was finally getting their happy ending. Then I winced as a pungent stench wafted up my nose. "I take it you guys had a successful hunt?" I pressed the back of my hand to my nose to try and block some of the smell.

"Oh, sorry about that," Ron said. "Yeah, we caught one and delivered it to the butcher so they can process it. They donate their services and the meat to local food banks. The thing is, Anne's not supposed to go hunting again without telling her parents first, and it was kind of unplanned today. So we were hoping…"

"That maybe you'd loan me the use of a garden hose and some water?" Anne finished with her best hopeful smile.

"Ugh. Fine. Have it. I'll get some bleach." I headed around the side of the house, entering through the back kitchen door where I thought I remembered seeing a bottle of bleach under the sink.

Dad blurred into the room, his face phone free for the first time in days. "Savannah. We have a problem."

Great. Now what?

I sighed. "What's up?" Had he read Anne's mind or something?

Melissa Darnell

"I just got off the phone with the council. They are coming here."

"Here, as in to Jacksonville and the Clann's *headquarters?*" It came out as a squeak.

He nodded. "They have already landed outside of Rusk and are on their way by car."

"What for?" Oh crap. Oh crappity crap! Had they figured out somehow that I could do magic now?

"They heard about the Clann leadership vote. However, they have been led to believe that the vote is a cover. They think the Clann is actually meeting in order to strategize the beginning of the next war."

My jaw dropped. "You've got to be kidding."

"Unfortunately I am not. I have been attempting all day to convince them that their intel is wrong, but none of the council members are listening to me."

So now the council was headed out to meet the Clann in the Circle. And Tristan was there….

CHAPTER 36

I vamp blurred out the back door, around the house and down the driveway, stopping at Anne's truck. "Sorry, guys, gotta go. Tristan's in trouble at the clearing."

Then I took off running before Dad, Ron or Anne could try to stop me.

I reached the edge of the Coleman property a few minutes later, my hands and face numbed by the cold wind I'd just run through. Carefully I climbed over the wooden fence that surrounded the property, and immediately my skin began to crackle. Either they were using magic to take the vote, or I was too late and the battle was about to begin.

The backyard behind Tristan's house was quiet, the front yard and circle drive filled with too many vehicles to count. When I reached the edge of the woods, I slowed to a crawl, choosing each step carefully so I landed on soft moss instead of pinecones or twigs that might give me away.

When I could see the clearing, I realized the fighting hadn't started yet. The Circle was filled with descendants, all turned toward the still empty stone chair in the center.

A familiar man's voice boomed out. "And our new Clann leader is…Tristan Coleman!"

I froze, my throat locking tight. So he'd gotten the majority vote after all.

Now I had to help him stop the war from starting here tonight.

I saw Tristan give the crowd a tight smile and sit down in the stone chair I'd once seen his father resting in.

"Good job, baby," I whispered, a tear slipping down my cheek. Tears of pride, I told myself as I wiped them away.

Then, beneath all the cheering of the descendants, I heard twigs snap close to the edge of the clearing.

Gowin approached the Circle with at least twenty vampires behind and at his sides. But I didn't recognize any of the other vamps with him. Had the council sent him and a small army to represent them instead of coming themselves?

And more important, how the heck were Gowin and the other vamps able to reach the edge of the Circle?

I understood that my Clann blood had allowed me to get past the vamp wards. But there was no way Gowin and his vamp buddies should be able to. Not unless a descendant in that clearing was consciously allowing them to.

Maybe I was panicking for nothing. If the council said they were personally coming here, they must be. So either Gowin was just leading the advance team to scout out the area for the council or…

Wait. Gowin was supposed to be investigating the descendant murders. Had he been invited here to reveal the identity of the killer to the entire Clann?

Hopeful that he had come with good news, I focused on him, working to read his thoughts.

He spread his hands palm out at his sides and thought, *Vamp wards down now.*

Familiar pinpricks of pain exploded along my neck and arms, and I joined all the rest of the descendants in a gasp of shock.

Oh my God. Gowin had just taken down the vamp wards. But how? He wasn't a descendant. He shouldn't have any Clann abilities.

While the descendants looked among themselves for the source of the use of power, I focused harder on Gowin, working to block out all others' thoughts. And when I succeeded, I almost wished I had failed.

Gowin was the killer.

He was preying on descendants because filling himself with their powerful blood also temporarily gave him Clann abilities. He was trying to turn himself into a hybrid like me. But why? The effects of drinking descendant blood was only temporary. Even if he drained every descendant alive, eventually he would run out of Clann blood. And unless the council had sanctioned his plan, they would kill him for this.

I dug harder through his memories, seeing each like a random movie scene…the descendants he'd drained, the walk-in cooler full of vials of Clann blood he'd amassed. His "armory," as he thought of it. I also saw shelves filled with the genealogy records he'd taken from Ron's mother, which he'd covered by making it look like an act of vandalism on the genealogical society offices. Those records were going to help him locate future descendant victims all over the U.S.

The shelves also contained numerous Clann spell books he'd stolen from his victims and studied to learn how to use power. He had been practicing spell after spell for days now. The fire spell was his favorite because it didn't burn him for some reason no matter how close it got to his skin. He planned to use it tonight on Caravass after the fighting began so he could blame the leader's death on the Clann and then take over the council with less resistance.

It wasn't the entire plan. Instinctively I knew I was missing a crucial part of it, but it was enough to warn the Clann with before the council showed up and the situation got out of control.

But then several yards to the right of Gowin's group, a larger second group of vamps, led by Caravass, approached the clearing. They moved in a more organized, almost military-like way, with more than a few hulking vamps in bulging suits within their force.

I was too late to warn anyone.

But I could at least reveal the truth and hopefully turn the spotlight on the real problem.

I ran into the clearing ahead of the vamps. The descendants all turned toward me, saw the vamps behind me. Hands rose up to throw spells at me.

"No, don't!" Tristan yelled, his hands flying out. I felt his magic form a wall between me and the descendants seconds before the others' spells flew. Fireballs bounced off Tristan's shield in showers of sparks like rockets hitting an invisible force field.

Everyone stopped throwing spells at their new leader's command.

"Please listen to me," I called out. "I know what you believe, and the lies you've been told. But the real killer here isn't all the vampires, and it's not the council. It's him." I pointed at Gowin. "His name is Gowin. He may be on the council, but he has not been acting with their approval. He hasn't been investigating the murders—he's been causing them, gathering descendant blood to give him the ability to use magic, not just against the Clann, but against his own kind, too."

"She's lying," Gowin answered calmly. "Obviously the witch boy has pulled her over to the Clann's side. Why would I want to act against my own kind? I've been a vampire and a council member for centuries."

"Because you're trying to create an army of super vamps," I said, picking the words out of his mind even as I spoke them.

"Obviously a Clann ally would lie against a vampire," Gowin said, still calm, even smiling. "I am here in support of my council. Unlike you. Exactly whose side are you on, Savannah?"

"Everyone's," I said. "There's no reason to fight, unless it's because you want to take out—"

Gowin moved so fast I never saw it coming. One second he was yards away with the others. The next second he was at my back, one of his hands wrapped around my throat, the other around my waist to hold me still.

"Gowin, let her go!" Dad shouted as he appeared at the edge of the clearing.

"But she's sided against us, Michael." Gowin sounded so calm. "She's making wild accusations against me that are completely unfounded."

Dad looked at me, his eyebrows pinched together.

"Dad, I read his mind and I swear to you he's the one killing the descendants." I had to fight for control over my emotions. Losing control would only make me look like an emotional teenage female, especially in the eyes of these centuries-old vampires. "He's using Clann blood to temporarily give him the ability to do magic. It's how he got through the vamp wards into this clearing and then took down the wards for everybody else."

"Or you could be the one who took down the wards," Gowin said. "You should be careful, little one. The council knows we can't force you to tell us the truth, nor can anyone here read your mind." He cocked his head and smiled. "Of course, you're probably betting on exactly that, aren't you? You know you can tell wild lies about anyone here, and no one will be able to read the truth in your thoughts."

My heart raced with panic. He was right! It was my word against his and his small army. Unless...

"I can prove I'm telling the truth." I held out a forearm toward the council. "Drink my blood. The blood memories will prove that I'm not lying."

Gowin froze behind me, and I smiled. *Called your bluff. Now what are you going to do?*

Dad turned to the council. "Well? My daughter is freely volunteering to allow you to feed upon her to support her claims. Surely one of you will accept this offer in order to prove or discount what she says about one of your own council members?"

"Gowin, please, don't do this," Emily cried out, pushing through the gathering, tears shining on her cheeks. She looked awful, with black circles under her eyes and her skin too taut and pale over her bones.

But Gowin didn't see her that way. He saw the possibilities she had given him, that first drink of blood that had allowed him to sneak up on his initial Clann victims. And the baby she carried within her now, his, the first of the true super army he was building. No, not building...growing.

This was the missing piece of the puzzle. He wasn't sharing the descendant blood with other vamps, and drinking Clann blood for the magical abilities wasn't his goal either; it was a means to an end. He planned to use the Clann's magic against its own members in order to force all the female descendants to bear his children. Children who would be hybrids like me but raised to obey him for all eternity. And then they would be bred together, and on and on in an endless hybrid army factory while he took over the entire world."Oh my God," I whispered. He'd gotten the idea from my dad and mom. He'd originally hoped to make me fall for him as his first hybrid broodmare, but when my heartache over the breakup with Tristan made me resistant to his charms, he'd gone for another Clann member young enough to still be impressionable to his flattery. One who would give him the first descendant blood needed so he could overpower other descendants for their blood. One who would also be smart enough to know about the Keepers' geneological records that would map out the location of the rest of his victims.

And Emily had completely fallen for him.

Gowin hummed in surprise. "So it's true then. You have learned to read everyone's minds. Well, in that case..."

Join me or die, he finished silently.

Oh crap. He could read my mind, too.

"You're kidding, right?" I hissed as his grip around my throat tightened, cutting off more of my air. "Who do you think you are, Darth Vader?"

"Well, Caravass, I tried," Gowin said to his maker. "But she's well and truly joined the other side, it seems. She refuses to side with the vamps."

"Not all vamps, just you, Gowin," I croaked. "Why don't you tell everyone here the truth and see how the sides line up then?"

I saw the answer in his mind. He'd already tried to convince Caravass, but the vamp leader had dismissed his ideas, preferring to keep the vamp race pure. Which was why Gowin felt he had to kill his sire tonight and take over the council for himself.

"Let her go, Gowin!" Tristan yelled.

Gowin turned us both so I could see Tristan standing on the throne's hill above the crowd, his hands raised.

"Careful, or she dies!" Gowin said, his fingers at my throat curling into claws ready to rip.

Tristan dropped his hands, his face more afraid and ticked off than I'd ever seen it.

He wasn't the only one. I was ready to tear Gowin's head off myself. If I could just get free…

"Gowin, you cannot win this fight," my dad called out.

"You're a fool, Michael." Gowin turned so he could see both Tristan and my dad. "You always were. Tonight, these descendants are going to pay for all the vamps they were arrogant and stupid enough to kill. Will you be on the winning side or not?"

"There are no sides here tonight," Dad answered. "Only many people seeking the truth."

Wait. Nanna had said all I needed to do was focus on what I wanted and inject those intentions with my willpower.

Well, I had plenty of willpower tonight. And Gowin had taught me something new about magic and vamps.

Closing my eyes, I envisioned becoming a living flame, and that flame spreading over me, but not touching me, from head to toe.

TRISTAN

When I saw the fire engulf Savannah, I yelled out in panic, thinking someone had hit her with a spell. Then I saw the smile on her face through the flames.

That's my girl, I thought with a whoop of pride as Gowin instantly backed away from her.

"She's using magic!" Gowin screamed. "There's your proof, councilmen. She's on their side!"

The vamp council must have believed him, because everything erupted into chaos then. Screams filled the air as Mr.

Colbert went after Gowin while Gowin's vamps led the council's army in an attack on the descendants from two fronts.

I raced across the battle arena that the Circle had become, ducking spell after flying spell until I could reach Sav. She was crouched on the ground, the fire gone from around her now.

"Are you okay?" I shouted over the screams and roars of angry vamps and descendants, patting her shoulders and arms and cupping her cheeks to be sure she wasn't burnt.

"I'm good! Just powering back up," she yelled, both her palms pressed to the ground.

A vamp came toward us, fangs and hands out. I started to raise my hands, intending to hit him with a ball of fire. But before I could release the spell, an arrow appeared in his chest and he fell to the ground thrashing. What the…

I looked in the direction the arrow had flown from, and there was a giant panther and a crazy-eyed Anne fighting back-to-tail against the vamps.

"Savannah!" I yelled and pointed in their direction.

Savannah turned and gasped, though the sound of it was lost beneath the screams and sizzling of flying magic in the air. "Are they *crazy?*"

They sure looked it. Panther teeth and claws and a compound bow and arrows might be cool, but they were no match against an army of vamps and magic.

And where the heck had Anne found a trained panther that size in East Texas?

I ran in a crouch toward the strange team, holding Sav's hand so we wouldn't get separated.

"What are you doing here?" I yelled at Anne as soon as we reached them.

"Savannah owed me a hunt!" Anne grinned even as she loosed another arrow. I turned to check. The arrow had found its home in the back of another of Gowin's vamps. The vamp screamed then burst into a cloud of ash that plummeted to the ground to form a pile. Anne had surprise on her side for now, but once the vamps caught on to her, she'd be toast. "Thank goodness I ran out of my carbon arrows and had to bring the wooden ones today, huh?"

"You've got to get out of here," Savannah yelled at them. "This isn't your fight!"

I tried to tell her that, believe me, Ron thought. *But she's too dang stubborn!*

A vamp launched itself at our group and the panther reared up to catch the vamp's neck between his teeth and paws.

I looked at Savannah. "I think... Did I just hear Ron—"

"Yeah, the panther's Ron," she shouted near my ear so I could hear her. "He's a Keeper, a shapeshifter the Clann created as allies centuries ago. He—"

Anne stood up so she could shoot over us. "Less explaining, more fighting!"

"It's a long story," Savannah finished. "I'll tell it later. But you need to know descendants and Keepers can read each other's minds, okay?"

"Albright!" Dylan screamed from several yards away. He threw his hands into the air.

Anne dropped like a stone, grabbing her throat as if choking. A second later, her eyes rolled up in her head as the veins beneath her skin turned black in snaking lines down the sides of her face and throat toward her chest. What had Dylan hit her with?

I whirled around to hit him with a spell, but a vampire had already found him. Good, I hoped the fanger ate him.

I turned back to find Ron, still in panther form, crouched over Anne and howling as Savannah pressed her hands to her unconscious friend's neck.

"Tristan, I can't stop it!" Savannah cried out. "Whatever he hit her with, it's like poison or something."

"Cover us," I told her and Ron as I dropped to my knees beside Anne and got to work.

The spell was as devious as its owner, spreading like wildfire through Anne's veins. It took all my concentration to push it back from Anne's heart, which seemed to be its ultimate target. Savannah and Ron worked to block us from more spells and vamps while too many seconds ticked by.

Finally, though, I could feel the poisonous spell fading as I drove it to Anne's lungs and out through her every breath. When it was fully expelled, she began to breathe again. She was still unconscious, but she'd live.

"Ron," I called out. The panther tossed aside the vampire he'd been ripping to shreds and leaped back over to us. "You've got to get her out of here somewhere safe. She'll be okay, but she's got to rest for a while."

The huge panther's head dipped once. He ran behind some nearby trees. A few seconds later he came running back in human form, still barefooted but wearing jeans and an un-buttoned flannel shirt. "Thanks, man. I owe you big-time."

He scooped Anne into his arms, cradling her limp body against him.

"Savannah, we've got to cover him so he can get her out of here," I yelled, moving to stand beside Savannah as she blocked fireball after fireball thrown our way from too many directions to track.

She nodded, and we split our focus between shielding our-selves and our friends as Ron ran with Anne in his arms through the woods toward my house, where I hoped their vehicle was parked.

Once they were out of sight, Savannah said, "We've got to

get to Caravass. He's the oldest. He can command the vamps to stop."

"Okay." Staying low, I kept a hand on her back, blocking spells as we ran toward the edge of the clearing where Caravass had taken a stand, weaving our way through battling witches and descendants on all sides.

Caravass and the other council members were engaged, too, though it looked mostly defensive now. They were dodging spells and hitting attacking descendants just hard enough to knock them out, unlike Gowin's small army who were breaking necks and slashing arteries as quickly as they could.

"Over there!" I yelled, using my hand at her back to nudge her toward the council.

"Not so fast," Gowin said into my ear a second before pain exploded in my chest.

CHAPTER 37

SAVANNAH

Pain exploded in my chest, and Tristan's hand at my back slipped away. I turned around, still crouched low, thinking he'd stopped to block the attacker who had just hit me with a spell.

But this attacker had caught him completely by surprise. And it wasn't my own pain I was feeling.

Tristan was standing fully upright and arched backward, his face twisted with shock and agony.

Then I saw Gowin at his back and what looked like fingertips sticking out of the front of Tristan's chest. As if Gowin had plowed his hand right through Tristan.

Please, God, no, I thought.

Just like that, my whole world ended.

I must have screamed or something. Gowin dropped Tristan as carelessly as if he were a piece of trash and moved on, probably to go after Caravass.

But I didn't care where he went, or how the battle was going around us, who was winning or losing. Even the whereabouts of my dad and Ron and Anne didn't matter in that moment as I caught Tristan before he could hit the ground.

He tried to speak, his eyes rolling to look at me as he gasped and choked.

"Please, don't," I cried, on my knees, cradling his upper body against me as I'd once held Nanna here in this same cursed clearing.

Once again, the Circle would claim someone I loved.

No. Tristan couldn't die. I wouldn't know how to exist without him in this world. He had to live.

I pressed a hand to his chest, but I couldn't stop the blood from pulsing out in a feeble rhythm to match his heartbeat. That rhythm was slowing even as I watched.

"Oh God. Tell me how to save you," I whispered in his ear, pressing my cold cheek against his, which was beginning to cool, too.

Nanna said I didn't need words. So I closed my eyes and concentrated on his heart, willing it to heal. I pushed energy into him, a little at first, then with everything I had as I grew desperate. I didn't care if I had to give him the last drop of energy within me, as long as he lived. "Come on, Tristan! You always told me to fight. Now it's your turn. Fight!"

I told his heart to repair itself, focusing on the magic and what I needed so much that I didn't realize Dad had joined us until his hand covered mine.

"He is dying, Savannah!" Dad yelled. "Turn him!"

Time slowed, until each of Tristan's heartbeats seemed to last several seconds.

"I can't," I tried to shout, but it came out as a mumble.

"You can. Do it now! He is wounded too much and los-

ing too much blood. Turn him before his heart stops and it
is too late!"

I shook my head. "I don't know how. You—"

"I cannot, his body will reject the pure vampire blood. You
must give him yours. It is the only chance he has."

"But he'll die!"

"He is already dying. There are only seconds left before
his heart fails. Turn him now or let him go." Dad pressed a
hand to my shoulder. "It is what he wanted. He loves you.
Do you love him?"

I nodded, my throat too tight for me to speak.

Tristan grabbed my hand, his eyes going wide, pleading
with me.

Praying I was making the right decision, I used my teeth
to open a gash in my wrist then held it to Tristan's mouth.

Leaning close to his ear, I whispered, "I'm sorry. I know
it's selfish. But I can't let you go. Not yet."

Then I did what I'd vowed never to do: I sank my fangs
into the side of Tristan's neck where his life pulsed and drank.

TRISTAN

I didn't know where I was, or even who I was at first. A cloud
of red filled my vision when I opened my eyes, giving me no
additional clues.

But that scent, the smell of warm lavender filling my nose
and lungs…that I knew. It meant home, and love, and everything I needed to be happy.

I reached up to touch that red curtain of softness across my
face. I knew that, too. It was hair, soft curly hair, long and
thick. My fingers remembered burying themselves in this curtain of red many times, always with joy.

The curtain slid away from my face and hands.

"Tristan?" a girl's voice whispered, low and husky, and it too was familiar and meant love.

Then a face came into view, and instantly I knew who she was.

"Savannah." The girl I loved and would die for.

Maybe I had died. I knew there had been pain, so much that I had been drowning in it. The pain had started in my chest, spread to every part of my body, then retreated back to my chest before fading away completely. In its place had come a flood of memories of Savannah as a little girl, playing in a tree house with a boy. Me. I was that boy, her best friend. And then the memories changed, showing us when we were older…the day I rescued her from someone named Greg outside a round brick building…the night we'd danced together under the moonlight, autumn leaves rustling around our feet, plastic armor covering me like a knight while Savannah flowed in a white dress with small white wings at her back.

"Are you an angel?" I murmured, trying to remember how to speak, to move enough to reach for her face.

She looked up at someone else, a man whose voice was less familiar, who said, "It will take a while for him to remember. Possibly days, even weeks."

I ignored the rest of what they said. None of it mattered. All that mattered was that the girl before me was Savannah, and I was Tristan, and I loved her.

And then another scent came to me. Something good, and warm. A smell that made my mouth ache and my stomach cramp with need.

SAVANNAH

"Tristan," Nancy Coleman screamed. She ran over to us and dropped to her knees beside him as the tears poured down her cheeks. "My sweet baby, are you okay? How do you feel? What happened?"

"Mrs. Coleman, he—" I began.

"Do not speak to me, vampire," she hissed in my general direction before ignoring me again. "Tristan, say something so I know you're all right."

She picked up one of his hands between hers. Her dark eyes widened. Slowly her gaze traveled up his arm to his pale face gleaming in the light from scattered fires in the clearing, then to his eyes, which were now a strange greenish-silver.

"Oh. My. God," she breathed out slowly, pulling her hands away. "You're…"

"He's alive," I told her. "It was either this or let him die."

Gasping, she dropped his hand. "What have you *done?*"

"He was dying. I did the only thing I could to save him."

Her gaze darted from me back to Tristan. Seconds ticked by as emotion after emotion rolled off of her. She couldn't decide whether to be happy he was still alive or horrified that he'd become the enemy she feared more than anything else in life.

"You should be killed for this," she snarled at me. "This is all your fault! If not for you—"

"If not for Savannah, your son would have died," Dad said.

"Stop this now!" Caravass shouted. "Vampires, come to me."

The fighting stopped as the vampires began to walk, some even backward, toward their leader. Even my father was pulled by the call and walked over to join them. The absolute control was both a relief and chilling. Thank God our Clann genes prevented the command from affecting Tristan and me.

But where was Gowin?

I searched the clearing and found Emily kneeling over a pile of ash two feet from Caravass, her shoulders shaking with her sobs. A quick read of her mind told the whole story.

Seeing her boyfriend try to kill her brother, Emily had made her decision and hit Gowin with a ball of fire as he tried to attack Caravass. She had saved the vamp council leader and killed her father's murderer. And her unborn baby's father.

Unfortunately, that left only me to hold Tristan as he sat up and inhaled deeply.

"Look at him, sniffing the air like an animal," Nancy said, scrambling to her feet and backing away from us. "He smells the blood. He already has the bloodlust!" Her gaze shifted back to me, her eyes dark and wild. "You've taken my son from me."

In the silence, the surviving descendants heard her and became aware of Tristan's change. Murmurs rose to shouts as their fury found a new target. Me.

"She turned our leader!"

"Tristan's a vamp now. He's on their side!"

"We should kill them all, punish them for taking our leader!"

The shouting grew, along with my fear. Would we survive Gowin only to be killed by the Clann?

Dad leaned over and whispered something to Caravass. The vamp council leader nodded, and Dad rejoined us at a slow and cautious human walk.

"Savannah, we must take Tristan away from here."

"But...his family." I looked at Emily, who was slowly becoming aware of the Clann's growing anger toward us. She stood up, saw Tristan and went pale. She might not be any help, either.

"Tristan, can you get up?" I whispered.

With Dad's and my help, Tristan got to his feet, still sniffing the air.

What is that smell? I heard his voice say in my mind. *It smells...good.*

Oh God, his mother was right. He was already feeling the bloodlust.

What is this bloodlust? he thought, and I jumped.

He could hear my thoughts.

Yes, just like you can hear mine. Right? He turned to me with a frown, his eyebrows drawn in confusion. He still held my hand, his grip tight.

Swallowing hard, I nodded. *Right. Um, listen, Tristan, this is really important. I want you to try and ignore that scent for now. Okay?*

But it smells so good. It makes my stomach hurt.

Emily walked over to us on unsteady legs. "Tristan? You're all right!" She stepped forward to hug him.

Dad moved to block her even as Tristan's head cocked to the side, his now silver eyes studying her without any trace of recognition.

"I would not do that," Dad murmured to Emily. "Gowin nearly killed him. Savannah had to turn him before he died. And he is already struggling with the cravings."

Her mouth opened, closed, and she jerked to a halt. Wrapping her arms around herself, she turned toward the still-shouting crowd of descendants, her eyebrows pinching together.

Mom, stop this, Emily thought. Mrs. Coleman's shoulders hunched as she turned to face her children from many yards away. *Don't let this get even more out of hand. I know you can't see it now, but your son's still alive. Let them get out of here safely so he can come back to us someday.*

Mrs. Coleman's jaw clenched for a moment, and my heart pounded hard in my chest. Finally, Mrs. Coleman nodded and faced the Clann.

"Descendants! I know you're upset over the loss of our newest leader. He..." Is. Was. Is. Was. Her mind struggled with the choice. She forced herself to say, "…is still my son, however, even if Clann law forbids him to continue as our leader now."

"Then I accept the leadership," Mr. Williams said, stepping forward to the front of the crowd.

Dr. Faulkner stepped forward. "Ah, but Clann law says you will not. Not as long as the parent of the previous Clann leader is still alive and willing to accept the role in their child's stead." He sounded like he had memorized every Clann law under the sun.

Silence as everyone waited for Mrs. Coleman to react. Finally she spoke. "As Tristan's surviving parent, I accept the leadership and will gladly take this position effective immediately."

Mr. Williams's face turned red then purple. But he said nothing, his thoughts revealing that he knew Dr. Faulkner was right and hadn't expected anyone to know such an old law. He would have to find some other way to become Clann leader.

It took a few minutes for the rest of the descendants to realize that the Clann leadership had once again changed. During that time, Tristan's grip on my hand grew steadily tighter to the point of near pain.

He read the thought in my mind and forced his muscles to relax. *I'm sorry. It's just that the smell is hurting me. I can't ignore it any longer. I have to—*

"Tristan, no!" Panicking, I blurted it out instead of only thinking it.

Tristan lurched forward and dropped my hand. Dad's hands darted out to grab his shoulders and hold him still.

Emily gasped. "Oh God. Tristan, no."

"Savannah, we must leave," Dad said as he pulled Tristan backward.

Tristan's eyes had narrowed, his lips pulled back to expose fangs as he growled.

I stood there frozen as for the first time I watched a vampire lose control over the bloodlust.

Mrs. Coleman turned to face us again, her eyes wide. She took a deep breath, and I heard her think, *I must do this, for my son and the Clann.* Then she said loud enough for everyone to hear, "Tristan Coleman, you are hereby banished from the Clann. Leave here, and do not ever return."

As if it were some kind of formal act, every descendant there except Emily and Mrs. Coleman turned their backs on us.

"Goodbye, my son." Mrs. Coleman silently mouthed the words, tears rolling down her cheeks.

"Come on," Emily muttered, grabbing my elbow and dragging me through the woods behind my father as he shoved Tristan down the path ahead of us.

The farther we got from the Circle and all that descendant blood on the ground, the less Tristan struggled against Dad. Finally Tristan began to have coherent thought again. *Why does it hurt so much?*

I know, baby, I thought. *But it'll stop if you keep walking with my dad.*

This man is your dad?

Yes. Trust him. He'll keep both of us safe and get you something to…eat, so your stomach will stop hurting.

Okay. I trust you, so I'll trust him, too. But Tristan's eyes still darted from side to side like a wild thing in spite of our reaching his own backyard.

"We will meet you at the house," Dad said, his tone allowing no argument. Then they were gone, Dad teaching Tristan to run for the first time, using the woods along the way as their cover.

"Oh my God," I whispered once I could no longer hear Tristan's thoughts. "What have I done?"

★ ★ ★ ★ ★

We hope you enjoyed COVET, Book 2 of THE CLANN!
Want to know which songs
Sav and Tristan listened to in COVET?
For the official COVET playlist and other information
about The Clann and Melissa Darnell,
visit www.TheClannSeries.com!

ACKNOWLEDGMENTS

I would like to thank my editor, Natashya Wilson, for your tireless and truly brilliant editorial guidance throughout this series, as well as your undying faith in Tristan and Savannah. I am convinced that no one on this planet could possibly adore Tristan more than you do!

I would also like to thank everyone else at Harlequin for their outstanding work on making each version of every Clann Series book so beautiful, as well as for spreading the word about it in so many wonderful ways. You guys are awesome!

As always, thanks goes out to my agent, Alyssa Eisner-Henkin at Trident Media, for choosing to represent me and for your enthusiastic support for this series.

And finally, I would like to say a heartfelt thanks to Walker Carrigan, Scheels Bow Technician, for taking so much time to not only teach me the basics about compound bows but also for going the extra mile and showing me how to shoot one correctly without taking out my foot (or anyone else in the store!). If I sound like a bow hunting genius in this book, it is due to your invaluable lesson. And if I got anything wrong, I'm blaming it on Savannah's lack of knowledge about compound bows!

Read on for an exclusive excerpt from
CONSUME by Melissa Darnell,
book 3 of The Clann.
Coming in 2013.

I stared at the surrounding forest on Rich Mountain, one hand braced against the trunk of a leafless hardwood tree at my side, my too quick breaths making puffs of fog in the afternoon air as the feeble sun edged beneath the winter-stripped branches of the treeline. The air was smoky, acrid with the false promise of comfort from the chimney of a cabin several yards behind me, which I was struggling to ignore during my few blessed minutes of solitude outside.

It should have been perfect…Tristan and me and a remote log cabin with a crackling fireplace nestled on a west Arkansas mountain in December. No Clann or vampire council members nearby to bother us. No more rules or secrets to keep us apart. No more risk of accidentally killing Tristan with a kiss.

Instead, it was all wrong, and I was staggering under the weight of what we now faced.

We weren't alone. My dad had come along, not for Tristan's safety or even my own, but for everyone else who might come too close and trigger the bloodlust within Tristan. Tristan's bloodlust could never be underestimated. If not for Dad holding him back, Tristan might have slaughtered his own family in the Circle, the Clann's clearing in our hometown woods where so much Clann and vamp blood had been shed only hours ago.

Just the memory of how Tristan had looked there—his once soft emerald eyes turned white-silver with need, his normally curved lips baring newly formed fangs as he snarled with rage—forced a shudder to ripple down my body. Until that moment, I'd never seen a vampire lose control to the bloodlust. Now that I had, I would never forget it.

Not coming to this isolated cabin hadn't been an option, and staying here promised to be anything but fun or peaceful. We'd had to load up Dad's car and come here immediately after the battle in the Circle just to get Tristan away from all humans before the bloodlust drove him crazy. Even stopping for gas had been a nightmare. Thank heavens the cabin was only a day's drive from our East Texas hometown of Jacksonville so we hadn't been forced to stop often. Now that Tristan was a full vampire like me, his strength was once again far beyond my own—becoming a vamp enhanced whatever each human had to start with, and unlike me, Tristan had worked out all the time for football before being turned last night. The one time we had stopped, I'd had to fill the car's gas tank so Dad could hold Tristan inside the car and away from all the humans at the gas station.

Afterwards, the mind connection had made it all even worse by allowing Tristan to pick up my every thought while I silently struggled not to freak out.

Dad couldn't read our minds thanks to Tristan's and my Clann genes, which gave our minds a natural block against all other vamps' minds. Unfortunately Tristan and I had zero trouble reading each other's every thought. It would have been great if there had been some sort of off switch to the ability. But for now, there didn't seem to be one. The only way we could block it was to be in separate rooms.

Which was why, after Tristan had fallen asleep inside the cabin, still hurt and confused by my reaction to him at the gas station, I'd snuck out here to the woods to catch a breath. And to finally give in to the thousand and one worries I hadn't dared think when he was awake.

I sighed, allowing the tree beside me to hold me up. I was so tired, but my mind wouldn't shut off and let me rest.

I refused to regret turning Tristan. He was the only one for me. He always had been, and he always would be. Holding his broken and bloody body that even magic couldn't save after the rogue vamp councilman Gowin had ripped a hole through Tristan's chest, I had known I couldn't let Tristan die no matter what the consequences. Right or wrong, turning Tristan had been the only decision I could possibly make at the time.

Now the question was whether we could survive that decision.

Tristan and I had been through so much to get to this point. And yet none of it had prepared me for the battle to come. Dad said the most danger for fledglings was in the first few days after turning, when the human mind struggled to assimilate the vamp DNA. During this phase, the brain tended to react as if to a concussion, shutting off the memory center and operating solely on the baser levels of senses and instincts. The memory would return in time, but it could take days.

In the meantime, Dad warned that Tristan might be highly emotional and irrational sometimes, and have difficulty concentrating for long periods. In addition, Tristan would have the vamp impulse to feed with no understanding of why he felt such cravings, and he'd have the speed, strength and re-flexes of a full vamp.

As Tristan's sire, or maker, it was my responsibility to fix him, to bring him back to some semblance of who he once was. If I failed, if Tristan revealed to human society that vampires really existed before I could help him recover his memories and self control, the council would kill him.

The cabin door creaked out in warning, and my shoulders tensed.

Just me, Dad thought as he slowly walked over to join me.

I couldn't stop a sigh of relief. Thank God I had Dad to turn to for advice on how to train a fledgling, because I was completely clueless here.

"Come to get some fresh mountain air?" Dad murmured.

"No, just needing some space to worry about Tristan. He can hear my every thought, whether I want him to or not, and I can hear his. He's so lost and confused right now. How are we going to tell him about everything?"

"We cannot," Dad said. "We must be patient and allow his memories to return to him on their own. He will never truly believe what he does not remember himself, and right now he is in much too volatile a state to handle all the ramifications of our current situation. You will have to protect him from your thoughts."

"He trusts me completely. What if he never remembers it all? What if I'm not strong enough, or smart enough, or we don't train him right or fast enough...?"

Dad rested a hand on my shoulder. "Now you know all that I have gone through with you. Becoming responsible for another's continued existence is the heaviest responsibility there is. But it does grow easier with time."

Time. How much did we even have? "Will the council try to find us out here?"

He shook his head. "They will simply watch the news reports for now. The Clann, however..."

"Tristan's mom is leading them now. Why would they be a problem?"

"We both know how she feels about our kind."

And how Mrs. Coleman blamed me for turning her only son into the very thing she feared the most in life.

"She might hate my guts," I agreed. "But she'd never send someone to hunt down her own son. She adores Tristan. And she knows he needs us to help him get better."

"True. But as the new leader, it might be a while before she regains full control of the Clann. When we left the Circle, the Clann clearly was not appeased by Gowin's death. Many descendants were voicing their belief that the council secretly sanctioned his actions, and it may take Nancy quite some time to convince them otherwise. In the meantime, it is reasonable for us to be cautious in case there are descendants who would wish to find us and seek retribution for turning their former leader."

After his father's death, Tristan had been voted Clann leader only minutes before Gowin, his rogue army, and the misinformed vamp council had attacked the Clann in the Circle. But even before the attack, the hatred and fear between the vamps and the Clann ran centuries deep, sparked by the danger each species presented the other and fed by the scars of loved ones lost in countless wars. Those wars had only ended after Tristan's father and grandfather worked for years to create a peace treaty with the vamp council. A treaty that now seemed on the brink of total failure in the wake of last night's battle.

I sighed and stared at the seemingly endless miles of surrounding woods now turning to shades of gray in the fast growing dusk. "Even if the Clann comes after us, they can't find us out here. We didn't leave a trail, and no one knows about this place, right?"

"They do not have to know about it. If the Clann is determined to find us, the odds are in their favor that they will. Do not forget, they have both spells and the Keepers to aide them."

Oh lord. I had forgotten about the Clann's alliance with the Keepers, a group of families also originally from Ireland who in the old country had agreed to have a permanent shapeshifter spell placed upon them that spanned generations. Once shifted into the form of giant black panthers, the Keepers could read Clann minds, including mine and probably still Tristan's, too. My best friend's ex-boyfriend, Ron Abernathy, was one of a long line of Keepers.

Could the Clann force him and his family to help them hunt us?

I swallowed the growing knot in my throat. We were deep in the woods hours away from Jacksonville. How would the Keepers scent us—by following the smell of our car exhaust?

"If we stay away from the surrounding towns, we should be fine here," Dad said. "But we must remain cautious. And if you sense any sort of magic being used, you must let me know at once. They may try to use a spell to track us down if they become truly determined."

Oh great. I hadn't thought of that. At a loss for words, I nodded.

I could sense when magic was used near me. It would hit me as a sensation of pins and needles stabbing the back of my neck and arms. But would I still feel it if it was being used far away? I had to hope so. To be on the safe side, maybe I should try to do some sort of invisibility spell on us to block any tracking attempts. Nanna told me once that all spells were simply willpower and focused intention. Surely I could cook up something to keep our location out here hidden.

"So about Tristan's training," I began, my fingertips drumming against the bark of the tree I leaned a shoulder against. "You've got a plan, right?"

"Not exactly. Every fledgling is a unique situation, and even the council members occasionally fail to help a fledgling overcome the initial bloodlust. And of course there will be the added problem of Tristan's magical skills to contend with, which I can assure you no sire before you has ever had to deal with."

"So we just have to figure this out on our own?"

The cabin door creaked open again, and my heartbeat raced even faster.

Tristan.

I forced my mind to go blank.

A second later Tristan was at my other side. "Hey. I woke up and no one was around."

"Just out getting some fresh air," Dad murmured. "It is a lovely sunset, is it not?"

Tristan watched me, trying to read my emotions when he couldn't read my thoughts. "Are you okay?"

I made myself smile. "Everything's fine. How'd you sleep?"

He shrugged. "Okay, I guess. I woke up thirsty, though."

Dad's gaze darted to meet mine. He turned toward us. "We should go back inside and feed."

But Tristan wasn't listening. Frowning, he raised his chin and sniffed the air. "What is that?"

I sniffed, too. "What?" I smelled the chimney smoke, the dead leaves under our feet, the dirt. But nothing more.

And then Tristan was gone. He was so fast even my vamp eyes couldn't follow his movements.

Shocked, I looked at Dad.

"Deer hunters," Dad growled.

Oh God. Tristan had scented humans somewhere in the woods.

We took off after him, with only the newly disturbed leaves to show us which way he had gone.

Be sure to read the first book in The Clann series

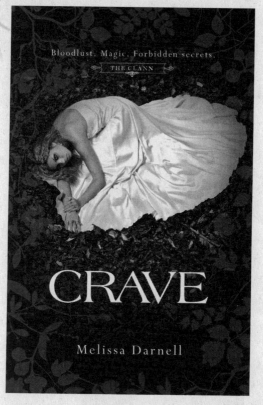

Bloodlust. Magic. Forbidden secrets.

THE CLANN

CRAVE

Melissa Darnell

The powerful magic users of the Clann have always feared and mistrusted vampires. But when Clann golden boy Tristan Coleman falls for Savannah Colbert—the banished half Clann, half vampire girl who is just coming into her powers—a fuse is lit that may explode into war. Forbidden love, dangerous secrets and bloodlust combine in a deadly hurricane that some will not survive.

Available wherever books are sold!

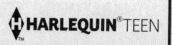